MW00887690

THE BUTTERFLY LEGACY

A Novel

By

Kathleen Marie Rice

For Pete & Carol,

I hope you enjoy reading this novel as much as I enjoyed writing it.

Love,

Kathleen

Kathleen M. Rice

The Butterfly Legacy

ISBN: 9781466227040

Published: December 2011

PRAISE FOR THE BUTTERFLY LEGACY

Karol Jackowski, New York City
Bestselling author of *Ten Fun Things to Do Before You Die* and *Forever and Ever, Amen: Becoming a Nun in the 1960's*.

"Rich in Irish history and riveting in its century-old murder mystery, *The Butterfly Legacy* is a brilliantly told story that I suspect will grip you, as it did me, from start to finish. Kathleen Rice has written a masterpiece that begs for a sequel. Enjoy."

David Faxon, Glastonbury, CT
Author of *Cold Water Crossing: An Account of the Murders at the Isles of Shoals*.

"Kathleen Rice has written a novel that will stir the hearts of Irishmen everywhere. From "The Great Hunger" of the nineteenth century to "The Troubles" of the twentieth, she skillfully weaves a tapestry of family secrets and tragic outcomes that define the Irish character. Told through the eyes of the families Hughes, O'Connell, and Buchanan, The Butterfly Legacy traces one family's rich history as it moves from generation to generation to a dramatic and thrilling conclusion in America of the 1970's. Throughout is crisp Irish wit that blends well with the characters and the times. A must read whether you're Irish or not."

Barbara Langell Miliaras, Winchester MA.
Author of *Pillar of Flame*; and CEO Triadha Productions

"A brilliant work. Rice's novel provides us with an historical view of the harsh conditions of Ireland's great famine of 1845-1850. The novel provides compelling psychological insight on how starvation, abandonment, and exile played out for a family over nearly 150 years, culminating in a murder committed in Haverhill, Massachusetts. The murder scene bears mysterious coincidences to a murder committed a century before. The final solution of the mystery involves a strange link between the murderer, his victim and a Boston detective. A 'must-read' for all those interested in the lasting effects of adversity, both positive and negative, upon a family."

ACKNOWLEDGEMENTS AND DEDICATION

Here's where a newly-published author has the opportunity to thank almost everyone. But, I'll contain myself. Above all I thank my sister Alice, who has always inspired me; and I thank all my Irish and French cousins, especially Cathy Eldridge Carey and Pam Rice O'Brien; and my friends, Peg Coughlin Allard, Peg Grady Guy, and Judi O'Brien Grant; and I thank especially my friends Karol Jackowski, who taught me a lot, and Judi Bednarz, who if she hadn't talked me into writing a novel I never would have attempted such a thing. Thanks also to John Corcoran for his comments on an early draft and David Faxon, who gave me invaluable advice and encouraged me to publish this novel. Special thanks to Eileen Kenneally, the cover designer, who would often say to me in perfect Irish lilt: "Tis hard work, this writing. Ye must be exhausted!" Finally, I thank Steve Wallace for his editorial assistance. He must have been exhausted!

This novel is dedicated to the memory of my two sisters, Pat and Peggy, my father, James – who told quite a few tall tales himself, my mother, Regina who kept James grounded, and my Great-grandmother Nelly, for whom Part One of *The Butterfly Legacy* is named.

AUTHOR'S NOTE

This novel is a work of fiction, drawn entirely from my imagination, including the 20th Century Neo2-Fenians. Exceptions include certain historical events, such as the existence of the 19th Century Neo-Fenians, who modeled themselves after the ancient Fenians; "Bloody Sunday;" the Great Irish Famine and the "coffin ships;" and the assassination of Lord Mountbatten in 1979. I bear sole responsibility if there are errors of fact regarding these events. In addition, the towns and counties as well as certain sites mentioned in the novel are real. These sites include the British Consulate-General, now located in Cambridge, Massachusetts, but, which during the time period of the novel, was located on the 47th floor in Boston's Prudential Center; Nun's Island, located in Galway City; Classiebawn Castle, located in the village of Mullaghmore, County Sligo; Winnekenni Castle and Raff's Restaurant, both located in Haverhill, Massachusetts. However, the events that take place at these sites in the novel are purely fictitious.

The surnames of the characters are in the public domain as far as I can tell. However, I did receive permission to name four characters after real people, they are: Catherine Eldridge Carey, Raleigh Buchanan, Mary Rafferty, and Monica Shellene. Finally, except for historical figures such as Lord Mountbatten, Queen Victoria, Prime Minister Peel, Prime Minister Russell, and Henry John Temple – better known as Viscount Lord Palmerston – any resemblance of the characters to persons living or dead is purely coincidental.

K. M. Rice

GLOSSARY

an Gorta Mór	The Great Hunger
Bodhrán	Irish Drum
Lazy Beds	A pejorative expression for the Irish potato beds
Ramhanni	Shovel
Piocoidi	Hoe
Díon fíor	A "real" roof
Cullaghs	Small wooden boats
Leamhán sléibhe	A native tree yielding wood sturdy enough to stand up to the West Coast's harsh, wet weather
Máthair mhór	My Grandmother
Lathair	A pit to store potatoes
The Tumbling	Irish peasants who could no longer pay their rent lost their homes in a despicable manner: Soldiers would tie a rope to the roof's center beam and pull, thus collapsing the walls inward.

PROLOGUE

"Coincidence is God's way of remaining anonymous."

~ A. Einstein

New Hampshire ~1952

The kid from Ireland jumped out of his Uncle Jim's "new for '52" Chevrolet, scrambled onto the cottage porch, stood on a chair, and lifted a ceramic half-moon nailed above the door. The Brooklyn boy's note was there! He could hardly wait to read it; but, just as he unfolded it, his Aunt Agnes hollered, "Tuckerton O'Connell, come down from there! Help your cousins carry these boxes." Reluctantly, Tuck stuffed the note in his pocket and helped carry things needed for two weeks on Country Pond. The note was the best part about his vacation for he found the place and his cousins boring; and he hated swimming in a lake, preferring the cold Atlantic waters off Ireland's West Coast.

"Here's the last box," Uncle Jim announced as he placed it with the others lying helter-skelter on the living room floor. He wiped his khaki pants off with his palms, dusted his hands, and gave Agnes a kiss. Ruffling his sons' heads he said, "Have a good time boys. You too, Tuck."

Tuck watched his uncle head for the car, thinking, *He doesn't look all that sad; probably hates it here too.* Then, while Aunt Agnes and the cousins were making a big fuss over Uncle Jim's leave taking, Tuck seized the moment and sneaked off into the pines behind the cottage. He sat down cross-legged on the fragrant pine needles. Anxious to read the note, but savoring the anticipation, he thought about the note he had left for the boy last year. He had described his Irish village in County Sligo and his older cousin's apartment in

Dorchester, one of Boston's working-class neighborhoods where he spent the first two weeks of his vacation. He had written that he'd rather stay with his cousin for the whole month instead of wasting time on Country Pond. He also told of his admiration for the 19th Century Neo-Fenian rebels and revealed that, when he grew up, he too would help free Ireland. He had asked if the kid liked the name he had given the cottage and signed the note "The kid from Ireland."

Then, hands trembling slightly, he unfolded the note.

Hey there, "Kid from Ireland! Sorry you don't like the lake. Check out the pet raccoons at the store. They're pretty cool. Last October we got a TV. Wish we had one at the lake. Does Ireland have TV yet? About those Neo-Fenians, I don't think wanting to be a rebel is such a great idea. I'm going to be a detective; but I like the sound of inspector. Maybe I'll move to England (ha ha). I like the name you christened the cottage. Half Moon Cottage has a nice ring to it. I hope we meet some day. Sincerely, the boy from Brooklyn.

Tuck thought that the note had an uppity sound to it. He mumbled, "Damn it! Didn't tink this vacation could get worse."

When he awoke the next morning, his cousins had already gone out to do whatever it is they do all day. Rubbing sleep crap from his eyes, Tuck overheard Aunt Agnes saying something to her neighbor. He leaned his elbows on the window sill to better hear what she was saying.

"...and this is the third year I've rented the cottage to the Buchanan family. You met them last year. What do you think, Mrs. Collins?"

"I met the aunt when she dropped them off. Nice woman. She lives up in Portsmouth you know. And Mrs. Buchanan is a lovely woman and the children are no trouble, Agnes."

"That's good to hear. I wouldn't want to rent the cottage to riff-raff." Then Agnes paused and lowered her voice.

Tuck no longer could hear what was being said; but, it didn't matter because the name "Buchanan" had caught his attention. He hopped off the cot, reached under it and withdrew an old wooden box filled with story sheets his grandfather had given him to keep him amused during the Country Pond portion of his vacation. Tuck had heard the stories many times, and so he was certain the name "Buchanan" appeared somewhere. He scanned through them, and exclaimed, "Ha!" as his eye caught the name. "I'll give ye a good mystery this year, boy from Brooklyn."

The two-week vacation went by interminably slow for Tuck, especially because it had rained almost every day. At last it was Friday, the night before they were to leave the lake. The weather had cleared and his cousins had gone to the outdoor theater to see "War Arrow," a Technicolor movie starring Jeff Chandler and Maureen O'Hara. But Tuck had feigned a stomach ache so he could remain behind to write his note to the Buchanan boy. He wrote the first paragraph in Gaelic to confuse him; then he drew something on the paper's right edge. Smiling to himself, he slipped the note into his pocket and checked to make sure Agnes was asleep in her chair. She was, so he pilfered one of her Camel cigarettes and sneaked out of the cottage.

He placed the note under the half-moon and, hearing music drifting in the air, he jogged over to the Country Pond Pavilion to see what was going on. Hanging onto a window sill, he watched a bunch of teenagers dancing. Then a sudden downpour drenched him; he slipped from the sill and fell to the ground. "*Céilí Mór go léir!*" he spat. And for good measure he translated the curse, "Damn it!" He crouched beneath the Pavilion's eaves, and, after several attempts to light the match, he lit the Camel. The rain stopped as suddenly as it had started. As he listened to the music drifting through the open window, he realized for the first time how the scent of pine calmed him, especially when it rained.

The next day, the vacation came to its soggy end when Uncle Jim pulled up to the cottage. "Tank ye God," Tuck whispered. For the next half hour Aunt Agnes hurried him and his cousins along as they piled boxes and suitcases into the Chevy's trunk and on the roof rack. They crammed the bedding onto the back seat and the three piled on top of them. As Uncle Jim accelerated, he said, "Another year gone by, eh?" Agnes mumbled an "Hmm" sound; the cousins didn't answer; and Tuck was busy looking out the back window, promising himself that someday he would meet the boy from Brooklyn.

Later that afternoon, a car pulled up to the cottage. The boy from Brooklyn jumped out and ran up the steps onto the screened porch, stood on a chair and lifted the half-moon. Ah! The note was there. Though he was nearly 15 years old, the idea of the note still intrigued him. As he unfolded it, his older sister Patricia yelled, "Raleigh Buchanan, get over here! I need help with these boxes." Raleigh sighed, stuffed the note into his pocket, and went to help his sister.

As soon as he everything was in the cottage, Raleigh unfolded it the note; but just then his mother called, "Raleigh, the rain stopped. C'mon now, you need to get to the store before everything's bought out." She handed him some money and a grocery list. "There's an extra dollar for you; but don't stay over there all afternoon."

"Cripe sakes," Raleigh thought, "I'll read the note by the waterfall."

He jogged to the cottage's boat and rowed across the lake in record time. After tying the boat to the dock he walked to the store's window to take a look at the pet raccoons. They didn't seem to do much except look at him. Nevertheless, he liked watching them watch him. He thought the animals' eyes were quite mysterious; and he loved a mystery.

Then he gathered and paid for the items on his mother's list. He nodded to the storekeeper and said, "How're you doing this year, Mr. Dawkins?"

"Good 'nough, son. 'Cept the rain this summer ain't doing much for sales. Don't know why 'cause folks gotta eat. Ain't that right?"

"Yes Sir, that's right. Say, I need to rent a bike. Would you hold onto the groceries 'till I get back?"

"Sure 'nough."

Raleigh handed the storekeeper his dollar and stuffed the bike key and 75 cents change into his pocket. He selected a bike and took off. He rode along the lake's contours until he reached the line between Kingston and Newton. With one foot on the ground, he looked around, trying to remember where the lake water flowed into the Powwow River. He leaned his bike against a tree and walked into the woods.

Shortly, he heard the sound of rushing water. Hanging onto small trees, he skidded down an embankment onto the lake's shore. He watched with amazement as the lake waters rushed toward the waterfall and down into the Powwow River. Someday, he vowed, he would go to Haverhill, an old Massachusetts factory town located north of Boston, to find the spot where the Powwow becomes one with the Merrimac River. Today though, he was content to listen to the waterfall's roar and read the kid's note, which he unfolded with great anticipation. But, he was brought up short by the first paragraph. "What the heck is this?" he said aloud and then tried to decipher the first sentence: *Má na póga Stork féileacán ar dhá bhuachaillí, cad iad na siad lena chéile?*

Having seen letters from his uncle living in Inverness, Scotland, he knew the words were Gaelic, Irish no doubt. But, no way could Raleigh translate it. It was irritating. He skipped to the part where English began. The kid had given him part of a riddle; Raleigh figured the other part was in the Gaelic paragraph. A rough rendering of what looked like a butterfly was drawn on the edge of the paper. Ticked off and confused, he said aloud, "Screw it! I don't know what the hell he's talking about." Maybe he was getting too old for note trading anyhow. He crammed the note into his pocket and climbed back up the hill.

He rowed briskly across the lake, feeling for the first time that he was about to be bored out of his skull on Country Pond. By the time he entered the cottage he had decided to try the dance at the Pavilion.

That night as Raleigh approached the Pavilion, he stopped short: A sudden feeling had come over him that fate had touched him that day. Maybe it meant that he'd meet *the* girl at the dance. He tried to picture what she would look like; but his mind’s eye could see only the kid's butterfly drawing. It had an odd familiarity to it. He shook his head and walked up the Pavilion’s steps. As he climbed them, he became aware that he was rubbing the nape of his neck. Slowly he pulled his hand away, shrugged, pushed the swinging doors inward and walked into the dance.

PART ONE ~ NELLY

"God had one son on earth without sin, but never one without suffering."

~ St. Augustine

CHAPTER 1 ~ THE POTATO

The Andean Countryside, South America ~1552

The Spanish sailor stooped for a better look at the tiny purple flowers swaying in the warm autumn breeze. He pushed aside the large, flat green leaves of one of the plants, and pulled at the thick stalk. Startled to feel its strength, he pulled harder. Nothing happened. He took a shovel-like tool from his sack and began to dig.

Later that year the Spanish Armada returned home bringing with it all sorts of treasure, including the sailor's potato plants. Soon the potato would be introduced all over Europe where, by the Nineteenth Century, it would become the main staple of people living in Ireland, a country dominated by England for over 800 years.

Mexico ~ 1844

Airborne spores of the pest Phytophthora Infestans*, Greek for "Plant Destroyer," landed on the potato plant's flat green leaves, releasing zoospores into the dew. The Destroyer began its assault, penetrating the leaves, causing dark lesions. Then a chilling drizzle washed the spores from the foliage down into the soil, causing most of the potato tubers to rot. Infected tubers were then hauled upon a Mexican ship set to sail for New York. Upon the ship's arrival, merchants unwittingly sent the blighted tubers throughout the United States and Europe where they would infect entire potato crops, first to be noticed in Ohio and in Belgium – and then England, from where they were carried across the Irish Sea to Ireland.*

For centuries the arable Irish land had been divided and subdivided by English and Anglo-Irish Protestant landowners seeking to increase rental revenues. By the 19th century Catholic tenant farmers worked meager plots of land that they could not own, but which once had been part of huge estates owned by their ancestors, the great Irish Kings. The potato had become the only crop that could grow in a small space abundant enough to provide sustenance for entire families. Tenants not only ate potatoes, but also used leftovers as barter or to pay their rent. Thus, by the time the infected potato tubers reached Ireland's shores, the vast majority of the country's population was almost completely dependent upon the potato. This dependence is why the historian, Cecil Woodham-Smith, would observe that "A potato crop failure in England would be serious, but for Ireland it would be a disaster."

Mullaghmore, County Sligo ~ August 1845

"Come down now, Thomas Hughes!" his Aunt Stella cried. Seven-year-old Thomas scrambled out of his cot and jumped from the loft, landing hard on the cottage's clay floor. As he skidded into the kitchen, his Aunt yelled, "No running in this house, Thomas!" She huffed through a pause and then, "I'm worried about the potatoes; and ye should be as well. July was hot one day, gloomy cold the next; and cold rain most of August."

"Aye and that's the truth, Aunt."

Stella gazed out the window and added almost to herself, "Tis the worst weather the elders in our village can remember." Then, "Go Thomas. Check the potatoes and be quick about it!"

Thomas slipped into his boots, threw his thin coat over his thinner shoulders, and left the cottage. He walked along the ridges of the lazy beds and was relieved to see the plants thriving, with their tiny purple flowers, large flat green leaves, and sturdy stalks. Excited, he ran back to the cottage.

"No rot spots the leaves, Aunt!" he hollered as he tumbled into the kitchen. Shivering, he added, "Tis very cold out there."

"Aye then, get yourself warmed up by the fire."

Stella breathed a sigh of relief for Thomas' report was the third good one this week. She whispered a prayer of thanksgiving with one breath and cursed her brother-in-law with the other. "Blast that Michael Hughes! Hailing the bad news told by his cronies. Surely the potato is not failing all over our dear land."

She tried to dismiss the thought, but in her mind's eye she saw potato fields blackened overnight in the south, and the rot creeping toward the west. Irritated, she nudged Thomas away from the peat fire, and slammed a pot into the hook dangling from the oven's bar.

Thomas gave his hands one more rub and got out of her way. Stirring the pot with a vengeance, she uttered, "And blast that man for scaring the children half to death."

She whiffed the steam, gave an approval nod, and poured broth into a bowl. She carried it and a hunk of bread to her younger sister, Fiona, who lay under a high window on a mattress stuffed with rags. Three weeks before, Fiona had given birth to a stillborn and had yet to recover. Stella gazed at her sister for a moment: a pale shadow of the lovely lass she had been. The roses gone from her cheeks. But, Stella marveled, those amazing blue eyes often revealing the pain still mirrored her good soul. She knew her sister should be up and about by now; she also knew that that wasn't about to happen. She stifled a sigh and handed Fiona the broth.

"Here then sister, ye must eat for the strength of it. Ach, but don'cha worry, the summer hungry months are almost over. The new potatoes are doing fine and will be ready to eat soon."

"Aye, Stella, tis good news." Fiona sipped the broth, then said, "God bless ye for coming all the way from Mayo to care for me." She took another sip and handed the bowl back to her sister.

Stella noted the effort such small movements demanded. She winced seeing sweat begin to bead upon Fiona's brow despite the chill leaking through the window. An icicle of fear melted down her spine for she had experience with this fever and knew the havoc it wrought.

Fiona's voice broke into Stella's thoughts. "I'd like to see the wee ones now."

Stella told Thomas to fetch his twin, who was still asleep on a bundle of straw in the loft. She thought about the older girls, Kathleen, 17, and Nelly, barely 16. They had been up half the night tending their mother. She called after Thomas, “Now don’t wake the others, they need their sleep.”

She fetched a damp cloth and, sitting on the edge of Fiona’s bed she wiped it across her sister’s brow. She said, “Tis a shame your eldest got himself involved in that ‘Young Ireland’ uprising. Gone in hiding he is for most of the summer. Dear Mother of God and sweet Jesus Himself!”

Fiona sighed. “Now Stella, Paul Tibertus must do what he must do.”

Stella huffed her disapproval as she straightened Fiona’s pillow. “He’ll come to no good end, sister, and that’s a fact.”

Up in the loft Thomas was pushing his twin’s shoulder back and forth, “Wake up lass! Mam wants to see us.”

Maeve pulled herself up by her elbows and scowled at her twin through sleepy, deep blue eyes. She shook her head, tossing her long, dirty-blond curls in his face. He ducked and jumped from the loft to the floor where he could hear his twin rising from the bed, sighing dramatically. He waited until she had climbed carefully down the rope ladder their father had made just for her.

Michael Hughes trudged up the hill from the valley on his way home. He had planned to spend the previous night at the harbor building project of Henry John Temple, better known as the Viscount Lord Palmerston, who ruled over County Sligo. Michael’s intention was good, for had he done as planned, he would have been among the first in line seeking work that morning. But, he had stayed too long at the pub and had awakened, hung over and dirty from sleeping in an abandoned scalp, a shelter built in a ditch and roofed with grass and twigs. Wondering what had happened to the builder of the scalp he mumbled, “Ach! This is what our country has come to. The peasants are shoveled from their homes and, if they have the strength, they build a scalp for shelter.”

With effort he reached the crest of the hill, squinted his eyes, and looked out over the valley at the Atlantic’s roiling white caps. His thoughts turned to earlier gatherings of friends and family. Life had always been harsh but never without joy. He thought about his gregarious countrymen who could turn a funeral into a festival. Folks would travel great distances to attend them as well as weddings, games, and races. There would always be two or more who could play the fiddle and the *bodhran*; and everyone else would dance and sing. Elders would tell stories about ghosts and fairies and, especially the Irish heroes and kings. Michael felt pride swell in his heart for he had made sure his children knew Ireland's proud history before they attended the Government-run school where their Irish heritage and language would've been threatened out of them.

He shook his walking stick at the sky and growled, *"Féadfaidh an Béarla fuilteacha, siad ag lobhadh in ifreann!"* And for the hell of it, he yelled the oath's English translation, "The bloody English, may they rot in hell!"

Turning from the Atlantic and facing east he could see the potato ridges of his farm and smoke rising from his cottage's chimney. He sighed with regret, knowing that he should've worked this morning so he could be walking home with a coin or two for his effort. Giving in to regret, though, was not Michael's style. So, he turned instead to rationalization and uttered a woeful litany: "Fiona is dying; Paul Tibertus is in hiding; Stella is a shrew; and the potatoes are failing all over Ireland."

He spat on the ground and carefully climbed down the hill toward home, thinking, *Tis a humble home, but better than many and surely better than a scalp.* He pictured his friend, George Ahern's house. Like most, it was a mere cabin with walls made of mud, clay and loosely placed stones. Michael smiled for the first time that morning as he pictured his two-story cottage with thick plaster walls, and a roof made with sturdy cross beams covered with straw mixed with mud. The floor was tempered clay; and the interior, lit by lanterns and a peat fire, was further brightened during the day by shafts of light through the cottage's windows.

Despite his neglect, Michael believed his family's lot was not so bad, being as it was close to the middle of the economic scale of Catholic tenant farmers. The family had a small vegetable garden, chickens, two pigs and a cow, whose milk they shared with their neighbors. His grandfather had had a few horses. But, with the passage of the English government's "penal laws," Catholics had been prohibited from owning horses, except ones that were valued at less than five pounds.

Michael shook his head and thought about the fact that Catholics could not hold office, nor could they vote or own land. They were nothing but tenants in their ancestors' land. He said aloud, "And then only if we can pay the damned rent. At least, before the drink got me, I built our cottage with walls that wind cannot pierce!"

With this on his mind, he was hardly aware that Thomas had sidled up to him.

"Da, where've ye been? Aunt Stella is steaming mad."

Michael let Thomas take his hand and lead him to the cottage door. Stella pulled the door open and spat, "Michael Hughes ye make an unholy sight! You're no better than an English soldier tumbling a tenant's home." She scowled through a pause. "Go wash that dirt off before coming into this home!"

Thomas sneaked under his father's arm into the cottage. Then it began to rain razor-sharp pellets that seared the skin and chilled the bone. Michael shielded his eyes and stumbled to the wash bucket filling with rainwater. His regret turned to resentment at Stella's imperious way with him.

He balled his fists and his mood blackened.

CHAPTER 2 ~ *an GORTA MÓR*

The following Wednesday Thomas bounded up the cottage's stone steps. He caught his breath and cried, "Aunt Stella! Da! Mam! Sisters! The potatoes are ready! George Ahern told me so. His Da and Granfar got them potatoes already today."

Thomas grabbed Michael's coat sleeve and pulled him to the door. "Hurry, Da!" Then he ran ahead toward the lazy beds. Michael, Aunt Stella and Kathleen followed. Maeve trailed behind, clutching Nelly's skirt. Each carried either a *ramhanni* or a *piocoidi* to turn the mossy turf. They dug the potatoes out of the ground, separating the larger ones from the smaller, intending to eat the latter right away. When they had as many potatoes as they could carry, and not wanting to drop a single one, they carefully walked back to the cottage. They reached the side of the cottage and placed the potatoes on the ground.

"Da," Thomas cried, "Let me help dig the *lathair*."

"Aye and I can use the help, lad."

When they finished, Thomas stood as tall as he could and told everyone to dump the large potatoes into the *lathair* and, as if they didn't know, he told them they must eat the new potatoes slowly until the October harvest.

That night the villagers gathered at O'Callaghan's Pub to celebrate a healthy harvest. Desmond McGrath and Padraig Shanahan played the fiddle and the *bodhran*; Margaret Moynihan poured the drinks; and each family brought some potatoes to bake on the hearth. Off to a corner young girls were flirting with the boys – all except fifteen-going-on-sixteen year-old Nelly Hughes who was in deep conversation with Cormac Daley.

"But why won't ye marry me, Miss Nelly? We have felt love, have we not?"

"Ah. Tis true, Cormac," she answered, feeling guilty as the lie left her lips.

"And Mr. Hughes approves, does he not?"

"Aye, tis also true."

"Then why won't ye marry me, lass?"

Nelly couldn't explain because she felt there must be more to love. *Cormac is like a brother*, she thought but did not say. Instead she said, "We can talk later, Cormac. Let's dance while we have the chance."

After a while, Nelly excused herself, and walked outside. The high, lopsided moon was bright, the potatoes healthy, and the fairies asleep. These thoughts rolled around her mind as the autumn breeze caught stray ringlets of her dark brown hair, tinged with auburn. She climbed the hill and then down the path between the hill and the cliffs rising high above. She stopped and looked out over the ocean, now calm as glass, with the exception of moonlit wrinkles racing toward the shore. Suddenly she felt someone nearby and turned quickly.

"Dear woman!" a deep, English-accented voice said. "I'm sorry if I frightened you."

Startled though she was, Nelly placed her hands on her hips, and said, "Ye eejit! How dare ye sneak up on a lass?"

"I wasn't sneaking for I didn't see you until I reached the crest."

The timbre of his voice bespoke sincerity. As he talked, Nelly was startled by his even, white teeth. She had never seen such white teeth. As he came closer she saw that his countenance was quite handsome; and his eyes, catching the moonlight, were kind. He stood tall in his English soldier's red and white uniform. She noted the shining medals attached to his tunic and, by the white sash across it, Nelly knew he held a high rank. She stepped backward, lost her footing on the side of a rock, and struggled to stay upright. The soldier's arm shot out and wrapped around her waist, breaking her fall. As he pulled her upright, their eyes met and the two gazed at each other for what seemed far too long to Nelly.

"Are you alright?" he asked.

"I'm fine then."

Letting her go he said, “I am Captain William Tuckerton, and you are?”

Nelly felt an unfamiliar flush rise from her breast to her face, and her heart beat so, she worried he might hear. Nevertheless, she managed to utter her name. She felt drawn to this man; and at the same time repelled. He was, after all, an English soldier.

“Sir, I must go back now.”

She didn’t wait for his reply and turned away. Though frantic she might fall again, she raced up the path and down the hill toward the pub. She went straight to the necessary room and washed her face hoping to remove any sign of the flush she still felt. She smoothed her hair, brushed her skirt with both hands, and then rejoined the crowd.

“And where have ye been, lass?” Michael asked.

“I was outside for a bit of air, Da.” And changing the subject she added, “The music is fine, is it not?”

“Aye and tis about time we have fun. Come, dance with me, daughter.”

As they swayed to the music Michael asked, “Do ye have a gentleman in mind, then? Could it be Cormac Daley?”

Recalling how she felt in the Captain’s presence, she hardly heard her father’s voice; but it finally penetrated: “Darlin, ye know that Kathleen will be married soon, and I fear…”

Feeling the flush rise again from her chest, Nelly interrupted her father.

“And where is Kathleen?”

“She’s with your mam.”

“Kathleen should be here dancing with her Mr. Ryan. I’ll go tend Mam.”

She pulled back and looked at her father with a mixture of love and sadness. She noted that his face was no longer handsome and his hair was thinner, as was his body. Her gaze slipped away from his.

And they finished the dance.

On her way back home, Nelly almost bumped into Father Malloy. The grave look on his face gave her a jolt. And she was surprised when he walked by her not saying a word. A fearful tingle ran down the back of her neck.

The next morning, Stella led the family in a thanksgiving prayer, ending with a traditional Irish blessing: "Health and a long life to ye; land without rent to ye; a child every year to ye; and if ye cannot go to heaven, may ye at least die in Ireland."

After breakfast of potatoes mashed with buttermilk and onions, Kathleen went to gather some potatoes for the evening meal. Upon reaching the *lathair* she thrust her shovel into the thrushes and clay, expecting to strike the top layer of potatoes. Instead, the shovel traveled downward with ease up to the handle. Alarmed, she moved to a different place and thrust the shovel in again. This time she brought to the surface a shovelful of foul-smelling black mush. The potatoes had become rotten overnight. In horror, Kathleen threw the shovel away from her and screamed.

Michael and Aunt Stella came running followed by the twins and Nelly. Within the hour, folks gathered from far and near. Father Malloy arrived shortly thereafter to comfort them.

And there, among the Hughes' potato ridges, the villagers prayed in their Christian way, said the Rosary in their Catholic way, and, in the ancient Irish way, they called upon the fairies to stop their nonsense. The praying and the sobbing and the wailing filled the air deep into the night, even though they could not know that an Gorta Mór, the Great Hunger, had only just begun.

CHAPTER 3
SHOVELING A HOLE IN WATER

October 1845

Stella sat at the edge the bed, holding a cup of tea near Fiona's lips. She helped her sister struggle upright saying, "Now, don'cha worry, Fiona. Aye tis true, the August potatoes went to rot; doesn't mean a ting darlin' for October's harvest will be ready soon."

Fiona took a few sips and gently pushed the cup away. Stella took it and helped her sister lay back down. She rose and skirted the clay floor, which Nelly and Kathleen were washing. Suddenly, an awful pounding on the door startled Stella and she dropped the cup. She went to the door in a huff. Her mood changed to fear at the look on her neighbor's face.

"Ah, Holy God!" cried Alice O'Keefe, tears staining her cheeks. "Ach! The potatoes are a ruin, they are."

"What are ye saying, woman?" Stella said in a tone higher than usual.

Nelly and Kathleen rose from the floor, wiping their hands on their aprons. Their eyes were wide with expectation; Stella wondered if they could see the dread in her own.

Fresh tears trickling toward her lips, Mrs. O'Keefe said, "Aye! Tis the awful truth, Stella. Me husband Terrance has already joined the villagers gathering at the Church." She took a breath. "Come with me now." She nodded at Kathleen and Nelly. "And take the twins as well." And with certainty she added, "Wee ones are close to God, ye know."

Kathleen stooped and wiped the tea from the floor, while Nelly picked up the broken cup pieces. As she tossed them in a barrel, Aunt Stella coughed and gave her a look intended to hurry her along. She sighed impatiently as the twins struggled with their coats.

Nelly went to her mother's bedside. "Mam, will ye be alright, then?"

"I'll be fine child. And I'll be praying to Saint Fiacre."

Aunt Stella tossed a stage whisper in Alice O'Keefe's direction: "A French Saint indeed. Just because his effigy holds a *ramhanni* doesn't mean he cared a wit about Irish potatoes."

As they approached the Church of Saint Brigid, the Patron Saint of Dairy, Stella tried to keep fear at bay by allowing her thoughts to wander to the Church itself. A simple handmade affair with great stones carried by men in an earlier day. Here and there a touch of marble, which had been added later and which old Danny and his nag had hauled all the way from Dublin. Trailing behind the others, she gazed at the roof, a structure that even a Dubliner would admit is a *díon fíor*. It was made from the *Leamhán sléibhe,* a native tree yielding wood strong enough to stand up to the West Coast's harsh, wet weather. She looked at the cross atop the roof's peak and blessed herself, aware of the depth of her fear.

She paused before opening the heavy door adorned with an oval, hand-painted stained glass window. And then she joined the others.

Father Malloy was in the middle of a sentence, "…therefore, keep in mind the beatitudes, especially those that tell us to give shelter to the homeless and food to the hungry." He sighed dramatically, and continued, "Many of our neighbors will suffer awful trials, for the Widow O'Reilly's constitution forebodes a terrible winter."

With that he blessed the congregation and said, "Ye must have faith that this misery shall end. The women brought some early harvest potatoes; they're on the hearth. Give thanks to our Lord, Jesus Christ!"

He stepped from the pulpit and the villagers silently followed him to the anteroom where they broke into frenetic, if solemn, conversation.

The next morning Aunt Stella was digging in the garden hoping to find a leftover turnip or two.

"Good morning madam," said Cormac Daley.

Stella craned her neck. "Aye, Cormac! And how is your Mam today? The women at Church said she is ill."

"That she is, but she's better than a week ago, and that's a fact." He paused and Stella noted the high color touching his cheeks.

She said, "Is there something else you wish to say?"

"Aye. Please may I speak with Miss Nelly?"

Stella saw Nelly peeking out the window, gave her a look, and called to her.

Shortly, Nelly came into the garden, tightening her shawl around her shoulders.

"Aye Cormac. And what brings ye this early morning?"

"Me Da and I are riding the horses to Lord Palmerston's harbor. I know of your liking for horses and would be honored to take ye with us?" Shifting his eyes toward Stella, he added, "Tis proper for sure."

"I tank ye, Cormac; but I am not feeling well this morning."

Aunt Stella noted the smile on Cormac's face dissolve so suddenly, she feared he might cry. She gave Nelly a look and her niece quickly added, "Another day riding the horses would please me, Cormac."

Cormac blushed, bent his head, and stuttered a farewell. As soon as he was out of earshot, Stella grabbed Nelly's arm.

"Miss high and mighty is not 'feeling well' indeed." She huffed through a pause. "Who do you tink you are, spurning that good lad? His father is at the top of the farmer scale. He has a strong house, cows and even horses! He earned his place rightful, as God is me judge."

She pushed a chicken out of the way with the tip of her toe, and said, "Ye cannot do any better than Cormac Daley! Tis time to stop your dreaming."

Shaking her grasp from Nelly's arm, she uttered, "Ah! Why do I bother? Ye father spoiled ye terrible. Go on, then."

Feeling a mixture of resentment and confusion by Stella's reproach, Nelly went into the cottage. Kathleen was tending to Fiona, and the twins were playing Jacks by the hearth; Michael was not home. She went directly to the second story and lay across the mattress. She didn't know why she was not attracted to Cormac. "He's a good lad; but so … so young," she thought. She imagined that there must be something more to love. *But, what 'more' is there?* Although, she conceded, she had felt something "more" whenever she was in the presence of Captain Tuckerton.

She recalled every encounter since they first met in August: The day she was walking along the strand when, it seemed to her, he suddenly appeared out of nowhere. They had talked briefly of the weather, the potatoes, and such things. Then he went on his way. She had felt a strange ache as she watched him leave; she remembered how her pulse had quickened when she placed her bare foot into the print his boot had made in the sand.

Now, in frustration, she began to cry in earnest.

The next day Nelly was stirring a pot over the hearth when Aunt Stella's voice broke into her daydream. "We need a talk, miss."

"Aye Aunt, sure and what is it then?"

"I tink I know why ye won't be with Cormac Daley." Nelly's face reddened as her aunt continued talking. "Sure tis gossip, but truth lurks there. The women are saying ye and that soldier have been seen keeping company more than once. This must stop!" She raised her voice an octave or two. "An English Soldier, no less. Ach! Have ye gone mad, then?"

Stella was a bit shocked when Nelly didn't respond. Instead, her niece placed her shawl around her shoulders and walked straight out the door.

Aunt Stella complained to Kathleen, "What are we to do with that one? She is not sensible. Not a 'tall like ye, Kathleen, having a proper courtship with Mr. Ryan. But that one tinks she's too good for Cormac Daley."

She walked to the window and saw Nelly running up the hill. "As God is me witness, that one will be trouble for sure."

"Ah! Stella!" Fiona said. "Why do ye listen to harpies' gossip? They should be busy praying over the loss of October's harvest instead of wasting their God-given breath berating the child."

Stella said nothing. Kathleen, finishing Nelly's task, poured steaming broth into a cup and brought it to Fiona. She said, "Mam, I tink Aunt Stella is right. I hear stories from folks other than the harpies."

"Now Kathleen," her mother cautioned, "take care of the plank in ye own eye."

Kathleen knew the Biblical phrase well, for it was her mother's way of admonishing her children not to gossip.

Stella watched as Fiona took a few sips of tea and handed the cup back to Kathleen. She lay back on her bed, appearing exhausted. Kathleen felt her forehead. "And how is the fever, Mam?"

"Ah, don't ye worry, me darlin'. I'm not about to leave this world while me family's in trouble."

Stella noted the ashen pallor of Fiona's face; and seeing Kathleen shiver, she knew her niece must be thinking that the end might be near.

Nelly reached the lazy beds and stopped to catch her breath. Then she walked along the ridges. Possible retorts to Aunt Stella's morning assault cluttered her mind. "Ah! Aunt Stella tinks I have no brain! I am more than a ..." Her thought faded as she became acutely aware of the ruin that once had been healthy potato plant foliage. The sight gripped her with fear. "What will become of us?" she whispered. She shook her head as though to shake the question and its answer from her mind and continued climbing toward the crest of the hill. She walked the path, took a breath and trudged her way upward to the top of the cliff. She gazed out at the Atlantic and watched the men in their *cullaghs* tossing their nets hoping to catch crustacea and herring feeding close to shore. Though she did not relish the thought of eating the likes of crabs, she chided herself aloud, "Tis food. Be grateful for it!" She sat on a large, flat rock, pulled her long skirt around her knees and held her shawl tight around her chest. The gentle autumn breeze brushed her cheek. "Ah! Holy Mother, please intercede with your Son for us." Then she began to cry.

Hearing a sound, she raised her head and saw the Captain drawing near, and quickly dabbed at her tears.

"So, Captain, tis true is it? Ye always do sneak up on a lass."

"I told you the night we met I do not sneak. I was down below riding my horse up the hill from the strand. I saw you up here on the cliff."

"And do ye have a sailor's telescope to see that far?"

"I couldn't see your face, that's true. But I recognized the dark length of your hair and imagined the way the auburn of it catches the sun."

Nelly blushed. And despite her effort to hide her tears, he asked her if something was wrong.

"I have someting in me eye." She explained. And in a teasing voice, she said, "And did her Majesty give ye special orders to spy on the Irish?"

"Yes, of course," he teased back, "But understand, our Queen Victoria does not hand out special assignments to just anyone." He paused and then added seriously, "Truth be told, miss, every time I come this way I hope to see you."

She stood and walked over to him. "Aye and I saw ye riding the crest of the hill above our cottage just a week ago." She quickly changed the subject and asked, "And what is your horse's name?"

"Her name is Ruffian; and she'd like to take you for a ride."

Nelly hesitated, feeling heat rush upward from her belly to her chest. Nevertheless, she nodded her assent. He reached for her hand, but she pulled it back saying, "I'm perfectly able to get meself off a mere rock, Sir."

Captain Tuckerton watched as the young Irish girl stood precariously. He grabbed her hand and was relieved when she didn't pull it back. He helped her as they picked their way carefully over the huge rocks, some flat and some dangerously jagged until they reached the flat face of the cliff. Then, together they half slid down to the dirt and rocky path below.

Letting go of her hand he said, "I'm sorry about the crops, miss. My soldiers say the same thing is happening in other counties, even in the east."

"Potatoes are fickle, sir. Tis hard when the crop fails; and they often do, and that's the truth. Worse, potatoes don't keep, ye know. So, during the hungry summer months, we eat meal until the August crop is ready. Meal tis awful stuff and not as filling as potatoes.

"Then we wait patiently for the October harvest. Sure and tis hard when that crop fails as well. As ye well know your countrymen fill ships with the wheat and oats and vegetables that we grow ourselves. I have seen hunger etched on my countrymen's faces while watching these loads sail away."

Appalled, the Captain bowed his head for he knew she spoke the truth. Then he lifted his gaze to her face and thought how beautiful she was. He knew she had been crying and her sadness brought out an even greater beauty. *A more mature beauty,* he concluded. He whistled to Ruffian, who was grazing on the side of the path.

"Ah! She's a wonderful animal!" Nelly exclaimed.

As he attempted to help her mount Ruffian, she surprised him by swinging her skirted leg over the saddle. He knew she had seen the look on his face, for she said simply, "Tis safer than side saddle."

He swung up behind her, wondering how he might gather the reins without improperly touching her. He gave a small shrug, simply wrapped his arms around her, and grasped the reins. He led Ruffian in a gentle gait down the steep path; and then a little faster as they descended. When they reached the strand, he urged the horse to a gallop along the edge of the surf. Ruffian's hooves splashed the hem of Nelly's dress, drenching it. The wind caught her hair and whipped it across her face and then around to smack the Captain's face. They both laughed and he urged Ruffian on. Then: "Whoa!" He guided the horse away from the surf and into the lowlands skirting the shoreline. Soon they found themselves deep in the woodlands. The sound of the surf receded, replaced by bird songs and high-pitched insect calls. He maneuvered Ruffian across several fresh water streams; and then, quite suddenly, halted her.

"Look Miss Nelly!"

He helped her dismount and they gazed in wonder at the sight before them: Acres of purple heather swaying slightly in the breeze. He reached for her hand, and was glad when she grasped his in her own.

As they walked, Nelly was mesmerized by the scent of the heather and the sounds emanating from the woods. A stirring she had never felt before rose from her groin to settle in the center of her belly, bringing with it a bit of fear. Suddenly, she stopped walking and withdrew her hand from his.

"I must be going back, Sir."

"Stay, miss. It's beautiful here, and so sad everywhere else."

"No," she answered firmly, "I must go back now."

She knew that the tone of her voice obviously caught the Captain by surprise. He said only, "I do not wish to offend you."

They walked back to Ruffian, mounted the grand horse and headed back to the sea.

Neither said another word.

Later that night Nelly lay sleepless, recounting every moment of that day. She realized that she couldn't remember when she had laughed so heartily or felt so fine. Then, unbidden, the memory of her morning encounter with her aunt pushed aside delight. She was suddenly sure that Aunt Stella was right, she was, after all, a dreamer – and this day may turn into a nightmare. She knew that even half-truths about scandal could bring out the worst in Irish women, especially the harpies who revel in scandal. She recalled a lass who, without proof, was accused of adultery. Her neighbors stoned her, and young girls tore her dress from her shoulders. And, holding her down, they chopped off her hair.

Nelly began to cry softly, trying desperately not to wake Kathleen asleep beside her. She prayed to the Virgin Mary to forgive her. She vowed that she would avoid the Captain. And, for good measure, she promised to be nicer to Cormac Daley.

At last she drifted off into sleep. But not for long for she awoke suddenly, fragments of her nightmare littered the floor of her mind: Ruffian rearing up against a threatening sky; bits of mangled heather flying from beneath his hoofs.

Parliament ~ December 1845

"Ach!" growled Parliamentarian George Moffet. "Frantic reports of potato rot in Ireland, my eye! It is just that: Rot!"

Another parliamentarian reasoned, "Now then, Sir Moffet, let us keep our heads. It is true that Ireland's potato harvest has always been uncertain, and crops often fail; but …"

Another interrupted. "Why are we wasting our time on this matter? A tempest in a teapot, as the great Bard himself would say. The Irish are a lazy lot. Why, they themselves call their potato fields by the name we gave them: 'lazy beds.' I agree with Moffett – this so called 'rot' will pass as always."

As more men began to speak at once, Prime Minister Peel shook his head in disgust and extended both arms. He looked around the room and, though he couldn't find a friendly face, his voice was commanding.

"Gentlemen, decorum please! The Scientific Commission we established to determine the cause of this strange blight has diagnosed it as wet rot."

He heard Moffett say in a stage whisper edged with sarcasm: "We established? No! You, Prime Minister, established it."

Peel shot a withering glance in Moffett's direction and said, "Village priests, and others who can read, must help people to follow the complicated cleansing instructions. But, the real problem is that the method the Commission devised to cleanse parts of the ruined potatoes has rendered them inedible.

"Remember that just one week ago our man in Mullaghmore, Captain William Tuckerton, informed us that many people who have eaten the 'cleansed' potatoes have developed severe dysentery from which many have died." He took a breath, and continued, "The Commission's abject failure to provide a source of food means that many more among Ireland's eight and a half million people will surely starve if England does nothing."

Then he delivered an impassioned plea, "Gentlemen, please! The Corn Laws must be suspended – or even repealed!"

The grand hall erupted with boos and hisses.

One parliamentarian yelled above the noise, "Whatever are you suggesting, Sir? Our economy is grounded in the 'laissez fair' doctrine! We simply cannot interfere with the free exchange of goods and services."

Peel replied, "Remember that the Corn Laws are an exception. They prohibit import of grain – wheat, barley, and oats. Ironically, as you very well know, the Corn Laws do not include corn for it is not grown in the United Kingdom. Thus we can legally import corn!"

He waited for a reaction, but there was none. In the end, Peel's plea went unheeded. However, whatever political reasons he may have had, he was determined to continue his efforts to assist the Irish, and he made a decision that would adversely affect his political career and his health. Despite Parliament's refusal to agree that importing corn would legally circumvent the Corn Laws, Peel decided to import American Indian Maize. He arranged to import enough maize that he thought would feed 500,000 people for months. When the shipments arrived, he issued the order to hide the corn in the main depots of Cork and Limerick, believing that the corn would be needed more in the spring.

He could not know that his reckoning would prove to be woefully inadequate, for though England's lack of response to the potato crop failure was a contributing factor, the root cause of the Great Famine was the Irish class system, based as it was on land ownership. English noblemen and Anglo-Irish Protestant land owners were at the top third of the economic scale; while landlords, like Lord Palmerston, who owned in excess of 60,000 acres, were at the very top. Farm laborers, comprised of the peasant class, were at the bottom of the scale, renting between 1/8 and two acres of land. The Hughes family was at the middle level of the "tenant farmer scale," which consisted of those who could rent between 10 and 30 acres. Thus, the Hughes family was not suffering as much as many of their friends and neighbors, many of whom were among the lowest class. So, while the corn sat in depots, the peasant laborers were forced to scavenge for food throughout the winter of 1845-1846. They would eat anything, from the bottom parts of leftover turnips they dug out of the frozen ground to seaweed that washed ashore.

The men of Parliament, who could have avoided the disaster to come, were certain – and some in good faith – that the potato crop failure of 1845 was just like the ones that came before. They could not know that this new and mysterious blight would attack crops all over Ireland. They could not know that crops would fail year after year for the next five years.

Mullaghmore - December 1845

"Michael, Fiona Hughes whispered, "I hear someone in the garden."

Michael's ear, attuned to his wife's voice lowered by fever, awoke immediately. He rose, threw his coat over his shoulders, stepped into his boots and grasped his walking stick. Holding the stick like a sword, he peeked out the door. He saw a figure trying to thrust a *ramhanni* into the ground.

"Aye there! What do ye tink you're doing digging around in me garden?"

As the man dropped the *ramhanni* Michael cried, "Eamon Ahearn! What are ye doing, man? Why do ye come sneaking to steal what we would gladly give you?"

"Aye Michael, I know ye would be kind; but I cannot bear the shame of ye knowing I cannot provide for me family."

"C'mere Eamon, there's nothing to be found under the snow 'cept hard earth. Follow me to the barn and stay quiet. We don't want to wake Aunt Stella, now do we?"

Michael climbed to the loft, pushed hay aside with one hand, and with the other handed Eamon two small potatoes, an onion and one turnip.

"Ye mustn't tell the others for they will surely come and be stealing what we have."

"Ah. Tanks, Michael. You're a God-fearing man, and that's the truth."

After his friend left, Michael thought maybe a bit of charity might make up for his sins. Then, not wanting to alarm Fiona, he told her that he had found nothing in the garden.

As 1845 slipped into 1846, the situation in Ireland became alarming. Given that food had been scarce since the previous year's crop had already been depleted, thousands of peasants began to starve. Worse yet, they lost all means to pay their rent, thus facing eviction from their humble homes. One bitter cold January afternoon Captain William Tuckerton rode Ruffian into the village. He entered the pub where Margaret Moynihan was wiping tables. No one else was there; yet Margaret ignored him. Finally, he asked where everyone was.

"And where do ye tink they are, Captain? Seeking warmth and food is where." She put her hands on her hips and snapped, "What do ye want?"

Will had not expected much, but the rude greeting stung anyway. Hating what was happening to these people, he had felt a growing depression since October when the blight hit the village. He was an English officer loyal to his Country, but he had begun to feel that loyalty waver. He said, "Ah, then, Madam, I will leave you to your work."

He rode Ruffian toward the eastern edge of the village, facing away from the Atlantic's blustery wind. His thoughts turned to Nelly, whom he had encountered only twice since that day when they discovered the magical field of heather. He knew she was avoiding him. Suddenly there she was. He dismounted Ruffian and walked toward a scalp thrown together on a hillside. Nelly was kneeling beside the humble mass of snow, mud, and twigs.

"Can I help you, miss?"

Nelly looked up in surprise; after a beat she said, "I don't tink ye can, Captain. These folks are dying of cold and congestion."

As he walked closer he could see that Nelly was gently guiding a cloth across the forehead of a scantily-clad woman. He peered into the scalp and could make out at least two other figures.

Nelly said, "One is dead as winter grass. And the other, a child but tree years of age is dying."

Ignoring her tone, as cold as the wind, he pressed on, "What happened to them?"

"They cannot pay their rent. T'was increased by the rate the damn British Government issued to their landlord. No landlord wants to pay the rate for his tenants. So, they tumbled their home as they have so many others."

She placed the cloth into a bucket of water, squeezed it and re-applied it to the woman's forehead. She looked up at Will and said, "Not bad enough that people are hungry and ill, but now they are homeless as well. This wretched family comes from Lord Edgley's estate and there will be more of it, God knows." She breathed in the cold air. "I have heard that England is doing this on purpose – kill us off and then they can have our Country to themselves alone. What do you say to that, Captain?"

Will said nothing, reflecting on the tumbling, which he had witnessed first-hand. Tenants who could not pay their rent were evicted from their homes and the very soil they tilled. If they refused to move, the landlord employed agents to scare them away. Sometimes angry peasants and farmers would come to the laborer's aid. If the agents could not handle the situation, they called upon Will's regiment for assistance. He had no choice but to send his troops. Once he had accompanied them to Edgley's estate, which consisted of a large English-style home, several smaller houses and 52,000 acres of land, a size almost equaling that of Lord Palmerston's estate.

Under the troop's watchful guard, the angry mob dispersed. Once they were no longer a threat, the agents went to work, tying a rope around the center beam holding the roof. He saw the man of the household huddled with the children while his wife knelt in the snow, hanging onto a soldier's leg, begging him not to destroy their home. Then, she began an awful keening as the agents pulled the rope, tumbling the roof down into the cabin, forcing the walls to collapse inward.

Ashamed at the memory, Will knew in his heart that Nelly was right, for there would be more tumbling. Hundreds of farmers and laborers lived on Edgley's estate alone. *Before winter's end*, he thought, *thousands more will be shoveled from their homes*. He felt ashamed that his countrymen could be so heartless. Yet, he could not bring himself to believe that England was intentionally killing off the Catholic Irish. Still lost for words, he tipped his cap toward Nelly and bade her farewell. As he rode off, he vowed to send two of his troops back to the place with some food, water and blankets. He would tell them to bring coats for the woman and the child who lay dying. He would order them to bury the dead, no matter how hard the ground.

Urging Ruffian to a tremendous gallop, he shouted into the wind, "Ah! I'm trying to shovel a hole in water."

CHAPTER 4
"THEY'LL MAKE DO, AS ALWAYS"

London ~ Winter 1846

"John," Prime Minister Peel said to his aid, "here it is only February and tenant farmers all over Ireland have become desperate. Captain Tuckerton sent word that more than a thousand in County Sligo alone have lost their farmer rank and have joined the lower class. And thousands in the lower-class have joined the peasant laborers."

Not knowing how to respond, John merely nodded. Peel sighed and leaned his head against the rattling window pane, his back to John. He said, "The Captain reported that thousands had to sell what little they had left – including babies' swaddling clothes and even fishing nets – so they could pay their rent. And children scour the hillside seeking grass hidden under the snow. John, the Captain said the children eat so much grass their mouths are permanently shaded the color of moss. God help them! We mustn't wait until spring to release the Indian corn. No! Tomorrow I will release it from the depots."

The following week, Peel received another dispatch from Captain Tuckerton. He wrote that thousands of starving people flocked to Cork and Limerick to buy the corn for two pence. Thus, the corn was depleted in no time. Weakened from their journey to the depots, many died on their way back to their own counties. The Captain wrote:

My Lord, those people lucky enough to buy the Indian Maize soon found that their luck was not without penance. The corn is extremely hard and requires extensive preparation. As you know, Ireland lacks the machinery to ground the maize into finer corn. And, these people simply do not know how to cook the maize. Mothers scoot their children outside when cooking the corn, for when the kernels come to a boil they pop like tiny explosions, scattering boiling water all over the kitchen. Because gnawing hunger assails them, and despite their inability to properly prepare the maize, people are eating the stuff half-cooked. Thus, along with other miseries that attend hunger, many who have tried to subsist on the corn have developed severe dysentery. Some have died when hard kernels punctured their intestines.

With deep chagrin, Peel read the Captain's last paragraph:

Sir, I know you have a keen interest in knowing everything that is happening over here. Therefore, pardon me for saying so, but the maize has become known in the popular mind as 'Peel's Brimstone.' I am truly sorry for that and regret that I do not have better news. Sincerely, Cap. W. T. Tuckerton.

Peel let the letter drop to the floor, brushed his hand across his brow, promising himself that he would speak to the Queen. He said aloud, "She can't possibly realize how bad things have gotten over there."

The next week during his regular session with Queen Victoria, Peel tried to convince her to repeal the Corn Laws. He finished by saying, "Their plight is too awful to witness, Milady. I beg of you, allow the grain the Irish grow themselves to stay in Ireland. I shudder whenever I picture the ships leaving Sligo Port loaded with grain grown by the very people who are starving to death."

In the end and to Peel's utter disappointment, the Queen approved the Majority's decision to uphold the Corn Laws. As the last Parliamentarian voted against repeal, Peel was so angry he declared, "Good God! Are you to sit in this cabinet and calculate how much diarrhea and dysentery a people must bear before it becomes necessary to provide them with food?"

Undeterred, Prime Minister Peel continued his efforts to aid Ireland. He proposed a public works program, which Parliament approved in late spring 1846. By early summer, the program employed over 100,000 people. Michael Hughes' friend, Eamon Ahearn, was one of them.

Eamon belonged to the farmer scale, but the previous April his rent was in serious arrears. Having bartered his scant possessions he had no choice but to join the works project. So, every day at six in the morning he hiked four miles to the Connaught Province public works project where he started the back-breaking work of road building with nothing in his belly. Halfway through the work day, which ended at 6 o'clock in the evening, a bell signaled dinnertime.

One day Seamus O'Reilly whispered to Eamon, "Ach! Can ye believe they expect us to eat this stuff?"

Washing his shovel as best he could, Eamon replied, "Tis better than nothing, Seamus." He placed some raw meal on the shovel, dipped his cupped hands into the drainage ditch and poured filthy water over the meal to soften it.

As Eamon began to eat it, Seamus wrinkled his nose. "How can ye do it, man? I'll starve first!"

After Eamon forced himself to swallow he responded, "And starve ye will, Seamus." Then he put his finger to his lips. "Shush! The ganger is comin' our way."

Cracking his whip at the slightest sign of slackness or weakness, the ganger – himself an Irish Catholic – pointed to a man and spat, "Stand up and pour that meal down the drain! I saw ye loafing before the dinner bell sounded. Get your tings if ye have them. You're knocked off."

Eamon muttered, "Knocking the man off doesn't matter to that bastard. One hundred or more are waiting to take his place."

A few days later on an unseasonably chilly morning, Eamon arrived late for work. "Ach!" sputtered the ganger, "There man! Tell me your name."

"Eamon Ahearn, sir."

"Ahearn, you're late and so ye'll be quartered."

And with that, Eamon lost one-fourth of his day's pay. His anger at himself for being late dissipated when he noticed that Seamus O'Reilly, pale as a ghost, was shaking. Eamon started to say something to him, but Seamus simply dropped his shovel, stumbled toward the side of the road, fell and died then and there. His wife and three children, who had accompanied him that day, took his place, not taking time to bathe or bury him.

Later, Eamon sneaked a look and saw Mrs. O'Reilly working the same tasks as the men, digging draining ditches, and carrying away clay in a basket tied to her back. Two of her children spent the day breaking up stones and hauling them away to the side of the road. The youngest child had joined other children as they crouched around a small turf fire by the side of the road.

Shortly after the death of Seamus O'Reilly, Eamon said to his wife, "Peg, I cannot go to the road works today, I cannot."

Though Peg was a kind-hearted woman, hunger and worry had taken their toll and so, she said, "How can ye not go, Eamon? Tink of the children!"

He tried to say something through a moan. Peg interrupted him, saying, "I'll tell George to go with ye."

Feeling weaker than he thought possible, Eamon pulled himself from his cot, dressed and, without a word, left the cabin. George threw his coat on and ran to catch up with his father. After they had walked two miles, Eamon whispered, "Lad, I cannot go on. Go, quickly and take my place. Save some meal for me."

George nodded and ran the rest of the way to take up his father's shovel. When he returned that night, he found his father lying on the side of the road. "Da?" He knelt down by Eamon. "Da!" he cried. "Ah. God help us! Da is dead, he is."

The boy ran the rest of the way home. He stopped short at the doorstep to catch his breath, dreading having to tell his mother the awful news. He said a quick prayer and then opened the door. Hearing of her husband's death, Peg Ahearn wasn't sure if what she felt was guilt for pushing Eamon off to work that day, or a sorrow so deep she could not speak. She gazed at her children for a moment, then took her coat off the hook and left the cabin.

The children would never forget the sound of Peg howling into the night.

To make matters worse for the Ahearn family, the public works program caused a coinage shortage and some workers went weeks without pay. Eamon Ahearn had been one of them. Peg testified that her husband had not been paid his daily rate of two pence for three weeks. She ended her testimony saying, "All during that time, me Lords, the only food me family had was what our friend, Michael Hughes, gave to us."

The head Magistrate asked, "And what would that be, dear lady?"

"Ah, sir," Peg replied, "Once he gave us two small potatoes, another time a turnip, half- head of cabbage, an onion or two. And once dear Mr. Hughes gave us some flour".

The Magistrate voted not to give Peg the wages owed to her family since she had "admitted" that her family had a source of food. He was not swayed by impassioned pleas from some his colleagues.

Throughout the spring of 1846 Prime Minister Peel continued to lobby for the repeal of the Corn Laws, predicting that repeal would stabilize prices. He finally won, but his success made him unpopular with the conservative party, members of which had booed and shouted at him. He endured their animosity until he finally resigned as Prime Minister. He died not long after his resignation. Though many historians would criticize Peel for holding back the corn when thousands starved, an equal number would credit him with saving the Irish people from the worst effects of the potato failure of 1845-1846.

By spring 1846 newssheets all over England and Ireland once again heralded a healthy crop. The headlines read: "The seed potatoes planted in February have taken hold with hearty green foliage." The good news resulted in reduced foreign aid; and Parliament continued to underestimate the likelihood of tragedy in Ireland. Benefactors and politicians alike did not realize that the seedlings were too few to feed millions of starving people. They couldn't know that the blight would return the following year as an Gorta Mor *continued taking its toll. Of course, some politicians saw cause for alarm for they recognized that millions had not had a decent meal for almost a year. But, their appeals to Parliament went unheeded.*

Peel's successor, Lord John Russell, deeply committed to laissez-faire, believed that citizens should not depend on the Government for handouts. Furthermore, he believed that the Irish were a lazy lot who brought misfortune upon themselves. He often spoke providentially: "God Himself has punished them for their bad habits." Russell, still miffed by Peel's decision to import Indian Maize, refused to import more even though it meant that millions would have little to eat, if anything until the October harvest.

"After all," he once argued, "the summer months are the hungry months, a time when Irish laborers are accustomed to less food. They'll make do as always."

With that, Lord Russell sealed Ireland's fate.

CHAPTER 5 ~ THE BETRAYAL

Mullaghmore - Spring1846

Pre-dawn brightened the unseasonably warm March night and the waning moonlight streamed into the window casting shadows crisscrossing the ceiling and walls. Nelly lay sleepless on the mattress she shared with Kathleen. Thoughts of her encounters with the Captain kept turning over in her mind. She could almost feel the weakness that would come over her whenever she was in his presence. She placed her palm over her heart and imagined it might burst from her chest. She sighed sadly, remembering how mean she had been to him when he appeared at the scalp where she was attending the dying woman. But, she thought, "Tis the only way that can keep me from him."

Kathleen moaned and turned on her side, crackling the mattress's chaff filling. Nelly held her breath, hoping that her sister would not waken. When she was sure Kathleen was still sleeping she carefully moved her half of the coverlet aside, knelt on the bed, and rested her forearms on the windowsill. Suddenly her heart skipped a beat for there he was on the hillside, standing still as a tree.

Without a second thought, for if she had one she would've stayed in bed, she quietly climbed from the mattress to the floor. She looked back at Kathleen's sleeping form, thankful that she had not stirred. She did not bother to remove her nightgown. She pulled her skirt to her waist, put her shawl around her shoulders, picked up her shoes, and quietly crept past the twin's loft. When she reached the lower level she glanced at her father's sleeping form on the floor next to her mother's bed; and she watched for any movement behind the curtain where Aunt Stella slept. Then she slipped out of the cottage.

The Captain ran down the hill when he saw Nelly emerge from the cottage. They met and embraced for the first time. Her chest heaving with fast and shallow breaths, Nelly burrowed her face into the crook of his neck. "Ah! Captain," she murmured. He breathed in her scent in quick gasps. Their lips met in hungry kisses. She thought she might die. He picked her up in one smooth motion and carried her up the hill. They mounted Ruffian and galloped as fast as the Captain dared, given the treacherous nature of the path leading down to the strand.

They did not see Aunt Stella slowly close the window curtain, whispering to herself, "Shame for sure will come upon this house."

Ruffian sped along the strand to the spot where the lowlands began to skirt the shoreline. Then Will called, "Whoa!" and guided the horse into the woodlands, across fresh water streams, and into the place where acres of heather swayed gently in the breeze. He dismounted, lifted Nelly from the horse, and carried her through the heather to a sheltering tree.

Kissing her neck, he removed her shawl. Then he kissed her fully on the mouth and she kissed him back. He slowly untied the string of her nightgown; she slipped the white sash from his shoulder. She felt his hand at the waistband of her skirt as she unbuttoned his tunic. For a brief moment Nelly got hold of herself, fearing she might be headed for Hell. But, she unbuckled his belt anyway as he tugged her skirt downward. Half-dressed they laid down on the fragrant heather. Will removed her nightgown from her shoulder, caressed and kissed her breasts. Then they made love – twice.

Will leaned back against the tree and Nelly lay against his chest. He whispered, "I love you Nelly Hughes."

"And I love ye dear Captain."

"I think now you can call me Will."

"Aye then, I love ye dear Will."

They kissed and made love again.

Spent, they fell away from each other and lay on their backs. After catching his breath, Will leaned on an elbow and took something from his tunic and pressed it into her hand. She sat up, opened her hand and gazed at the solid gold ring resting in her palm.

He said, "That's my family's crest."

Nelly peered at the crest and made out the name "Temple." Horrified, she cried, "Your family? But your name is Tuckerton! Are ye now tellin' me that you're kin to Lord Palmerston?"

Will sat straight up, fully realizing the problem for the first time. "Ah, please listen, Nelly. Lord Palmerston is merely distant kin. I hardly speak to him except on matters of government."

"And how distant are ye from that awful man?"

"The man is my second cousin once removed. We share an ancestry and nothing else, I promise you. Please, I want you to have this ring as a sign of my love."

At length, satisfied with Will's explanation, Nelly's initial reaction subsided. She said, "I must hide the ring from me family."

"Yes, I know that. It is our secret for now; but one of these days, we will marry. You will marry me, won't you?"

Nelly could not speak. She closed her fist around the ring and lay back in Will's arms, finally knowing what "more" there is.

A week later, Will's attendant woke him earlier than usual.

"Sorry for the bother, Sir."

"What is it Nelson?"

"A dispatch from London arrived this morning with the Frigate, *HMS Marianne*. I was told to give it to you promptly." A bit awestruck he added, "It boasts the Queen's seal, Sir."

"Right, Nelson. Thank you."

"Shall I prepare your breakfast?"

"Just tea please."

Placing the letter on the desk by the window, Will washed his face and put on his trousers, letting the suspenders hang down by his sides. Turning to the window he gazed out over the hillside. A smile played upon his lips as he fantasized Nelly thinking of him at that very moment. The smile folded into a frown as he reluctantly picked up the letter and broke the Queen's seal. Signed by an assistant to the Prime Minister, the letter informed him that he was to return to England to provide a first-hand account of conditions in the West, particularly Counties Sligo and Mayo. The letter contained his orders to return when the *Marianne* sets sail for its return trip.

"Ah!" Will sighed "Damn the luck!"

"What's that, Sir?" Nelson said as he held the door open with the toe of his boot while struggling not to drop the tray he was carrying.

"Come in, Nelson."

"Yes Sir. I'm trying Sir."

Will noted with amusement the high color creeping up from his assistant's neck and relieved him of the tray.

Stifling a smile he asked, "When does the *Marianne* set sail for home?"

"It sets sail tomorrow at first light, Sir."

"Ah." Will breathed and turned away. "I'll be leaving with the *Marianne*. I don't know how long I'll be gone, so please pack my trunk accordingly."

"Your trunk will be ready after supper, Sir."

"Thank you, Nelson. That will be all for now."

"But your breakfast?"

"I'll not be taking breakfast. Good day, Nelson."

"Yes, very good Sir." And with that Nelson left Will alone.

Later that morning Will halted Ruffian on the hill above the Hughes' farm. He dismounted and tethered Ruffian to a tree. Stroking the side of her head, he whispered, "Stay girl, I shan't be long." Then he strode down the hill toward the cottage. Without hesitation, he knocked on the door.

Kathleen opened the door and seeing the Captain her eyes grew wide. Her voice was touched with awe, "Sir! What do ye want then?"

"I would like to talk with Mr. Hughes for a moment."

Suddenly Aunt Stella grasped Kathleen's arm and pulled her inside.

"Captain what could ye possibly want with me brother-in-law?"

"I have been called back to England and I…"

Noticing the twins at the window, Stella interrupted him. “Come, walk with me.”

Neither saw Kathleen slip out of the cottage.

Half way up the hill Stella took hold of Will’s sleeve. “Tis far enough. Now then, why would your trip interest me brother-in-law?”

Will had been unsure if he would have the temerity to ask for Nelly’s hand. Nevertheless, he cleared his throat and came right out with it: “Madam, I love Miss Nelly and wish to ask for her hand in marriage.”

For once Stella was speechless, but recovered quickly. “Mr. Hughes is quite indisposed, Captain. And the mother is too ill to receive company.”

“Then Madam I will ask you for her hand for I have no time to spare.”

Completely taken aback, Stella loathed the idea of a marriage between her kin and an Englishman, a soldier at that. Will noticed the angry flush that suddenly appeared on the woman’s face, but he didn’t skip a beat: “Therefore, I would be grateful if you would grant me permission to marry Miss Nelly.”

He dug into his knapsack and removed a pouch. Holding it by its string, he said, “I will give your family this money as a sign of my good faith.”

Stella’s eyes widened at the thought. He continued, “Also, I do not know how long I will be gone, but I will send money each month until I return.”

Stella glanced at the pouch, not wishing to stare. The idea of the money and Stella’s cunning nature set her mind reeling with possibility. At length, she said, “Aye then Captain, you have my permission to marry me niece … if she will have ye.”

“Thank you, dear Lady. May I see her so that I can properly ask for her hand?”

Stella hesitated briefly. Then, she lied, “Nelly went to the village early this morning with Mr. Ryan.”

A bit crestfallen, Will said, "I see. Please tell her that I will come for her upon my return; that is, if she will have me."

"Aye," Stella replied as she reached for the pouch. And now I must bid you good morning."

Will bowed, thanked her again, and walked up the hillside.

Nelly came out of the cottage just as Will was mounting Ruffian. She ran past Aunt Stella, but stopped half way up the hill. Will had not heard her calling to him.

She ran back to the cottage where she confronted her aunt. In a tone an octave higher than usual, she cried, "Aunt Stella! What did the Captain want?" Not waiting for an answer, she asked, "What tis that in ye hand?"

"Tis a pouch."

"I can see that, Aunt. Tis for me, is it not?"

Stella replied, "Tis for later." Turning away from Nelly, she nodded to herself for she had decided what she must do.

Just then Kathleen came into the cottage carrying a jug of milk. Stella noted the red blotches on her cheeks and said, "And what have you been up to, miss?"

In answer Kathleen held the jug at arm's length. Stella gave her a puzzled look, but let it go for she had other more important things on her mind.

For the remainder of the day and into the night, Kathleen wanted to tell Nelly what she had overheard but she didn't want to admit to eavesdropping. Also, she thought it better to let Aunt Stella do the telling.

Nelly went to bed that night not knowing the reason for Will's visit.

Early the next morning she climbed the crest of the hill, down the path and up to the cliffs. She gazed northeast toward where she knew the barracks were. Though she could not see them, she imagined what they looked like in the moving shadows cast by the rising sun. She imagined Will galloping toward her hill. Then she saw something out of the corner of her eye and turned to see a ship heading south. She could not know that Will was on that ship and was, at that very moment, gazing upward toward the cliffs of Sligo. Nelly watched the ship until it sailed past the promontory now graced with Lord Palmerston's half-finished home, which was christened Classiebawn Castle. She turned away and walked back home.

Entering the cottage, she practically tripped over the twins. Without pausing she said, "Aunt Stella, ye must tell me now what the Captain wanted."

"Aye, I must and I will. Come, let's walk."

"They're walking up the hill, they are," cried Maeve.

She and Thomas were on their tip toes looking out the window. Busy as they were, neither saw Kathleen once again slip out of the cottage. She knew the gist of Stella's conversation with the Captain; and she wanted to hear what Aunt Stella would say to Nelly. She hid behind a tree when Stella paused to catch her breath. She heard her aunt say, "See here?"

Nelly looked down at the pouch in Stella's hand.

"Tis full of money from the Captain."

"Why …" Nelly began, but Stella interrupted her.

"That man is an English nobleman. He has no need for the likes of Catholic tenants."

Nelly stared at her Aunt, clearly baffled. Stella continued, "Can't ye see it, child? He is gone! He left on the ship this morning."

Nelly's breath caught and she turned as if to run, but did not. Stella continued, "He gave me money for our family. Payment I should tink for whatever evil he has done to ye."

The awful sharpness of her aunt's words stung Nelly and she cried out, "No Aunt Stella! This cannot be true. The Captain loves me and I love him."

"Tis folly," Stella said flatly. But seeing her young niece's pain, she thought twice about what she had put into motion. *No*, she said to herself, *Tis the right thing to do*. Then aloud, she said, "Calm yourself, child. Tis a cruel thing the man did, going off like that. But soon, I promise, ye'll be glad tis all done with."

As Stella started to embrace her niece, Nelly simply collapsed into her arms. Unaccustomed to such shows of emotion, Stella unfolded herself from Nelly's embrace, took her hand and said, "Come home now."

Neither saw Kathleen run back toward the cottage. Though shocked by the lie Aunt Stella told, she had to believe that the woman must have her reasons. She simply was not sure what she should do; or if she should do anything at all.

A few minutes later, as her aunt and sister drew near, Kathleen shouted, "Maeve, Thomas get down from that window!"

The twins scrambled away from the window. Fiona asked Kathleen to come by her side. "Kathleen, I don't know what the Captain could want with us – with Nelly. And, only God knows what Stella could be doing about whatever it tis. Stella is a good sister, Kathleen, but she is a hard one. Aye! And that's the truth of it."

Kathleen wanted desperately to confide in her mother; but she simply was too confused and, anyway, could not bring herself to admit to ill-gotten knowledge. And so she said nothing.

Stella and Nelly entered the cottage and Nelly went straight to her room. She took Will's ring from its hiding place, clenched it in her fist and flung herself across the mattress. Tears streaming down her face, she ignored the ring's sharp-edged crest cutting into her palm. She thought her heart would break. "How could this be?" she said aloud, "Why would he give me his family's ring and then betray me?"

With the question on her lips, Nelly threw her hands to her mouth muffling a sudden keening sound rising from her throat.

CHAPTER 6 ~ A SLENDER EDGE

Throughout May and June, the Hughes family continued to assist their neighbors in a way that far exceeded what their ordinary circumstance would allow. But no one asked about the source of the family's bounty. On the last day of June Nelly came into the parlor looking pale and a bit shaky. Stella took her aside and said, "I heard the retching again this morning, lass. I have no doubt what ails ye."

Mystified Nelly said, "I don't feel well is all, Aunt."

With uncharacteristic tenderness Stella said, "Ah, ye hardly eat what little you're given. Don'cha know what's wrong?" When Nelly didn't respond, Stella said flatly, "You're with child, lass. And we must make a plan." Under her breath she added, "Drat that man!"

Aghast, Nelly bounded up to the second floor.

Later that day Mr. Ryan brought Stella to the barracks to collect the mail. Unseen by Mr. Ryan, she tore open a letter from the Captain. She shook several coins of high value into her hand and then scanned the letter meant for Nelly. She stuffed it and the money into her apron pocket, intending to burn the letter in the hearth as she had the one before and the one before that.

She lifted the hem of her skirt and climbed into the cart.

"Mr. Ryan, I need to purchase your service."

"Ma'am I am Kathleen's betrothed. Tis me family soon! No need to pay me."

"Tis kind of ye, but I need ye to take Miss Nelly down to Galway. Tis far away and more than a mere favor. Tis a secret as well. So, Mr. Ryan, ye shall be paid, and that's that."

"Aye Ma'am. And when do I do this, er, favor?"

"All will be ready after Sunday Mass."

Upon her return to the cottage, Stella said to Kathleen, "Mr. Ryan is waiting for you to fetch your Da. Take the twins, they need a ride. Where's Nelly?"

"She's in bed, Aunt. I fear she has the fever."

"She'll be fine, I promise you. Now go."

After the children left, Fiona said to Stella, "Sister I might be ill all these months, but me eyes and ears are fine. I know the lass is with child." She caught her breath. "And so, we must make a plan for her."

"Tis all taken care of, Fiona. Mr. Ryan is in my confidence and will take Nelly to the Sisters of the Good Shepherd. There she will be kept safe to deliver the child."

"I fear what ye have in mind, Stella. Nelly and the wee one must come back home."

"Tis not possible, sister. Hungry though our neighbors are; they have strength enough to wag on about a child with a child, but without a husband." She paused. "And can't ye just see Cormac Daley and his good father and mother? Ach! I won't stand the shame of it, Fiona."

In her weakened state, Fiona managed to lean on her elbow, saying, "I don't care what Cormac Daley and his kin tink, Stella. Are ye forgetting Nelly is not your child? She belongs to Michael and me. And I …" Exhausted with the effort, she lay back on the pillow.

Stella felt Fiona's forehead. "Ah! You're not up to this. Ye speak of Michael, do ye? And where is that no-account husband of yours?"

Her sister's words stung like a bee and Fiona started to respond. But Stella took no notice, saying, "Mr. Terrance O'Keefe sent a letter with me sign to our cousin in Prince Edward Island."

"And ye did this without telling me, Stella? How could ye?"

Stella didn't respond; instead she held out a letter. "This is Mr. Seamus O'Connell's answer."

With as much strength as she could muster, Fiona said, "I don't want to know."

"Fiona, be sensible. Nelly cannot bring the child home. Mr. O'Connell says he will marry her; and with no dowry, mind ye. He will take care of the wee one as his own." And in a more gentle tone, she added, "Fiona, dear sister, tis the right thing to do."

When dawn broke on Sunday morning Nelly crept out of bed and dressed quickly. She kissed Kathleen's forehead and whispered, "Stay on sleeping dear sister; I cannot say goodbye to you." She picked up the satchel she had prepared the night before and crept to the loft. She placed her hand lightly on Maeve's brow, and gently kissed her cheek. Thomas turned in his sleep and Nelly whispered, "Take care Thomas, ye are in my prayers always. When our brother Paul Tibertus comes home, tell him I love him and will miss him."

Then she went down to the first floor. Michael was waiting for her. She saw tears in his eyes and immediately embraced him. She held his hand for a moment, let it go, and walked to her mother's cot. She touched Fiona's brow, feeling the awful heat of the fever. Fiona opened her eyes, but could not speak.

"Ah! Mam," Nelly whispered, "I am sorry to bring ye shame."

Tears filled Fiona's eyes. Nelly felt her own tears sting the back of her eyes.

Just then the door swung wide. A bitter wind brought rain and Aunt Stella tumbling into the kitchen. Michael took his leave through the open door.

"Tis time lass," began Aunt Stella, "ye mustn't delay, Mr. Ryan has his schedule. Meet him at the crossing just beyond the school house."

Nelly kissed Fiona's cheek, tasting the salt of her mother's tears, barely holding back her own.

Stella said, "Now don't carry on. The good sisters will care for you. After the wee one is born they'll see you both off on the ship sailing to America." She took a breath. "Mr. Ryan will give the sisters your fare on a good ship, the one that sails to New York first and then on to Canada."

Nelly nodded, picked up her satchel and left the cottage.

Kneeling on the mattress, Kathleen looked out the window. Since the day she overheard Aunt Stella talking to the Captain and later to Nelly, she had been in a colossal moral debate with herself. On the one hand, she wanted to tell Nelly that the Captain intended to return to her. On the other, she had decided that her Aunt must be doing the right thing. And so, Kathleen had held her own counsel and now it was too late.

She watched Nelly walk down the cottage path, wind nipping at her hem. Kathleen knew that she would never forgive herself for not telling her sister the truth. And, she would never forget the sight of Nelly walking away from home, holding her back straight and her head high. Kathleen wanted so much to wave good bye; but Nelly did not look back.

When Nelly arrived at the school house she went in and walked straight to the back wall. She knew that Father O'Malley had carved her name there so all would know that one more has left the village and will never return. She traced her finger under the letters that spelled her name. Then she left the schoolhouse and turned into the wind.

Nelly did not cry and she did not look back.

After a week of trekking 135 kilometers of rough terrain and taking rest in welcoming homes, Mr. Ryan's carriage entered Galway City, the only actual city in the Province of Connaught. Obtaining directions from several helpful citizens, Ryan found the path that would lead to the Sisters of the Good Shepherd. When they reached O'Brian's bridge, Nelly gazed across it to "Nun's Island," and pulled her shawl tighter around her shoulders. The Island seemed entirely composed of the medieval convent's massive walls.

Mr. Ryan's deep voice broke into her thoughts, "Ah! We're finally here miss."

Nelly's heart took an odd tumble; but she managed to whisper, "Aye so we are, Mr. Ryan."

Though the bridge did not seem sturdy enough for the weight of his cart and its passengers, Ryan gamely urged his horse forward. Hardly had they crossed the bridge when two nuns, clad in white habits, came running to meet them. Nelly was a bit shocked to see nuns running, for she didn't know they could, or should. The younger nun, hardly older than Nelly, stretched her hand to help her climb from the cart. The older nun grabbed Nelly's satchel before Ryan could climb from the cart. She introduced herself as Sister Aloysius and the other as Sister Judith. Aloysius handed the satchel to Ryan and took Nelly's hand. The four trudged up the hill to the convent. Aloysius told Ryan to stay put while she and Judith ushered Nelly into the convent. Ryan winced as the massive doors shut loudly. Within moments the doors re-opened and Sister Judith placed a tray of tea and sandwiches on a table. Maintaining custody of her eyes all the while she nodded and went back into the convent.

After taking the refreshments Ryan lit his pipe and wandered about the grounds. Half an hour later he was skipping stones on the river's surface when a sudden wind scattered leaves and blew clouds across the mid-day sun, blocking its warmth. Anxious to get on his way, Ryan thought this weather change might give him an excuse to take his leave. Just as he was about to knock on the door, it opened and Aloysius stepped onto the porch.

"Mr. Ryan, Miss Nelly is settled now." She scowled at the sky. "Ye best be on your way, sir."

"Aye, and that's the truth. Would you be telling Miss Nelly goodbye for me then?"

"Aye of course. Watch the bridge now."

Ryan walked down the hill, turned and waved. Sister Aloysius called, "Godspeed to ye."

He climbed into his cart and off he went across the bridge.

Mr. Ryan didn't see Nelly peering out a second-floor window of a nun's cell where Sister Judith had taken her. She gave a small wave and watched his carriage until she could no longer see it.

Sister Judith was saying, "This was Sister Mary Brigid's room. She was our superior for many years; and some people tink she's a saint in heaven. The Pope is considering whether her name should be placed among the potentials for canonization."

Fussing about the room, she continued, "We give this room to wayward girls to inspire them."

"I see." Nelly said, suddenly feeling tainted. She hadn't thought of herself as wayward. Her passion for Captain Tuckerton and the ache over his betrayal had overshadowed everything else. She had never thought of the child whose heart beat in her womb as illegitimate.

Sister Judith's voice broke into her thoughts. "Well, then, Sister Lucy will bring ye some tea and bread. Then, ye must rest until you hear the bell ring. When it rings come down to the Main Hall and join us for evening prayer." She looked around the room, nodded her head in satisfaction, and left Nelly alone. As she pulled the door almost closed, a cat with a glossy gray coat slipped into the room.

"Ah! And what do we have here?" Nelly said, clearly pleased. She picked up the cat and looked into her face. The cat, purring loudly, placed one paw on Nelly's cheek. Nelly's soft chuckle suddenly turned into a sob. Tears began to flow and she held the cat close. "Ah cat! What am I to do without them? I miss Kathleen and the twins, Mam and Da." Another sob escaped from her lips, "Cat, I miss Captain Tuckerton..." The cat squirmed free of Nelly's embrace and leapt from her arms.

Nelly willed herself to stop crying and began to unpack her satchel. She pulled a small piece of the satchel's lining; and then more frantically she tore a larger piece. With a sigh of relief she grasped Will's ring from beneath the lining. Since the ring wasn't exactly where she had placed it, she thought that Aunt Stella may have found the hiding place. But she knew she would never know for sure. Her thoughts were interrupted by a soft knocking at the door.

"Tis Sister Lucy with tea, child. May I come in?"

Nelly stuffed the ring under the pillow and before she could answer, the nun pushed the door open and held it with her copious backside. As she bent down to pick up the tea tray, the cat sauntered out of the room.

"Ah. I see ye and Victoria have met. She's an imperious thing that cat. So we named her after the Queen."

Nelly couldn't help but smile at this plump and merry vision awkwardly kicking her habit out of her way as she walked toward the window shelf. Nelly hadn't known many nuns, but her cousin was a nun with a sour expression, always on the verge of anger, it seemed. Nelly didn't know that some nuns could be merry.

Sister Lucy brought a cup of tea and bread to Nelly.

"Here, eat and drink, lass. I tink ye'll enjoy the bread. Made it me self, I did." Her gaze fell on Nelly's face. "Ah, child, ye must be exhausted. But ye must eat for the strength of it." She looked around. "Did Sister Judith tell you whose room this used to be?"

"Aye that she did."

"Then ye'll be fine. Sleep a bit if ye can. Come down at the bell."

She turned and left the room as awkwardly as she entered.

Though eating held no appeal, Nelly knew she must eat; and so, she ate the bread and drank the tea. Then she fell into blessed sleep; but woke up suddenly to a loud clanging noise.

Disoriented, she sat straight up. She looked at the threatening sky filling the single window in the room. Remembering where she was and why, a lump formed in her throat. She pulled herself together and saw that a basin had been placed in her room while she slept. She went directly to it and washed her face. Then she looked at her reflection in the window, fussed with her skirt and hair, and left the room. She turned on her heel and walked back to the cot. She removed the ring from under the pillow and put it back into the lining of her satchel. Then she found her way to the Main Hall.

After Vespers, accompanied by the Gregorian chant, the nuns led the way to the dining room. Everything was so different from what Nelly knew. She marveled at the spacious rooms and was amazed when a middle-aged nun actually served their supper. During the meal Sister Aloysius sat at the head of the table and read aloud from the Bible. Except for Sister Aloysius reading, there was no talking. When a nun wanted salt, for example, she would make a small gesture and another nun would mysteriously know to pass the salt.

Nelly did not gesture for anything. Sister Judith had told her that silence would reign for the rest of the night and would be broken only after Morning Prayer and breakfast.

Later that night, Nelly did not check her tears. She cried silently until the strain of the trip took its toll and pulled her into a deep sleep.

The next morning she awoke to the shrill clanging of the bell and the frightening feeling of displacement. She dressed quickly and went to the Main Hall. After breakfast, Sister Aloysius took Nelly's hand.

"Come child, walk with me."

As they walked down the front steps, Aloysius said, "Ach! There's that foul smell again. Tis that most sinister Fairie, '*Fear Liath*,' that awful, formless creature made from fog itself."

Nelly raised her eyes to the sky. "Aye and they say he creeps from the bogs, bringing the rot to the potatoes."

Wrinkling her nose, Sister Aloysius said, "We once could breathe good clear air after rain, but no more."

She led Nelly down to the river. "And what did ye mam tell ye about being with child?"

"I helped bring the twins into the world so I know what happens. The sickness will go away soon, but I don't know how it feels to bring a child forth. Mam yelled a lot."

"Aye tis painful child. And were you sick this morning?"

Nelly was surprised to realize that, though she was heartsick that morning, she had not been sick with the child.

The two were quiet for a while. Then Nelly asked, "What happens to the wee ones who are born here?"

"If families do not come for them, there are good folks who care for orphan children."

Crestfallen at the thought of losing Will's child, Nellie said, "Ah! But I can care for him."

"And how do ye know tis a boy, then?"

"I don't know how. I just know."

"Stella McBride gave me several pounds for ye to sail to New York and then on to Canada. Ye must go when the last boat leaves Sligo Port. It will come here and then on to America. Ye cannot take a wee one on the boat."

"Tis a ship, Sister."

"Ship. Boat. Tis all the same."

"A ship is safer than a boat, Sister." And then she added emphatically, "The lad will come with me and that's that."

Sister Aloysius patiently replied, "We'll see. For now, ye'll work and pray along with us. When your time comes, Sister Lucy will care for ye." She paused, and added proudly, "She's a nurse from Dublin, ye know.

"There's the chill. Come let's go back."

Nelly thought, *Good! The merry nun will care for me and the child.*

As the weeks passed, Nelly enjoyed the small comings and goings of convent life – even the silence at meals and during the night. Her child grew within her and often she felt glad; but her moments of happiness fled with the thought of Will's betrayal. The cat named after the Queen had become her constant companion. But Nelly did not like to use the Queen's name, so she renamed her "Cat."

The summer months passed quickly and the new potatoes were healthy and remained healthy. Even the second crop in October was healthy enough that year. But, since there had not been enough seedling potatoes to plant in February, the harvest did not yield nearly enough to feed the whole Country. So, all over Ireland, millions continued to starve. Since the Sisters of the Good Shepherd did not have to contend with a landlord, absent or otherwise, they were able to keep the grain they grew and the milk from their cows. So, they had oats to make oaten cakes, wheat to make bread, and plenty of milk to make cheese and butter. They had plenty to eat and to share with their neighbors.

Then one day a very strange thing happened – snow fell in October, which was unheard of in Ireland. Though light, the early snow presaged the winter of 1846-47, the worst winter anyone had ever seen. It would go down in history as "Black '47,"the year Ireland's population would be decimated by famine, disease, and emigration.

Sister Judith, who had been gazing at the snowfall, saw the postman's cart. She wrapped her shawl around her shoulders and went to meet him. Walking back to the convent she flipped through the mail. One piece was from Mullaghmore, addressed to Sister Aloysius. She picked up her pace and went quickly to her superior's cell. Rapping lightly on the half-opened door, she said, "Tis Sister Judith. I have a letter from Mullaghmore."

"Enter," Sister Aloysius said. She took the envelope from Judith and tore it open. She read the note aloud:

Dear Sisters of the Good Shepherd, Mr. O'Keefe is writing this for me as I cannot read nor can I write. We received news of my niece's progress and we are grateful. But my news from Mullaghmore is not so good. My dear sister, Nelly's mother, has died. Fiona left this sorry world just two days ago. Mr. O'Keefe says she will be dead almost two weeks by the time you get this letter. Her parting was a blessing, for my sainted sister was sick from birthing a child, still born was he. And then we all came on hard times, with no potatoes, so Fiona did not gain strength. A month ago, she fell into a very deep sleep and did not awake. She suffered just like the martyrs in heaven. And now she has joined them. Mr. O'Keefe says that my name, Stella, means star. He is a smart man, he is. Because I cannot write, then, I will make a star so you will know this is from me. I thank you for caring for my niece, and for caring for the wee one when the time comes. Yours in Christ,

Next to the star, Mr. O'Keefe had written "McBride," Stella's last name.

Sister Aloysius dangled the letter loosely, and said, "Judith, bring Miss Nelly to the parlor."

Upon entering the parlor with Judith behind her, Nelly could tell bad news was coming her way.

"Child" began Sister Aloysius, "come sit down." She told Sister Judith to fetch the tea.

Aloysius gazed at Nelly with eyes full of compassion. "I am sorry to give you this news." Then she read the letter aloud.

Stricken, Nelly stood, but immediately sat down, shaking her head from left to right. Sister Aloysius got up and placed her hand on Nelly's shoulder. She stood that way until Sister Judith returned with the tray of tea and biscuits. Judith handed a cup to Nelly.

"Here, the tea will help."

Nelly took the cup and sipped. She handed the cup back to Sister Judith.

"I do not feel well, sisters. May I go to my room?"

Sister Aloysius nodded to Sister Judith. Taking the hint, Judith took Nelly's hand. Once in the room, Nelly said, "Sister Judith, ye need not stay with me."

"I'll get ye settled, and then we'll see."

"Sister, I will sleep. Please leave me."

Judith nodded and reluctantly left the room.

As Nelly lay down, "Cat" leapt onto the cot. Grief stricken though Nelly was, she did not cry. Neither did she stir at all that late afternoon; nor did she appear for evening prayer and supper.

Later that night, Sister Judith rapped on the door, saying, "Miss Nelly, ye must eat. Tink of the wee one." Not hearing a response, she went into the room. The cat was asleep at the foot of the cot and Nelly appeared to be sleeping. Judith placed the tray on the window shelf and left the room.

Satisfied that Judith was gone, Nelly opened her eyes stared out the window into the night.

The sisters understood why Nelly did not appear at Evening Prayer, but were very concerned when she did not appear for Morning Prayer. Sister Lucy went to Nelly's cell and rapped on the half-opened door. "Tis Sister Lucy here, child."

With effort, Nelly swung her legs over the side of the cot and bent in sudden pain. Sister Lucy was aghast by the sight of Nelly's pale face sweating profusely.

"Ach! And how long have ye been like this?"

Before Nelly could answer, she cried out in pain. Sister Lucy rolled up her habit's sleeves and helped Nelly lay back on the cot.

Nelly whispered, "It hurts so much, Sister."

Feeling Nelly's brow Sister Lucy said, "I can't tell if ye have the fever or if you're hot from exertion."

Then Nelly suddenly sat up, her arms across her stomach. "Tis another cramp," She said weakly. Lucy was concerned because, by her reckoning, Nelly was not yet ready to give birth.

Sister Lucy put a finger to her lips in thought. Then she exclaimed, "Ah! I see. I tink the child will come early." She tucked the covers up to Nelly's chin. Nudging the cat out of the way, she said, "I'll be right back."

A short while later, she returned with sisters Judith and Aloysius, followed by "Cat." The three nuns were carrying things Nelly recognized as things she and Kathleen gathered when their mother was ready to deliver the twins. She cringed and shut her eyes tight. Aloysius gave Sister Judith a look and said, "Take that cat downstairs. She mustn't be around the sick bed or near the wee one."

Throughout the day, one or the other sister attended Nelly. Sister Lucy had cautioned them to be prepared for a still born child. By nightfall, an exhausted Nelly dealt with the worst cramp of the day. Her cry echoed through the room, to the ceiling and died in a whimper on the floor.

Sister Lucy said, "I tink the child is ready to come, lass. Take heart now and do exactly as I say."

Twenty minutes later a premature child was born. Sister Lucy sighed, "Ah! Tis a boy, just like ye said."

"Humph!" Huffed Sister Aloysius clearly displeased at Sister Lucy's apparent acceptance of clairvoyance. She took the baby from Sister Lucy and gave him a whack. The baby yelled in protest. She said, "He's a healthy one, he is."

As two sisters tended the baby, Sister Judith concerned herself with Nelly, who still appeared to be in great pain. Judith suddenly cried, "Oh dear God! Someting's happening here. Come Sisters, hurry."

Aloysius said, "Go to her Lucy, I'll tend the wee one."

Lucy rushed to the cot saying, "Open your legs, child. I need to see what's happening here." Without taking a breath, she exclaimed: "Sister Judith! Did'ja take out the afterbirth?" Before Judith could answer, Sister Lucy cried out in jubilation, "Tis another wee one, Sisters! Twins they are."

After what seemed to her like an eternity, Nelly delivered the second child, an identical twin, but smaller than his brother. She fell back exhausted and drenched in sweat. Sister Lucy gave the baby a gentle whack; but he did not respond. She took him away from the cot and nodded to Sister Judith. With a damp cloth Judith gently wiped Nelly's face, neck and chest. Sister Lucy gave the tiny twin another whack and this time he cried out. She sighed with relief and asked Sister Aloysius to bring the other child to Nelly.

Nelly looked down at the tiny being at her breast. She touched the small hand and the baby's fingers grasped hers. Not knowing that this action was a mere reflex, she was enormously touched. She felt a swelling in her chest as unchecked tears streamed down her cheeks. This time, her tears accompanied a happiness she had never known before. Then, the baby began to fuss.

Judith said, "I don't tink your milk is ready, lass. Tis the strain of the two of them coming early. But don'cha fret. Until your milk is ready he will have good cow's milk to nourish him."

In a small, exhausted voice, Nelly said, "And the other?"

Sister Lucy brought the baby to Nelly's cot. "He's a weak one, he is. God knows he worked very hard coming to ye."

As Nelly reached up to the child her fingers lightly touched his hand. She was saddened when he did not grasp her fingers. Seeing this, Lucy said, "We'll watch him while ye take care of his brother. And what are their names?"

Nelly looked first at the child at her breast and said, "His name is William Tuckerton Hughes. He will be called Will." She looked up at Will's twin and said, "His name is Christopher, after the Saint who helped us cross the bridge to ye Good Shepherds."

Sisters Lucy and Aloysius took the twins down to their quarters to care for them. Sister Judith remained behind to watch over Nelly until she fell asleep.

When Nelly entered that state between wakefulness and slumber, she thought of the famine raging throughout her homeland and of the friends and relatives who had been its victims. She imagined the face of her mother who she would never see again. And she thought of Will, almost able to smell his scent as he made love to her in the midst of sweet heather. She thought of his promise with the ring he had given her. She could not fully believe that he had betrayed her; and so she had given their strongest son his name. During the past year Nelly had come to an understanding of the slender edge between happiness and sorrow.

She had become intimate with edges.

CHAPTER 7
A VOYAGE IN A COFFIN SHIP

Mullaghmore ~1972

Mayor Daniel Fahey pulled the rope unveiling the memorial to those who perished in the wreck of *The Forrester*, which sank off the coast of Quebec Province in 1847. As soon as the crowd's applause died down, the local historian, Gregory McGowan intoned, "Today we remember those who died during those awful years when burying the dead was the way of life in Ireland. Death was so prevalent during the Great Famine that corpses were carried on special carts whose bottom would drop so the poor souls' bodies would fall into a mass grave … there to be covered with lime.

"We gather especially to remember those who fled our great land in ships meant to carry only lumber. In County Sligo alone, Sir John Temple, who you all know as the Viscount Lord Palmerston …"

Boos and hisses rose from the crowd.

McGowan departed from his prepared speech, "Please Ladies and Gents give credit where credit is due. As twice England's Prime Minister, history attributes great accomplishments to Lord Palmerston. Remember, he was the first landlord to step foot on Sligo's conquered land."

Waving an arm toward Donegal Harbor sparkling in the sun, he said, "The man built that harbor, which carried the West Coast into the 19th Century."

Then he turned dramatically toward the cliffs, saying, "And you'll agree that his Classiebawn Castle added grace and beauty to our rugged landscape." Not wanting to lose his audience he quickly added, "Aye of course I agree that overshadowing all of it, Lord Palmerston's record during the worst years of Ireland's Great Hunger is utterly shameful."

The crowd cheered its approval.

"Under his orders more than 2,000 people from County Sligo alone were shipped off to North America in ships designed to carry only lumber. Though the poor souls' bodies and spirits were broken with fever they held out hope for a new life. But irony so evil, instead of a new life many of their lives ended in a watery grave at the bottom of the Atlantic. Such was the fate of our brothers and sisters who perished 125 years ago when *The Forrester* crashed into the rocks of Cap-de- Rosiers."

With a flourish he pulled his handkerchief from his breast pocket and touched his cheek as if to wipe away a tear or two. Then said, "If a bridge were made of the corpses of our countrymen lost in the Atlantic, it would span from Eire all the way across to the Americas."

As McGowan continued his eulogy, a young woman with dark brown eyes and skin the color of mocha, lifted her crying two-year-old son. The child stopped crying immediately and grabbed his mother's long dark hair. Claire Sheain anxiously looked around at the crowd and whispered, "Shush Will, Da is here somewhere."

Just then a roughly handsome man about 30 tapped her shoulder. "So, here you are lass. I was looking all over."

"Ah! Blarney, Tuckerton O'Connell. We've been right here where you left us. The lad's crying for you and I've had enough of the doldrums today."

Tuck ruffled his son's hair and kissed him.

Claire said, "Do you tink it all could be true?"

"Aye tis true, darlin'," Tuck said.

He took Will from Claire's arms and guided his small family away from the crowd. He observed, "McGowan will probably tell a tale for each of the 125 years that passed between then and now. But tonight when the lad's asleep I'll tell you a tale of all tales."

"You're full of tales, man. Could this possibly be a tale I've yet to hear?"

"You've not heard it all, not by a long shot."

Later, settled on their hotel room's balcony, Tuck held up his bottle of Guinness, toasted the crowd, which had begun to disperse. He said, "My Granfar, Paul Tibertus O'Connell, told me a grand tale about his Great Grandmother, Nelly Hughes, and her son, Will."

He took a hefty pull of Guinness and began his story with a dramatic account of the Great Famine's toll on both his and Claire's ancestors. He told her of the brief affair between Captain William Tuckerton and Nelly, of the birth of their twin sons in a Galway Convent, and of Nelly's determination to take both sons with her to Prince Edward Island.

"But that wasn't to be, Claire. And therein lays the tale of all tales."

Galway - November 1846

Until the very morning Father Carroll arrived at the Convent to take Nelly to the dock, she held out hope that she would take the twins with her to America. The sisters had prepared her to face the fact that Christopher, the weaker one, would have a better chance of survival if he remained with them. Sister Lucy had said, "Christopher will fare much better with us then on that boat."

Nelly had responded, "Sister, I keep tellin' ye tis a ship; tis safer than a boat."

Ignoring the comment, Sister Lucy had continued: "He is too fragile, child. I tell ye he cannot live pass Galway Bay. We'll send him to ye when he's strong enough."

Now holding Will under her cloak she stood on the dock watching a ship drop anchor. She held Will closer to her breast as a biting gust of wind slammed into her, tearing her bonnet from her head. She caught it and went inside the waiting room.

"Aye, ye there!" yelled the ticket agent. Nelly turned toward him. "Aye missus. You're the one the good sisters sent are ye not?"

"Aye that I am, sir. I have me ticket here."

He looked at her ticket, which was for passage on an American Ship. He said, "I'm sorry to tell ye that American captains refuse to make the crossing until winter's end. Tis the worst winter ever seen in Ireland and ye should wait 'til spring to cross over."

He held a match to his pipe.

Pointing to the ship in the harbor, Nelly said, "But we can go on that ship, can we not?"

The agent blew a ring of smoke.

"That would be *The Forrester*. Tis a lumber ship ready to return to Canada. Tis a strong ship, but the American ship is more comfortable." He paused and added, "Anyway, they say the Saint Lawrence River might be frozen early this year."

A touch of panic, Nelly said, "Sir, I must go now! Family waits for me on Prince Edward Island."

"Ah! Why didn't ye say so? *The Forrester* is what will get ye there quicker than an American ship. Look here." he pointed to the ticket in her hand. "Ye see that? For the money ye save taking *The Forrester*, I can get ye a good berth. Leave it me."

And with that he exchanged her ticket, showing her the red mark indicating a higher level berth. He said, "Alright then?"

Nelly thanked the agent and sat down on the only free bench in the building. The rafters were moaning with the wind, and ice began to form ghostly sculptures on the windows. After a while, the man sitting next to her said, "See there, missus? The longboat is here to take us to the ship."

The man, carrying a *bodhran* and little else, said, "Me name is Martin Ashe."

She shook his offered hand and told him her name, adding, "And this wee one's name is Will."

"And a fine looking lad he is."

When the agent announced departure, Mr. Ashe helped Nelly to her feet, and picked up her satchel. As the agent ripped the stub off their tickets, he looked directly into Nelly's eyes and said simply, "Godspeed to ye and the lad."

He watched until all ninety Galway passengers had left to join the 197 souls already on board. He shook his head sadly from side to side and reflected upon what he knew about the lumber ships. In the past two years *The Forrester* had made three voyages from Quebec to the British Isles transporting logs from the Canadian forests. The ship's return trips would have been quite fast given there was no cargo on board; but, without ballast she surely would be unstable. However, he knew that now her return trips, though not as quick, were stable enough because instead of lumber, her hold was laden with human cargo. "Perfect ballast!" he said aloud and with disgust. He knew that most of the Irishmen aboard *The Forrester* had been shoveled out of their homes, their passage paid for by Lord Palmerston himself. "To get rid of them!" He mumbled. He looked at the mandatory portrait of Queen Victoria on the wall, and spit on the floor.

His thoughts returned to what he knew about lumber ships. After a ship delivered its lumber, the bins were torn down and replaced by 6 x10-foot berths for passengers. There were no amenities, not even toilets – just a bucket here and there that may or may not spill before their contents could be tossed overboard. The agent wondered whether the berth he had been told about and had given Nelly really existed. He seriously doubted it; but, he countered to himself that his intentions were good. Then he went to work counting the ticket stubs of the Galway citizens now gone forever.

The bitter wind began to whip snow and sleet as Martin Ashe helped Nelly and her son to board the ship. Once on deck, they were shocked to see a mass of their countrymen in nothing but rags huddling together for warmth.

A few minutes later, Captain Maurice Lemieux addressed the throng. In heavily accented English he yelled above the wind, "Each family of four will share a berth. Those without family will come together in fours and share one berth.

"None of you are allowed on deck, except those fit young men who will be chosen to assist my crew. If any one of those goes back into the hold for any reason, he will not be allowed back on deck."

He paused holding onto his cap, and then continued, "We have one pound of food for each adult. Two children below the age of 13 are counted as one, so they will be given one pound to share. Each of you will have three quarts of water and no more. Be warned that you must not be greedy with water. We don't expect complaints. Do not fail to follow the crew's orders. The slightest disobedience will be dealt with harshly."

Fearful and angry murmurs rose from the crowd.

Captain Lemieux took his pipe from its pouch and held it unlit. He yelled, "Quiet! Save your questions. There will be plenty of time for them later." He removed his cap and concluded, "God save the Queen!"

At mention of the Queen several Irish men in the back of the crowd spit on the deck.

Then crew members immediately marshaled the crowd as they would cattle toward the four hatches that led to the hold below. Nelly stepped aside and called to one of the sailors in charge of her group.

"Sir!" The sailor turned toward her. "See here," she said, "I have a ticket for a special berth."

The sailor snatched the ticket from her hand, looked at it and laughed.

"Come now, Mademoiselle, there is no … what was it you called it, a 'special berth'? No such thing aboard a lumber ship. Are you Irish as stupid as they say? Your berth is down the hatch like the rest. Move on now. You're blocking the way."

Nelly looked about for Martin Ashe, but he was nowhere in sight. Then, with unnecessary roughness, the sailor pushed her toward one of the hatches. One by one, men, women, children and mothers carrying babies descended a steep ladder leading to the hold below. Once settled into their 6 x10-foot spaces and despite the suffering they had already endured, many still had the strength of mind to be shocked by what they were about to endure: weeks in the ship's hold not fit for animals, without space to walk around or fresh air to breath. They feared they would die in the stifle of their beds of filthy sawdust and straw.

As Nelly took her final step on the ladder, a hand grasped her elbow. She was relieved to see a familiar face. Martin Ashe said, "Here, missus, come take me berth. Tis closer to the hatch and God's clean air."

Not waiting for her to refuse his offer, he led her to his berth. Holding his *bodhran* in one hand he helped Nelly and Will climb onto the berth. Though people were put together regardless of sex, age or physical condition, Nelly was relieved to see that the berth Mr. Ashe offered her was occupied by a middle-aged woman, a teen-aged girl and a small boy with hair as black as night.

The woman said, "I am Mary and this is my daughter, Caitlin. The lad is Desmond. He's an orphan, he is."

"Hello Caitlin. Hello there, Desmond. I am Nelly and this wee one is Will."

She craned her neck and saw the top of her benefactor's *bodhran*. Humbled by his generosity, she silently said a prayer for him. And then his drum disappeared from her sight.

Mullaghmore ~ 1972

Tuck took a sip of his now tepid Guinness and tossed the rest over the railing. He got another and refreshed Claire's tea. Then he lit a Camel, cartons of which an American friend had sent to him.

He said, "So many died on the crossing from the famine fever, typhus, delirium, and whatnot. But not Nelly and Will … she was a strong one, she was.

"Claire, only eight lanterns lit the ship's filthy hold. Granfar told me that when they flickered on a person, Nelly could see a ghost-like figure … a mere shadow of a man or a woman. One day, a man, mad with fever, suddenly up and ran through the hold past Nelly's berth. He scrambled up the ladder onto the deck. And didn't Nelly run right after him followed by the man's daughter. When they reached the top steps of the ladder they saw the man jump overboard without the least hesitation. His daughter let out a small cry and threw her hand to her mouth. Without a word, she climbed back down into the hold."

In between sobs, Claire said, "Ah Tuck, no matter how often I've heard such stories I am still shocked by them. It's so… so… awful! Too awful to believe."

He took his handkerchief and gently brushed tears from her cheeks, saying "Aye tis hard to believe, but tis the truth handed down from Nelly to her son, all the way to Granfar Paul Tibertus, and then to me. My family is known for telling tall tales, but this is not one of them."

Then he dragged deeply on his cigarette and tossed its end over the railing.

The North Atlantic ~ December 1846

For over a week tremendous gales had been assaulting *The Forrester*. Finally, the weather calmed down and Captain Lemieux and his second in command, Emil Leduc, were walking on deck.

"Captain," Leduc began, "by now we should have already been docked in Quebec. Those damn gales set us back almost a week."

"Aye and we've yet to meet up with the icebergs," the Captain responded.

"Do you think the Saint Lawrence is frozen over?"

"Who's to know?" Lemieux paused to light his pipe. "Those wretched Irish. How many dead have been sent overboard?"

"At last count 82 of them died of something – typhus, dysentery and God knows what else. Sir, the count was only seven when the sailors first refused to touch the dead."

"Mon Dieu! Think of it, Leduc, the Irish themselves sent 75 of their own to their watery grave."

"They are a brave lot, Captain. Did you hear the drum and fiddle at Christmas?"

"Yes, I did. The poor wretches can hardly walk, yet they could sing the joyful Yuletide songs. It is amazing."

"It is that. They sing all the time, Captain. And some even dance. There's a man … I think his name is Ashe … he plays the drum like none I've ever heard. The sailors listen to their songs. I saw some of them toss food down the hatches. I didn't write them up, Captain."

Upon revealing that fact, Emil's right eye twitched. Captain Lemieux noticed, and smiling wryly, he said, "I myself have tossed them some food from time to time. Most of their food ran out over a week ago. I cringe, Emil, when I hear the moans of the sick crying out for water. The damn dock overseer fouled that water. It's nothing but filth now." He took a breath and added, "I have changed my mind about them, Leduc. God help me."

At that moment, the crow's nest sailor cried, "Icebergs! Icebergs dead ahead!"

An excellent seaman, Captain Lemieux traversed the iceberg fields expertly. Some of the Irish boys, including Desmond, climbed the ladder and opened the hatch a crack. Seeing that the sailors were about doing their tasks, the boys crept onto the deck. The sheer magnificence of the stars hurt their eyes; and the sight of the icebergs filled their imaginations.

After having his full of the wondrous outdoors, Desmond climbed back into the hold. Reaching his berth and hardly containing his excitement, he exclaimed, "Ye won't believe a word I say! Ye'll tink tis the fever. I tell ye there are more stars then there are fairies in all of Galway. And the ice tings are taller than Galway's cliffs, they are. And, we saw two ships stuck on them."

Hardly without taking a breath, he asked Nelly, "Will the people on the ice die missus?"

"They will surely die if they can't get off the ice. We must pray for them."

"Will we die, missus, will we?"

"No, no dear Desmond, we won't die. Our Captain has nerves as strong as Connemara marble. He's French, ye know, that means he's Catholic. He won't let the ice get us."

Nelly's berth-mate, Mary, said, "Surely the ice won't get me daughter for I don't tink she'll last the night." Her voice cracked with emotion as she said, "Look! The darlin' is barely conscious."

The next morning Nelly told Desmond to hold Will. "Watch him until Mary and I return from the deck."

Together they managed to carry Caitlin's frail body up the ladder. Upon seeing them struggle to place the body on deck, a sailor went to their aid. He carried the body to port side and gently lifted it over the railing. Since coverings were long gone, he simply let Caitlin's body slip from his hands into the freezing waters below. Then he made the sign of the cross. Nelly crossed herself as well. Then she helped a grief-stricken Mary climb down the ladder.

For his kindness, the sailor met only derisive shouts from his crewmates – and like others before him who had dared touch an infected Irishman, he was ordered below deck for the remainder of the trip.

Later that afternoon Captain Lemieux had maneuvered his ship through the last of the iceberg field. "Well that's finished," he reflected. As Leduc had said, by this time the ship should have reached Quebec, having already dropped its human cargo off at the Gross Isle disinfection center. Instead, gazing at the sky, the Captain felt a familiar unease. He felt sure that *The Forrester* was about to engage in an epic battle with gigantic North Atlantic waves.

And he was right. Not half-hour later, seeing a huge wave, he yelled, "Leduc, get those men aft! The main sail must get into the wind."

No sooner had they safely maneuvered the ship, Captain Lemieux barked another order, "Leduc port side! Another big one's coming our way."

Leduc's men handled the sails as best they could, and the monster wave barely missed broad-siding the ship. Captain Lemieux managed the steerage so that the ship's bow crawled up the underside of the wave. The ship just made it over the crest as the monster wave began its descent. For a few moments all noise ceased; the sailors and their captain looked to the sky; their ship seemed suspended in thin air.

And then it plummeted into the roiling sea.

The wind's roar returned bringing with it torrents of snow, sleet and even lightening. One bolt struck the main sail, causing it to crash to the deck. Then, the ship fell violently into the hollow of an on-coming wave. She rocked bow to stern and port to aft, as if shaken by a giant's hand. Below deck, almost two hundred Irish immigrants, some dead or near death were being tossed about. Lanterns crashed to the floor erupting small fires; privy buckets toppled over; and the beds of hay and sawdust and human beings tumbled to the floor in filthy heaps.

Suddenly all was quiet. The passengers and the crew could not know that at that moment they had entered the eye of a "perfect storm" off the coast of Quebec Province. When *The Forrester* emerged from the storm's center the wind and waves renewed their assault. The steerage had frozen solid and Captain Lemieux had lost complete control of the ship. The force of nature alone drove his ship into the rocks of Cap-de-Rosiers where it capsized. *The Forrester* was torn apart by the rocks and the raging tide. Screams of terror competed with the wind …

And then there was just the wind.

Aided by flashes of lightening, Father LaPorte, the village priest, watched in horror as the storm ravaged the ship. He left the safety of his cottage and struggled headfirst into the wind. Once in the church's belfry, he frantically rang the huge iron bell signaling an alarm. As soon as he saw some villagers making their way to the shoreline, he left the belfry to join them. For the next horrifying hours the priest and the villagers did what they could to help the survivors reach the safety of the shore and the warmth of their homes. When there was no more that could be done, the villagers, except for John Hagen and Father LaPorte, left the shore. Soaked and exhausted, the two remained behind even though they held out little hope of finding more survivors.

Father LaPorte started to leave when Hagen yelled above the wind, "Father, I see something. Look there!"

With that Hagen shucked his boots and tore off his coat. Without hesitation, he dove into an oncoming wave. He struggled toward the rather large object he had seen. As he reached it he could see it was a cask. He grasped one of the straps wrapped around the thing. He thought his struggle had been in vain; but then he saw another's hand holding onto the strap. He worked his way around and saw a woman hanging on for dear life. He yelled something to her and began to pull his burden toward shore. Father LaPorte joined Hagen and the two of them were able to get the cask and the woman ashore. Father LaPorte quickly covered Hagen and the woman with blankets.

"My baby…" The woman whimpered, "…inside the tub."

Hagen unstrapped the cask and there, swaying in a small amount of water and crying loudly, was an infant boy. His tiny hands and legs were scraped; and blood, mixed with sea water, flowed from a cut on his forehead. Father LaPorte tucked the infant inside his jacket while Hagen helped the woman to her feet. They brought them to Hagen's home where Mrs. Hagen took immediate charge of Nelly Hughes and her son, Will.

The next morning several villagers were about hoping to find more survivors; but they found only bodies that had washed ashore during the night. Father LaPorte was taking stock of the storm's damage when he saw something fluttering in the breeze. He walked to the rocks and bent to pick up the torn Canadian flag. He quickly drew back, thrusting a hand across his mouth. Bodies of two men were impaled upon the rocks. These would later be identified as the bodies of Captain Maurice Lemieux and his second in command, Emil Leduc. Most of the crew had also perished. Later that morning, by some incredible miracle, Martin Ashe walked out of the sea carrying his *bodhran*. One of the villagers rushed up to him offering aid. Taking the proffered blanket, Mr. Ashe explained that he had spent the night huddled on a rocky outcrop because he had been too exhausted to swim ashore. As the villager led him to shelter, Mr. Ashe saw the empty cask swaying back and forth in the tide.

"There was a woman and child in that ting. Do ye know what happened to them?"

The villager told him that they had survived. Ashe said a prayer of thanksgiving.

A week would go by before the bodies of Mary and young Desmond washed ashore. Of the initial 287 Irish Immigrants, 90 had died at sea, 46 died just prior to, and during the storm, and 85 souls went down with the ship's wreckage. Twenty-four men, 26 women and 16 children survived the wreck of *The Forrester* in December, 1846.

CHAPTER 8 ~ MARTIN ASHE

Mullaghmore ~ 1972

Claire dabbed her eyes with Kleenex and blew her nose. Tuck put both hands on her shoulders and kissed her forehead. He stretched, walked over to the balcony railing and leaned over it.

"The crowd's gone home now, and I tell you, Claire, those folks will go about their business and forget what they heard today. They don't want to remember even though Ireland's 'Troubles' go on to this day."

She took hold of his hand and pulled him away from the railing.

"Come, please don't get into it today man."

Tuck knew she was referring to his erstwhile membership with a band of men and women on the fringes of the Irish Republican Army. He said, "Claire, if it were not for my involvement with the Neo2-Fenians, we would not be together."

Noting that she was about to provide a rejoinder, he quickly added, "I've gotta go to the loo. Be right back."

Claire thought about what he had said which got her thinking about the 1960's – a time when many people lost faith in the greatest political, social and religious institutions. The women's movement spread across America; Blacks struggled to win their rightful place in American society; the Irish "Troubles" hit new highs; and the Vietnam War protests captured the hearts of tens of thousands of young men and women. Vatican II was convened under Pope John the XXIII in 1962 and closed in 1965 under Pope Paul VI. During that short time the way Catholics practiced their 2,000-year-old faith gradually, but profoundly changed. Eventually, many of them lost their faith; others merely misplaced it. Nuns and priests began to leave their communities, a movement that, by 1972, had begun to deplete the clerical ranks of the Catholic Church.

Claire recalled the awful struggle she had endured deciding whether to leave Dublin's Sisters of Mercy. In the fall of 1967, just two months before making her final vows, she had made her decision. She left the order and joined a group of lay sisters whose purpose was to work for peace. The following year she traveled with them to United States to attend an international peace rally in Boston. And there she met Tuck O'Connell and his cousin, Paul Tibertus O'Connell. Though she was attracted to Tuck, it was Paul T. who occupied her time that day.

When Claire's group returned to Ireland, she stayed behind and obtained a working permit. Within a short period of time she and Paul T. had become an item. She had not known then that Tuck had backed off in deference to his older cousin. Though, she learned later, Tuck was acutely aware of his own feelings toward her, but had held his own counsel – until that fateful night in 1969.

Until that night Claire had been unaware of Tuck's and Paul T.'s involvement with the Neo2-Fenians operating out of Boston. Disavowed by the IRA, the radical group named itself after the Nineteenth Century "Neo-Fenian" movement in Ireland and America, itself an off-shoot of ancient warrior bands that lived apart from Irish society but could be called upon by kings in times of war. The Neo2-Fenians, a loosely organized, clandestine band of men and women, was formed in the early '60's. In mid-decade, prior to its migration to the United States, the gang had been involved in violent terrorist activities in Northern Ireland.

Claire winced at the memory.

Then Tuck's voice pulled her from her reverie, "God lass! What're you tinking about? Your beautiful face mustn't freeze that way."

"And do you need to ask, Tuck?"

"Come, lass. You're the one who said don't get into it."

She gazed at him a moment and then her eyes drifted from his. After a brief silence she asked him to tell her what happened to Nelly and Will.

Relieved, Tuck lit a Camel.

Claire said, “Those tings will be the death of you, Tuck.”

Ignoring her comment, he said, “Granfar told me that Martin Ashe made sure that they didn’t get sent to the Grosse Isle Disinfection Center, which was as bad a fate as going down with the ship … maybe worse.”

Warming to his subject, he told her that Martin Ashe had pricked a little blood from each of their fingers and rubbed it on their cheeks so that they would look healthy enough not to be sent to Grosse Isle. “Granfar told me that Ashe lied to the immigration officer, tellin’ him that his brother had a job waited for him in Sherbrook.”

Tuck dragged on his cigarette, looked at it as if it were a bug, and then crushed it in the ashtray.

“Ashe’s story must have seemed reasonable to the officer because he sent them on their way. Granfar says the guy let them go because he didn’t want to place three more on the public dole. You see, Claire…”

She interrupted him. “The boy’s crying; I’ll be right back.”

When she returned, Tuck held out his arms. Will twisted his hand free from his mother’s and, squealing with delight, scrambled into Tuck’s arms.

“Well lad, tis time you heard the story.”

A moment later the boy wriggled free and ran back to his mother.

Cap-de-Rosiers, Quebec Province ~ New Year’s Day 1847

The citizens of the town of Gaspe had hastily constructed a hostel to house the survivors. The structure contained a curtain fashioned from birch bark which served to separate the men from the women and children. Though the citizens were terrified they might catch disease, they were generous with their food and water, medicine and clothing. Father LaPorte celebrated Mass each morning just outside the hostel.

One morning after Mass Mr. Ashe joined Nelly and Will for the morning meal. On the way Nelly asked him to help her get to Prince Edward Island.

"Ah! Do ye know how far that is, lass? Tis over 750 kilometers south!"

He paused and Nelly could tell he was making up his mind about something.

"Well then, I'm going to Bathurst; tis about halfway from Gaspe."

Nelly looked expectantly at him.

"Tis done then, ye both will come that far with me."

Nelly bent her head into Will's blanket and whispered, "God bless Mr. Ashe."

A few days later, as the coach to Bathurst rumbled over rough terrain, Nelly was reminded of the road to Galway. She pressed Will closer and whispered, "Was it really that long ago, darlin'?"

"What's that?" asked Mr. Ashe.

"I wish it were spring, Mr. Ashe," Nelly responded, "for t'would be good to see the roses they say cover the whole Cape. Wouldn't it be grand for the souls' of our lost brothers and sisters to have roses for their burial beds?"

"Tis true, lass. But even in the gray of winter, the Cape is a wonder, is it not."

"Aye and that's the truth."

Tears she had been holding back slipped down her cheeks. Through her sobs she managed to say, "The cliffs remind me of home, they do."

"So you're missing home, are ye?"

"Aye, Sir. I miss wee Maeve and Thomas. I miss Kathleen and Da. And even Aunt Stella."

"And …"

She stopped talking, a sob escaped her lips, and her eyes glistened with tears. "… and I miss Mam. She died, Mr. Ashe, and I haven't given her or any of them a thought in weeks."

In a comforting tone, Mr. Ashe said, “Tis to be expected, lass. Of course ye couldn’t be tinking about anyting on the crossing we suffered. And then losing our brothers and sisters to the sea. People twice your age haven’t seen what ye’ve seen.”

He put his arm around her shoulder and she leaned into him. They remained silent until the coach made its first stop. Mr. Ashe climbed from the coach and helped Nelly and Will to the ground.

“It’ll do us good to stretch our legs, lass.”

Though it was a cold day, the sky was bright with early afternoon light and so they walked a bit. Mr. Ashe stooped and picked up a stone. He tossed it from one hand to the other. After a while, he said, “I hope I do not intrude, but when we first met in Galway Port I thought ye might be crossing to join your husband. But ye do not speak of him.”

His words hung in the air as a deep crimson crept from Nelly’s neck to her face. Mr. Ashe tossed the stone over to the side of the path.

“Ah! I am a dolt! I am sorry that I said such a ting. Please forgive me.”

Seeing tears leaking from Nelly’s eyes he came to her side.

“Mr. Ashe, I am ….”

She couldn’t finish the sentence and her tears fell unchecked. Mr. Ashe pressed his handkerchief into her hand. He looked around and saw a boulder just right for sitting.

He put his arm around her shoulders, which were shaking with her sobs. Will started to wail.

“Shush baby,” Mr. Ashe cooed. “Here, let me take him.”

He lifted Will from Nelly’s arms, not sure how to hold him and feeling more awkward by the second. Nelly grasped the handkerchief with both hands and pressed it against her face. She wiped her cheeks, blew her nose and composed herself.

“Mr. Ashe, Will has a twin who was too frail to come with us. Christopher stayed behind with the Sisters of the Good Shepherds.”

She caught fresh tears with the handkerchief; then said, “God forgive me but I’m glad he did not come for he surely would have died on that Godforsaken voyage. I know in me heart that I shall never see him again!”

She continued to sob quietly, thinking not just of Christopher, but also of her family; and of the Captain, who she believed had abandoned her; and of the man whom she was to marry but did not know. In between sobs, she said, "I am betrothed to the distant cousin I told ye about. Seamus O'Connell is his name."

Mr. Ashe maneuvered Will into the crook of his elbow and with his other arm he pulled Nelly to his chest. She let herself cry with abandon.

Shortly the driver yelled, "All aboard! The coach is leaving in five minutes."

Five days later the coach arrived at Bathurst in the Province of New Brunswick. Mr. Ashe went to the customs office. He told the officer that their papers were lost in the wreck of *The Forrester*. The officer could hardly doubt Mr. Ashe's veracity. He issued papers allowing Mr. Ashe to travel to Quebec City, 663 kilometers to the west; and then further south to Sherbrook. The officer gave him papers for Nelly and Will to continue to the town of Notre Dame, about 188 kilometers to the south. From there they would cross Bedeque Bay to Port Borden, Province of Prince Edward Island.

While in the customs office, Mr. Ashe noticed a strange contraption and asked the officer what it was. The man explained the magic of the telegraph, which had been introduced to the area earlier that year.

"It can send messages everywhere without need for boats or horses or nothing."

Amazed, Ashe asked if he could send a message to Seamus O'Connell on Prince Edward Island. The man proudly responded, "Yes, this marvel can do that. But it will cost you a pretty penny."

Before the storm hit *The Forrester* Mr. Ashe had sown his coin and paper money inside his woolen shirt. Though most of the paper money had been ruined with sea water, he had coins of high currency; so he had money to pay for a message to Charlottetown. The officer telegraphed Seamus O'Connell that Nelly would arrive in Port Borden in a week's time.

Pleased with himself, Mr. Ashe left the customs office and joined Nelly, who was waiting for him in the town's café. He came in, brushing snow off his coat. He sat down and, in great detail, told Nelly about the marvelous invention.

"Now, Mr. O'Connell will know that you're coming soon. And, lass, I asked him to get word to your family that ye and the wee one survived the crossing."

Nelly, clearly impressed, thanked Mr. Ashe for his kindness.

"Mr. O'Connell will care for us I know that." She hesitated, thinking about Captain Tuckerton. "Can we talk some more, Mr. Ashe?"

"After all this time, and now ye want to talk. Well now, the officer told me that the coach is leaving for Notre Dame in less than fifteen minutes. So, if you are to meet this man O'Connell on time, we cannot tarry."

Astonished, Nelly said, "So soon?"

"Aye and I leave for Sherbrook tomorrow morning. We should go now, we don't want ye to miss that coach."

Nelly took a final sip of her tea and bundled Will in his blanket. They left the café and headed toward the Notre Dame Coach.

"Well, this is goodbye, then."

"Aye, tis that lass."

Nelly handed Will to the driver, turned and wrapped her arms around Mr. Ashe's neck.

"I shall never forget ye dear Mr. Ashe, not as long as I live! I will tell Will every day of his life that God sent us a guardian angel, truly He did."

Mr. Ashe gently disengaged himself from Nelly's embrace. Holding both her hands, he pressed a pouch of coins into one and kissed her on both cheeks.

"I don't know if ye have enough money or not; but I want ye to take this for the coach fare."

She nodded, thanked him and turned away. The driver helped her into the coach and handed Will to her. As the coach began to move, she looked out the window and gave Mr. Ashe a small wave. With his *bodhran* slung over his shoulder, Martin Ashe waved back. Then he turned away so that Nelly would not see the tears gathering in his eyes.

Several days later the coach pulled into the town of Notre Dame. The driver yelled, "A quick lunch is all we have time for. So snap to it!"

As soon as the passengers climbed from the coach, the driver immediately ushered them to the town's café. After they were seated he said, "The boat to Prince Edward is set to sail in one hour. I do hope arrangements have been made for you because there's no hostel or hotel in Port Borden."

With that, he sat down at a table with the café's cook who had coffee waiting for him. The two began to catch each other up on a fortnight's worth of gossip.

Suddenly, a cold wind blew snow and a man into the café. Nelly knew it was him. Seamus O'Connell wore a hound's tooth cloak and a black cap that tipped to the left. His gait was hesitant as he looked about the café. When his eyes fell upon Nelly and Will he removed his cap and walked toward them.

"My name is Seamus O'Connell; and you must be Nelly Hughes."

Nelly's face had reddened and not from the cold. "Aye, sir. And this is Will. I tink Aunt Stella told you he would be with me."

"That she did. May I sit? "

"Of course."

Seamus motioned to the cook, who reluctantly stopped what he was saying to the driver. He called from his table, "What will you have?"

"Tea for the lass and coffee for me; and some biscuits then."

He spoke with a confidence Nelly found comforting. He looked up as the cook brought their drinks and biscuits.

Will made a tiny sound, and Seamus said, "He's a fine looking lad." He looked at Nelly and smiled a smile, though a bit crooked, enhanced his handsome face. His eyes were brown, almost black, his eyebrows and sideburns were the color of fog. Most of the hair on his head was still dark brown with that gray fog slicing through it. His chin had a prominent cleft. His cheeks were bright red partly by nature and partly by the cold. To 17- year-old Nelly, who had expected an old man of 32, Mr. O'Connell didn't appear old at all. And though she found his dark good looks a bit unsettling, she did not find it difficult to talk him.

"I was told ye would meet us in Port Borden."

"I thought you might have had your fill of boats and so I came to keep you company."

Changing the subject he told her that he had received the telegram from Martin Ashe and handed it to her, saying, "The postman brought me this odd looking paper. I don't have to tell ye how amazed I was."

Then he asked her about Martin Ashe. She told him how much help he had been to her and Will throughout their long and difficult journey.

"Mr. Ashe made sure we always had something to eat on that crossing. And, when the big storm hit, he knew before anyone that the ship would run afoul."

"How in the good Lord's name did you survive?"

"Mr. Ashe took a cask and leather straps from the deck. He split the cask so it looked like a tub with a cover. He told me to place Will in the tub and, when the time came, to cover it. He told me to wrap the strong leather straps around it. And when the time came, didn't that tub float with Will in it and me hanging on. Can ye imagine that, sir?"

"No lass, I cannot imagine it. Tis a miracle and I'm glad for it."

Shortly they boarded the Port Borden ferry.

Once settled, Nelly said, "I'm sorry if ye might've looked for me on a ship headed for New York."

"I didn't lass because my friend in the States told me that the American ships wouldn't be making the crossing again 'til spring. I didn't know what ship you boarded, but I knew it would be Canadian. I don't mind telling you I worried about that. I've heard tales."

He took a sip of his coffee. "I did travel to Quebec Province and watched four ships sail up the Saint Lawrence River, hoping you would be on one of 'em. Then the river started to freeze over. When you didn't come, I was sure they put you off at Grosse Isle. I went there … awful place. One of the priests taking care of the poor wretches told me he had not seen nor heard of anyone with your description. So, I gave up and went back home."

He took out his pipe, and began the ritual of lighting it.

"By the time I arrived home, the postmaster had delivered a message from your Aunt Stella. The good sisters in Galway had told her that the American ships were not sailing and that you left on a Canadian ship."

He paused and then looked straight into Nelly's eyes.

"I learned the name of the ship you were on the day Father Michaud announced at Mass that a Canadian ship, named *The Forrester,* had been wrecked on the rocks of Cap-de-Rosiers. I thought you and the wee Will were gone.

"Then I got Martin Ashe's telegram saying that you both had survived and were on the way to Prince Edward Island."

"And does me family tink I'm dead?"

"No, no. As soon as I got Mr. Ashe's message, I sent a letter home that you both had survived after all."

Nelly gazed at her son and said softly, "Aye we survived, dear Will, we survived."

CHAPTER 9 ~ KELLY CROSS

Mullaghmore ~ 1972

Tuck said, "So Claire darlin' if it hadn't been for Martin Ashe, Nelly and Will would not have survived that awful voyage. And you wouldn't be with me; and that grand darling boy of ours wouldn't have been born!"

He held up his fingers one at a time and counted, "My Great-great-great Grandmother Nelly was quite the woman, was she not?"

Claire nodded. "Aye, no doubt there." Then, without taking a breath, she said, "Tell me about Seamus. Did Nelly love him? Did she forget about the Captain? Did the nuns send Christopher to Prince Edward Island?"

"Hold your horses, lass. I'll get to all of it. Tis a long story."

Claire looked at him askance as he lit yet another Camel.

Prince Edward Island ~ 1847

Seamus pulled the reins hard to the left. The horse reared turning away from the edge of the bluff. The carriage swayed violently, sending a whirlwind of dusty snow and small stones in its wake. Nelly, one hand on her bonnet and the other clutching Will, was tossed back and forth; but, by sheer will power, she didn't fall off her seat. Seamus corrected the reins and the horse settled down.

He hollered, "Sorry for that, a rabbit spooked this old nag."

"Aye then," Nelly weakly responded.

"We'll be at Saint Mary Road soon." When Nelly didn't respond, he said reassuringly, "Tis close to home."

Earlier they had turned off Kelly Road, which had taken them across the small Island. They were now close to the end of Cascumpec Road heading north. Seamus' farm was located in an area called Kelly Cross, a place not on any map. Nelly almost dropped Will when the carriage suddenly stopped.

Seamus explained, "Sheep lass."

Excited, Nelly leaned out the window and saw sheep crossing the road, a sight she had seen often at home. She leaned further out the window so Seamus could hear her.

"Ye have sheep here crossing roads like home, then?"

"That we do, lass."

Ten minutes later Seamus maneuvered the carriage off Cascumpec Road onto Saint Mary Road. Five minutes after that, almost by rote the horse pulled the carriage through a hand-made gate into the area called Kelly Cross.

"Here we are!" Seamus said as he guided the horse to the back of the cottage that was his home. He jumped from his seat, took Will from Nelly's arms, and helped her climb from the carriage.

"Come, see this sight."

He guided her around the carriage to the edge of a bluff. She gasped as she gazed over the Gulf of Saint Lawrence and at the bluffs higher than the one she was standing on.

"Ah, tis like home!"

Her eyes suddenly glistened with tears. He placed his arm around her shoulder and led her to the cottage where they entered through the mud room door.

Once inside Nelly said, "I'm fine now. Ye see t'was such a shock to see the bluffs and the sea. Here, let me take the child." She looked around, and said, "And where should I put him?"

He pointed to one of the doors. "Your room is just there. I'll fetch your tings."

Nelly carried Will into the room, which she found pleasing. She went to the window with a view of the Gulf. Holding onto Will with one arm, she opened it to let the cold breeze freshen the room. Through the other window she could see Seamus tossing hay and seed to several cows and horses. A large chest of drawers took up one wall.

Nelly ran her free hand along the ornate carvings. She would later learn that it was made of Red Oak, valued for its strong, fine-grained wood, perfect for furniture and barrels. A mirror, the likes of which she had never seen, adorned the wall next to the chest. The bed, on the opposite wall, was covered with a large, colorful quilt. An oil lamp was on top of a small table next to the bed. And, on the other side was a cradle, which had begun to rock slowly from the Gulf breeze. Inside it, to Nelly's delight, was a smaller version of the quilt.

"Ah! Will darlin' we'll like it here, I tink."

Calling through the door, Seamus asked if he could come in.

"Aye," Nelly answered.

Seamus entered the room, balancing a pitcher of water with one hand and her satchel with the other. Squeezed between his side and arm was a soft, stuffed sheep he had purchased for Will in Port Borden. Nelly took hold of the toy so he could put the satchel on the floor.

Laying Will on the bed, she said, "The lad will sleep soundly in this room, and that's a fact."

Seamus poured water from the pitcher into a milk-glass basin resting on a table situated near the door. As he turned to leave, he said, "When you're done, come to the parlor and I'll show you the rest of the cottage. Then we'll have some supper."

"That will be fine."

He softly shut the door behind him.

Will began to fuss. Feeling the chill, Nellie shut the window. She laid her son on the bed, undressed, washed, and then fed him at her breast until he fell to sleep. She placed him in the cradle and whispered, "Aye me darlin' we will like it here for sure."

She quietly left the room. Entering the parlor she heard Seamus exclaim, "And what's this?" He knelt and picked up a letter that apparently had been slipped under the door. "Tis from Sligo," he said.

Nelly ran to his side. "Open it, quickly." Then added hopefully, "Ye can read, can ye not?"

"Aye that I can."

He read aloud the Gaelic script.

Dear Niece, Mr. O'Keefe is writing this down for me, for as you know I cannot write a word. He sent a message to Mr. O'Connell that you left Galway Port on a boat called the Forrester. We have yet to hear back.

Seamus stopped reading and explained that his letter crossed Stella's and that her family would know by now that she and Will had survived the crossing and the wreck.

Though we have heard nothing but bad news from across we have hope that you are alive. I do have bad news, I fear. Our family does not fare as well as you might remember. The money from the Captain no longer comes. Tis no surprise a 'tall.

With mention of the Captain, Seamus stopped reading again, bowed his head, pressed his lips together and took a breath. "Then, Aunt Stella says…"

Your father is weak but not in danger. Except, you know well, for what he does to his own self. Kathleen and Mr. Ryan wed on Christmas Day. Old Danny played the fiddle and Frank Lucy brought his bodhran and even Mary Moynihan danced. Now that Kathleen is gone the food we have goes further but not far enough. Paul Tibertus came back home but was immediately captured, and wasn't he put into Lord Palmerston's jail for no good reason a'tall. The twins are very hungry, no doubt; but they'll survive. Cormac Daley comes round now and again to bring food. We are all alive and thank God for it. Now, child, I must tell you…"

Seamus paused and gave Nelly a look, which by experience she knew nothing good would come of it. With rising alarm she said, "Who died?"

"Nelly, lass, I'm so sorry…"

"Read it, man."

Seamus took a breath, and then continued to read.

Now, child, I must tell you that Christopher, who was not well as you know,

Nelly's hand flew to her lips muffling a small sound. Seamus motioned for her to sit down. He stood behind her with his hand on her shoulder and continued reading.

... the lad succumbed, he did. The good sisters tried to save him, but God wanted him more. I am sorry to send this news. But with all of it, we hope and pray that you are alive and well and that the other wee one is healthy. Please send word as soon as you can. But if, God forbid, you cannot, sure tis true that Mr. O'Connell will. And thank God for him. You will know tis me by my sign. God Bless!

Next to the star Stella had drawn, Mr. O'Keefe had written her last name, "McBride."

Seamus folded the letter and said, "A star is drawn at the end. It means..."

"I know what it means."

The harshness with which Nelly responded surprised both her and Seamus. More softly she said, "Sister Aloysius explained it to me when Aunt Stella sent word that Mam died."

Then something hard dropped into Nelly's heart. She named it her Druid ... *that will dance on me ribs and darken me heart the moment happy comes me way.*

Aloud, she said, "I'm tired, Mr. O'Connell. I'll sleep for a bit," and she left him standing there, the letter dangling by his side.

At the bedroom door she turned and said, "I am sorry."

She gazed at him for a moment, and he saw in her eyes a terrible sadness that belied her age. Then she went into the room and shut the door. She leaned over Will's cradle and touched his cheek. Then she went to the window that faced west. She watched as the cold winter's sun began its descent over the small island off the coast of New Brunswick.

Nelly did not cry.

Mullaghmore ~ 1972

Undone by Christopher's death, Claire said through a sob, "Holy Mother Tuck! I cannot imagine losing our Will."

Tuck decided he'd better give her a preview and said, "Darlin' Christopher did not die then."

Claire glared at him, "How could you!"

"No, no. Really, there's a story there; but I don't want to get ahead of my tale."

"C'mon Tuckerton, don't tease. Tell me what happened to him."

"Let me tell you what happened to Nelly and Will first, OK?"

Claire grimaced. "Ah, but tis getting late, Tuck."

They fell silent and watched the sun begin its descent over the Atlantic, a triangle of which could be seen from their balcony. The warm, salty breeze took on a late afternoon chill. At length, Claire said, "There's the chill. Let's go inside."

Tuck picked up his glass and Claire's tea cup. She carried their sleepy child into the room.

After supper Claire said, "Alright, then, tell me what happened to Nelly and Will."

"The story will keep darlin'. Tomorrow we'll be starting our long trip home. There'll be plenty of time for storytelling. OK?"

He cleared the dishes from the table and they went to bed, but not necessarily to sleep.

"Are you comin' woman?" Tuck called as he placed the last of their luggage into his 1966 Renault.

"Needn't shout, Tuck. We're right behind you."

They piled into the car, and took off in a southeasterly direction. Within a short time, Will fell asleep in Claire's arms and she nodded off. Tuck welcomed the quiet. He was taking the long way to Dublin and liked the idea of the drive southeast, then west toward Galway where he had made reservations at a bed and breakfast. He intended to take Claire and Will to the ancient Aran Islands, a cluster of three islands created by "storm beach," composed of huge rocks, smaller stones, mud and limestone that had been cast by gigantic waves eons ago. Tuck loved these Islands, seemingly untouched by time and where Gaelic was the primary language.

On the way to Galway City, Tuck thought about the same trip Mr. Ryan and Nelly had taken to the Sisters of the Good Shepherd. While it had taken them almost a week, it would take Tuck a mere two hours. He whistled softly at the thought.

He pictured the drive southwest of Galway to the majestic Dingle Bay where they would stay in Tralee. From there he looked forward to driving the Ring of Kerry. Though the drive would be about 170 kilometers long and wouldn't take them any closer to home, he didn't care.

Claire was a Dubliner, who had never been west of the River Shannon, nor further south than Limerick. While in the area of Tralee and Killarney, Tuck planned a special treat for her. He knew she would delight at the unexpected sight of palm trees on hilltops overlooking the Killarney countryside. He knew she would love the sultry heat simmering over the Muckrock House and the Rose Garden.

Tuck loved his homeland.

An hour after they had settled in the Galway Inn, they were off to the Aran Islands. Tuck enjoyed the chance to practice his Gaelic with children returning to the Islands from their holiday, the woman behind the ferry's concession stand, and the man who asked him for a cigarette. As they walked back to the ferry, Tuck picked Will up and nuzzled his neck.

"Such a good traveler, you are lad."

He kissed him and said to Claire, "Let's go on a picnic tomorrow. I know just the place."

The next day they picnicked on the green across a narrow strip of water from Nun's Island, dominated by the ancient convent where Nelly had given birth to her twins. The Sisters of the Good Shepherd were no longer there. For the past 50 or so years the convent had been inhabited by a contemplative order of discalced Carmelite nuns. Claire wondered if there was a "merry" nun like Sister Lucy among the shoeless, silent Carmelites.

It was a perfect summer day. Vanilla ice cream clouds skimmed across the azure sky. Sunbeams bounced off the convent's stain glass windows shooting prisms of color. Little scavengers surrounded the three begging for a treat. Ducks appeared to float serenely on the surface of the water, while beneath it their webbed feet paddled furiously.

Claire said, "I'm trying to imagine how Nelly felt when she first saw that convent looming over there."

Ruffling Will's hair, she said, "Darlin' boy, this is where your ancestors were born."

Will gave her a look and ran off chasing a duck.

After they finished eating, Tuck said, "I tell you the sight of the convent over there has 'me' story tellin' juices goin'. Our son seems content enough chasing that duck."

He lit a cigarette and blew several smoke rings.

"Where was I?"

Her words dripping with playful sarcasm, she said, "Nelly had just learned that Christopher had died … but not really."

"Ah," he replied, "but Nelly didn't know that, so suspend disbelief for now and I'll tell you about Nelly and Will. About six years after they arrived on Prince Edward Island ..."

Kelly Cross ~ Six Years Later, 1853

Seamus leaned against the door, fragrant smoke drifting up from his pipe. He gazed at Nelly working her spinning wheel. He was still amazed by her beauty: the strong line of her jaw, the Grecian line of her nose, the dark brown of her hair streaked with fiery auburn, the impossible blue of her eyes. Now as he watched her deft handling of the spinning wheel, he noted sadly that she never showed that intensity for him. But, he reflected, the comings and goings of their life together were not without joy, and they were not without love. He was certain she loved him in her fashion and she never refused him his marriage rights. She had borne him two sons, five-year old Desmond named after his father, and three-year old Michael named after her father.

Then he listened to the lilt of her voice as she spoke to her six-year old son.

"Ah there Will, catch the wool for Mam."

The child was a handsome lad with blond hair, wild with curls; and his skin was fair, like his English father, Seamus supposed. But, the blue of his eyes were his mother's. Will slid to the floor and scooped the excess wool from under the wheel. He twirled the yarn expertly from one small fist to the other.

"That's it, Will. Aye that's it!"

Then, in sing-song fashion, she sang: *"We will make a lovely blanket; and the blanket will make money ..."*

In a childish soprano, Will finished the verse: "*...and half the money goes for me schoolin' in Quebec or New York City."*

As he bent to grab more wool he slipped on some, falling and laughing in a pile on the floor. Nelly whooped with laughter, a laughter touched by the same lilt that made her voice so pleasing to Seamus. He asked himself, *And did she laugh like that with the younger boys?*

Will, aware of his step-father's presence, looked up.

"Da! Come see the blanket me and Mam are spinning."

Nelly turned ever so slightly, a smile playing on her lips.

Seamus said, "Lad, go fetch your brothers, and bring them to the kitchen. I'll speak with your Mam and join you soon."

Reluctantly, Will placed the yarn carefully near the wheel's pedal, nodded to Seamus and squeezed past him through the doorway.

"So, do ye tink spinning is good for the lad, Mrs. O'Connell?"

"Tis a way to be together, Mr. O'Connell. Back home both girls and boys play a game called 'Sheep Crossing.' The older children sing songs and draw pictures of wee ones with wee lambs. And they all prepare to spin for the 'Sheep to Shawl' competition."

She paused to catch some yarn slipping from the wheel.

"I've been tinking to start the competition here on Prince Edward Island. So, ye see Mr. O'Connell, tis not so strange for the lad to learn the spinning."

"Tis very well and good. But don'cha ye be teaching the wheel to our Desmond or Michael. Do ye hear me?"

"That I do." A slight pause, then, "Not all children take to the spinning."

"The woman doesn't give an inch of it. Always the last word," Seamus thought but did not say.

He turned and left the room, hoping she had not seen the red blotches attacking his cheeks. The red of anger or sadness, he didn't know which. *But could it be shame?* Yes, he concluded, it could be shame. For whenever he was in her presence he felt awkward, and in his own home, no less. Better to be away from her presence. But, of course, he knew he could not stay away from Nelly. And he didn't. Two years later another child was born. They named her Flannery, a traditional Irish name, but also his mother's maiden name.

Kelly Cross ~ Eleven Years Later, 1864

On an early spring afternoon, Seamus was feeding the horses and cows. He stopped his labor, took off his hat and wiped his brow. He gazed up at the window of the second floor, recalling how Nelly would leave her spinning and come to this window to check on his whereabouts. If she saw him feeding the animals she knew he was almost done with his chores, so she would stop whatever she was doing to prepare supper. That was her routine for the 17 years of their marriage.

Until a few months ago.

Seamus sighed, put on his hat and went back to his work. When he finished he went upstairs and leaned against the door to the room where Nelly lay. He held his unlit pipe by his side, wondering if she were sleeping, not wanting to disturb her. He hated that this woman – this beautiful woman who had weathered deep loss, and who had braved the mighty Atlantic in the horrific hold of a ship – he hated that this woman now lay desperately ill, the bloom of youth gone from her cheek. He gently smoothed her hair, now mostly silver caught in a braid that fell over her shoulder. He put his palm on her forehead. The heat of it seemed to scorch his hand.

She opened her eyes, still impossibly blue, and smiled weakly.

"Dear Seamus, ye've finished your work then?"

"Aye darlin' tis finished for the day. How do you feel?"

"I am tired with the fever."

"Are you in pain?"

"Aye, just a bit. I want to tell ye some tings."

"Now, don't go tiring yourself out."

He held a glass of water to her lips, saying, “Take a few sips, lass.”

“Ah such blarney! I’ve not been a lass for a very long time.”

He smiled and said, “You’re still the most beautiful lass anywhere on God’s earth.”

“Listen to me, husband. Ye’ve been so patient with me. So kind, more kindness than I ever deserved. I hope in some way I have made ye a happy home.”

“Ah! Of course you’ve made me happy; you’ve made my life.”

He blinked back hot tears. “I love you Nelly. So much I cannot describe.”

He turned his head slightly so that she wouldn’t see the tears gathering in his eyes.

She whispered, “And I love ye, dear Seamus.”

Then she looked up as Will and his brothers entered the room.

She took in every inch of their countenance.

Will was tall like his natural father, Captain Tuckerton; his eyes Dresden blue, like her own. His hair, wild with curls still held the shadow of youthful blond. On his forehead she could still see a trace of the scar he earned as an infant swaying in a life-saving cask in the cold waters of the North Atlantic. Desmond and Michael were shorter and stockier than Will. Both had brown eyes, almost black like their father’s; and both had unruly dark hair.

In a weakened voice, but still with that lilt Seamus loved, Nelly said, “Ah! There ye all are me boys. And where is Flannery?”

“She’s coming, Mam.” Desmond said.

Michael added, “She’ll be here in a wink Mam.”

They did not tell her that Flannery remained in the parlor, having refused to come upstairs. She had said some spiteful things to her brothers. But they knew it was because their little sister was overcome with sorrow knowing that her mother was dying.

Desmond took a few steps forward, but stopped. Michael went passed him to Nelly and kissed her. Then Desmond did the same, followed by Will.

Nelly said, “I couldn’t be more proud of ye boys. I have some tings to say…”

But she began to cough. The coughing began slowly and softly, like hiccoughs. But the boys and Seamus knew what was coming. Her cough rose in a crescendo and fell, leaving Nelly struggling for breath, drenched in sweat, her face reflecting exquisite agony.

When she recovered she motioned to Seamus to come closer.

"Husband I must tell me son some tings before the angels come for me."

He understood exactly what she intended to do. He told Desmond and Michael to kiss their mother and leave with him.

Nelly motioned for Will to come near her. He leaned close to Nelly, not wanting her to strain her voice.

"Will, me darlin'. Ye used to ask me why ye had blond hair and such light skin, while the rest of us seem so dark."

For the next hour or so, in between coughing fits, Nelly explained to Will the circumstances of his birth. In great detail, she described his natural father, Captain William Tuckerton. She didn't tell him of the Captain's betrayal, which she would never know had been a lie. She hastened to remind him that Seamus is, and always would be his "true" father. She told him that he had had a twin, Christopher, who was too fragile to cross over with them. She told him that Christopher had died from his struggle to live. She would never know that that too was a lie.

Following a particularly painful coughing spell, she whispered, "Go over to the spinning wheel and lift the yarn spindle."

Will did as she instructed. He was surprised that the spindle covered a small depression in the wood.

"Lift what's inside that little piece of wood."

Holding something small wrapped in cloth Will said, "Mam, what is this?"

"Bring it to me, son."

She leaned on her pillow with effort, but fell right back onto the pillow.

"Unwrap the cloth."

Will shook the cloth and an object fell into his palm. The look he gave his mother held a mixture of puzzlement and amazement.

She murmured, "Tis a gold ring, is it not."

"Aye Mam."

"And do ye see the engraving of the Temple Family Crest? Tis your father's crest and so tis your crest as well."

The effort of talking brought on a coughing spell. Will came closer and took her hand in his. She whispered, "Your father gave this ring to me to prove his love. Tis your ring now and tis proof of your birthright."

Nelly's energy was finally depleted. She seemed to sink into the bedding as though she might disappear; and then she fell into a deep sleep.

Will remained at his mother's bedside for a long time, allowing his hot tears to fall unchecked on his hand holding her hand.

PART TWO - WILL

"When one plans revenge, he must dig two graves."

~Confucius

CHAPTER 10 ~ THE APPRENTICE

Across from Nun's Island ~ 1972

"No more today, Tuck," Claire began, "it's too damn sad! No wonder our elders don't tell us much … except, apparently for your Granfar. Whenever someone dies in my family, *Máthair mhor* always says 'The good Lord has taken him from this veil of tears' …"

"…and now the faithful departed is in heaven," Tuck said, finishing her thought. "And the old folks really believe it. Tis why there's so much gaiety at our funerals."

Will had stopped chasing the duck some time ago and had fallen asleep in Tuck's lap. He asked Claire to take him for a moment. She did and he stretched and said, "Aye and the story doesn't get much happier." After a pause he said, "Tis enough for now I tink."

She agreed.

The following morning, as they headed for the Dingle Peninsula, Tuck concentrated on driving, Claire remained silent with her son snuggling comfortably in her lap. They made several stops to enjoy the magnificent landscape of their native land. After registering at the Tralee Inn, they ate a light supper and planned the remainder of their trip home.

The next day, Tuck gassed up the Renault and they took off for the drive around the Ring of Kerry. Within a short time he cranked the engine of the small car, enjoying the way it handled the Ring's curves. Will squirmed in Claire's arms, not liking her tight hold on him.

Tuck down shifted often, telling Claire, "Tis better to use the clutch rather than the brakes on these curves."

Holding her breath, Claire didn't respond. When he slowed down, she smiled to herself thinking how much Tuck loved to drive fast. Her smile faded as she thought about the reason he drove as though he were on a race course. He'd been in some tight jams with the Neo2-Fenians back in the States. "But," she said to herself, "at least he's out of it now." Then she shook the memory from her mind.

Within a few hours, Tuck took the last curve of the Ring and headed back to the Inn.

"Claire, you haven't said a word all during the drive around the Ring."

"Will enjoyed the Ring; I was helping you drive."

Tuck chuckled, downshifted, sped up, but suddenly slowed to a crawl. "Damn tourists." He muttered.

It took them twice as long to get back to the Inn. As he pulled into his designated parking spot he muttered, "Turasoiri damnaigh!"

Later that night, after their son had fallen to sleep, Claire poured herself a cup of tea and joined Tuck on the veranda.

"The lad's settled is he?" Tuck said.

"He is that. Now you can tell me about Will."

He told her that, shortly after Nelly's death, Will said goodbye to the only family he had ever known in order to find the family that he'd never known existed. He traveled south to New York City where he learned the printing trade. About two years later he boarded a steam ship, headed for England. From there he traveled across the Irish Sea to Dublin.

Dublin ~1866

The impending summer storm whipped waves over the hull of the paddle steamer as it made its way from Liverpool to Dublin. No easy task since the Irish Sea is rough even in calm weather. Paddle steamers were relatively new crafts on the seas, so masts and sails were a necessary backup. So, when the engine failed shortly after leaving port, the captain ordered his crew to hoist the sails. Most of the passengers were tossing their sickness over the railings; and Will O'Connell was among them.

After several harrowing hours, the steamer sailed into Dublin Harbor. The pale and disheveled passengers filed onto the dock and dispersed. Some met relatives, while others entered pubs that lined

Dublin's Docklands. Will went straight into a rooming house, which charged an outrageous sum for a vermin-infested room with one window that faced a brick wall. Will didn't waste any time finding more suitable lodgings.

He loved Dublin. The City's hustle and bustle reminded him of New York, but with the bonus of hearing the lilt of Irish-accented English and Gaelic's musicality. Hearing the ancient language reminded him of his mother and Seamus. But, Will's first experience in their homeland was dampened by Ireland's political unrest, particularly in Dublin and Cork.

One night, after two weeks looking for work, he was in a local pub sipping Guinness. He lifted his eyes from the news sheet in front of him and, in the mirror above the bar, saw a man with a cane approach him. The man placed his hand on his shoulder, and said, "Hello there, Mr. O'Connell."

Surprised, Will looked over his shoulder and said, "Aye then, how do ye know my name?"

"Tis me business to know many tings. As a matter of fact, I know that you're looking for a job in the printing trade."

At this revelation, no longer caring how the man knew his name, Will said, "Tis the truth, sir."

"Me name is Malachy O'Sullivan."

"Well then, Mr. O'Sullivan, have a seat." He held his hand up signaling the barkeep to pour his new acquaintance a draught.

No sooner had the barkeep placed the glass in front of him, Malachy picked it up, drank deeply and burped loudly.

"I happen to know that Donavan O'Casey, Dublin's master printer, is in need of some help." He looked slyly at Will and continued, "I can arrange a meeting."

"Now then, why would you be interested in my employment, Mr. O'Sullivan?"

"Tis no secret that ye've been asking around about a family named Hughes. I had a friend with that name. A Young Irelander was he. Executed by the British bastards back in '47 or '48. I owe him. Ye might be related, eh?"

Will knew his Uncle Paul Tibertus Hughes had been in hiding when Nelly left Ireland and that he had been captured and imprisoned. But, his great-aunt Stella's letters had stopped coming, so he didn't know whether or not Paul T. had been executed or not – or even if he were otherwise alive or dead.

Will said, "The man you speak of could be a relative."

Malachy said, "Could be an uncle?"

His time in the rough and tumble of New York had toughened Will up and he had become circumspect with strangers. He merely replied, "Aye could be."

Malachy drank deeply from his second glass of Guinness and began talking, not seeming to care whether or not Will was listening.

"Many brave former Young Irelanders joined up with the Fenian cause. I did meself. And, sure as there are fairies in the West, if the bloody Brits hadn't done your uncle in, he would've joined us."

Will gave him a look. "I didn't say the man was kin, Mr. O'Sullivan."

"Tis not important what ye say, tis important what ye know. Whether Paul Tibertus is your long lost uncle or not, he would know that the Brits will not bend without force. No, he would'a seen that the Fenian way is the only way that Ireland can be free and independent from the Crown."

"And what way would that be, Mr. O'Sullivan? I heard that the Fenians are no longer a threat to the Crown."

Malachy responded hotly, "Are ye talking about the uprising last year, then?"

"Aye that I am."

"Well then," Malachy said proudly, "ye most likely know that 100,000 or more Irishmen served in the American Civil War. On the side of the North, of course, since the Brits was tinking about lending a hand to the South. If ye know that, ye know that some Irish officers came back home with money and a plan for the rising in '65."

Malachy tipped his empty glass and motioned for another one.

"Our patriots were betrayed, O'Connell. A blasted traitor informed the Brits of the Fenians' plan for the rising in'65. In a wink of an eye, the Brits arrested our leaders."

He picked up his fresh drink, and continued, "We will find the bloody traitor. He's a dead man and that's a fact."

Will raised his glass in mock salute. Malachy ignored the gesture.

"Do ye know the names of our leaders, O'Connell? Paul Tibertus Hughes' nephew should know the great Fenian names."

He didn't wait for Will to respond.

"In 1859 James Stephens from Kilkenny, a former Young Irelander, named himself chief of the New York Fenians and when he came home, he organized the Dublin Fenians. And there was John O'Leary; Thomas Clarke; and Jeremiah O'Donovan Rossa."

Will had heard his mother recite these names often enough, and gave a slight nod in recognition.

Malachy, who Tuck noticed was becoming quite drunk, continued talking, "The Fenian organization and methods were secret, with local cells led by local leaders. There were, and most likely still are, more than 50,000 members, Mr. O'Connell. Tink of what that number can do."

"Tis a large number for a secret organization to remain a secret, Mr. O'Sullivan."

Malachy, ignoring the sarcasm, said, "Most everyone now sees that Fenianism is the only way. Ye will come to see it too, Mr. O'Connell."

With that he climbed from his stool and stood unsteadily. He placed his hand once again on Will's shoulder, but this time for balance.

"I'm off now; but I'll be seeing ye again."

He bowed slightly, picked up his cane, and swayed toward the door. Will watched the big man's reflection in the mirror until the pub door closed behind him. Then he took a long pull of his Guinness, dropped several coins on the counter, and left the pub.

The next morning Will awoke later than usual, having had a fitful night's sleep. As he got out of bed, he noticed an envelope on the floor, apparently slipped under the door while he was sleeping. He ripped open the envelope and read the short note.

Mr. Will O'Connell, nephew of P.T. Hughes, you are to meet with Mr. Donavan O'Casey. He will discuss his need for an apprentice. He lives at 73 Westland Row. Tis not far from your accommodation. Come at Noon. Don't be late. Do chara nua, Malachy O'Sullivan

"Your new friend ...," Will translated aloud. O'Sullivan's affiliation with the Neo-Fenians concerned him. Though he was glad to have a job prospect, he was unnerved by the means through which it had come to his attention. "Mmm," he mused, "What would Seamus tink about this."

During his childhood and adolescence, Will had been torn between two points of view. Whenever his mother talked about the brutish manner in which the British treated the Irish during the famine, she bestowed honor upon Young Ireland's efforts to win back their homeland. On the other hand, Seamus would counter eloquently, speaking of the ideals and wisdom of pacifism. Will weighed these opposing points of view; then he re-read Malachy's note.

In the end, because he needed a job, he decided to see what Donavan O'Casey had to say.

The walk was a bit longer from Will's Stable Lane flat than Malachy's note indicated. Nevertheless, he found his way to Westland Row, a street bordering the Trinity College campus. O'Casey's house was so large that Will thought it must contain several flats. He climbed the steps and knocked on the door.

A young woman opened the door and said, "Good afternoon, sir. Ye must be Mr. O'Connell."

"Aye that I am miss."

She opened the door wider. "Mr. O'Casey will be with ye shortly. Come in then."

Will entered a foyer larger than his flat and gazed for a moment at the grand staircase straight ahead of him. She motioned for him to follow her to a room beside the staircase.

"Please wait in the library."

"I tank ye, miss."

Then she left him.

Stepping into the library, Will stared in awe, unaccustomed as he was to such luxury. Shelves lining the walls from floor to ceiling held hundreds of books; and heavy oak furniture dominated the room, softened by light-colored velvet drapes. Will had never seen so many windows in one room. He had no idea that a printer could be a wealthy man. He turned when he heard the door open.

"Good afternoon," said a middle-aged man as he strode into the room. He had a mop of wavy gray hair on his head and mostly gray throughout his handlebar mustache. He swung a mahogany, silver handled cane back and forth. Reminded of Malachy O'Sullivan swinging his cane, Will wondered if every important person carried one. As wide as he was tall, Mr. O'Casey extended a beefy hand toward Will, saying, "A friend of Malachy O'Sullivan is a friend of mine. Come, sit down. O'Sullivan says ye need a job and we have a need for an apprentice."

"Aye, tis the truth. Thank you for seeing me, Mr. O'Casey." And after an awkward silence Will ventured, "Mr. O'Sullivan said you're the master printer."

O'Casey laughed so heartily, Will wondered what he had said that was so funny.

"O'Sullivan never gets it right. I am the owner and editor of the *Dublin Times*. I employ master printers at the two largest newspapers in the area. The other paper is in Cork. George O'Gorman, master printer at the *Times,* is the one in need of an apprentice."

He noticed that a blush the color of a ripe apple crept across Will's cheeks. Smiling to himself, O'Casey said, "Tell me about your printing experience."

Will explained that he had apprenticed for two years at New York City's *New Amsterdam Sentry.*

"And why have ye returned to Ireland then?"

Though he knew he was born in Ireland, he said, "I am not from Ireland, sir. I come from Prince Edward Island."

"Ah. But, ye don't have an American accent. Your folks must have the Irish accent, eh?"

"Aye, that they do, sir; and they spoke Gaelic often, both originally the West, you see.

But to answer your question, I intended only a visit; but, though I've been here only a short time, I feel quite at home."

They talked along these lines for an hour, interrupting their discussion once when the butler, Grady, brought tea. At length, Mr. O'Casey ended the conversation, walked Will to the front door, and said, "George O'Gorman will contact ye." He gave Will a quizzical look and added, "Ye do want to stay in Dublin, don'cha?"

"Aye sir. That I do."

"Tis done then."

"Thank ye sir. I appreciate the job, sir."

"A good day to ye now, Mr. O'Connell."

After the door shut behind him, Will glanced up, marveling at the height of the house. His gaze fell on the second floor bay window and he saw a curtain slowly close. He wondered if the young woman who had let him in had been at the window. He reflected upon their brief meeting and thought she was lovely in that way of his mother, except her eyes. They were the deepest brown like those of Seamus and his brothers. He wondered who she was and hoped he would see her again.

Later that night he wrote a letter to Seamus. He asked about his step-father's health and about the affairs of Desmond, Michael, and Flannery. He told Seamus of his adventures since leaving New York; and about his new job. He described Donavan O'Casey in great detail and explained that he was the boss of his soon-to-be boss. And he described O'Casey's grand home. He didn't mention Malachy O'Sullivan nor did he mention the young woman.

CHAPTER 11 ~ THE END OF INNOCENCE

On the Road to Kilkenny ~ 1972

As Tuck had predicted, Claire had been transfixed by the sight of palm trees atop Killarney's vast, rolling hills; and had delighted in the Muckrock House and the Rose Garden.

As he drove northeast toward Kilkenny, an hour's south of Dublin, he said softly, "*Baile Átha Cliath.*"

Claire responded in English, "Dublin: the Town of the Ford of the Hurdles."

Tuck smiled. Suddenly he downshifted as the flow of tourist traffic came to a snail's pace.

"Damned tourists!"

"Ah Tuck! Use the time to tell me more about Will's life in Dublin.

"Although, it's starting to sound familiar. A little too much like you and that … that..."

"Claire, as you're always saying, let's not get into that."

She didn't respond, so he took up his tale.

Dublin ~ 1866

During Will's first month in Dublin he was preoccupied with his new job, save for the times he met Malachy O'Sullivan for Guinness and conversation. He also attended Mass at O'Casey's parish, feeling a bit ashamed that his ulterior motive was to catch a glimpse of the young woman who had opened O'Casey's door for him on his first visit.

One Sunday morning, on a whim, he decided to attend Mass at the Chapel located at Cardinal Newman's newly found University School on Lessing Street. He didn't have a horse and couldn't afford a carriage ride, so he walked the two kilometers from Stable Lane to the Chapel. He was late, so he slipped in through a side door, sure that he must've been seen by several Marist priests and nuns, though they kept custody of their eyes.

As was his habit during Mass he looked about, hoping to catch sight of the young woman. He took Communion, knelt in his pew, and folded his hands over his face. He peeked through his fingers to scan the communicants returning to their seats. And there she was! His heart beat a little faster as he watched her enter her pew and kneel. She kept her veiled head bowed in prayer.

After Mass he left quickly and waited across the street from the Chapel. He watched her walk in a westerly direction. He waited a minute or two, and then jogged to catch up to her.

Extending his own prayer book, he hollered, "Miss! Did you drop this?"

"No sir. Tis not me book." Then, with surprise she said, "Why, tis Mr. Will O'Connell himself, is it not."

With equal but feigned surprise, he said, "Ah! The lass who opened Mr. O'Casey's door for me!"

"Aye that I am."

Will was taken aback by the sheer loveliness of her smile. Nevertheless he managed to ask if he could walk with her.

She answered, "Father's livery man, Mr. O'Leary, will be bringing the carriage right off."

She noted the astonished look on Will's face. Though he didn't mean to, he blurted, "Then, you're not Mr. O'Casey's maid?"

"I am certainly not, sir! I am Mr. O'Casey's daughter."

If there had been a hole nearby big enough, Will surely would've jumped right in. But, recovering quickly he said, "I'm sorry for my presumption, miss."

"No harm done. Do ye have a carriage, then?"

"No, I enjoy the walking," he lied.

"Come, ye can ride with us. Father said ye live on Stable Lane. Tis on our way back.

"Ah! There's Mr. O'Leary now."

Once seated inside the carriage, Will said, "Miss O'Casey you know my first name, but I don't know yours."

"Molly," she responded and held a gloved hand toward him. He held her hand lightly, raised it toward his lips, not sure whether or not one kisses a gloved hand. But he kissed it anyway. She smiled, guessing at the reason for his hesitation.

A few days later Will's boss, George O'Gorman, told him that Mr. O'Casey had requested his presence the following Saturday. Thinking it must be a party and excited that he might see Molly again, Will bought a new set of clothes. He wanted to buy new boots, but couldn't afford to do so. He promised himself that someday he would buy two pair.

On Saturday night he climbed the steps of the grand home and rang the bell. This time the butler opened the door. Taking Will's coat, Grady greeted the young man and walked him to the library door. He nodded, and left him standing there. Not quite sure what to do, Will shrugged, opened the door and walked into the room. The room was filled with the scent of fragrant pipe smoke and several men, including Mr. O'Casey and Malachy O'Sullivan. They were not dressed for a party. Feeling awkward dressed as he was, nevertheless Will extended his hand toward Mr. O'Casey's outstretched hand.

"There ye are, me good man. Tank ye for coming. Ye know Malachy O'Sullivan; and these are some new friends."

He introduced the four other men gathered in the room. Each shook Will's hand, their eyes lingering on his outfit. Will was sure they knew that he had misunderstood the purpose of the meeting. If so, they hid their amusement. That evening Will learned how to smoke a pipe, which Mr. O'Casey had given him. And he learned about things he'd come to regret, for they would change the course of his life forever.

During the first half-hour or so, the men drank, smoked and talked about the weather and such. Finally, Mr. O'Casey said, "Malachy tis time we tell Mr. O'Connell the purpose of his visit."

Malachy tapped tobacco into the bowl of his pipe and took his time lighting it. Then he said, "Mr. O'Connell, I tink ye must realize by now that we all, Mr. O'Casey too, are loyal to the Neo-Fenian cause. Our question is can ye be persuaded?"

Will was not shocked by the question, for he had listened to Malachy's political views often enough. However, his stomach muscles tightened with the thought of being in the company of men, who he now knew for sure were Neo-Fenians, or at least on their fringe. Gamely, he stared right back at Malachy, and said, "I'm not a fighting man as you must know. I came to Ireland to see my parent's homeland; and I earnestly like my job for Mr. O'Casey…"

One of the men interrupted him, "Tis exactly the reason we need ye, O'Connell. Ye have no past here."

The man had an ugly scar that curved from his forehead, through his eyelid, which was permanently shut with scar tissue, and down his right cheek. He was a burly man with obvious body odor. His name was Padraig Riagan. His first name means "of noble descent," his last, "furious and impulsive." For reasons that would become obvious to Will, the man chose to be called by his last name. However, unbeknownst to Padraig Riagan, even his friends called him "Paddy" behind his back.

Riagan walked closer to Will. "Ye don't have much choice now that we have taken ye in our confidence, now do ye?"

Mr. O'Casey held up his hand. "Now, Riagan, no sense in threatening the lad."

Will hadn't heard anyone refer to him as a "lad" since he stepped foot in Ireland; he wondered what O'Casey's use of the term could mean. He was staring at Riagan, but felt O'Casey's gaze upon him. He shifted his eyes and looked straight at O'Casey, who said, "Ye are doing a good job at the *Times*, so says me man, George O'Gorman. But the job we have in mind for ye is far more important; and tis a man's job. Tis not a job for a mere lad. Ye understand me meaning?"

Will understood O'Casey to mean that, if he turned down the assignment, he would be forever thought of as a lad – or worse, a coward. He thought he'd probably lose his job as well. Otherwise, he reasoned, why would O'Casey have mentioned the job? His thoughts jumped ahead imagining that O'Casey might even prohibit him from courting Molly. In the end he acknowledged to himself that he had already made his decision by accepting that night's invitation.

"What do you want me to do then?"

Malachy clapped Will on the shoulder saying, "That's me man!"

O'Casey told Will to sit and gave Malachy a high sign to pour the drinks. The men lit their pipes, sipped their drinks and talked only of neutral subjects. Shortly four men left the room through a door hidden near the bookcases. Will stood; Malachy remained seated.

"It's time for me bed," O'Casey said to Will, "Malachy will tell ye about the assignment."

He touched Will's shoulder. "Good night then, Mr. O'Connell." And, swinging his cane, he walked out of the library.

This time, Will noted that O'Casey put the emphasis on the "Mr." Pleased, but not sure what to do, he remained standing until Malachy told him to sit.

"On September 16, pretending to be a vagrant, go to Clontarf, north of the Docklands." Pulling roughly on the sleeve of Will's new coat he added, "But don'cha be wearing this getup."

He continued, "At quarter to midnight ye'll light a fire facing Bull Island. Be sure to make it a big fire, Mr. O'Connell."

The man's emphasis on the "Mr." sounded sarcastic to Will.

"If a constable or a soldier comes by he will tink you're just another vagrant lighting a fire for warmth against the autumn chill. When the Church bell tolls the midnight hour, ye'll signal the lads waiting on Bull Island by swinging a flat board back and forth in front of the fire. Do this tree times – very slowly." He drained his glass and said, "Ye can do that, can ye now?"

Will nodded for the task seemed simple enough. He didn't ask the ultimate purpose. He didn't want to know.

Malachy rose from his chair, picked up his cane and slapped Will on the shoulder. "Good man!"

He walked to the secret doorway and left the room.

Will was puzzled, not sure which door he should use. He felt a slight dizziness, perhaps from the pipe tobacco; but, more likely from the events of the evening. Was he now a Fenian, he wondered.

Thankfully, Grady opened the library door, gave a slight bow and motioned Will to follow him. Once outside, Will breathed the sweet late summer air. He looked up at the window where he thought Molly had been the first time he visited the grand house. There was no movement. He walked home, thinking all the while about the men who left through the secret door.

A few days later, Will worked up the courage to ask Mr. O'Casey if he could court Molly. Though O'Casey was not happy about the prospect, he knew that Molly was fond of Will and so gave his permission, "Once in a while, no more, and only when Mrs. Mirran chaperones, ye understand?"

During the next few weeks Will courted Molly to Mass, a Bach recital, and a picnic on the banks of the River Liffey. On these outings, Peg Mirran always remained a discreet distance crocheting or reading.

So engrossed in his job and courting Molly, Will was stunned when the time came for him to prepare for his assignment at Clontarf. That morning he woke feeling hung over from a restless sleep. Before getting out of bed he ticked off things needing to be done, as well as the tasks he had already completed. He had scouted the Clontarf beach from the South Wall halfway to the North Wall. Decades before these were barriers built to aid the tide deepen the mouth of the River Liffey. He had chosen a secluded spot in the shadow of the South Wall near where O'Sullivan had said the boys from Bull Island would land their boat. He forced some breakfast down, got dressed and went to work.

Throughout the day he tried thinking about Molly, but thoughts of Midnight interfered. After work he had a light supper and tea, though he longed for something stronger.

At 11 o'clock that night Will dressed in old clothes, darkened his face and hands with dirt, and put on an old hat his step-father, Seamus, had given to him as a keepsake. He tipped it just right to cast a shadow over his eyes. Satisfied that he hadn't forgotten anything, he picked up a parcel filled with plenty of flint and kindling for the fire. He slung it over his shoulder and climbed out the window.

When he reached Clontarf he scaled the South Wall and laid flat on his stomach. He saw several vagrants warming their hands over their fire. He crawled toward the spot he had chosen the week before, confident that the vagrants would be unable to see him given that his spot was behind the wall's curvature. He retrieved the wooden slat he had hidden in the brush and lit a fire. He lay back in the brush, all the while casting his eyes about looking for intruders. Occasionally, he gazed across the water to Bull Island. He imagined that he could see the Fenians climbing into their boat. A few minutes before Midnight, he picked up the wooden slat and made a few practice swings. He felt the heft of it, but thought of the weight on his shoulders.

Then he called to mind Malachy's instructions: *The British Militia changes shift at quarter past Midnight; so at midnight ye must give the signal and then hide yourself good. Wait there until ye see the lads come ashore. As soon as the last one passes, leave that place and meet me at the Pub. Remember, do not approach the lads and do not let them see ye. And for God's sake, don'cha let the militia see ye either! Ye understand, then?*

Now he jumped when the Church bell struck midnight; but he did as Malachy had instructed. He swung the slat back and forth over the fire and tossed it into the flames. After he thought the Militia must've changed the guard, he tossed sand on the fire and spread the ashes around, retreated to his hiding place and sat down to wait. Just as the bell struck half past Midnight, he heard water splashing softly. He watched two men, then four, then two more walk out of the mist. They each carried what looked like a very heavy load on their backs. Will guessed their loads contained guns and ammunition.

Once on shore the men walked in the general direction of Will's hiding place. They passed but a few yards in front of him. One man kicked at some ash that had continued to smolder. He looked around and spat on the ground. Will watched as the men walked single file toward the wall's curvature. Then, using ropes with three pronged hooks on the end, three scaled the wall. Once on top, they pulled the munitions up. Then the others scaled the wall.

Will stood and carefully climbed his way to the top of the wall. On his belly he maneuvered across the top until he could see the vagrants' fire on the shore side of the wall. Through the mist he strained to see the lads atop the wall. Instead, movement on the village side caught his attention. He peered through the mist. With the aid of the village lanterns he could see soldiers making their way stealthily toward the wall. He looked back toward the vagrants just as they began to shed their outer clothing. They were soldiers! They raised guns that their clothes had hidden. Then they knelt as one, taking aim at the top of the wall. Will looked back at the soldiers on the other side of the wall. They too knelt as one, taking aim at the top of the wall.

He was horrified, but there was nothing he could do to stop what was happening. A shot rang out and he saw one of the soldiers on the village side fall forward. Will could barely make out the outline of one of the lads; the soldiers saw him as well and fired. The man tumbled over onto shore side. The mist cleared for a moment so Will could see three other lads kneeling on the wall. Then, gunfire erupted and two of them fell forward from their kneeling positions. The other crawled toward the edge of the wall.

Then, everything seemed to move in slow motion. Will was appalled by the violence he was witnessing. He scrambled down the village-side of the wall, lost his footing and fell hard on his right shoulder. Pain shot down his arm, wrapped around his elbow, and straight down into his hand. He hoped that the noise erupting all around had concealed his painful yelp. When he recovered, he leaned on his good elbow and saw that the soldiers had circled the lads. Four of the eight who had come ashore were holding their hands up in surrender. The soldiers who had posed as vagrants were walking toward the others.

One shouted, "Two more of them bastards are dead atop the wall." Another was roughly pushing a wounded man forward. "This one here was with them." Two others were carrying the body of the one who had fired the first shot that had killed one of the soldiers.

Lying flat on his stomach and wincing with pain, Will feared he might vomit. Suddenly, a gruff voice commanded, "Don'cha move, boyo!"

By sheer instinct, Will flipped himself around, blindly kicked toward the voice, and was surprised that he had made contact. The man's gun fell to the ground with a thud. A second later he whimpered – the only sound a man can make from a terrible blow to his shinbone.

Will leapt to his feet and prepared to run; but realized he'd lost Seamus' hat. He made an about-face and saw it poised on top of a bush. He glanced at the injured man, ran to the bush and scooped up the hat. Then, holding his right arm bent at the elbow, he ran like a bat out of hell, leaving his would-be captor behind.

The man was holding his shin with both hands, and bobbing his head up and down, not able to raise his voice to alert the others. Then anger overtook his pain. He crawled to his gun and took aim at Will's fleeing form.

Suddenly, he fell forward.

A man walked from the shadow of the wall toward the prone body and slung his bow over his shoulder. Nelly's young brother, Thomas Hughes, now a 28-year old man, knelt beside the fallen man and felt for a pulse. There was none. He placed his boot on the man's back and, with some effort, pulled the arrow from his neck. Thomas wiped his arrow on the soldier's pants and walked away into the night.

Unaware that his Uncle Thomas had saved his life, Will ran as fast as his injured shoulder would allow. He scrambled up and then down a small hill and jumped onto a dock. But, misjudging the distance, his left leg grazed the top of a piling and he fell hard on his right ankle, which made a sickening sound. Wincing in pain he stood and gamely skirted Clontarf heading toward Dublin Centre.

Over an hour later, limping, his arm bent to his chest, Will arrived at the Pub. He sat on the bench near the door, his head bowed. Despite the chill in the air, he was sweating profusely.

"Ach!" Malachy's angry voice called out from the shadows. "You're late, O'Connell. Where in hell have ye been?"

In between gasps for breath, Will told Malachy what had happened. Malachy's face contorted with anger. He spat on the ground and growled, “Ye did someting, O’Connell! Ye did someting that tipped them bastards.”

Then he took notice of Will’s injuries. “You’re a sorry mess, and that’s the truth.”

Pulling him roughly from the bench, he added, “We’re going to O’Casey’s.”

Will’s stomach tumbled with anxiety and pain and he vomited.

As Malachy jumped backward, he grumbled, “Ach! Don’cha get that mess on me shoes.”

He dragged Will through streets and alleys and finally into the alley behind O’Casey’s house. He reached behind the brick wall and pulled something. Will watched in amazement as a section of the wall moved slowly outward.

O’Casey’s large form filled the entrance way.

“What the fuck are ye doin’, Malachy! Ye know better than to come here tonight of all nights.”

“The lads fell into a trap. Will here got himself wounded.”

O’Casey stepped aside and they entered the library. Once inside, with his back to them, he said, “Ye’ve done it now for sure; and I’m speaking to ye both. I want an explanation.”

Before Malachy could respond, O’Casey rang the butler’s bell. He poured himself a finger of whiskey and sat down. He didn’t offer the same to the other two. Shortly, Grady came into the room. He had that sleepy, disheveled look to him. O’Casey barked, “Get that Chinese pharmacist over here to take a look at the lad.”

Through his pain Will thought, *There’s that word again.*

Grady didn’t dare express his opinion as to the lateness of the hour. O’Casey seemed to read his mind: “He’s a Chinaman, Grady! No need to worry about bothering him.”

Grady left the Library with Will leaning heavily against him.

Earlier Molly had awakened and went to the necessary room. The chamber’s window was open a crack and she had heard talking. She looked down and had seen Will and O’Sullivan in the alley below. Now she was at the top of the stairs and watched as Grady half-carried Will toward the kitchen.

"Father's dragged him into it," She whispered in dismay. Then she tiptoed back to her room. Shortly, she heard a noise again. She went to the hallway railing and saw Grady walking toward the kitchen again, this time with the Chinese Pharmacist. She went back to her room, knowing she wouldn't sleep. Just before dawn she had made her decision. She got out of bed, dressed quickly, and went to Peg Mirran's room. Sleepy-eyed and disheveled Peg opened the door. Without preamble, Molly said, "We need to wake Mr. O'Leary to take me to Mr. O'Connell's flat."

Astonished, Peg said, "What are ye tinking, lass? Ye cannot do such a ting at this ungodly hour!"

"No back talk, Mrs. Mirran. Tis an important errand I must make."

Reluctantly, Peg dressed quickly, threw on a cloak and the two of them crept down the staircase and slipped out of the house. Peg awakened O'Leary and gave a brief explanation. Mr. O'Leary knew when not to argue.

O'Leary pulled the horse-drawn carriage to a stop outside Will's flat. Molly jumped from the carriage, ran up the stairs, and banged on the watchman's door until it opened a crack. Molly demanded to know which room was Will's. "2A," he said, and slammed his door. Molly took the stairs two steps at a time; then banged on Will's door.

After a moment or two, Will opened the door, his eyes widened in surprise.

"Molly! What on earth are you doing here?"

She pushed her way into his sparse room. She looked around and made a face. With hands on her hips she spat, "An unholy sight ye are!"

Will started to say something; but she spoke over him.

"Don't bother to lie to me, Mr. O'Connell! I saw ye and that awful Mr. O'Sullivan tonight. And did the Chinaman give ye herbs that are like fire in the belly?"

She took a breath. Will seized the moment and, speaking in rapid phrases, he did his best to convince her that he had been in a terrible brawl.

"Malachy came in the nick of time, lass. He saved me from further injury."

He limped to the table by the bedside and put the sling over his shoulder. For the first time since entering the room, Molly took note of Will's pale face beneath the retreating blush of sleep. Gingerly she touched the sling and in a softer tone, asked him what happened to his arm.

"Tis my shoulder."

Then Molly's glance traveled down the length of his right leg. She gasped at the sight of the bandage wrapped around ankle.

"Will…" She whispered.

"T'was an awful brawl, truly it was."

He stretched his good arm toward her. And, leading with her heart instead of her head, Molly allowed him to draw her close. With the softest touch she had ever felt, his left hand traced her face from her forehead, along her jawbone to her chin, which he tilted upward. He kissed her fully on the mouth. And she kissed him back.

CHAPTER 12 ~ THOMAS

Kilkenny ~ 1972

Claire breathed, "Dear Jesus!" Claire breathed. "Thomas lived through the famine."

"Aye, that he did," Tuck said as he maneuvered the Renault into a parking spot nearest the inn's door. He said, "Wait here, Claire, while I get us registered."

After they were settled, Claire couldn't wait to hear more about Thomas. Tuck told her that he would get to that, "… but let's get back to Will for now."

He related that the Chinese pharmacist determined that two bones in Will's ankle had been badly cracked and that he needed to use a brace for an indeterminate time. He had given Will a cane to use, and by mid-November the ankle and shoulder felt good enough for Will to be able to swing his cane as he walked.

Tuck said, "Ol' Will enjoyed the effect of walking around swinging a cane, like other important men in his life."

He went on to say that Will's shoulder healed nicely; but his ankle never healed properly and gave him a lot of pain. At first Will was hesitant to drink the Pharmacist's herb concoction; but soon enough he liked its pain-easing power. "Or…" Tuck mused, "…maybe he just liked the loopy way the brew made him feel."

Dublin ~ 1866

One day shortly before Christmas, Molly rapped lightly on her Father's study door saying softly, "Tis me, Father."

"Ah Molly! Come in then."

O'Casey's shirt was unbuttoned at the top, the sleeves rolled to his elbows. He poured Molly a cup of tea, and hesitated. Then he put a few drops of brandy into it and said, "Just the ting to take the chill off a cold afternoon."

She took a sip and made a face; then she said, "Father, I know ye are a bit chary of Mr. O'Connell since he got in that brawl. But ye know that I fancy him."

"Aye lass that I do." A beat, "So then, what is the question?"

She took another sip of the tea, but didn't make a face this time.

"Father, please invite Mr. O'Connell to the Christmas Ball. Tis the only present I want for me birthday and even for Christmas."

O'Casey got up from his chair and walked to the window overlooking his broad lawn. He sipped his tea and gazed at the threatening sky. "I can feel the snow in me bones."

Keeping his back to Molly, he said, "I've been meaning to tell ye … and I should've told ye before this…" He hesitated and took another sip of tea, also laced with brandy.

"I don't tink tis a good idea for ye to keep seeing the lad, daughter. He's in my employ and tis unseemly to bring employees into our personal life. Tis bad enough ye talked me into letting him court ye in the first place."

Truth be told, he was far more anxious about having brought Will into his clandestine affairs than he was about the fact that he was an employee. But he couldn't voice that deeper concern. Molly put her teacup on the table, got up and walked over to her father. She touched his arm. He didn't look at her right away, knowing he would melt.

"Tis more than just a fancy, Father. Mr. O'Connell has become dear to me and is all alone in the city and will be so at Christmas. Please invite him to the Christmas Ball."

"Doesn't look right, daughter."

She put both hands on his arm. "Father, t'would please me so."

And that did it. He puffed his cheeks and blew air through his pursed lips. "Alright, then." Under his breath he added, "Ye'll be the death of me yet."

She understood his exasperation, but thought a hug might do the trick, so she threw her arms around his neck. He held his tea cup aloft but it spilled anyway. Then she literally danced from his study.

"Ach!" he said to himself, "I cannot seem to say 'no' to the lass. But this! This is not good." Sighing, he poured a hefty two inches of brandy into the dregs of his tea.

On Monday morning George O'Gorman leaned into Will's cubicle. "Hey, Will. Ye got another message from the grand house."

Will noted the sarcastic edge to his voice. O'Gorman handed him an envelope saying, "T'wouldn't have anything to do with that time ye hurt yourself, would it?"

Will didn't like O'Gorman's tone or the possible meaning behind his words. He said only, "I don't know what you mean, Mr. O'Gorman."

"Ah, tis probably just another invitation." After a pause he said, "Ye know, O'Connell, O'Casey never invited me to one of his shindigs." As he started to leave, he added, "Just as well, though. I wouldn't want to break me leg for the man; tis enough I break me back for him six days a week."

Will ignored the remark, but his concern about what O'Gorman might know deepened. He limped over to his desk and leaned against it. He looked at the envelope, noting that it was quite plain without even his name. He tore it open, still hoping it might be an invitation to the Christmas Ball. But, the note consisted of one line: *Come tonight at 9 o'clock sharp. Use the alley door. M. O'Sullivan*

That night Will reached behind the side of the brick wall as he had seen Malachy do on that terrible September night. Just as the Trinity Chapel bell tolled 9 o'clock, he felt a handle and pulled it. Stepping back he watched the brick wall slowly moved outward.

Malachy leaned forward through the opening and looked up and down the alleyway.

"Come in quickly."

Padraig Riagan and Mr. O'Casey were seated by the fireplace and looked up when Will and Malachy entered the library.

O'Casey said. "C'mere Will and sit down. And how's ye ankle doing?"

"Tis coming along fine, Mr. O'Casey, though the Chinaman says I will need the cane for a long time. My shoulder is better, and that's a blessing."

O'Casey motioned to Malachy. "Pour the man a whiskey."

Will took a sip and looked expectantly at Mr. O'Casey. But the man didn't speak – no one spoke. Will became more nervous by the minute as the men continued to drink their drinks and smoke their pipes, not saying a word.

Finally, O'Casey said, "The need for the cane won't be a problem for this job."

Then, as he did the first time, he excused himself. "Riagan and Malachy will tell ye what ye need to know. I'm off to me bed."

After the door shut, Malachy said to Will, "Ye need to leave tonight for the Round Tower in Swords, not far north of here. O'Leary is even now preparing a horse for ye." He turned to Riagan and said, "Do ye have the letter?"

"Aye," Riagan replied, pulling an envelope from inside his jacket. He handed it and a piece of paper to Will. "Ye'll need this map; tis drawn large to get ye to the Round Tower in the dark. Ye'll have a lantern, but don't use it unless ye must."

Malachy pointed to a spot on the map that had been circled. "This here is the tower. Our man, Devon, will be waiting. Ye must arrive no earlier or later than Midnight. Devon will give ye a package of goods, might be heavy. He'll show ye where to rest the horse; but ye must leave in time to get to work in the morning. Ye got that?"

The job was completely unexpected, and Will was overwhelmed by the thought. But, he managed to reply, "I understand. Do I bring the package here then?"

Riagan snapped, "No! Tis a stupid question. Bring the package to me. I'll be waiting at Saint George's Quay ... I'll be there earlier than ye're expected. Then ye must get to your job on time. We don't want O'Gorman to start his tinking."

Turning to Malachy he said, "Someting's got to be done about that man, Malachy. He…"

Malachy gave him a look that halted further comment. Then the three of them walked to the secret door. As Will walked down the alley he smiled wryly to himself, thinking, *Now I'm one of them for sure.*

He circled around to the main yard on his way to the stables, acutely aware of pain shooting from his ankle and shoulder to his head.

O'Leary led a horse out of the stable. He nodded to Will, pointing to the oversized saddle bag fixed on the horse's back. "I'm told tis quite a load ye'll be carrying."

Will nodded, tied a strap to his cane, slung it over his shoulder like a bow, and mounted the horse.

"I pray ye know what you're doing, lad."

Not minding O'Leary's use of the term "lad" he tossed a half smile in the old man's direction and took off.

As he rode north to Swords and its ancient Roman tower, he was unaware that his Uncle Thomas was following him. Arriving at the Tower, he dismounted and let the horse graze freely. Thomas was already hidden where he could see his nephew, but Will couldn't see him.

Then the man called Devon appeared. He sized Will up and said, "Are ye sure no one followed ye?"

"I'm sure." Will answered with more confidence than he felt. Then he gave Devon the envelope. Devon tore it open and scanned the note. He looked at Will, then back down at the note. It simply verified that Will was indeed O'Casey's messenger.

"Wait here."

Instead of a mere package, Devon came back dragging a very heavy looking bundle. He unfastened the saddle bag and dropped it to the ground. "Tis too small for this load, man."

Will helped him fasten the bundle in back of the saddle.

Noting their struggle, Thomas shook his head, thinking, *That would be guns, no doubt. The lad's a gun runner now.*

Without stopping to rest the horse as he had been told to do, Will headed back. Thomas followed him until it was clear that Will was headed for Saint George's Quay; so, he took off on a different route to the Quay. When he saw lantern light ahead, he dismounted. From his vantage point he could see Will and Riagan struggling to unleash the bundle from the horse. Both men jumped back as it fell to the ground. Thomas recognized Padraig Riagan.

"Ach!" He whispered in his horse's ear, "Even the Fenians don't acknowledge that bastard as their own."

And then he rode off.

Will drove his horse hard all the way back to O'Casey's stable. As he began to remove the saddle, a stable hand suddenly appeared. He was not pleased. He furiously pulled the saddle from Will and, taking the reins, he spat, "I didn't tink you'd come for another two hours. Ye may not need the rest, but the horse surely does. Wait here while I dry the poor beast."

In a few minutes he returned leading a fresh horse from the stable and said, "I was told to take ye home. This fellow can carry us both."

Will was relieved that he wouldn't have to walk home, for his ankle hurt badly from his foot's pressure on the stirrup during his round trip. He mounted the horse and rested his right foot lightly against its side until they arrived at his flat. As soon as the young man rode out of sight, Will gingerly climbed the lattice and into the window of his room. He breathed a loud sigh, leaned his cane near the door, and removed his coat and suspenders, letting them hang down his sides. Fading moon light tossed soft shadows through the window. He sat on his bed and prepared himself for the ordeal of removing his boot from his injured ankle.

From out of the shadows a voice said, "So, Will O'Connell, I beat you home from the Quay, eh?"

Startled, Will leapt from his seated position, landing hard on his right foot. He fell, gasped and twisted his head toward the voice. "Who the hell are you?"

"I tink the better questions are 'Who the hell are ye? 'What has become of the lad who left Prince Edward Island?' And, do ye even know yourself?"

Will lifted himself from the floor and began to say something.

Thomas barked, "Sit down, nephew!"

Will sat down heavily onto his bed. "What do you mean 'nephew?' Are you mad, then?"

Walking over to Will's bedside table, Thomas said, "I see ye got a nice stock, nephew."

He poured an inch of whiskey for them both and handed a glass to Will.

Will's mind was reeling, but he managed to say, "First, I'm taking off this damn boot."

He painfully removed his boot and took the other off with ease. Taking the glass Thomas offered, he said again, "Who the hell are you?"

"I am your Uncle Thomas, Nelly's *little* brother. And, before we get into what ye need to know about those associates of yours, ye will tell me everyting ye know about me dear sister, Nelly."

Amazed, Will could only stare at Thomas.

"Speak, nephew while there's still time. With the shenanigans ye've been up to, t'would not be a surprise to hear militia banging on your door."

Will drained the whiskey from the glass and signaled his desire for more. Thomas obliged, aware of Will's shock and pain.

Will said, "Tell me first what happened to the Hughes family. When Aunt Stella's letters stopped coming, Mam thought everyone was dead."

Thomas nodded and said, "There was so much tragedy after Nelly left us. First our mother died; and soon after Aunt Stella told us that Nelly's son Christopher had died."

Will lowered his eyes at the mention of his twin's name. He wasn't sure why, but he didn't tell Thomas that Christopher did not die then or that he was most likely still alive.

Thomas said, "And our brother Paul Tibertus was executed for nothin' a'tall. Then one day Aunt Stella fell to her death from Maeve's

Knockneara. Some thought she did herself in but I don't tink she'd commit such a sin. T'was the famine fever for sure."

He went on to say that one day his father, Michael, left the cottage and never returned. "I tink he died from fever; I don't believe he left us on purpose. Then there was just me and me twin Maeve at home. But our sister Kathleen and her husband, Mr. Ryan, took us in.

"There was hardly enough food or us all. Their baby died straight off from the famine fever. T'was an awful ting to witness."

For a long moment Thomas stared off into the middle distance; and then he said, "One day Mr. Ryan wandered off to find food or work. And like me Da, he never came back. Two weeks later, I woke up and found no one else in the cottage. I went into the barn and found Kathleen and Maeve laying on straw, bound together in death. I was eight years old and alone."

Will thought he saw tears gather in Thomas' eyes.

"I left the village, wandered about, taking crumbs and stealing what I could. Finally I ended up in Limerick."

Then he told Will about his early years, how he came to use the bow and arrow, and ended his tale with his arrival in Dublin a year or so before his nephew arrived.

"When I heard that a man named O'Connell had arrived in Dublin looking for a family named Hughes, I knew it must be Nelly's son. When I found ye and saw what ye've been up to, I decided to watch out for ye from a distance until tonight. But I won't get into it with ye just yet."

He leaned back on the chair and said, "Tis time for ye to tell me about Nelly."

Will was surprised that Thomas hadn't mention Captain Tuckerton. The realization dawned on him that, of course, he was probably the only one alive who knew about the Captain and Nelly, save perhaps for Seamus O'Connell. For the time being at least, he decided to leave the Captain out of his story.

Tired and drained, he told Thomas the short version of life on Prince Edward Island. He stopped talking for a long moment, watching dawn's light seep through the window. And then, he told Thomas about Nelly's sickness and death. The retelling of her final days brought hot tears to his eyes. Pain thudded in his head and ankle and he longed for sleep. He looked at Thomas and saw tears sliding down his cheeks.

Thomas swiped at his tears. "Ah. Tis a sad tale, and that's the truth."

He reached into his vest pocket, withdrew something, and said, "A year before Nelly left us a man came to our village. He had an odd looking thing he called a calotype. He told us it was invented in Edinburgh and could take pictures of important men. The man wanted to take a picture of our Nelly for she was so beautiful."

He handed the picture to Will. Both men remained silent for quite a while.

"Enough!" Thomas said. "We both need our sleep."

He dropped to the floor and looked around, "Toss me that pillow."

Within minutes they were both fast asleep.

Will awoke to sunlight casting prisms of color through the stained glass window. He stared for a moment at the window, the one piece of beauty in his flat. As his bad foot touched the floor exquisite pain shot up his leg. So, he sneaked a sip of the pharmacist's brew. He was not at all sure why he didn't want Thomas to see him do it. Then he prepared a light breakfast as Thomas began to stir.

While they ate Thomas said, "Nephew, I decided t'was time to show me face because I needed to tell ye to leave Dublin. Ye must come west with me before it's too late."

Despite the urgency of his Uncle's tone, Will resisted. "Aye, uncle, I know I must get out of it. And I will, but only with Molly."

Thomas rejoined, "Ye may not have the time ye tink ye have, nephew. That September mess in Clontarf should have been enough warning for ye."

Will said, "And how do you know about that?"

Seeing no need to tell Will about the soldier aiming to shoot him in the back, Thomas replied, "Tis not important how I know; tis only important that I know.

"Enemies surround ye, nephew; and not just the Brit … although, there are plenty of them to worry about for now ye are a gun runner. Danger is everywhere, believe me. That bastard, Padraig Riagan hates the ground ye walk on. Not to mention that coward George O'Gorman! He's trouble for ye nephew, no doubt about that."

Will stared at his tea grounds as though by doing so he could change their nature. He hated the truth spoken out loud.

Thomas continued, "Malachy O'Sullivan is a friend only when it suits him. And ye tink O'Casey's a friend, nephew."

It wasn't a question.

"That man ye hope to be your future father-in-law is an enemy of your spirit."

Suddenly, Will looked up from the tea cup and yelled, "Stop! I won't hear anymore."

Then, he said more softly, "I won't accept any more assignments, I promise."

"Tis not a promise ye have power to keep."

"I can keep that promise; I am my own man."

Thomas smiled wryly.

Then Will changed the subject saying firmly, "I cannot leave without Miss Molly, and that's that."

Thomas splayed his hands in defeat.

"I need to go."

He put on his cloak and slung his bow and quiver over his shoulder. He walked over to Will and kissed his brow. Placing his hands on both sides of Will's face he said, "The child of me dear sister, Nelly. Ye don't have her coloring, and that's a fact. But ye do have the blue of her eyes."

He pressed the picture of Nelly into his nephew's hand and said, "Take care, Will O'Connell."

With that he climbed through the window and was gone.

Will whispered into the fleeting night, "Will I ever see you again Uncle Thomas?"

He gazed longingly at his mother's picture. And, then he reverently leaned it against the stained glass window.

CHAPTER 13 ~ THE FENIANS

After Thomas left, Will lay sleepless on his cot until the church bell tolled the 7 o'clock hour. He dressed, pulled on his left boot, and, more slowly and wincing in pain, pulled on his right boot. He grabbed his cane and left the flat. He nodded to the watchman as he passed by his open doorway.

"Wait! There's an envelope for ye," the man hollered.

Will turned on his heel, took the envelope and, noticing the watchman looking at him strangely, he said, "I didn't sleep well last night, sir."

"Aye, I heard noise up there at all hours. Ye must be quieter in the future, Mr. O'Connell."

Will didn't take the time to open the envelope, which was embossed with his name. He knew what it was; and he knew he was right this time.

Kilkenny ~ 1972

Claire sighed and said, "Well, at least the poor fellow got the invitation to the Christmas Ball."

Then as Tuck walked toward her, she said, "What have you got there?"

He handed her the photograph of Nelly, now cracked with age.

"Ah, I can see how beautiful she must've been."

"Tis true enough."

Holding onto the picture, she said, "Paul Tibertus was executed after all. And how awful the way Thomas found his twin and Kathleen."

Tuck said, "Granfar thought that that part about Thomas finding Kathleen and Maeve together in death might be a stretch. Actually, he believed that Kathleen may have survived the famine. More than once his father had searched for any sign that she did; but he found nothing."

Claire thought back to their time in Sligo when they had searched for the Hughes family graves. They had not found a trace of them, save for Fiona's and Stella's proper graves.

She said, "Tis likely Kathleen's bones are with the rest, lying under those rocks heaped over mass graves still standing in the West."

She shuddered at the thought and then fell silent.

Tuck said, "I tink my tongue is tied up, Claire. Are ye tired? Or not …"

He feigned a wicked smile and they went to bed – but not to sleep.

Long after Tuck fell asleep, Claire remained awake, thinking about the tragedy that had befallen their ancestors. She got out of bed and picked up Will, who had been sleeping on the floor in a comfortable bundle. She held him close.

She nudged Tuck several times.

"Are you still awake?"

"I am now."

"I just can't understand how Thomas survived the famine."

"T'was meant to be, Claire. If he hadn't saved Will, I wouldn't be here telling the tale. And you wouldn't be holding onto Will's grand looking descendent with the same name."

Claire tightened her hold on Will, and then laid him back into his bundle. After a moment she said, "But you must wonder how Will survived, being involved in all that mess. Did he take Thomas's advice?"

Tuck rolled over. "Not at that time, Claire. I tink he wanted to say 'no' to O'Casey, but he was in too deep."

"So," Claire said slowly, "what happened to him?"

"I'll tell you tomorrow." He reached over and tenderly kissed her on both cheeks and her forehead and said good night.

The next day, after breakfast they took tea on the veranda. And Tuck took up his tale.

Dublin ~ 1866

Will arrived at the *Times* late, hoping he wouldn't run into O'Gorman. But, he walked into his cubicle to find the man seated with his feet upon the desk.

"Tis about time. And did'ja goes to a party at the boss's house again?"

Ignoring the sarcasm, Will said, "Sorry to be late, Mr. O'Gorman."

O'Gorman gave a shrug, plopped his feet on the floor, saying, "Mr. O'Casey does not suffer slackers, O'Connell." With that he strode from the cubicle.

As soon as O'Gorman turned the corner, Will opened the envelope carefully, wanting to preserve it for he had never seen his name printed so elegantly. *Hope I can dance despite this damned ankle.*

Throughout the day he found it hard to concentrate, his head was full of Thomas' warnings. When his work day ended, his ankle and shoulder sent painful signals to his head. Nevertheless, he sat a while longer at his desk and wrote a note asking for an appointment with O'Casey. He treated himself to a carriage ride to the grand house and gave Grady the note.

The next morning, as he started walking to work, Mr. O'Leary pulled the carriage to curbside. "Hop in here beside me, lad. Today you go to the *Times* in style."

O'Leary halted the horse in front of the *Times* building. "There ye go, lad. Mr. O'Casey will see you Sunday afternoon at 3:00 sharp."

As Will walked up the steps he saw O'Gorman at the window. He noted the angry red blotches tainting his cheeks.

Precisely at 3 o'clock on Sunday afternoon Grady opened the door and greeted Will, "Good after afternoon Mr. O'Connell."

"And you as well, Grady."

The butler led him to a room he hadn't been in before and told him to wait in Mr. O'Casey's study. He set a tea tray on a side table and left the room.

A huge desk made from the *Leamhán sléibhe* stood stately in the center of the room. Will went to the bay windows behind the desk and gazed at the rolling lawn, hedges and gardens now covered with snow.

An hour later he was staring into his empty cup when O'Casey finally walked into the room. Without a greeting, he said, "So, Mr. O'Connell, what's so important? I'm a busy man, ye know."

Will was so put off by this greeting he feared he might stutter. And he did. "Mr. O'Casey. Sir. Um… I…"

O'Casey strode to the bar and poured himself some brandy. He sat heavily in his chair and said, "C'mere Will and sit down."

Encouraged by the use of his first name, Will sat down.

O'Casey touched the brandy glass next to his cheek. "Get on with it, man."

"Mr. O'Casey. Sir …"

"Ye said that already."

"Aye, sir, I know, sir." He cleared his throat. "Miss Molly will have a birthday two days from now … on Christmas..."

"We all know that, don't we?"

"That we do, sir."

Will longed for some brandy, but gamely continued, "I purchased a ring for Miss Molly…" Then he blurted, "Please, sir, I came here to ask for Miss Molly's hand in marriage."

There, he said it.

"Molly has already brought to me attention her affection for ye, O'Connell. I had hoped she would marry a man of means, but that's the way of love, so the poets say. Truth be told, I don't remember the last time I said 'no' to the lass. She was only 10 years old when her mother died, and I have spoiled her."

He lit his pipe and didn't say another word for a long while. Will wondered if the man was thinking about his dead wife or purposely taking his time. Then O'Casey stood and began to pace the room, swinging his cane as he did so. He stopped at the windows and gazed out at his vast, snow-covered lawn. The sun glinting off the snow cast a strange light upon the hedges. "See here O'Connell, the hedges look a bit like Pagan sculptures, don'cha agree?"

Will strained to see what O'Casey was talking about, but saw only snow-covered hedges shadowed by the late afternoon sun slanting toward the western horizon.

"O'Gorman says you're doing a fine job at the paper. Though he might tink tis what I want hear."

Will felt off balance, which he thought might be O'Casey's intention.

"But, more important, and we mustn't speak of this again, ye have done a good job for Ireland. Your first try was a fiasco; but I learned that yc did nothin' to cause it. Mind ye, Malachy was not at fault either."

Then O'Casey turned from the window and poured more brandy for himself. After a moment, he put the glass down, slapped his knee and stood up, and said brightly, "Tis done! Ye may marry me daughter."

Will's face lit up as he reached for O'Casey's extended hand. He thought the man actually winked at him.

O'Casey thought that Will's smile might hurt his teeth; but he hid his amusement and walked him to the door.

"O'Leary will drive ye home. One more ting, when ye first arrived in Dublin, ye asked about the Hughes family. Tis fine; but I heard ye also asked about a Captain Tuckerton. He's kin to the Temple family. I want no more of that, ye hear?"

Will was taken aback for he thought his inquiries about Captain Tuckerton had been forgotten.

"I meant no harm, sir. I won't be mentioning the man or his family again." The lie flew easily from his lips.

"Good day then, Mr. O'Connell."

"And a good day to you, Mr. O'Casey."

Road to Dublin ~1972

After a light breakfast in Kilkenny Tuck and Claire and Will were on the last leg of their journey home. Claire was holding their son, who was contentedly playing with a toy truck. Tuck reached over and tickled him. Then he told Claire about the Christmas Ball at which Mr. O'Casey announced Molly's engagement to Will. He invited the gathering to the wedding that would begin on New Year's Eve day with the Mass of Holy Matrimony in the Trinity College Chapel.

"You know, O'Casey was a show-off at heart, so he also announced that his Christmas present to the young couple were keys to a grand house on the western side of the Trinity College's campus. He told his guests that Christmas Day was also Molly's birthday and joked that her birthday present was his approval of her marriage to Will.

"But," Tuck continued, "he didn't mention that he would give his son-in-law a hefty raise in salary. You can bet he wanted Molly to live in the style she was accustomed to."

He took a quick look at Claire, and then said, "I know most of this because Granfar gave me one of the letters Will had written to Seamus."

When he didn't offer more, Claire said, "Well, are you going to share it?"

He told her to look into the glove compartment. Claire found the letter wrapped in plastic. She read it aloud in flawless Gaelic.

Dear Father, I am writing to tell you the good news of my marriage to Molly O'Casey this past New Year's Eve day, December 31 1866! All the grand folks in Dublin celebrated with us. For Christmas, Mr. O'Casey gave me keys to a grand house near Trinity College; I don't know all the rooms yet. Molly reminds me of Mam as I have told you before. She is a good wife and she attends daily Mass. Mr. O'Casey also gave me quite a wonderful pay increase. Please tell me if ye need anything, for I want to share my good fortune with you. I wish I could talk to you about marriage things, for I know so little, having been too busy what with the printing at O'Casey's paper. But,

Christmas and our wedding days were wonderful. I am grateful. Your loving son, Will O'Connell.

"Humph!" Claire mumbled, "I see he didn't mention his injuries, or his Fenian friends."

Tuck countered, "Maybe he did in other letters we don't know about, Claire. I'll bet you he told Seamus about his Uncle Thomas."

"I would hope so." Then, changing the subject, she said, "Imagine telling his father he doesn't know a ting about sex."

Tuck tossed her a wink. "No I cannot imagine such a ting."

He placed his hand on her thigh and gave it a squeeze. They both laughed. Will dropped the truck and Claire retrieved it. She looked up and said, "Ah! I just saw a sign for a picnic grove up ahead. Let's stop."

A kilometer or so later, Tuck pulled off the highway onto a dirt road and then into a cul-de-sac near a stream. Claire leaned toward the windshield. "Perfect, Tuck. Just right."

For an hour or so they ate, played with Will, and talked about anything that came into their heads. Tuck was lying on his back with his hands behind his head. He started to nod off when Claire said, "Tell me more about Will and Molly."

He leaned on one elbow and, with the other arm, shielded his eyes from the sun. He intended to tell her about Will's next assignment. "You know the history of the Fenians, eh?"

"Aye, the Fenians. I didn't know much about that movement, until that madness in '69, Tuck."

She stared off into the middle distance and her face darkened.

He sat up and put his arms around his knees.

"Claire, do you want to hear the story or not?"

When she didn't answer he said, "You're the one who's always telling me 'don't get into it,' am I right?"

Fighting back tears, she turned her gaze upon him and said softly, "Oh, Tuck."

She reminded him of those awful days following the doomed Neo2-Fenian plan to attack the British Consulate in Boston, Massachusetts.

"You could have died."

"But I didn't tanks to you, Claire. I promised to get out of the movement. And I did."

"Aye tis true; but, sometimes when you're listening to news about Ireland's 'Troubles' I see it in your eyes."

"And what do you tink you see, Claire?"

"I see a longing to be part of it. And sometimes I feel it in the excitement of your voice when telling me about Will's escapades. I tink I'll always see it."

"Ah, lass," Tuck began.

Claire interrupted him saying, "You dropped out of it for me, Tuck. And I tink you stayed out of it for our son. I don't tink you left it for yourself."

Tuck picked up Will's ball and tossed it to him. Will rolled the ball back to him. Tuck pretended to be bowled over by it. Claire smiled a bit sadly as she watched this exchange. Finally Tuck said, "Come son, time to get going."

He picked up the giggling boy and slung him over his shoulder. Claire packed the picnic basket. She smiled wryly, and whispered softly, "Ah, that man!"

Tuck drove the Renault back onto the highway.

Claire said, "I'll be glad to be home, Tuck."

Will snuggled against her breast, and fell asleep almost immediately.

Except for a few comments about the weather and the sights along the way, they drove in silence. Tuck knew that Claire had spoken the truth, but he didn't know what to do about it. After a while, he stopped struggling with that truth. He glanced at Claire and saw that she had nodded off. His thoughts turned to the Fenian uprising a century before his own involvement in "The Troubles."

After their failure in 1865 to disrupt targets such as British fortified positions or to conduct arms raids, the Neo-Fenians conducted lesser skirmishes. These occurred mainly in Dublin and Cork, and to a lesser extent in Tipperary and Limerick. Tuck knew now what his great-great grandfather had not known then: Donavan O'Casey's band of rough necks was on the fringe, their purpose being to aid the Fenian attacks that included the "March Rising" of 1867, which concentrated on capturing or disrupting targets such as railway and coast guard stations.

Like the ones ol' Will got himself into, Tuck thought.

In the end the plan failed. But, the Fenians would reorganize; and, like Young Ireland before it, the Fenian ideals would remain alive in the popular imagination. And those same ideals would fuel the mid-Twentieth Century Neo2-Fenian movement.

Then Tuck recalled that fateful day when he left Ireland for Boston to stay with his cousin, Paul Tibertus O'Connell. He had visited his grandfather to tell him he'd be gone for a while.

The old man was in the middle of one of his endless diatribes against the British, ending with, "…them bastards! They'll be the..." Exhausted, he leaned back in his chair and shut his eyes.

Exasperated, Tuck put his hand on his grandfather's knee and said, "Granfar, I don't tink you heard a word I said."

Through hooded lids he stared at Tuck for a moment. In a soft, slightly fearful tone he said, "Me ears are fine, lad. You're still tinking of goin' off, eh."

"Granfar, tis only two weeks! You'll be fine 'til I get back."

But it would be a much longer time before he was able to return to Ireland.

A few days before his two-week holiday ended, Tuck and his cousin were standing across from the Boston Common where a peace rally was just breaking up.

Paul T. said, "Tuck, tink what we could do if we could get that many people together for our cause!"

Tuck merely nodded for his attention was on four young women walking toward them. As they drew closer, the men could hear their Irish accents. Paul T. poked Tuck's side, "Hey, they're our country women lad. Maybe they need directions, eh?"

An hour later Claire Sheain and her friends were singing and drinking with Paul T. and Tuck in an Irish pub nestled on a narrow street on Boston's waterfront. Though Tuck was immediately attracted to Claire, it was Paul T. who occupied most of her time. Nevertheless, as the group left the pub, Claire pulled Tuck aside and said "I'm not given to being forward, but *carpe diem* I always say."

With that she gave him a slip of paper with her name and address.

On their way back to Dorchester Paul T. had talked of nothing but Claire Sheain. Crestfallen, Tuck knew he couldn't interfere, and handed Paul T. the note Claire had given him. Nevertheless, he decided then and there to extend his stay in the States.

Before long Claire's presence in Paul T.'s apartment seemed natural. Tuck kept his distance in deference to his cousin's designs on her. He would learn later that she was puzzled and hurt by his inattentiveness. At the time, both were unaware of Paul T.'s clandestine activities as a key member of the Neo2-Fenian terrorist group. However, it wasn't long before his cousin told Tuck about his involvement with the group. A romantic soul, enamored by the older man, Tuck was an easy recruit and soon became indoctrinated. And soon after that he was totally committed.

In time, Paul T. told him that the gang planned to attack the British consulate located in Boston's Prudential Center. He said, "We chose the anniversary date of the Neo-Fenians' failed attempt to attack Canada protesting England's long rule over our land."

Now, Tuck was pulled from his musings when a car swerved past, its driver blasting his horn. "Shit!" he exclaimed, realizing he hadn't been paying attention to the road.

Claire woke up and said, "What happened?"

"Guess I was driving too slow."

"Tuck O'Connell driving slow? That's a new one."

Will had also awakened and started to fuss. Claire sniffed and winced. "The lad needs a stop."

He pulled into the next rest area where they freshened themselves, bought some ice cream, and walked a bit.

At length Tuck said, "I was tinking of Will and his new bride."

"Ah, then, no more talk of 1969," Claire responded.

Feeling guilty but ignoring the comment, Tuck began by telling Claire that Will and Molly enjoyed only six weeks of married life before his new father-in-law gave him what would turn out to be his last assignment.

CHAPTER 14 ~ THE TRAITOR

Dublin ~ February 1867

Early on a brilliant Sunday morning, sunshine streaming into the bay windows of their bedroom, Molly turned over and tossed her arm around Will's waist. He shifted his position and turned toward her. They gazed at each other through sleepy eyes, and without a word, they made love. Since their marriage Will had learned quite a bit about "marriage tings."

An hour later, he swung his legs over the side of the bed.

"Ouch!" he cried.

"Ah! There ye go again. After all this time, Will O'Connell, you'd tink you'd remember the bad ankle."

"Ah, lass, I don't forget. I just don't like taking heed of it."

He leaned over and grasped his flask from the bedside table, almost knocking over the lantern. Molly noticed that he took more than a sip, and placed her hand on his back.

She said, "I worry about that stuff the Chinaman gives ye, Will. It makes ye a bit off, it does."

"It helps the pain."

"But at least ye shouldn't take it before Communion."

When he didn't respond she sighed and got out of bed, saying, "I'll see to the breakfast table for after Mass."

"Let Mrs. Mirran do it."

"Mrs. Mirran is more like kin, husband. Let her sleep at least 'til time to get ready for Mass."

After Mass, as the three walked out of the Church, Will grimaced when he saw O'Leary's stable boy leaning against a post smoking his pipe.

"I'll be right back," he said.

Molly was talking to the Priest and didn't notice when Peg Mirran arched her eyebrows, giving Will a disapproving look. He returned the look and walked across the street.

"Aye then, what is it?" He said to the stable boy.

"Mr. O'Casey wants ye to come to the library tonight at 7 o'clock."

Will was abashed and said, "He's summoned me on a Sunday night?"

"Tis what he told me," the boy answered as he mounted his horse. Then he rode off, leaving Will standing there.

Molly came up behind him. "And what did he want, Will?"

"Your father needs me to go to the *Times* tonight after supper." Lies came easily these days; and he elaborated, "I need to set the print for an article he just received." Seeing the skeptical look on her face, he added, "Tis important, lass."

Not wanting an argument, Molly simply gave him a look that revealed she knew it was a lie.

That night, as Trinity's Chapel bell tolled 7 o'clock, Will entered the library through the secret door. Seated by the fire were Malachy, Riagan and the three other men he hadn't seen since his first visit to O'Casey's home. He went directly to an empty chair near the fireplace and warmed his hands.

No one said a word.

At length, O'Casey entered the room. He was disheveled as if he were recovering from a binge. Will noted that, with each step, O'Casey leaned heavily on his cane, unlike his usual jaunty manner whenever he entered a room. The others didn't appear to notice. O'Casey got right to it, telling them about the Fenian "Rising" planned for 4 March through 6 March.

"Our part is simple enough," he said.

Then, except for Will's assignment, O'Casey described what each one was to do on each day of the Rising. Then he dismissed them, telling Malachy to wait nearby for Will. "I want ye to take him home when we're finished here."

O'Casey offered Will a brandy, which he declined, still feeling the effects of his herb drink. Then he detailed Will's assignment.

Will asked, "How real should we make the fight?"

"Just follow the man's lead and ye'll be fine."

Then the older man motioned for Will to take his leave.

After the secret door swung closed, O'Casey went to his study and wrote a note. "Ach!" he exclaimed, and viciously crumpled the paper. With it in his hand he walked to the window overlooking his lawn. His mood was reflected in the foreboding sight of the strange shadows cast by the moonlight, reminding him once again of Pagan sculptures.

Reflecting on the reality of the mission he had just given his men, he was especially concerned about the assignment he had given to his son-in-law, which was far more dangerous than he had acknowledged. He paced around the room, stopping at the fireplace. He directed his anger at Will for having fallen in love with his daughter. Then he acknowledged that he was angry at himself as well. *Putting me daughter's husband in harm's way!* Then he whispered, "What next dear God, what next?" Pulling himself up straighter he said aloud, "God damn it! God damn the British to Hell."

His anger unabated, O'Casey shook his head and tossed the crumpled note into the fire. More desperate by the moment he poured himself another whiskey, sat back down at his desk and wrote another note. Satisfied, he put the note in an envelope and sealed it with a seal he used only on these occasions. Then he rang the bell for Grady, who almost immediately knocked on the door.

"Come in." O'Casey said impatiently.

"Fetch O'Leary. Tell him to bring the carriage 'round the alley in 15 minutes."

Once in the carriage, he directed O'Leary to drive to one of the bridges that crosses a tributary of the River Liffey. As they approached the bridge, O'Casey said, "Tis a nice enough evening, O'Leary. I'll walk for a while. Stay with the horses."

O'Leary watched O'Casey until he had walked the length of the bridge and turned the corner. Then he reached down to the floor and brought his flask to his lips. Taking a swig he said to his horse, "The man is up to no good, and that's the truth."

O'Casey looked furtively around, and then walked toward a small building with boards nailed across its windows. He stared at each of the five windows. Then, following instructions he knew by heart, he knocked a signal on the third window from the doorway. Shortly, the door opened and an old man holding a lantern motioned O'Casey to follow him. They entered the building and walked down a dark hallway. The lantern's light suddenly dimmed, sputtered and died. Ever superstitious, O'Casey took this as a bad sign. He breathed easier when, after some trouble, the man re-lit the lantern; and they continued down the hallway. Then the man stopped and pointed to a door. He turned and left the way they had come in. O'Casey wished fervently that he could be anywhere else but here. He said a prayer, though not thinking it would do any good at this point. Then he knocked on the door.

"Come in."

O'Casey entered the room and was surprised to see that, since his last visit, the room had been completely furnished. A British officer was seated at a desk. He looked up as O'Casey entered.

"It is quite cold out there and you're sweating, man."

O'Casey did not respond.

The captain raised his voice, "O'Casey, it's cold and here you are sweating like a pig. Take off your coat before you faint, man. C'mon, have a drink."

O' Casey replied hotly, "I'll not be taking off me coat, captain. And I'll not be having a drink with ye."

"Right you are! You can't be associating with the likes of us now can you?" Winking at his associate, he said, "Isn't that right, sergeant?"

With some effort, O'Casey eased his breathing, wiped his brow, and said, "Tis the last time."

Mocking the Irish accent, the captain replied, "Tis the last time, is it? Tis what ye said the last time, and that's a fact." Then in his normal accent he said, "Take off your coat, man. If the sweating doesn't bother you, it sure bothers me."

O'Casey ignored him and reached into his inside pocket. He handed the captain the envelope containing the note he had written. He spat, "Here, take it!"

The captain smiled wryly as he slowly reached for the envelope, which O'Casey had dropped on the desk. The captain picked it up and swung it back and forth. Then he bowed his head slightly and said, "I thank you, Mr. O'Casey and the Queen thanks you."

The captain didn't think O'Casey's face could get much redder, but it did. He supposed anger and self-hatred could do that. Handing O'Casey a pouch he said rather harshly, "Here's thirty pieces of silver for your trouble."

"I'll not be taking that from ye anymore, starting tonight."

The captain noted that, just before O'Casey turned to leave, he had gazed a bit too long at the sergeant's bottle of Scotch. After the door shut, the captain tossed the pouch to the sergeant.

"Make a note of this transaction and put the money back in the coffer."

He sighed, and with disgust said, "No wonder the bastards can't win a skirmish, never mind a war! Time after time, generation after generation scum like O'Casey betray their own."

With that he tore open the envelope O'Casey had given him and read aloud the details of O'Casey's plans to aid the Fenian Rising in March.

When he finished, the sergeant said, "The Wicklow Railway Station plan is pretty bold, don'cha think, sir?"

"Yes. But, they've got a surprise coming."

"I'll bet you a pint and a quart that those dates have some grand significance to them. Some martyr's execution most likely."

"Or maybe some ancient King's 'valiant' deed," replied the captain. He spat on the floor, drained his glass, and said, "Let's get the hell out of here."

As O'Casey walked back to the carriage, he recalled the details of the note he had given the captain. Though it contained essential information about the Wicklow plan, O'Casey had altered the timing somewhat. He took comfort knowing that at least his daughter's husband will have the chance to escape before the Brits foil the plan.

Then he thought about his own dangerous position between two wholly different worlds: The British, who could imprison him or betray him at any moment; and the Fenians, who would slit his throat if they discovered that he was the traitor they had been seeking.

CHAPTER 15 ~ DISASTER AT WICKLOW

On the Road to Dublin ~ 1972

"Oh my God!" exclaimed Claire. "O'Casey's the traitor. I can't believe it."

"Believe it, Claire. Thomas called it when he told Will that O'Casey was a coward who would harm his soul.

"After his 'talk' with the Brits, O'Casey went home to drown his guilt in whiskey. Fuckin' coward. You haven't heard the worst of it yet."

He paused, then, "Granfar told me that, earlier that same day, Malachy had dropped Will off at his house …"

Dublin ~ February 1867

Will opened the door to find Molly standing there, hands on her hips. Stepping back he said, "What are you doing? You nearly knocked me down."

"We need to talk, husband."

"You never asked before you start talking. Must be important, eh?"

By the look on her face, he realized this was no time to tease, so he said in a more serious tone, "Let me take off my coat and get warm first."

Molly followed him as he placed his cane in the umbrella stand, limped to the coat rack, and hung up his coat. She followed him as he limped into the parlor, and stood near as he took a seat by the fire.

"What do we need to talk about then?"

"Ye must tink I'm a dolt, Will O'Connell. I knew Father wouldn't be sending ye off to the *Times* on a Sunday night."

Will started to protest, but she talked over him.

"I saw O'Sullivan drop ye at our door. So do not lie to me. I know you're up to no good."

His voice edged with anger, Will retorted, "And what is it you tink you know about my affairs, woman?"

Molly spat back, "I couldn't say. But I fear what I imagine. I know Malachy O'Sullivan's politics full well, husband. He's been in the library with Father more times than I can count. And, through me chamber's window I've seen those other roughnecks sneaking around the alley. Father tinks I don't know what they're up to.

"And that foul-smelling Padraig Riagan with his scarred face! Don't tink I don't know ye've been with him often enough. I can smell him when ye come to bed."

Will's anger rose for he knew she was right to be wary about these men with whom he never intended to become so deeply involved. In measured tones he said, "I tink that's enough, Molly."

"I'm not finished, Mr. O'Connell. Not a'tall finished! Ye disappear, once for a whole day and night. Ye make up some lie and ye tink ye have me fooled. More than once ye come home depressed and disheveled, do ye really tink I didn't notice?"

Will poured himself whiskey. Keeping his back to Molly, he pulled his flask from inside his jacket and shook a few drops into the glass. He knew that Molly knew what he was doing, but he didn't care.

"And don'cha tink I know how you really hurt your shoulder and that ankle of yours. Ach! A brawl indeed. All these months later ye still take that devil water, and even in the morning."

Will slammed his glass down and headed for the stairs. Molly yelled, "I am not finished, husband!"

He stopped and slowly turned to face her, anger touching his features.

Unabashed, Molly continued, "Whenever I ask where ye have been, ye tell me, 'tis man's business.' Ha! Tis the Devil's business. Ye must know that nothing good will come from associating with those good-for-nothing rebels. Not even the Fenians will own up to them!"

Will lost control and for the first time in their life together he shouted at Molly, "Tis not your business Mrs. O'Connell!"

She shouted back, "Tis me business! Some night ye won't be coming home a'tall."

She lowered her voice, "Tis not just meself I'm tinking of."

She lifted her hands in supplication, but quickly dropped them by her side, a stance of defeat. Then she said bluntly, "I am with child, Will!"

Will stood still as a post staring at her. At length he said, "Molly, darling…"

He went to her and wrapped his arms around her. Her struggle against the embrace didn't last long. She whispered soft womanly things in his ear; and he whispered soothing things into her hair, which was tickling his chin. He kept raising his head from the tickle. She looked up at him and started to laugh through her tears.

"You're an eejit, man!"

"And I love you too, Molly."

He kissed her fully on the mouth. Took her hand and led her to the bedroom.

After they made love Molly fell asleep almost at once. Will slipped out of bed and crept down to the parlor. He sat by the window and stared at the falling snow. He was filled with dread about his assignment.

Then, quite suddenly, he said aloud, "A child!" And joy co-mingled with dread. He felt nothing but confusion as he entered into a moral debate with his conscience.

Wicklow ~ 1972

Tuck drove into the southern outskirts of Wicklow, consulting his map only once. He stopped when he arrived at the spot he sought.

"Wake up, Claire!"

She awoke and tightened her grasp around her son.

"Claire, I don't want you to miss this sight. Take a look."

Claire had been to Wicklow before, but had never seen the magnificent headlands from this vantage point. Gazing at Bride's Head she said, "Ah, tis an amazing sight indeed. Let's go out there."

"No darlin, it will be dark soon, so we should keep moving. But, we can take a few pictures. Then I'll tell you about Will's last assignment right here in Wicklow."

Will had awakened when the car stopped and now he started to fuss. Claire fished a cookie out of the bag and gave it to him.

After taking pictures they drove into Wicklow, which forms a rough semicircle around its harbor. They stopped for Petro and a visit to the WC. Then they took off for Dublin, forty-two kilometers northeast of Wicklow. Claire gazed at the wondrous scenery, while Will sat sleepily on her lap. After a while, she said, "So, what was Will's decision?"

"Knowing Molly was with child, Will had a hell of a fight with his conscience. But in the end, he decided to tell Molly that O'Casey told him to go to his Newspaper in Cork, which would require an overnight trip."

Claire's face screwed into a mask of disgust. She said, "Another lie."

Wicklow ~ March 4, 1867

Will hated lying yet again to Molly; but he rationalized that this mission would be his last. He awoke early the next morning and gazed a long moment at his sleeping wife, thinking of the child whose heart beat within her. He kissed Molly gently. She stirred; but, to his relief, she remained asleep. After a quick breakfast, he fetched the hidden bundle containing his vagrant clothing and left through the back door. Less than half hour later he was galloping south toward Wicklow.

When he arrived at the town's outskirts he stopped to consult the map O'Casey had given to him. He followed a circuitous route around the town, with the Irish Sea constantly in sight. He stopped when the headlands came into view in the distance. He had seen them before, but he never ceased to be amazed by their magnificence. Then he urged his horse forward and soon, losing sight of the sea, he entered a forest. Shortly, he found the spot O'Casey had marked on the map. He went around the back of a small cottage and tethered his horse to a tree near a stream. "Plenty of water and grass for you to eat," he whispered to his horse.

He changed his clothes and left the cottage. A short time later he limped into the town. The Wicklow Railway Station loomed straight ahead of him. He entered the building and went directly to an empty bench and lay down, pretending to fall asleep.

As noon approached, the station bustled with people going to and coming from the track area. When the clock tolled 12 o'clock Will braced himself waiting for the constable who, O'Casey had told him, would rap his leg with a club. Will was to pretend being miffed at the constable for arousing him. Then the two of them were to engage in a fight.

As the echo of the last toll bounced off the granite wall, a constable walked over to Will and swung his club hard onto Will's bad leg. Given the unnecessary strength with which the constable had hit him, Will had no trouble hitting him hard on the shoulder with his cane. Both lost all sense of pretense and engaged in a loud ruckus.

Two other constables, busy watching the struggle with amusement, didn't notice four men enter the station from different directions. Dressed in proper Sunday clothes, the Fenians appeared to be ordinary travelers heading for their train.

However, the constable had seen the men even as Will pummeled his back. Knowing timing was essential, he maneuvered away from Will just far enough to swing his fist, which glanced off Will's cheek. Then he tackled him, got up quickly, pulled him to his feet, and dragged him toward the exit. On the way he shoved Will's cane into his chest. The other two constables clapped and whistled their approval.

The constable nodded to his colleagues, saying, "I got him, lads. I'd be grateful if ye take care of the mess while I take this bum to the station."

Will growled, "You didn't have to hit my leg so hard, man!"

The constable spat back, "Ah! Don't be such a pussy." Something was nagging at the back of the constable's mind.

It was irritating.

Then two dozen or more British soldiers rushed toward him and Will. *Were the soldiers late, or were the Fenians early?* At that moment he became aware of what bothered him: Ha! The Fenians had entered the station almost 10 minutes earlier than O'Casey had informed the British Captain. Now anything could happen. The constable, actually a double agent loyal to the Crown, had a sudden insight and mumbled, "Fuck O'Casey! He betrayed the Crown as well as them bastards."

With unnecessary roughness, he hustled Will into an alleyway.

"C'mon! We must make this look real."

Alarmed, Will asked, "How did the British know to come here this morning?"

"We have traitors among us. Ye especially should know that, O'Connell. C'mon, ye must get to the safe house!"

Just as they headed for the alleyway exit, an explosion from the direction of the train station shook the ground beneath them, tossing them back and forth against the alley walls. When the dirt and dust began to clear, the constable screamed, "The rats! They were to disable the train, not blow the fuckin' thing up."

He ran out of the alley, holding a kerchief to his bleeding head. He knew his superiors would have no trouble believing that his prisoner had escaped in the chaos following the explosion.

Will was dazed and hurt. He pulled himself to a sitting position and saw tiny stones and pieces of glass embedded in his hands. He lifted his pant leg and saw the same had happened to his knees. He rose painfully and looked around for his cane. He found it at the opposite end of the alley from where he had fallen.

A woman ran into the alley screaming, "Oh God! They murdered women and children!"

Will was aghast. O'Casey had assured him that the Fenians would not hurt civilians. Their mission, he had said, was to disable a train chock full of British munitions and other supplies. Will would later learn that the rebels had intended all along to attack a passenger train they believed carried only weaponry and a few British soldiers.

As it turned out, two soldiers on leave, the train engineer, and 22 British and Irish civilians perished that day in March 1867.

On the road to Dublin ~ 1972

Tuck glanced at Claire and could see her anger rising. She said, "Ah, Tuck. That disaster reminds me of your own."

A bit sheepish, he replied, "Enough story for now, eh?"

Frustrated, he turned on the radio hoping to find some music; but each station was carrying a news bulletin. He selected one. The newscaster was providing an account of yet another bombing in Northern Ireland. He reported that an IRA splinter group had taken responsibility. The station cut to a live announcement by the group's spokesperson who was giving condolences to the families of unintended civilian victims. He stated emphatically that his group was not in the business of targeting civilians, "...not like British soldiers who massacred peaceful, unarmed Catholic demonstrators in Derry last January. Collateral damage is expected in time of war."

The host of the regular program came back on the air. In disgust he said, "Collateral damage my ass! The man calls this a war? No, ladies and gents, tis terrorism, and that's a fact."

Claire turned off the radio. "When will it ever end? Today the rebels killed innocent people just like the Fenians did a100 years ago. They're nothing but murderers, Tuck!"

"Tis a hard word, Claire."

"What else would you call them? Do you call them patriots as you called yourself in '69? For God's sakes, man!"

Tuck pulled the steering wheel hard onto the shoulder, spitting gravel into the traffic. Several passing drivers blasted their horns. Tuck killed the engine and pushed his door open. He walked fast, jumped the guard railing and entered the woods.

Claire leaned her head out the window and yelled, "Jesus, Tuck! Get back here."

The sudden stop had startled Will and he had begun to cry.

Pushing branches out of his way, Tuck ran straight into the branch of a small pine, tripped and fell hard. "Shit!" he murmured.

He remained seated and lowered his head. He admitted to himself that by suggesting the trip to Sligo he had hoped to soften Claire's heart as well as her attitude toward "The Troubles." Surely, he had thought, the unveiling of the memorial to those who had died in the coffin ships, particularly *The Forrester*, as well as the drama of their ancestors' suffering, would do the trick. But, it seemed, it hadn't.

Tis no use. She'll never see it.

He recalled that night in 1969. The Neo2-Fenians' plan to bomb Boston's British Consulate was devised to avoid human casualties. Nevertheless, as they later learned, staff schedules had been changed and two cleaning crew members and a guard had been killed in the explosion. Several people on the street had been hurt, but not fatally.

That night they had driven their motor cycles to the vicinity of the Prudential Center. While the others stayed with the cycles, Paul Tibertus simply took the elevator to the 43rd floor, climbed three stairwells to the 46th where he incapacitated a Consulate guard. He then broke into the stairwell leading up to the 47th floor where the Consulate was located. The package he was carrying contained an explosive device set to trigger an explosion in 20 minutes. He placed it in a maintenance closet located outside of the Consulate offices. Then he took the stairs two at a time back down to the 43rd floor where he took the elevator down to the lobby. Not wanting to attract attention, he forced himself to walk across the plaza and onto the street. Then he half-ran to join the others.

They took off heading north away from the Prudential, thinking they'd be able to make a clean getaway.

But, they were mistaken. As they raced their cycles north on Route 93, somehow the Reading police were aware of their flight and caught up to them. Soon, they were joined by the Malden and Boston police, as well as the FBI. Tuck recalled riding beside Frankie Gallagher when suddenly Frankie was no longer there; and Paul T. and Tom Shaughnessy were nowhere in sight.

He motioned to Alicia Burns and Kevin McAvoy to enter a rest stop. Motors still running, they hopped off their cycles and ran in different directions into the woods. Tuck ran headlong into a small pine branch and received a painful cut from his eyebrow to his temple.

Now he touched the scar and felt the phantom pain, thinking, *The same stupid thing happened today*. Then he recalled what happened next that night.

He had reached an embankment, and, wiping bloody sweat from his eyes and face, he peered through the bushes. He saw a man kneeling beside the body of a woman. He knew it must be Alicia Burns. Furious, he jumped up and ran headlong into the man. They fought and stumbled through the bushes and tumbled down the embankment.

The man straddled Tuck and held a gun to his face. Tuck immediately recognized him as the man he had seen the year before in a pub. He had recognized him then and he recognized him now as the "the boy from Brooklyn." But, he couldn't tell if the man's eyes held the spark of recognition.

Then the man gathered his wits and roughly pulled Tuck to his feet. Smiling wryly, Tuck said, "So, Lieutenant Detective Buchanan, did you ever figure out the riddle?"

Seeing the look of fascination on the man's face, Tuck seized the moment. He wrested the gun from his hand, and ran like hell into the woods.

Now he got up, brushed leaves and dirt off his clothes, and pulled twigs from his hair. He wrapped his handkerchief around the cut on his forearm, stemming the bleeding. When he returned to the car, Claire was sitting on the guard rail holding Will. Without a word Tuck got into the car and started the engine. He looked out the window and stared at Claire until she got back in the car. She didn't ask him what had happened to his arm or his face. Tuck maneuvered the Renault into the traffic flow headed toward Dublin. Neither spoke for a long while.

Finally, Claire put her hand on his thigh. “I hate fighting with you, Tuck. I’m just so afraid that you’ll get back into it.”

“You’ve got to let that go, Claire. I love you and our son and I won’t put you in jeopardy. I promised before and I promise you now.”

After a few moments of silence, Claire said softly, “Is your arm OK?”

“Better than Will’s shoulder and ankle.”

Then she said, “Well OK then, tell me what happened to Will.”

CHAPTER 16 ~ FALL FROM GRACE

Dublin ~ March 4, 1867

The Trinity Church bell tolled the 10 o'clock hour as Malachy galloped into the outskirts of Dublin. He rode directly to O'Casey's house, tethered his horse, and ran into the alleyway where he frantically pulled the handle in the brick wall's crevice. He watched impatiently as the wall swung outward. He pressed the bell summoning the butler to the library. When Grady arrived, Malachy said tightly, "Fetch O'Casey." To the butler's questioning look, he added, "Now Grady!"

Shortly, O'Casey barged into the library and growled, "Malachy! Have ye gone mad, then? What the hell do ye mean, coming here tonight of all nights?"

Uncharacteristically, Malachy brushed O'Casey aside, and went straight for the bar. He poured himself a whiskey and drained half of it in one gulp. He burped, and said, "The boys killed dozens of civilians; and Irish among them! And sure didn't the soldiers track them lads down."

He finished off his whiskey and poured another and one for O'Casey, who seemed to be in shock. "Drink up and listen to me. We were betrayed again; and, I don't mind tellin' ye I don't trust that son-in-law of yours. Less than one year ago he came out of nowhere and in a wink he's married to your daughter. Tink about it man!"

O'Casey put the whiskey on the table and fell into the chair next to Malachy, covering his face with his hands. Malachy reached over and touched the man's arm.

"Donavan, we've been friends a long time. As ye know, I was for the lad right off. But, lately I've had me doubts. And ye can bet your horses that Padraig Riagan won't stand for it. Paddy's still in Wicklow and I tink he's goin' after O'Connell …"

He let his words hang in the air, realizing that O'Casey was not listening.

Then O'Casey said, "I cannot wrap me mind around the horror ye describe, Malachy. Ye see …" His voice faded a bit; and his eyes took on a faraway gaze as he completed his thought, "… they were only to disable a munitions train. And maybe a few soldiers would get in the way. Tis expected."

Then, he looked startled and breathed, "Oh God!"

Alarmed, Malachy got up from his chair and put his face in front of O'Casey's.

"Donavan!"

O'Casey's eyes drifted to Malachy's, who could not see a single spark of light in his old friend's eyes. He rapped O'Casey's arm; but didn't get a rise out of him. In frustration, he said, "Ach! For God's sakes, man, get a grip! I must go. Get some rest or someting."

He leaned down by the side of his chair, picked up his hat and eyed his unfinished drink. He grabbed the tumbler, took a final gulp and left through the secret door.

An hour later, Grady was suddenly awake. Puzzled, he got out of bed to look for the source of what had disturbed his sleep. He slipped into his robe and slippers. Knuckling sleep from his eyes, he shuffled downstairs to the second floor, which contained the family's bedrooms. O'Casey's door was ajar and Grady peeked in. O'Casey was not there. He went down to the ground floor and checked the library. Not there either. His alarm growing, he opened the study door. Flooded with relief, he saw O'Casey, apparently asleep, his head resting on the desk, his arm hanging down by his side.

"Mr. O'Casey?" The butler ventured.

He walked closer to the desk, and, peering down at O'Casey, he saw a co-mingling mess of blood and grayish stuff forming a jagged path from the side of the man's head to the front edge of the desk. Grady jumped back, almost falling out of his slippers. He stepped gingerly to the side of the desk. O'Casey's silk pin-striped pajama top was soaked with blood. Grady's gaze slipped down the length of O'Casey's arm. A pistol was lying on the floor.

As Grady's mind registered what had happened, he shrank back in horror, and clapped his hand across his mouth, stifling a scream. He backed out of the study into the foyer, and stumbled toward the kitchen. "I'll get O'Leary, he'll know what to do," he said to no one at all.

In his panic, Grady didn't see Thomas standing still as a tree near the walkway.

Thomas entered the house through the door Grady had left opened. He crept silently through the mudroom and through the kitchen into the grand foyer. He looked around and saw a door ajar. He looked in and saw what Grady had seen. Though he was surprised, unlike Grady, he was not shocked for he had seen his share of violent death. He walked over to the desk and noted that a whiskey bottle had toppled over, apparently when O'Casey fell forward. He saw a blood-spattered envelope that hadn't been sealed. He picked it up and carefully pulled out the note, and read it.

I ask my dear wife in heaven, and my daughter on earth to forgive me. And I ask them to pray for my soul. With the deepest regret, Donavan Sean O'Casey.

Thomas put the note back into the envelope, wiped the drying blood from it as best he could, and put it into his pocket. At the door, he glanced once more at O'Casey's body. He blessed himself and said the prayer for the faithful departed, after which he thought, "Lot of good that'll do."

Upon entering the foyer, he heard a carriage bell. *That would be the constable.* He trotted over to the only other doorway in the foyer and entered the library. From his surveillance of Will, Thomas knew there was an entrance from the alley to O'Casey's house. He deduced that it might lead into the library; and, if so, he reasoned, an exit would be there as well. He spent several frantic minutes touching, pushing, and pulling at the floor to ceiling bookcases. Finally, he pushed one just right and a portion of it began to move outward.

The March chill filled his nostrils, clearing the stench of blood from them. He stepped into the alley. Then he realized that he didn't know how to get the door shut. For a moment he stared at the bookcase on one side of the door and the brick wall on the other. He shrugged. *Let the constable figure that one out. Maybe he'll tink murdering intruders had entered through that door.* He decided he would not let Molly see her father's note, saving her from the disgrace of her father's suicide.

He turned away from the door and jogged the length of the alley, peeked around the corner and quickly pulled his head back. The chief constable and two others were running up the front steps. When he was sure they were inside, he ran to where his horse was hidden. He took off across the Trinity College campus headed for the O'Connell home.

After the mess at Wicklow Station, Will had made his way back to the safe house. Oddly enough, through the fog of anxiety and pain, his thoughts had focused on the well-being of his horse. He limped to where he had left him that morning. Satisfied that the beast was content enough, he went into the cottage and directly to the cot. Every bone in his body ached; his hands and knees stung from myriad cuts. Steeling himself against the pain and the guilt steadily mounting in his soul, he soon fell into a long, dreamless sleep.

As dawn broke Will woke up with a start. "Who's there?" he cried.

Thomas said, "You're in it deep now, nephew. Dozens of human beings died yesterday; an English soldier or two, but mostly citizens. Irish among them."

Will whispered, "No, please God!"

Ignoring Will's supplication, Thomas continued, "You're now an accessory to murder."

He walked closer to the cot, saying, "British soldiers came upon the scene just before the explosion rocked the station. When they recovered from the blast and realized what had happened, fire ignited their blood. They captured those boys soon enough. And, against their Country's rule of law they shot two of them… and, for good measure, slit their throats."

In shock Will remained stock still. Thomas pulled him from the cot, ignoring his nephew's painful yelp, and said, "Pull yourself together. We've got to get out of here!" And then he let him go. Will promptly sat back down on the cot. The room had brightened and Thomas noticed the blood on Will's hands. He looked closer. "Ach! That's not good. And those knees don't look any better."

With the tip of his knife he carefully worked the stones and glass from Will's hands and knees. Then he gently wiped the cuts with a cloth drenched in whiskey and covered them in make-shift bandages.

"There," he said with satisfaction, and added, "Come then, get your tings. Tis not safe here."

"Tis a safe house," Will replied.

"Get up! We're leaving now."

After an hour they dismounted their sweating horses and led them through rough terrain with a terrifying drop on one side. Thomas halted his horse, and pointed east. "We'll see Bride and Wicklow headlands soon enough. But first, we must find water for these poor beasts, they need their rest."

Will gave his uncle a look, feeling a great need to rest himself.

Shortly they came upon a stream and led their horses to drink. Unlatching his saddle bag, Thomas said, "We'll rest here for a little while." Then, he pulled a small package from the saddle bag and tossed it to Will. "Here then, take some nourishment."

They ate bread with cheese and drank the refreshing water. Feeling a bit sheepish for his folly, Will hadn't said much up to this point. Now, he gathered some courage and said, "Uncle Thomas, I can see that we're not headed for Dublin. You must tell me what your plan is. Molly must be sick with worry." And, almost to himself, he added, "Or wild with anger."

Wiping his mouth, Thomas said, "Or in the depths of despair."

"What do you mean?

Thomas sighed, and said, "There's more to tell, nephew." He picked up a few stones and tossed them aimlessly. Then: "O'Casey was a traitor. More than that, he was a coward and he shot himself dead last night."

Eyes wide with shock Will got to his feet and began limping in circles. He said, "I don't believe it. No, no, no."

Thomas stopped his nephew from pacing, forced O'Casey's note into his clenched fist, and said, "Then read this!"

It took a couple of seconds before the meaning of O'Casey's note registered in Will's brain. Then, he dropped his arms to his side, letting the note dangle from his hand.

"Now do ye see why we must leave?" Thomas said.

"I cannot leave Molly," Will responded.

"With or without her, ye cannot stay here or anywhere in the east."

"I cannot leave her, Uncle Thomas."

"Ye won't have to leave her."

"What do you mean?"

Ignoring the question, Thomas said, "C'mon, we need to get to a safer place."

And without another word, they led their horses back into the woods.

They had been riding for less than an hour when Thomas reined his horse to a stop. They entered a clearing, and Thomas said, "Here we are."

With a puzzled expression Will looked around, saying "What's here?"

Suddenly, Molly's voice rang out from behind a stand of trees, "Husband!" As she began to run toward Will, he dropped the reins and cried, "Good God, Molly! What are you doing here?"

She didn't answer; instead, she flung her arms around him.

"Will," Thomas called, "…a moment."

Will gave Molly a squeeze and walked over to his uncle.

"Aye then, Uncle Thomas?"

"Will, give me O'Casey's note. It must stay out of sight for Molly tinks her father was murdered, and it must stay that way. Do ye understand?"

"Aye, that I do," Will answered, looking back at Molly.

Then, he rejoined his wife and the two of them followed Thomas behind the stand of trees. When Will and Molly entered the clearing beyond the stand of trees, he was surprised to see Peg Mirran standing in the doorway of a shack.

Once inside, Thomas told Will that, after following him to Wicklow and witnessing the whole mess, he went back to Dublin to fetch Molly and Mrs. Mirran. He said, "I don't tink I'll ever know why I stopped at O'Casey's home first. I was debating whether or not to ring the back door bell, when O'Casey's man came running out of the house mumbling to himself. He left the door open, so I went in and found what he was running from."

He paused, looked at Molly. "I'm so sorry, lass." He turned back to Will. "Then I went to fetch Molly. I told her who I was and that I'd been keeping an eye out for ye."

Molly interrupted him. "Thomas told me about father." She nodded toward Peg Mirran, saying, "Mrs. Mirran heard me scream and came running."

When she began to cry, Peg put a comforting arm around the younger woman's shoulders, but addressed Will: "Thomas had to do a bit of coaxing, but he convinced us to come with him to Wicklow."

With that she squeezed Molly's shoulder and walked over to an alcove. She picked up a basket, and said, "I'll put up something to eat."

After they had eaten, Thomas lit his pipe and asked the women if they had brought whiskey, adding with a smirk, "Will's stock is on his hands and knees."

Peg gave him a look but pulled a bottle from her satchel. She poured an inch or two for each one of them. Thomas said, "We will be safe here for the night." Then he added pointedly, "From the Fenians as well as the British!" He took a sip of whiskey. "We leave for Bray tomorrow at first light. And then we head west to Sligo."

Then he raised his glass and said, "To Sligo!"

The others raised theirs as well, and in unison, they said, "To Sligo."

CHAPTER 17 ~ REQUIEM

Just before dawn the next morning, Thomas rose and tended the horses. Peg prepared breakfast, after which they left headed for Bray. Thomas led the way, Will handled the carriage, and his tethered horse brought up the rear. The carriage rumbled precariously down a steep path, a wake of small stones and dirt trailing behind. Soon, Thomas pivoted in his saddle, halted his horse and yelled to Will, "Tell the women to look east!"

Will pulled the reins bringing the carriage to a stop.

"Molly, Mrs. Mirran, look!"

From their vantage point they were able to view the full majesty of the headlands, which left them breathless. Thomas hurried them along and led them through a circuitous route around Wicklow. An hour later they reached Bray and headed roughly northwest. Almost a full week and 116 kilometers of rough terrain later they entered the outskirts of Tullamore, County Offaly where they made camp.

Early the next morning Thomas nudged his nephew awake, and whispered, "Will, I tink we're being followed."

Rubbing sleep from his eyes, Will said, "How do you know, then?"

"Tree days ago I thought there might be someone behind us. I checked, but didn't see anyting. But this time … nephew, I've told ye about that no good Padraig Riagan's hatred for ye."

"Aye, that you did," Will said, leaning on his elbows.

"True, O'Casey was the betrayer the Fenians have been seeking; but, I tink Riagan blames ye for the Wicklow betrayal … and for O'Casey's 'murder' as well. Though t'was a good ruse to keep the truth of it from Molly, tis not so good for ye."

Seeing the confusion on Will's face, he added, "Riagan will use any trumped-up story to come after ye. But I will get him first. Ye must guide the women from here."

Will started to say something, but Thomas put his finger to his lips. "Shush. Get up! I have someting to show ye."

As Will watched, Thomas drew circles in the dirt. Pointing to the lowest circle, he said, "Look here. Tis Tullamore, ye see? Today ye go north from here, then northwest."

Then he traced a line from one circle to the other, to a third and stabbed the stick into its center. He said, "Tis the village of Mullingar on the eastern shore of the River Shannon."

He drew a curved line representing the great river that forms a natural border between the east and west of Ireland.

"Stay one night in Mullingar; and, if I haven't caught up to ye by then, cross the grand river." And thrusting the stick into the dirt, he added, "Make camp here. Tis a wooded area just outside *Ros Comain*. Wait for me there.

"Tis more than 75 kilometers from here to there, so be sure to let Molly and the wee one she bears get plenty of rest."

He reached into his saddle bag and retrieved a pistol and a bag of ammunition. He said, "I hope ye know how to use these, nephew."

Thomas stood then and slung his quiver and bow over his shoulder. He mounted his horse, tossed Will a wink, and was gone.

Ros Comain

Four days later Will pulled the carriage to a stop at the top of a hill. Gazing at the great River Shannon, he said, "Well, would you look at that!"

Mrs. Mirran said, "Tis as beautiful as I imagined."

Following Thomas' instructions, they made camp outside the village of Mullingar. When Thomas didn't appear after a full day and night, they went into the village. Molly was lost in her own thoughts about her father's violent death and her husband's narrow escape from his no-good associates. Peg, on the other hand, was clearly excited to see so many people bustling about, trading, buying wares, and purchasing ferry tickets. The ferry was a paddle-wheel affair without much capacity. Because they had horses and a carriage, they couldn't board it until the next day. So, Will rented a room for the women, who were grateful to have a decent bath and a bed. Will stayed in a barn with the horses.

The next day, as they ferried across the River Shannon, the women oohed and aahed at the sights, while Will napped. He woke to the harsh sound of the ferry's horn announcing their arrival. He was tired and disturbed by Thomas' extended absence and was not looking forward to making yet another camp. Nevertheless, shortly after they disembarked he searched for, and found a place that seemed to match the wooded area Thomas had drawn in the dirt.

Early the next morning Will awoke to the sound of snapping twigs. Peering into the morning mist, he reached under his bedroll and grasped the pistol, saying, "Who's there?" And then he saw him.

"Uncle Thomas!" He exclaimed. He leaped out of his bedroll and ran to his uncle, who fell into his arms. Will was horrified to see a terrible gash on Thomas' forehead, and noted that he was holding onto his side.

The women came running and were aghast to see Thomas cradled in Will's arms. Molly knelt down. "Thomas, where is your horse? I'll fetch him."

Thomas murmured, "The poor beast gave up the spirit days ago."

Will carried Thomas further into the camp and laid him on a bedroll. Peg cleaned and bandaged his wounds as best she could; and Molly gave him sips of whiskey mixed with water.

In a voice steadily weakening, Thomas told them what had happened. He had retraced their journey from Tullamore back toward Bray. He hadn't gone far when he found a camp he thought might be Riagan's. He found a hiding place for his horse, and one for himself that afforded a clear view of the camp. He waited half a day before he heard laughter and talking coming from the western edge of the camp. He watched as Riagan and two other men sauntered into the camp.

Cramped and hungry, Thomas waited while they tended their horses; while they ate; while they smoked their pipes. He waited while they drank and told bawdy stories. And he waited until he felt sure they were asleep. When their camp fire spat its dying embers, Thomas crept from his hiding place, and without the least hesitation, slit the throat of one of the men. Before he could turn to the other, Riagan jumped him.

As Thomas heaved Riagan off him, the third man thrust a knife into his side. Thomas fell and Riagan viciously kicked him. Riagan howled as Thomas' knife sliced his leg. In that instant, ignoring the pain in his side, Thomas rolled himself away just as the other man was almost upon him. He reached for his quiver and grabbed an arrow. He rolled onto his back, holding his arrow like a spear. And the man charged straight into it, piercing his lung. His knife fell harmlessly to the ground. With ebbing strength, Thomas grabbed another arrow. He turned toward Riagan, who had recovered and was limping toward him. Thomas stood as Riagan gained momentum. He charged Thomas and dragged a knife across his forehead, just as Thomas thrust an arrow into the man's throat.

Riagan held onto Thomas in a death grip. Then, Thomas managed to wrest himself from the dying man's grasp, and Riagan slipped, writhing to the ground. When his body was still, Thomas spit on him, and pulled his arrow from his throat. He tore his own shirt, tied it around his forehead, hoping to stem the bleeding. Then he limped over to the third man, who seemed to be in convulsions. Thomas picked up the man's knife and, without hesitation, slit his throat. He put his boot on the man and pulled the arrow from his chest and limped away to the place where he had left his horse.

Now a coughing fit seized Thomas. Then, his face contorted in pain, he whispered, "I'm sorry I killed me horse, forcing him to ride so many hours." Then he managed to say, "I had to be far away before the bodies were found … and I was desperate to see the tree of ye once more."

Both Peg and Molly started to cry. Will was on the verge, but checked his tears when Thomas motioned to his pocket. Will fished inside and took out a blood-spattered envelope. Thomas said, "The note leaves all me possessions to ye, nephew."

Will listened intently as his uncle's lips continued to move; but he heard nothing.

Then Thomas leaned back and closed his eyes.

Five hours later Thomas Michael Hughes breathed his last. After burying him, Will and the women said prayers from the Requiem Mass, which they knew by heart. Atop the grave Will placed a roughly-hewn cross upon which he had carved a simple phrase: *A brave and good man, T. M. H. died here on 24 March 1867.*

Road to Dublin ~1972

Obviously touched by Thomas' death, Claire said, "What a tragedy. The man survives the famine to grow up and save his nephew; and then he gets himself killed."

"Sure, tis a tragedy, Claire. But, according to Granfar, better days were ahead for Will and Molly once they reached Mullaghmore. I'll tell you more if you want?"

She did.

CHAPTER 18 ~ HOME AT LAST

Ros Comain ~ 1867

After putting Thomas to rest, Will and the women set out for *Mainister Na Buille,* heading north by northwest. Late that afternoon, having made camp, Peg and Molly went into town to gather supplies. Waiting for Molly outside a store, Peg picked up a news sheet. The massacre at Wicklow Station was still news in the west. Her eyes grew wide when she spied Donavan O'Casey's name near the bottom of the page. She looked around, folded the sheet and went into the store.

"Come Molly, we must get back."

"Aye Mrs. Mirran. I'm almost done here."

Upon entering their campsite, Peg cried, "Mr. O'Connell, Mr. O'Connell!"

"Aye! I'm right here." He stared at the frantic look on Peg's face and then glanced at the news sheets she was shaking in his direction.

Peg said, "Mr. O'Casey's name is in the news!"

Will grabbed the sheets and read the piece aloud.

Donavan O'Casey, a prominent Dubliner, was found murdered in his home. A hidden doorway in his library was wide open to the elements. The authorities believe this was how O'Casey's assailant(s) gained entry into the house. It is believed that O'Casey was slain by the Fenians, who were responsible for the Wicklow Station massacre that same day.

The authorities have been unable to locate O'Casey's daughter Molly and her husband, Mr. W. O'Connell. Their housekeeper, Mrs. P. Mirran, is also missing. Dublin's chief constable said that the O'Connell family may have been murdered as well. However, he also acknowledged that they could have been kidnapped. This reporter spoke to another constable who wishes to remain anonymous. He said that the Dublin authorities have a third theory, which concedes that the family may have fled for their lives. But, if so, no word has been heard as to their whereabouts.

"Housekeeper indeed!" Peg Mirran huffed.

Will smiled and said, "I don't tink that error tis the important part of the story, Mrs. Mirran."

Then he took notice of the tears that had sprung in Molly's eyes, and grabbed her hand. "Ah, Molly darlin', I'm so sorry.

"But, don'cha believe for a minute that the Fenians killed your father. They would have no reason." He cringed as the lie left his lips, for he now knew that O'Casey was the traitor the Fenians had been searching for.

He kissed Molly's hand, and continued, "At least, the authorities might stop looking for us, and that's a blessing."

The next morning they left *Mainister Na Buille* and headed for County Sligo. Six days later, after an arduous trip through some of Ireland's wildest and most beautiful land- and seascapes, Will guided the carriage onto a cobble-stoned path that led into the village of Mullaghmore.

"Whoa!" He commanded his horse, and exclaimed, "Molly! Mrs. Mirran! Look up!"

They gazed at a magnificent castle situated on a promontory high above the village. Will said, "That would be Classiebawn Castle! Tis as beautiful as Mam said it was, and it wasn't even finished when last she saw it."

Molly replied, "Aye, tis a sight husband, and that's a fact."

Peg brushed her skirt and tossed her head.

She said, "Tis true. But we mustn't tarry. Me bones can't stand another night on the ground…," and in a stage whisper she added, "…or in this damn carriage."

Not a soul had ever heard Peg Mirran curse before.

On the Road to Dublin ~ 1972

Tuck stopped talking, pulled the car to the side of the road, and got out to relieve himself. When he returned, Will was fussing, so he lifted the boy from Claire's lap and tickled him. The fussing turned into a delightful squeal. As they drove off, Tuck asked Claire where he had left the story.

"Will and the women finally arrived in Mullaghmore. And we're almost home too."

"Aye, it won't be too much longer." Tuck responded.

They remained quiet the rest of the way home. Soon Claire was lost in thought, thinking about that night in 1969 when the Neo2-Fenians attacked the British Consulate. Ironically, that awful travesty led to the first time she and Tuck acknowledged their love for each other.

That morning Claire's roommate, Suzanne, and her boyfriend were leaving for New York to attend a wedding. Suzanne had leaned into Claire's room and said, "We'll be gone for almost a week, Claire. I can be reached at the number I put on the fridge if you need me for anything."

And then they were gone.

Claire had welcomed the prospect of having the place to herself for a few days.

By Midnight she was fast asleep in a chair, her book on her lap. The shrill sound of the phone startled her awake. She fairly jumped from the chair, sending the book flying across the room. Reaching for the phone, she glanced at the clock – it was 4:15 a.m.

"Who is this?" She hissed.

Breathlessly, Tuck responded, "Tis me, Claire. Can you get a car?"

"Of course I can't get a car! What on earth has happened?"

In staccato sentences he gave her the short version of the British Consulate attack and its aftermath. They were cut off for a moment. Claire heard the clinking sound of coins dropping into the pay phone. Tuck's voice came back on the line. He told her where Paul T.'s car was parked.

"A spare key is in a magnet box under the right front fender. Please Claire, I hate involving you in this mess, but I need your help."

More coins dropping, then: "I have to get off this phone … cops are everywhere on 93. I'm outside Reading. I'll stick to the woods and get myself to Route 125. I'll find a phone and call you back. I'm counting on you, Claire."

At 7:45 a.m. Claire had been waiting almost an hour in the parking lot of a closed ice cream stand outside the town of North Andover. She had just about given up when Tuck rapped on the car window. She was horrified by his appearance. One of his hands was covered with a bloody handkerchief, and his face was a mess of dried blood and dirt. She unlocked the passenger door and he got in. As he lifted his right leg into the car, Claire noted that his movements were deliberate. He tossed the stick he had been using into the back seat. He gave her directions to Country Pond and promptly fell asleep.

Claire crossed the Bradford Bridge and drove up Haverhill's Main Street. She stopped the car and nudged Tuck awake. Her voice shaking with emotion, she said, "I don't know how to get to that lake from here."

Tuck looked out the window and said, "Where are we?"

Once he got his bearings he told her to follow Main Street into New Hampshire and continue on Route 125. "I'll tell you the trickier turns when we get closer. I tink my ankle is broken."

"I tink a hell of a lot more is broken, Tuck. A doctor can fix your ankle; but he can't fix your soul."

"No doctor. I'm not faring as badly as I look.

"Frankie was shot dead. Alicia Burns, too. I wrestled with the man who killed her."

He paused and then added, "I recognized him, Claire; but that's another story. I got the best of him and ran like hell into the woods … and right into a ditch. That's how my ankle got all fucked up."

He took a breath, then said, "I don't know what happened to Paul T. or Shaughnessy. And I lost track of McAvoy in the woods."

Fear overshadowed Claire's anger as she said, "For God's sakes, I can't hear this right now. I need to concentrate on driving."

For the next half hour they drove in silence, save for Tuck's directions. Then he told Claire to pull onto a narrow dirt road. The car lumbered along until he directed her to pull into a clearing where they camouflaged the car. Then, with Tuck leaning heavily on her, they carefully climbed down an incline to the shores of Country Pond.

"The cottage is over there," he said weakly.

She helped him mount the steps onto the cottage's porch. He told her to fetch the key behind the ceramic half-moon nailed above the door. She unlocked the door and said, "Tis not the way I expected to see Half Moon Cottage for the first time."

She helped him onto the sofa and covered him with a blanket. Following his instructions, she built a fire in the potbelly stove. Then she inspected the ice box and was surprised to see food, beverages and water jugs. "Is this stuff fresh?"

"I stocked the place last week," he answered.

She brought him water, which he drank slowly with three aspirin. She inspected his wounds, determined that his ankle was not broken, but expressed concern about the gash from his eyebrow to his temple. He yelped when she cleansed the wound with hydrogen peroxide. Attempting to hide her fear, she said, "Men are such babies."

Then she gave him some broth. He sipped a bit and ate a half piece of toast. And then he lay back and fell asleep.

Several hours later he awoke with a fever that Claire thought signaled infection. For the next few days she nursed him, fed him broth, and forced him to drink plenty of water. She gave him antibiotics, the prescription for which she had finagled from a local doctor. Within four days he was clearly on the road to recovery.

Now Claire thought, *Most clearly on the road to recovery!* She recalled the tenderness with which he had made love to her, apparently knowing that it was her first time. Though his injuries had had an awkward effect on his ability, their lovemaking was at once passionate and gentle and they couldn't get enough of each other. Despite the circumstances in which they had finally acknowledged their love for each other, Claire had told him she would do anything for him; but she had one condition: he must completely disassociate himself from the Neo2-Fenians. At the time her condition had not been a tough pill for Tuck to swallow.

After several days, she determined that Tuck could fend for himself, and they left Half Moon Cottage. She drove back to Haverhill and, following Tuck's plan, dropped him off at the train station, where he would buy a ticket for Boston, and get on the train. Then she ditched Paul T.'s car, returned to the station, bought a ticket for Boston, and sat a few seats behind Tuck. When they arrived at Boston's South Station they said a tearful good bye, promising they would meet in Dublin three months to the day.

Tuck had told her that he would take a circuitous route, via trains, busses and at least one taxi to Maryland's Friendship International Airport. He would go on to Chicago and from there to Dublin.

Now, as they arrived at Dublin's City Centre Claire sighed, thinking about their reunion in Dublin, Will's birth later that year, and the few years of peace they enjoyed. And for that she was grateful.

Noticing her complete concentration, Tuck said, "We're almost home"

Pulled from her reverie, Claire blinked. "So we are," she said faintly.

Tuck made the turn onto their street near the Docklands where he worked. He double-parked while they emptied the car; and then he hunted for a parking space. When he came into the flat, Claire was putting things away and Will was whining.

Tuck picked him up, saying, "Tired lad? And hungry too I bet."

He looked in the refrigerator and selected an egg. He called out, "Claire, how old is this egg?"

"T'won't kill the lad. Hunger will get him first."

While the egg boiled, Tuck tore some mold off a piece of bread and prepared toast with jam for Will.

"Claire, what do you want to eat?"

"There's nothin' in the place. I'll go to the market."

She came into the kitchen carrying a bunch of laundry, which she tossed in a hamper inside a kitchen closet, and then left for the market.

Tuck sat Will in his high chair and placed the toast on the high chair's table. He said, "Now watch this! Here comes the egg." He made zooming sounds as he circled the spoon around causing Will to giggle.

Claire returned with some prepared food and ice cream. Tuck had already put Will to bed. He said, "The lad fell asleep the moment his beautiful head hit the pillow."

After supper they carried ice cream onto the porch of their second floor flat.

"Remember the quiver Thomas had?" Tuck began.

"Aye, of course I remember," She said, deftly catching a bit of ice cream dripping from her lip.

"I saw it once at Granfar Paul Tibertus' house. I was about 10 years old."

He swirled the last of his ice cream and scooped it into his mouth, made a smacking sound and said, "Good stuff, lass."

"Aye, tis that."

"The leather was so old that when I touched it I thought it would fall apart. Thomas' initials had been carved into the base." Then he added thoughtfully, "Thomas Michael Hughes. Now there was a man, eh?" Busy with her ice cream, Claire simply nodded.

"There were two arrows and the bow in the quiver. The bow was broken into two pieces. Granfar showed me the note Thomas had written. It was yellowed with age, but you could still see the dark smudges that Granfar said was Thomas' blood."

He put his empty dish on the table and walked over to the railing. Leaning against it facing Claire, he continued, "That's when Granfar told me about Thomas for the first time. My imagination ran amuck, I can tell you that. I still have Thomas' note he gave to Will. But my Dad, the old bastard, took the quiver and sold it, even though it wasn't worth a ting. He had no sense, and that's the truth."

Bringing him back to the subject, Claire asked him what happened to Will and the women.

Tuck responded, "Will got himself a job with some news sheet or other. Nothing as grand as the *Dublin Times*, mind you. But, remember Thomas had given Will his possessions, including money. So, Will did OK for himself and his family."

He paused and asked Claire if she wanted more ice cream. She declined, touching her waist, sighing dramatically.

Tuck returned from the kitchen eating ice cream. After polishing it off he took up his story. He told Claire that Will purchased a cottage in the outskirts of Mullaghmore where their first child was born in October 1867. They named him Seamus O'Connell II after Will's step-father. Their daughter, named Flannery after Will's little sister, was born two years later. Then he went on to tell Claire about Will's inquiries about Captain William Tuckerton.

He said, "The man got nowhere. Most people simply didn't want to talk about anyone related to the Temple family. But," he added ominously, "there were others who viewed Will's interest in the Temple family as very suspicious. After a while Will simply stopped asking about the Captain."

He lit a Camel and exhaled slowly. Through the cloud of smoke Claire could see his eyes move with memory. Then he said, "Claire, remember Alice O'Keefe, the Hughes' neighbor?"

"Aye, of course I do. And who could forget her husband who wrote down Aunt Stella's letters?"

"Well, you won't believe it, almost 10 years after settling in Mullaghmore, Will received word that Alice O'Keefe wanted to meet him, which is how he found out what really happened to Christopher. Tis a long story and I'll be in it for the pound, not the penny. Do you have the heart for it?"

Claire did.

And, as it had been ever since that afternoon at Sligo's Famine Memorial, Tuck's story had a hold on her.

PART III ~ CHRISTOPHER

"Memory is a complicated thing, a relative to truth, but not its twin."

~ Barbara Kingsolver

CHAPTER 19 ~ A TWIST OF FATE

Mullaghmore, County Sligo ~ December1877

Molly cried, “Seamus! Get down from that post this minute!”

A handsome 10-year old scrambled down the post and ran, slipping in the snow, to his mother. Named after Will’s step-father, Seamus had inherited Will’s blue eyes; but he had Molly’s brown hair, so dark it seemed almost black. In fact, he looked a lot like his uncles, Michael and Desmond who, his father had told him, lived in North America – Prince Edward Island, Canada, to be precise.

“Here! Right, Da?” Seamus had said pointing to the globe he received for Christmas five days before. His finger touched an approximation of where Prince Edward Island was situated in the Gulf of Saint Lawrence.

“Aye son.”

Seamus’ eyes lit up. “You were a lad there, right, Da?”

“Tis true, son.”

Seamus tossed that thought around his young mind, trying to fathom the distance his father must have come from Prince Edward Island to Ireland. He traced that distance on the globe with his finger. His eyes grew wide and he whistled as his finger crossed the Atlantic Ocean.

Now his mother grasped his hand. “Da will be waiting to take us home; but I have one more errand. Stay put right here on the Baker’s bench.” She turned and walked down the street.

An old woman pulling her shawl tight around her shoulders crossed the street. She shuffled over to Seamus and said, “Lad I wish to speak to ye.”

Seamus looked around. “Tis me ye mean, ma’am?”

"You're the only lad around, are ye not?"

"Aye, tis true."

"What is your name, then?"

Seamus hesitated but told her his name. Leaning toward him, she said, "Your Da would be Mr. William O'Connell?"

Seamus nodded, "Mam calls him Will."

"Aye. He's been heard asking about a Captain Tuckerton, a relative of a family named Temple."

And, pointing toward Classiebawn Castle, she added, "Tis an important family that owns that grand home. And do ye know where your Da comes from, lad?"

"Aye. That I do. I even touched the place on me globe."

Her eyes twinkled as she said, "On a globe, ye say. And where on the globe did ye touch?"

"Canada. That's in North America, ye know."

"Aye, that I do and tis a fine place for sure. And do ye know his mother's name? That would be your *Mathair.*"

"*Mathair mhor*'s name is Nelly O'Connell."

The old woman nodded. "Aye, but do ye know her name before she was married to Mr. O'Connell."

Seamus thought for a moment. "Oh. I see what ye mean. Da talks about the brother of *Mathair mhor*. He was me great-uncle Thomas Hughes." Then, quite satisfied with himself, he said, "So, that means *Mathair Mhor* had that name too!"

"Aye! Very good, lad. I knew her, and I knew your great uncle, Thomas, when he was just about your age." She looked him up and down and said, "Maybe a bit younger." After a pause she said, "I must go now; but ye must do a favor for an old woman."

She sat down next to the boy and scribbled on a piece of paper. She folded it twice and handed it to him. "Give this note to your Da when ye get home. Tis very important."

She looked down the street and saw Molly walking toward them. "Now don'cha go lookin' at the note; and ye mustn't show it to anyone else. Understand?"

Seamus nodded his understanding and put the note inside his coat pocket.

The woman shuffled away. She looked back once and saw Molly leaning down to Seamus, but looking her way.

Molly said, "What did that woman want, Seamus?"

"Nothin' Mam." He shivered a bit, thinking that telling a lie to his mother might be a mortal sin.

After the evening meal, Seamus went into the parlor to say good night to his father. He nervously gave him the note.

Will asked, "And where did'ja get this, son?"

"The old woman gave it to me."

"An old woman, ye say?"

"Aye, Da. She told me not to show it to anyone else. Mam asked what she said to me and I said, 'Nothin'. Tis a mortal sin, is it?"

"No, no. The old woman told ye not to show anyone else and ye didn't. So tis not a sin."

Then, Will called to Molly, "Tis time for the lad's prayers and bed."

He kissed Seamus goodnight, and then read the note.

Mr. O'Connell, for a long time I lived in a lovely town called Andover in Hampshire County, England; and then I returned to Ireland to live with my cousin in County Claire. A month or so ago I came back home to dear Mullaghmore. You must know that talk of the Temple family gets noticed here. When I heard that a young man was asking about Captain Tuckerton I knew it must be you and I have looked for you ever since. When I saw your carriage bringing the Mrs. and the lad to town, there was someting about you. So I talked to the lad. And a fine young man he is. He told me what I hoped to know. I knew the good Lord would help me find the son of Nelly Hughes if I were patient enough. I have someting to tell you that I have kept close to my heart for a very long time and I must tell you before the good Lord takes me. Please meet me at O'Kelly's shop on Friday after the New Year. Three o'clock would be fine. God bless ye. Mrs. Alice O'Keefe.

Will knew that a man named O'Keefe had penned Aunt Stella's letters and he was intrigued. He told Molly he couldn't think what the old woman would have to tell him.

"Ye'll know soon enough, husband," Molly answered.

On the Friday after New Year's Day 1878, Will limped into O'Kelly's shop and saw the old woman right away. He introduced himself, and was startled with the strength with which she grabbed his hand in both her hands. Tears sprang to her eyes.

"Dear Mr. O'Connell, such a handsome man ye are; though ye don't look much like our dear Nelly." Then she peered into his eyes and said, "Ah, but ye have the blue of her eyes."

She pulled him toward a table where they sat down. She nodded to Mrs. O'Kelly who brought tea.

Will took a sip. Staring at Alice O'Keefe over the cup's rim, he said, "Mam got letters from her Aunt Stella. The words were written down by a man named Terrance O'Keefe?"

"Aye, Terrace was me husband … a good man and very smart. He taught me to read and write. So, I can, but not as good as himself."

Then she began to tussle a bit with her shawl. Reaching inside, she pulled out an envelope, which was folded and torn in places. She gazed at him for a moment.

"Did ye Mam ever tell ye about her life before she crossed to America?"

"Aye. She told me about the good times before the potato rot; she told me about the dying and about her crossing in a doomed ship. She told me about Martin Ashe."

Mrs. O'Keefe said, "I don't know about all that. But never mind, did she tell ye anyting about your birth?"

Will eyed the envelope and leaned forward, "Aye that she did. She birthed a twin to me, but he died. Christopher was his name."

Mrs. O'Keefe squinted, and smiling wryly, she said, "Tis true that's what she was told."

Will looked at her expectantly; but she had taken notice of the other patrons. As he started to say something, she put her finger to her lips. "I should've known that there'd be too many ears here. We will go to me cottage."

She stuffed the envelope back into her shawl and got up.

After a short walk, Mrs. O'Keefe said, "Here's me cottage."

Upon entering, Will looked around at the comfortable two-room affair, dominated by a large fireplace. As Alice prepared tea she asked Will to bank a fire against the chill.

Pouring the tea, she said, "As ye know, dear Terrance wrote letters for people; but…" She paused and took a deep breath, "… Mr. O'Connell, two of those letters shamed him 'til his death. The telling your Mam that Christopher died weighed heavily on his heart …" She paused again. "…because it was a lie."

The tea cup shook in Will's hand; red blotches touched his cheeks. Then, he blurted, "What's that you say?"

"Me husband wrote down the words that Christopher died for your great-aunt Stella. But, Mr. O'Connell, Christopher did not die."

Will started to get up, spilling a bit of tea; but then sat right back down.

"He's alive then?"

"Aye, that he is … at least he was when I last heard from him a year or so ago."

Will had hardly heard Mrs. O'Keefe's words. He simply cried, "Oh! Oh dear Jesus. Christopher is alive! Explain, Mrs. O'Keefe. Do you know where he is? Did you know the Captain?"

"One ting at a time and I will tell ye what I know," She said, laying her hand gently on Will's arm. She peered at him, saying, "Ye look a bit pale, Mr. O'Connell. Here then, let me take your cup."

She got up, retrieved a bottle of Courvoisier Cognac and put it on the table.

"Tis the brandy of Napoleon, ye know. I don't have much money, but sure I know how to spend it."

She tossed their tea into the fireplace and poured the brandy into their cups and sat back down.

"Christopher doesn't know about ye or his real mam and da."

She reached into her apron pocket and handed Will the envelope, saying, "This letter is the second one me husband regretted writing for that woman. Be careful, tis more than 30 years old."

He noted that it was addressed to Lord Palmerston. Though his mind was reeling, he had the presence of it to ask how she had gotten the letter.

"I was told to burn the letter." She gave him a sly look, and said, "But, as ye see with your own eyes, I did not burn it. By a twist of God's fate I kept it all these years for t'was meant for ye Mr. O'Connell."

CHAPTER 20 ~A TERRIBLE SECRET

Dublin ~ 1972

Tuck stopped talking and rummaged through his knapsack.

Impatiently, Claire said, "Well?"

He handed her a piece of paper, safely wrapped in plastic. "Be careful. Tis the letter Alice saved for Will."

Claire looked at him in surprise. "Man, I can't believe you never told me about this. You are full of secrets, aren't you now."

She began to read the letter, but Tuck said, "No, Claire. Just hang onto it and I'll tell you what Mrs. O'Keefe told Will."

Mullaghmore ~ 1878

Will dangled Stella's letter from his hand, and with the other took a hefty swallow of cognac; Alice sipped hers, and then said, "Dear Terrance had taken Stella to Galway to fetch Christopher. On the way back to Mullaghmore they ran into a snow storm. Ah, t'was a fierce one once they reached Connemara. As ye know, the mighty Atlantic all but surrounds the place. So, they had to take shelter in an Inn ..."

Connemara, County Galway ~ January 1847

Aunt Stella and Mr. O'Keefe were seated in the inn's parlor while they waited for a room. She was saying, "But ye must put these words down for me!"

Terrance responded, "I cannot do it. I don't tink God forgives me for writing to Miss Nelly that Christopher is dead." He wiped his brow with his sleeve. "And now this! I tell ye woman, tis the devil's work."

Aunt Stella shifted Christopher on her lap, and said, "Shush! The others will hear." She leaned closer to him. "Ye could take the money quick enough before; just one more letter and ye'll be done with it."

He said, "Aye, I took the money before, hoping t'would be best for the lass to tink the wee one is dead so she wouldn't yearn for him." He made a sound somewhere between a sigh and a whimper, and continued, "But this awful lie ye ask me to write down."

Stella dug into her cloak pocket, saying, "Ah! Go on with ye, Mr. O'Keefe. Here! Take the pouch and be done with it."

When he didn't take the pouch, she placed it on the sofa next to him. At length, he picked it up, making a quick sign of the cross. He put it in his satchel and removed his ink and quill. Then he wrote down the words as Stella dictated them.

Mi'Lord Palmerston, with this note your groundskeeper, Mr. O'Keefe, gives you the infant Christopher to care for. He is flesh of your kin, Captain William Tuckerton. Ye must make amends in his place for he violated my niece and left her with child. She is now in Canada; and the wee one cannot be cared for by the family. I spied the ring the man gave her. It has your crest upon it. To prove what I say I draw it here. I will keep this matter secret for my family's sake and for your sake. As you know, we are all starving; and the money the Captain promised to send has not come. Most important, you must pardon Paul Tibertus Hughes who, as you surely know, is the Young Irelander you hold in your prison awaiting execution. You say he violated the law. I say tis your law only. You do as I ask, and I will not tell of your kin's crime, except for this man, Terrance O'Keefe who writes this down. He told me the star I draw here means my name.

As always, Mr. O'Keefe wrote Stella's last name next to the star she had drawn.

Stella shifted in her seat. "Tis done then," She said.

Mr. O'Keefe exclaimed, "How can ye be so cold, woman? "Christopher is your kin!"

"Ah! Stop it Mr. O'Keefe. He is the bastard child of an English soldier!"

Shocked by her own words, Stella abruptly stopped talking. She tightened Christopher's blanket around him, laid him on the seat next to Mr. O'Keefe, and growled, "Watch him!"

She walked over to the window and stared at the whirling snow. Stella McBride's rationalization powers were in top form on this stormy day in Connemara. Though she knew what she was doing seemed cold hearted, she felt her reasons were good enough. Mentally she counted them off: First, Christopher would always be too weak to survive the voyage to Canada. And, most likely the famine would take him, so why not let Nelly believe he's dead now rather than later. Secondly, the Temple family had committed terrible crimes against her friends and family. The plan she had put in motion would hardly balance things, though it would make her feel better. Third, she and her sister Fiona's children were starving already and they needed the money; and, fourth ....

And there she stopped counting her reasons, for she could not bring herself to acknowledge the main reason behind her plan. She gazed at the storm, its energy causing snow to swirl in scary likeness to typhoons she had only heard about. Stella McBride had kept her emotions in check half her life, never speaking of her own tiny deaths. But, watching the angry storm, her pent-up emotions broke through her defenses. She savagely brushed away tears that had suddenly gathered in her eyes. *And fourth*, she thought, *Paul Tibertus mustn't die.*

After a while, willing the tears to stay put, she composed herself, marched back to Mr. O'Keefe, and sat down.

"I will tell ye someting that ye must never repeat. Do I have your word?"

"Couldn't be worse than this letter!"

"Don'cha be putting on the high-and-mighty act with me, Mr. Terrance O'Keefe. I am not moved by your self-righteous disapproval.

Not for the plan this letter puts into motion, or for what I am about to tell ye."

She straightened her skirt and wrapped her shawl tighter around her shoulders, and then she said, "Paul Tibertus does not belong to Michael Hughes and me dear departed sister. He belongs to me!

"There, I've said it! And don'cha tink for a minute to judge me. Paul Tibertus is the son of a good Irishman, loyal to our country. And for that loyalty he was butchered by the bloody English before he could marry me. So, to spare the shame of it, Fiona and Michael brought up Paul Tibertus as their own."

Mr. O'Keefe's eyes grew wide with shock. He sat there stock still, speechless.

Stella's cheeks were beet red, and, as she continued to speak, her voice shook with emotion, "And now me son is to be executed by the same evil that killed his father; and that is now killing our beloved land." She took a breath.

"And that is why me letter demands the trade, Mr. O'Keefe! Christopher, who may not live anyway, for Paul Tibertus, who should live to help Young Ireland save our country."

She held out her arms. Mr. O'Keefe hesitated briefly; and then he handed Christopher to her. She scooped him into her arms and left the Inn's parlor.

Mr. O'Keefe watched her climb the stairs toward the concierge desk. A look of amazement was frozen upon his face.

Dublin ~ 1972

Claire dangled Stella's letter in her hand, too stunned to speak. Tuck simply waited. Finally, she said, "Oh, that woman! How could she commit such treachery?" After a pause, she added, "But, t'was her own son she was trying to save." She blessed herself, saying, "God forgive me, I almost feel sorry for her."

She lowered her head in thought. A moment later she looked up and gave Tuck a playful punch on the shoulder and said, "I cannot believe you never told me that two women in your family gave birth out of wedlock. And over a century ago at that."

Tuck gave her a look, "So?"

"So, I tink those ancestors of yours give you permission to keep me in common law. That's what I tink, you cad you." She had to smile at her use of the word.

Tuck chuckled, and said, "Tis getting chilly, let's go inside."

Claire responded, "Now don't leave me hanging! I want to know what happened to Christopher."

"I'm getting to that; but, first Mrs. O'Keefe told Will a hell of a lot more."

Connemara, County Galway ~ 1847

The look of amazement on Terrance O'Keefe's face faded into a mask of anxiety; his hand began to shake, and the letter slipped from his fingers. He became aware of the other travelers and, realizing they may have taken notice of the exchange between him and Stella, he looked around rather sheepishly. He picked up the letter and folded it into an envelope. He wondered what kind of sin he had committed by helping Stella trade Christopher for Paul Tibertus. *Tis so cruel*, he thought. He knew the shame of it would haunt him for the rest of his life.

And he didn't sleep well that night.

By the following morning, the storm had lost its power and snow was falling in mere flurries. Two days after that, the sun's bright warmth had melted enough snow to allow travelers to be on their way. Stella and Mr. O'Keefe didn't say much to each other on the final leg of their journey home.

When they reached the hill above Michael Hughes' farm, Stella said, "Mr. O'Keefe, leave me off here. The family mustn't see the wee one." She tucked Christopher snugly into his blanket and placed him next to Mr. O'Keefe.

She climbed from the carriage and started to walk, but hesitated. She turned back and looked in on Christopher. O'Keefe watched in wonder as Stella's face softened. She leaned down and kissed the baby on the forehead and brushed his cheek. She looked up at Mr. O'Keefe with an expression touched with sadness. He thought of her star-crossed life and, for a moment he felt sorry for the woman. But, his pity dissolved as he watched her pull herself up to her full height, the sadness vanishing from her face.

"No misgivings about that letter Mr. O'Keefe. Ye must take it and wee Christopher straight away to Lord Palmerston's estate."

With that she turned and trudged down the hill to tell Nelly's family that Christopher had died.

CHAPTER 21 ~ LADY CATHERINE

Mr. O'Keefe walked up the path leading to his cottage. Alice was standing in the doorway looking as though she was ready to hit him. But, when she saw he was carrying a baby, she quickly made an about-face and cried, "And what on earth are ye doin' with Nelly's wee one, husband?"

"One ting at a time, woman! Tis cold out here and I need a spot of tea before I tell me tale."

As soon as they entered the cottage, Alice took Christopher from her husband. He watched her as she bounced him lightly, making cooing sounds. She looked to him as though she had been doing that all her life, barren though she was. He went back out and, when he returned with his satchel, Alice had already placed Christopher in a straw basket. Shortly, she poured tea for herself and her husband. The moment he brought the cup to his lips he knew she had put a dollop or two of whiskey into it. He sighed with relief.

Alice took a sip of tea, grimaced, and said, "Ye told me t'was a trip to Galway and back. Instead, ye've been gone almost a month. And here ye come back with this wee one. Husband, ye have the tea. Now out with it!"

So, he told her that after Nelly had given birth to the twins, she left for America with one of them, pointing to Christopher he said, "As ye can see, this one was too fragile to make the crossing, so I took Stella McBride to Galway to fetch him. On the way back, we ran into a fearsome snow storm in Connemara and we got stranded in an inn."

He paused, not wanting to tell Alice why Christopher was with him. He took a sip of tea, got up and poured more whiskey into his cup. Alice could tell he was making his mind up about something. He turned and faced her. He told her about Stella's letter telling Nelly that Christopher had died.

Alice's face turned a variety of red, and she said ominously, "The witch! She is on her way to hell, and that's the truth of it. For God's sake, man! How could you use your writing talent to tell such a lie?"

"Tis even worse than that, Alice." He handed Stella's letter to her, saying, "Here then, take a look."

After reading it, Alice fairly yelled, "Ach! And now ye'll be asking for Lord Palmerston's wrath upon your head."

She got up and tossed the tea into the fireplace, and exchanged it for straight whiskey.

"Terrance! Oh, Terrance I fear for your soul."

He pleaded, "I cannot bring the child to Lord Palmerston. I am a simple groundskeeper to him. But you're head mistress for the wife of Lord Palmerston's land agent, Lord Eldridge, and ye do not fear her. Please, bring the letter to Lady Catherine Eldridge."

Minutes seemed to fall into oblivion before Alice answered him. "So, ye want me company in hell, eh?"

"No, no, woman. Tis not your sin; tis mine alone. Please bring the wee one to Lady Catherine."

"Fetch the midwife for the poor little ting; and I'll tink about it."

By nightfall, after caring for Christopher's needs, Alice had warmed to her husband's idea. She rationalized, as had Stella, that the baby may not live anyway. For the trade, Paul Tibertus could continue his patriotic work with Young Ireland. And it was true that she was in Lady Catherine's confidence.

The next morning, after they arrived at Lord Francis Eldridge's estate, Terrance waited in the carriage, while Alice brought the letter and Christopher to Lady Catherine.

As Lady Catherine read the letter, the color drained from her face. She folded it and handed it back to Alice.

"Mrs. O'Keefe, I cannot abide even burnt embers of that letter in my home. I want you to go home and burn it. You may return to your usual schedule on Tuesday. In the meantime, the child will be well cared for."

But, when Alice arrived home, she did not burn the letter, though she didn't know why at the time. Instead she hid it behind a fireplace stone.

On Tuesday the following week when she arrived at the estate, the maid, Mairead, informed her that Lady Catherine wanted her to go directly to her chambers. Unnerved though she was, Alice was anxious to see Christopher again.

She knocked softly on the door, saying, "Tis Mrs. O'Keefe, madam."

She entered the room and saw Christopher asleep in a proper crib. She blushed, thinking of the meager straw basket in which she had placed him. Though she wanted to go to him, she stood still waiting further instruction.

Lady Catherine said, "Come and sit down, Mrs. O'Keefe."

Alice did as she was told, folding her hands in her lap.

"I'll get straight to the point," Lady Catherine said. "Lord Palmerston is not in Ireland this month or next; but even if he were here, my husband Lord Eldridge…"

A knock on the door silenced her. "That would be Mairead with the tea. Please get the door, Mrs. O'Keefe."

The moment Mairead walked in the room she saw Christopher and tossed Alice a puzzled look. She placed the tray on the table, and Lady Catherine thanked and dismissed her in one breath. Then, she poured tea for herself and Alice.

"As I started to say, my husband will be away for another week. He must not know anything about this matter, which is why I instructed you to burn that letter. He would have been honor bound to give it to Lord Palmerston. I can assure you, he would not take kindly to blackmail."

She noted fear creep into Alice's eyes, and quickly added, "I do not mean you or your husband; though I cannot abide by his willingness to pen such a letter. No, you nor your husband are to blame. Stella McBride alone attempted this blackmail." She paused, took a sip of tea; and then said, "Is Christopher's mother involved in this deceit in any way?"

"Oh no, madam. Stella McBride told Miss Nelly that the child died."

A sudden crimson touched Lady Catherine's cheeks. "She will pay for her treachery in this world, or in the next."

Regaining her composure, she picked up her tea cup and looked over the rim at Alice. She put the cup down. "You're staring, Mrs. O'Keefe. Do drink your tea."

The two women drank in silence for the next few minutes. Then Lady Catherine said, "Mairead knows of the child's presence; but I will instruct her to keep her own counsel, as I expect you will."

Alice responded weakly, "Of course, madam."

"I have dispatched a letter to a distant cousin living in England," Lady Catherine began, "Rose and her husband Walter cannot have children of their own. I suggested that they adopt Christopher; and I know they will be delighted to do so. They are unaware of the circumstances, of course. I caution you to keep it that way."

"Of course, madam."

Lady Catherine lowered her eyes, and said, "They are Scottish, so of course, they're Protestant."

Alice felt a shudder ripple through her at the thought of Nelly's child being brought up Protestant. Lady Catherine reached across the table and placed her hand on Alice's. "Mrs. O'Keefe, you have been with me for a very long time and I have grown fond of you. So please keep that in mind as you hear what I'm about to say."

Alice's heart pounded; her eyes grew wide as Lady Catherine continued, "You will accompany Christopher to England as his governess. You are to stay with the family until Christopher is sent away to school. That would be about twelve years hence."

Seeing the shocked expression on Alice's face, Lady Catherine quickly added, "I will see to it that you have a holiday twice each year to visit with your husband and friends."

Alice was aghast, but in no position to argue. Her immediate thought was that her exile from home and husband was penance for her part in the betrayal that Stella had wrought. Tears sprung to her eyes and her hands began to shake. Lady Catherine stood, walked around the chair and placed a comforting hand on Alice's shoulder.

Dublin ~ 1972

"Oh, dear Jesus," Claire said, "Poor Alice."

Tuck replied, "But, look at it this way … if she hadn't been Christopher's governess we would never have known anyting about him."

"What about the Captain? Did Alice know what happened to him? Did she tell Will?"

"Aye that she did. But, first I need to tell you about the scheme Mairead and her lover dreamed up."

Mullaghmore ~1847

Always on the lookout for herself, Mairead had her ear pressed to the door, and had heard the exchange between Lady Catherine and Mrs. O'Keefe. When she heard movement, she pulled away from the door, ran down the back stairwell, and out the back door. She entered the stable and ran to Jack Dolan, one of the Lord's grooms. He smiled wickedly and grasped Mairead's hand. She giggled and he helped her climb the hayloft where they met as often as they dared. He immediately shed his pants; she tore at her blouse; he lifted her skirt and they made wild love as quietly as wild love could be made.

After their tumble in the hay, Mairead told Jack about what she had heard. In a tone that gushed with conspiracy, she said, "Jack, don'cha see the chance we have?"

Jack, being on the slow side of things, didn't see at all. So, Mairead clarified until he understood.

"Aye! I see what'cha mean. Tis a chance to get in the Lord's good graces."

That's it, Jack. The letter has been burnt so there'll be no blackmail; and Paul Tibertus will be executed. Then, Stella McBride will carry out her threat to bring shame on Lord Palmerston." She gave Jack a sly look, and added, "Though tis true that the Lord is known to be quite the philanderer, himself. It runs in the family, ye know."

She pushed Jack away as he tried to kiss her. "No more of that, man. We must plan."

Dublin ~ 1972

Tuck said, "Shortly after Alice and Christopher left for England Stella's body was found at the bottom of Maeve's Knockneara. The chief constable told Michael Hughes that Stella had either fallen accidentally, or she had committed suicide. The constable knew the word 'suicide' was anathema to Michael, so he assured him that, if Stella had done herself in, God would forgive her, for surely she suffered from famine fever.

"But to be sure that Father Malloy would give Stella a Catholic burial, the constable reported that Alice's fall was an accident. And …"

Seeing Claire's look, Tuck abruptly stopped talking.

"Wait a second, man," she said. "That part about Mairead and Jack doesn't ring true. Alice O'Keefe couldn't have known about that, so she couldn't have passed it down. Am I right?"

Tuck winked and said, "Tis a fair observation, Claire. Granfar told me that Alice found out what Mairead and Jack were up to, though he didn't say how she knew. Then, she handed the story down to Will when she caught up to him in Mullaghmore."

Smiling to himself, he added, "On the other hand, maybe ol' Paul T. made it up to explain how Stella had been found at the base of Knockneara. No loose ends, you know."

Claire chuckled, "Well, tying up loose ends does make for a good story."

Tuck looked at his watch and said, "Tis a lot more story to tell. I thought I could be in it for the pound, but my tongue is tied up."

"Don't leave me hanging, man. I want to know what happened to Christopher."

"Well, darlin' as it turned out Mrs. O'Keefe's tongue was tied up as well, so just a bit more story for tonight."

Mullaghmore ~ 1878

Will had listened in awe to Alice's account. Seeing tears gather in her eyes, he leaned toward her, and took her hands in his. After a few respectful minutes, he asked if she knew what had happened to Captain Tuckerton. He said, "He abandoned me Mam, you know."

"Ach!" She hissed, "The Captain did no such ting. Tis another lie Stella McBride told."

"And how do you know this?"

Not long after Nelly left home, her sister … that would be your aunt Kathleen … asked to speak to me. Poor child was ridden with guilt that she had not told your mam what she knew."

Her pause was a bit too long, so Will prompted, "Please go on Mrs. O'Keefe."

"Kathleen said that she overheard the Captain ask Stella for Nelly's hand. The very next day she overheard that woman lie to the lass, letting her believe that the Captain had abandoned her."

"My God! Why would Kathleen keep such a thing from her own sister?"

"Ye must understand the times, Mr. O'Connell. Stella was in charge of that family; and the lass was filled with confusion. The Captain was an English soldier, after all. The child thought Stella must know what she was doing. But, the guilt wouldn't let her rest; and that's why she told me the truth. Ye must believe that your father meant to marry your mam."

"Then why didn't he come back for her?"

Alice poured a bit more cognac into both their glasses, and then she said, "Since I was Lady Catherine's head mistress I heard many tings not meant for me ears. Tis how I know that Captain Tuckerton went to England on an assignment. But, less than a month after he left Mullaghmore he was on his way back to Ireland."

She touched Will's hand, and said softly, "T'was a nasty twist of the Devil's fate that your father could not return to Miss Nelly. His ship went down during one of those awful squalls that rise up in the Irish Sea for no reason a 'tall. Ye see he did not betray your mam."

Will was devastated by the irony of it all. Alice watched as his features clouded with despair. She pointed toward his cognac; he nodded, and took a few sips. Then he reached into his pocket, removed a small pouch, and shook its contents into Alice's hand.

"Mam gave this to me just before she died. Tis proof, she said, of my true heritage."

Alice held the Captain's ring reverently and lightly traced the Temple Crest with her finger. She pressed her lips together, shook her head sadly, and handed the ring back to Will. And then she gave him Stella's letter, saying, "Take this and keep it safe, for tis also proof of your heritage.

"I am weary with all this excitement; so I cannot finish Christopher's story tonight. But, …" She walked over to the cupboard and retrieved a sheaf of papers tied length- and width-wise with red ribbon. Handing him the sheaf, she said, "But, every chance I had I took up me quill and wrote down everyting I knew about Christopher. Tis all there in those papers. When you finish reading come back to see me."

"I promise I will, Mrs. O'Keefe. But…"

She put her finger to her lips as if making up her mind about something. She went back to the cupboard and withdrew a book, saying, "Your twin became a famous writer … as good they say as Lewis Carroll. Mr. Carroll is a made-up name, ye know, and didn't Christopher use a made-up name for his books too."

She handed him the book, saying, "Last year he sent me this gift … t'was the last I heard from him. But, this book is meant for ye, Mr. O'Connell."

He opened to the first page of *The Wreck of the Highlander*.

Alice pointed to the inscription. "See there? Christopher signed his name, though he wrote Walter MacPherson. T'was the name he was given by his adopted parents. How I wish he had known to sign 'Christopher.' Ah, go to him, go to your twin. Ye'll find him in Edinburgh. He's a professor at that fine university up there."

Will nodded, hardly able to speak.

"Now I must say good night, Mr. O'Connell."

Will placed the book and the sheaf of papers under his arm, and picked up his hat and cane. At the door, Alice touched his cheek, saying, "Be careful, Mr. O'Connell."

Will thanked her and gave a slight bow and said, "God bless ye, Mrs. O'Keefe. I will see you again soon."

Dublin ~ 1972

"But, they never saw each other again," Tuck said.

"What happened?" Claire asked.

"Tis another sad tale; are you sure you want to hear it?"

"I'd rather hear about Christopher."

"I have the story sheets Alice gave to Will. We can read them together tomorrow. For now I'll tell you what happened to Will and Alice."

Feigning resignation to hide her curiosity, Claire said, "Go on then."

"Granfar told me that Will had been watched ever since his arrival in County Sligo. The surveillance intensified after he and Alice O'Keefe met, and his every move was reported to a person interested in keeping Will's heritage from being revealed. Anyway, when Will returned to Alice's cottage the police were milling about. He was told that Mrs. O'Keefe had died in her sleep."

Claire said sardonically, "Ha! Died in her sleep, I bet."

"Aye, you're right. Will overheard a constable tell another that Alice's death was quite suspicious."

Claire said, "Here you go again with the loose ends, Tuck O'Connell. If Mrs. O'Keefe was dead, how would that bit of information come down to your Granfar?"

Tuck just smiled, took a Guinness from the fridge, and said, "Pay attention now, the plot thickens."

CHAPTER 22 ~ VENGEANCE

Mullaghmore ~ 1878

Crestfallen, Will went back home and told Molly the sad news that Mrs. O'Keefe had died. Then, he asked her to fetch Seamus.

"Ah then lad, come sit by me. I have sometings to show you."

He handed the captain's ring to Seamus, saying, "Hold onto this while I tell you tings you need to know."

Seamus held the ring tightly in his hand, and Will told the boy about his true heritage, including lively as well as sad tales about his ancestors, Fiona and Michael, Paul Tibertus, Kathleen and the twins, their Aunt Stella, and especially Nelly and the captain. He told him about Nelly and Seamus O'Connell, for whom the boy was named. He told him stories about his life on Prince Edward Island, and Seamus' half-uncles, Desmond and Michael, and his half-aunt Flannery.

Will rose, went to the side of the fireplace, and pulled several bricks out of their place.

"C'mere Seamus. Take a look."

The boy peered inside. Will said, "Reach way in lad."

Seamus reached inside and touched something. He looked at his father. Will nodded approval, and Seamus pulled out a wooden box.

"Open it."

The boy opened the box. One by one he picked up its contents as Will told a story for each: paper money, torn and faded beyond recognition; Thomas' arrowhead; and the letter Aunt Stella had intended for Lord Palmerston's eyes.

Then he told Seamus to take a look at the sheaf of papers. With his finger Seamus traced the handwritten name on the cover page and said softly, "Christopher." Beneath it, he pointed to Alice O'Keefe's name. A question formed in his eyes.

"Aye, the old woman wrote this down … tis all about my twin, your uncle Christopher."

Will reached behind his chair and retrieved the book, *The Wreck of the Highlander.* "When you're old enough, son, read this book. See here? The writer's name is 'Alastair Ferguson.' Tis a made-up name by Walter Macpherson. His real name is Christopher. He didn't know that; but we do, don't we, lad."

He paused, hoping Seamus would not see the tears welling up in his eyes, and then said, "I will go to Scotland and find Christopher if God wills it; but if it is not His will, maybe you'll find him someday, eh?"

Seamus nodded vigorously.

One month later, Dannel Kenneally, Lord Palmerston's groundskeeper, was doing his morning chores near the southwestern corner of Classiebawn Castle. Something glittering in the anemic February sun caught his eye. He drew closer; then recoiled in horror. A man's body was sloppily covered with sod. Then he gamely bent forward to see what had caught his attention. He saw a gold ring engraved with the Temple crest on the man's finger. Kenneally fell back on his haunches and slapped his hand across his mouth. His right hand landed on the dead man's clothing, which had been placed in a pile. He caught sight of a silver knife protruding from the man's chest.

He got hold of himself and moaned, "Murder!" and leapt to his feet. He ran from that place to tell the gatekeeper of his discovery.

Later, the chief constable, accompanied by the village priest, knocked on the O'Connell's door. The priest spoke in low tones to the inconsolable Molly. Seamus and Flannery stood by, wide eyed.

The next day, the news sheet where Will was employed headlined the death of one of its own.

Mullaghmore 12 February 1878

The body of Master Printer, William T. O'Connell, was found on the grounds of Classiebawn Castle. A spokesperson for Lord Palmerston said that the Lord regretted that such a terrible thing could happen on the grounds of his home. He was sure it was the work of the rogues associated with the Neo-Fenians, who had been seen in County Sligo of late. The Chief Constable agreed with that conclusion, given the ritualistic appearance of the scene. He cited the silver knife driven through O'Connell's heart, the fact that his clothing had been removed, and the sod that covered his body. However, this writer was approached by a source who believes that O'Connell's death was meant only to resemble a rebel-type execution. The source reported that O'Connell was murdered because of his rumored connection to the Temple family. This writer reports only what he has heard; he was not given proof of this tale, and does not report the tale as true.

Molly was about to rip the news sheet to shreds, intending to toss them into the fire, but stopped when Seamus came into the room. He said, "Mam, I will find the man who killed Da. I promise."

"Ah! Seamus, no good will come from vengeance," she answered. Then she hugged him tightly and began to cry.

"Mam, you're choking me!"

"She loosened her grip and wiped tears from her cheeks, trying desperately to control herself for the children's sake. Flannery peeked into the parlor. Molly opened her free arm wide and Flannery ran to her crying, "Mam, don't cry. Please don't cry."

Molly held her children close.

Dublin ~1972

Tuck stopped talking. Claire could tell that his mood had changed. And she was right. He said roughly, "Claire, do you have any doubt that the bloody Temple bastards killed Alice and Will because of what they knew?"

And Claire's mood had changed as well. With simmering anger coloring her cheeks, she said, "Ah, God! Will it ever end, Tuck?"

"Do you mean the violence that touched my family?"

"I tink you know what I mean."

"You're talking about me, then?"

"I guess I am."

She stood up then, a study in resignation. She said, "Tis a bit chilly on the porch. I should check on Will." With that she walked into the flat.

Tuck lit a Camel and stared into the night for several long moments. He flicked the end of the cigarette over the railing and went inside. Claire was sitting at the kitchen table. He sat down, saying, "Claire, I promised I'd stay out of it. I won't go back on my word."

"I don't want to talk anymore tonight, Tuck. I'm sorry, but the end of that story did me in."

A bit roughly, he said, "I won't be tellin' you anymore stories, I can tell you that."

"Goodnight, Tuck." She stood and left him sitting at the table.

The next morning, Claire kissed Tuck on the forehead and said, "No more stories?"

"Not if they make you mad at me, and that's the truth."

"I love you, Tuck. From all that you told me, Will O'Connell was, at bottom, a decent man. But look at it! He got himself involved with those 'wannabe' Fenians, and in the end he was murdered ... and most likely by those ruffians. I worry you'll go back and end up just like him."

Tuck sat up straight. "Claire, Granfar Paul T. said the Temple family made it look like the Fenians killed Will."

"Of course he did. He would rather have thought the Brits did it."

Holding back his anger, he said in measured tones, "Well, the British Army had their rogue soldiers then, just like now, you know. The Temples needed to shut Will up and they could've hired one of them."

"Enough talk of it, eh? Let's not spoil the day." She sighed through a pause; and then said, "But, I do want to know what happened to Christopher."

"OK," Tuck answered, "But, we need more food in the fridge. We ate everything you bought last night. I'll go to the store, then we can read Alice's story sheets together. OK?"

He leaned toward her and kissed her lightly on the cheek. "I do love you so much."

"And I love you."

He pulled her closer and kissed her fully on the mouth. And she kissed him back.

Will came running into the kitchen, and Claire pulled back from Tuck, smiling. She scooped Will up and swung him toward Tuck. He caught hold of him and lifted him toward the ceiling. Will giggled with delight.

"Aye and you're such a good lad," he said, snuggling his son's neck. Then he put him down and bowed toward Claire. She laughed and said, "Go on with you."

Then, he left for the store, taking the stairs two at a time.

A short while later, as he left the store a man appeared out of nowhere, and almost bumped into him. The man continued to walk briskly down the street. Tuck started to walk the other way, but paused for a moment, lowering his head in thought. He looked back just as the man turned the corner. Something nagged at the edge of his awareness, but he couldn't place what it could be. He gave a small shrug and started for home.

Suddenly, an explosion rocked the earth beneath him. The eggs seem to sail in slow motion to the ground, spewing white and yellow stuff across the sidewalk. Tuck found himself on the ground. He heard screaming. A man tripped over him. Trying to catch his balance, the fellow slipped on the splattered eggs and fell hard to the ground. He and Tuck looked at each other with shocked expressions on their faces.

Tuck stood up and helped the other man to his feet.

The man said, "What the fuck was that?"

Tuck just looked at him, full of sudden dread. He yelled something and began to run. As he turned the corner onto his street, he murmured, "Oh. Oh no! No!" And then he screamed, "Oh God, no!" His apartment building and the one next to it were in flames. He ran forward but a constable restrained him. Tuck fell into the man's arms.

His scream became a whimper.

The next day the headlines reported that several civilians were killed in a terrorist "mission." A senior officer of the British Army stationed in Dublin laid the blame for the conflagration on the IRA; the IRA blamed the Neo2-Fenians.

A reporter said that an anonymous source laid the blame on the activities of rogue English soldiers, "...who have been known to be operating in this part of Dublin. The source said that the rogues had planned to capture, not kill, a group of Neo2-Fenians believed to be hiding in one of the buildings."

Another said, "In answer to this reporter's question, an Army Officer distanced the Army and the Government from the alleged activities of the rogue soldiers. He also revealed that the IRA is not suspect in this case." The reporter quoted an IRA spokesperson's words of sympathy for the families of the civilians whose lives were cut short. Claire and two-year old Will O'Connell were among them.

Tuck was beyond consolation.

The day after the funeral, Tuck walked to where he had parked his car the night they had returned from their trip. He whispered a prayer of thanksgiving that he had not found a parking space near his building that night. He opened the trunk and pulled out his satchel. He unzipped it and lifted his grandfather's old wooden box. He touched the plastic bags containing the letter written by Stella McBride and a note Peg Mirran had written to Will, but that he'd never received.

Then he carefully removed the sheaf of papers penned by Alice O'Keefe that Will's son, Seamus had handed down to his son, Paul Tibertus, who handed it down to Tuck. He placed the sheaf back and removed two plastic bags containing Thomas' arrow and Captain Tuckerton's gold ring, which he placed on his finger. Then he shut the trunk, zipped his satchel and slung it over his shoulder.

He walked around the block to the street where he and his small family had lived for the past three years. His building and the other were both in shambles. Smutty smoke still simmered in places. Crime scene tape circled the area, and several constables guarded the site. Crime scene techs were milling about doing whatever it is they do. He watched them for a while. Then, he stepped back a few paces. He whispered, "I love you, darling Claire. And you, my son, I love you beyond words."

He turned abruptly and walked away from that place. Though tears of sorrow streamed down his cheeks, his heart was filled with hatred. He resolved that one day he would exact his revenge.

For the next month, Tuck tried unsuccessfully to identify and locate the man who had murdered his family. Desperate for information, he decided to go to Belfast to see if his Irish Nationalist acquaintances could help him. He traveled under his assumed name, Chris McBride, which he thought was a clever use of the names, Stella McBride and Christopher: the betrayer and the betrayed.

On his drive north he recalled how dearly Claire had wanted to know about Christopher's fate. An ineffable sadness overwhelmed him. He pulled over and jumped out of the car, heedless of the traffic whizzing by him. He ran as fast as he could, tears blocking his vision. Then he leaped over a guard rail into the woods whereupon he fell to his knees. He howled to the sky, tears streaming unchecked down his cheeks until they were spent.

After he gained control of himself, he walked back to the car, filled with renewed determination to find the man whose horrible act had wrenched joy from his life.

CHAPTER 23 ~ WHISPERED TRUTH

Belfast ~ 1972

Tuck registered at an inn on the outskirts of Belfast, ate a light supper, and went to his room. He sat on the edge of the bed, removed *The Wreck of the Highlander* and Alice O'Keefe's story sheets from his satchel, and placed them on the bedside table. He picked up the sheets and lay back on the pillow. With his index finger he traced Alice's delicate Gaelic script as he read the first few sentences. He was glad that Alice referred to Christopher as "Christopher," rather than "Walter," his adoptive name.

He whispered, "Here's to you, darlin' Claire," and began to read Alice's first entry in diary form.

She wrote that Walter and Rose Macpherson met her and Christopher at the dock; and she described the trip through the English countryside to the Macpherson home in Andover, County Hampshire. She noted that, while not as stately as Lord Eldridge's estate, the home was beautiful, and that, "To me t'was a mansion; not a'tall like me humble home in Ireland."

Andover, Hampshire County, England ~ 1847

The Macphersons adopted Christopher almost immediately, naming him Walter after his stepfather. Rose had transformed the maid's parlor into a nursery, which, Alice soon learned, did not sit well with Cleona. In the months ahead, the maid would give Alice a hard time over the slightest matter. The nursery and the kitchen were equipped with everything a baby needed to grow strong and healthy. Alice vowed that she would see to it that "Walter" would do just that.

She also vowed that she would continue to call him Christopher when no one else was about.

Walter and Rose were tolerant of Alice's need to attend daily Mass, allowing their groom, Peter, to take her to the only Catholic Church in their vicinity. Though Alice missed her home and husband, within a few short weeks she felt comfortable, thoroughly enjoying her duties as Christopher's governess. One afternoon while Christopher was napping, she ventured into the library. Upon opening the elegant oak door, she was immediately struck by the warm, pungent, yet pleasant scent of carpet, furniture oil, and books – hundreds of which graced floor to ceiling bookcases. Alice walked along the cases, lightly running her fingers along the books' spines. She stopped and stared at *Aesop's Fables,* and opened the book to "The Tortoise and the Hare," and then to "The Ant and the Grasshopper." They reminded her of her husband, who could recite them from memory. He once told Alice, "These are moral lessons for children. Mr. Aesop was wise, ye know."

"And why is that, Terrance?" She had said.

"Because he used animals instead of people. T'would be dangerous to be so truthful if he used people to tell the lessons."

Tears sprung to Alice's eyes as she thought of Terrance's patience when teaching her to read and write. She blew her nose; then shook her head. She continued to move along until her finger touched the spine of "The Story of the Three Bears." Holding her finger on the book, she looked ahead and spied Daniel Dafoe's "Robinson Crusoe," "Moll Flanders," and "Gulliver's Travels" by the Irishman, Jonathan Swift. Proud of his knowledge, Terrance had told her that these books were probably among the first novels in the English Language.

"Ah!" she murmured, "I will read these stories to Christopher soon enough."

Whenever she could she would spend an hour reading everything she could handle – even struggling through more difficult ones, including Shakespeare's sonnets, "The Cherrie and the Slae" by the Scottish Poet, Alexander Mongomerie, and a 1787 edition of Robert Burns' poetry, especially careful handling the 60-year-old book. She read "The Gentle Shepherd" by Allan Ramsay several times, and loved anything by Sir Walter Scott. She tried and failed to work through various sections of Milton's "Paradise Lost." At night she would make a chronological list of works with which she would teach Christopher to read.

The MacPhersons were pleased that their son's governess could read and write and that she took on such scholarly endeavor in her free time.

One evening in July, 1848 Alice had just finished the extra chores she shared with Cleona when she heard Christopher crying loudly. She picked him up, held him close, and he stopped crying almost at once. He reached his hand up and grasped the cross on a chain around Alice's neck.

"Ah, baby," she cooed. "you're a handsome one, for sure. I tink your twin across the ocean must bc as handsome."

Then, as twilight's soft shadows played against the walls and ceiling, Alice began to speak Gaelic into Christopher's tiny ear. It was a ritual that she had begun on their first night in Andover. She whispered tales of his true home in Ireland, his mother, Nelly, his twin on Prince Edward Island, and his true father, Captain William Tuckerton. As she whispered tales of the famine that the Irish were enduring, its horrors were in stark counterpoint to the soft lilt of her voice.

Though she felt shame betraying Christopher's benefactors, she felt certain telling Christopher the truth was the right thing to do.

Andover, Hampshire County ~ Four Years Later

One bright Saturday afternoon in November 1851 Rose invited neighbors and friends to help celebrate "Walter's" fourth birthday. The boy was thrilled with the toys he received that day. His friend, five-year old Jonathan, gave him a Bilbo Catcher, the object of which was to swing the attached ball and catch it in the cup. Walter/Christopher soon found out that it was not as simple as Jonathan made it seem. Another boy gave him a spinning top. Christopher looked at the toy for a moment. Then he held the spindle between his thumb and forefinger and snapped his fingers, expertly spinning the top. Walter and Rose were delighted at this show of dexterity. The boy's maiden Aunt,

Lisbeth, gave him a slate board, chalk and an eraser made of wood and felt. A neighbor lady gave him an abacus. Though he demonstrated his understanding of the purpose of the slate and chalk, he was perplexed when he picked up the abacus.

Alice took it from him, saying, "Tis a wonderful present, lad, but tis for another day." Another child gave him a wooden yo-yo. Two years older than Christopher, Bonnie patiently explained how to do "sleeper" tricks. Christopher wasn't able to master the art – at least not that day.

While the children enjoyed cake, Rose and Walter left the parlor. Before Christopher noticed they were gone, they came back carrying a pony-sized rocking horse made of solid mahogany. The saddle and bridle were made of soft leather; the stirrups and other hardware were made of brass. One by one Christopher and his friends took turns on the horse, squealing with delight. While they played the adults sipped brandy and spoke in low tones.

Once the guests left, Rose took her son's hand and, as she did most every night, walked him to his room. The nursery had been transformed into a room full of toys, pictures, books and mobiles appropriate for a four-year old boy. They sat together on the window seat and she read from one of his gifts, a small child's version of "Gulliver's Travels." When he started to nod off, Rose rang the bell summoning Alice. As soon as Alice entered, Rose kissed Christopher and said, "Walter, darling, I will come back to tuck you in." Alice helped him bathe and dress in his nightgown. He hopped into his bed and Alice tucked the blanket under his chin.

As always, when Rose returned she sat on the edge of Christopher's bed and helped him say his prayers. As she began the prayer, Alice made a quick, clandestine sign of the cross. When Rose finished the prayer, she kissed Christopher and said, "Goodnight dear boy. Sweet dreams."

At the door she said, "It was a good day, Mrs. O'Keefe."

"Aye t'was that, madam."

"I thank you for your help as always."

Rose left and shut the door softly behind her. As it closed Christopher said, “Mrs. O’Keefe, now tell me the stories about that place.”

Alice sat down on the edge of the bed and said, “Ah, Christopher, you’re no longer a wee one. Ye’re a big lad now and I cannot be telling me tales any more after tonight. Ye must never speak of them to anyone but me. Understand? And ye must never tell your good parents that I call you Christopher.”

Christopher’s eyes widened. “Aye, and that’s the truth.”

“Good. We have an understanding, then.”

He giggled because that exchange was what he and Alice said to each other each time she began her tales. She tickled him and said, “Ah! You’re such a good boy.”

Then, for the last time in her Gaelic tongue, which Christopher now understood, Alice began to whisper the truth about his heritage. When she finished, she said in English, “Dear Christopher, ye will remember what I’ve told ye all these years because someday you’ll need to know them. And always remember that you’re loved by people ye’ll never know.”

He reached up and touched the cross hanging from the chain around Alice’s neck, and pushed it gently back and forth. Then Alice bent down and kissed his brow. He reached up and wrapped his arms around her neck. “Good night, Mrs. O’Keefe.”

“Good night, lad. God bless.

CHAPTER 24 ~ THE RIDDLE

Andover, Hampshire County, England ~ April 1858

As the years went by, Alice was increasingly amazed at Christopher's wit and intelligence. She read increasingly learned books to him. By his sixth year he was able to read beyond his years; and, by his tenth, he had mastered ever more difficult books. Alice had shown him how to use the abacus for simple arithmetic. But as his questions became too difficult for her, Mr. MacPherson hired Angus Stewart to tutor the boy. By his eleventh year Christopher had mastered simple algebra and geometry.

One afternoon, the boy ran to the library holding Aesop's Fables. He pushed open the heavy door and paused to catch his breath.

Alice looked up from her desk, saying, "Ah, Christopher, what brings ye in such a hurry?"

"I discovered something, Mrs. O'Keefe. You won't believe it."

He laid the book on Alice's desk, saying, "The stories remind me about things Mr. Stewart is teaching me."

He leafed through the book until he came to "The Dog and the Shadow."

"Look here, Mrs. O'Keefe. The dog is running with a piece of meat in his mouth. He crosses a plank over a brook and looks into the water; and he sees his shadow, but thinks it's another dog that also has meat in his mouth. When he tries to take the meat from the other dog, he drops his meat into the water. Do you see that?"

"Aye, child I see that. Nothin' wrong with me eyesight."

Frustration touched his features as well as his voice, as he said, "It's like the idea Mr. Stewart taught me about things with three dimensions."

Then he rapidly turned the pages to "Counting Crows."

"See here, Mrs. O'Keefe?"

She stared at the drawing accompanying the text. Christopher said, "Don't you see it?"

"Child, I don't see what you see. Explain it to me."

Tracing the lines with his finger, he read the short tale aloud, and said, "It's like what Mr. Stewart taught me about solving problems and taking measurements, you see?"

Alice held up her hand. "Shush, child. I don't know what you're going on about."

Christopher looked at her quizzically. He didn't understand that his mathematical acumen was far beyond his years – and way beyond Alice.

He said, "How about this one, then?" He pushed the pages to the next marker. "This story is like the reasoning Mr. Stewart teaches me in logic lessons."

Perplexed, Alice simply smiled.

Noticing her expression, he said, "Oh, you don't know mathematics."

"That I don't, child. But Mr. Stewart will delight in your discovery about Mr. Aesop's tales."

Wanting to please her, Christopher said, "It's alright about mathematics, Mrs. O'Keefe. Mr. Aesop fools with us about morals too. And I know you know about that!"

Alice smiled. "Tis almost time for supper, lad. Go wash your hands."

Later that night, Rose invited Alice to take coffee and brandy with her and Walter, an invitation they often extended, much to Cleona's chagrin. Settled in the parlor, Alice related Christopher's excitement about his discovery.

Walter said, "Mr. Stewart told me that he had almost reached the limits of what he could teach the boy."

Rose nodded agreement, and said, "Thankfully he'll be going to the Cavendish School up in the Highlands in the fall."

Though Alice wanted to return home to Ireland and her husband, she also knew she would not be ready when the day came to leave the Macpherson home. She had become part of the family and loved Christopher as her own.

Her mixed emotions would best her desire to sleep that night.

On a blustery Friday of the last week in August, Walter brought the carriage to the front of the house. Rose and Alice boarded the front seat and Christopher climbed into the back. As the carriage started to move, he knelt backwards facing the window. Though he welcomed the adventure he was about to embark upon, he felt bereft, for he knew he was leaving his childhood behind. Knowing he'd have holidays when he would see his parents did not assuage the sadness he felt, because he knew he would most likely never see Alice again. And tears sprung to his eyes.

Earlier that morning, he had found his governess in the parlor and had sat down next to her. He told Alice that he would always remember her and that, next to his father and mother, he loved her most of all. After a brief silence, he said, "Sometimes I remember things you told me when I was young; but I don't know what they mean."

She leaned toward him and whispered, "*Má na póga Stork féileacán ar dhá bhuachaillí, cad iad na siad lena chéile?*"

He translated loosely, "If the stork kisses a butterfly upon two lads, what are they to each other?" He thought for a moment, and said, "They are brothers, right?"

She said, "Níos mó ná sin, Criostoir. Tá siad cúpla comhionann."

"More than that, Christopher," the boy translated, "They are identical twins." And, with a bit of frustration, he added, "But the answer doesn't help me understand my memories."

Alice said, "When the time comes, our riddle will help you understand, darlin' lad."

Though her explanation didn't satisfy him, Christopher had learned his manners well and didn't persist. Instead, he leaned toward Alice and touched the cross hanging on the chain around her neck. He pushed it gently back and forth. Then he wrapped his arms around her neck and said, "I will miss you, dear Mrs. O'Keefe."

Holding back her tears, Alice told him to fetch his satchel and bag of favorite books. He did as he was told; and before he left his room he penned Alice's Ireland address into his new notebook.

Now, as he watched his home and his childhood disappear from his view, he vowed that he would write to Alice often. And he would keep his vow. In several letters he would ask her about the stories she had told him. Each time she answered in the form of her riddle about twins and a butterfly.

1972 ~ The Belfast Inn

Tuck became aware that he was rubbing the back of his neck. "Twins and a butterfly," he said aloud. His eyes smarted from fatigue and restrained tears. He rubbed them and laid Alice's story sheets on the bedside table. His stomach growled, so he went to the Inn's bar and ordered a sandwich and Guinness. Later in his room, he took up the sheets, found his place, and read a diary entry that Alice had inserted out of place.

I was to be Christopher's governess only until his twelfth year. Shortly after the dear lad left, t'was a rainy September morning, Mr. Macpherson brought the carriage 'round to the front of the house, and we took another tearful ride to the docks. This time to the ship that would take me home for good. Though I could not know then that I'd return one day to look for Christopher. Terrance and I enjoyed a peaceful life for many years. Then dear Terrance suffered mortal injuries in a carriage accident. T'was a painful time. But, I am thankful that Christopher sent me letters from time to time so I could write more about his life.

CHAPTER 25
SPEAK MEMORY! (V. Nabokov)

Cavendish Boarding School ~Autumn 1860

"No use denying it Macpherson, if that's your real name."

Hugh Mackenzie, in the midst of taunting his roommate, paused for a moment to see if he was getting a rise out of Christopher. It didn't appear he was; so, using the slang for an Irishman, he said, "As I was saying, you're an Irisher for sure. You even talk Irish in your sleep. I've been hearing that mumbo jumbo for two years now."

Christopher raised his eyes from the book he was reading, and glared at Hugh, but said nothing. Hugh said, "Ha! Look at'cha! I see the red of shame on your face."

Christopher's face was red, but from anger, not shame. He had learned well from Mrs. O'Keefe not ever to feel shame.

His tormentor continued, "You even lie in your sleep. Sometimes you mumble something about your father being a British Captain. You're a bloody idiot, Macpherson."

With that, he turned back to his desk, feigning disgust, but really miffed that he was never able to goad Christopher into reaction. He grimaced and mumbled, "You're sure no Scot,"

Unable to concentrate on his book, Christopher closed it and left the room. Hugh's comments made him painfully aware that his re-occurring dreams were not the norm. He was increasingly desperate to know their meaning. His letters to Mrs. O'Keefe often contained questions about the things she had told him. In his latest letter he had asked her to explain words, phrases and names dredged from his memory. But, Mrs. O'Keefe's answer was, as always, in the form of the riddle about twins and a butterfly.

As Christopher walked along the arched walkway bordering the courtyard, he wished he could talk to someone about his dreams. *Maybe I'll speak to my Mathematics instructor. No, that wouldn't do.*

Because of his unusual talents, Christopher was not a very popular boy, nor did he seek popularity. He was not comfortable talking about himself even to the one true friend he had. He met Wallace Stevenson the previous spring term when he joined the debate team. *Maybe I'll give Wallace a try.*

The Chapel bell tolled the half hour. *Or, maybe prayer will help.* He walked across the courtyard and into the Chapel. But, the pesky partial memories skirted the edges of awareness. He left the Chapel, no more enlightened than when he first entered.

As he walked across the courtyard, Wallace called out, "Hey there, Walter, wait up!" When he reached Christopher's side, he gave him a playful punch on the shoulder, and said, "Have you become deaf over night? I've been yelling your name."

Christopher said, "I was thinking about things."

"You're always thinking about things, ol' chap."

Christopher took Wallace's appearance as a sign that he should talk to him about his dreams; but they had reached the dining hall, went in and took their assigned seats. While waiting for the headmaster to say grace before dinner, Christopher wrote a note to Wallace and passed it to his table mate, who passed it to the boy on the end of the next table, who passed it down to Wallace. Wallace unfolded the note and read, "*Wallace, there's a matter I need to discuss with you. Please meet me in the courtyard following evening prayer. Thanks, Walter*"

Wallace leaned back until his eyes met Christopher's and nodded. Christopher was relieved that he finally felt the courage to confide his concerns. He was also anxious, and hardly touched his meal. Suddenly, the crack of the headmaster's ruler startled him. He quickly bent over his plate and began to eat. His table mates snickered; and the headmaster gave each a stern look.

After dinner, Wallace met Christopher in the courtyard, and listened as Christopher talked about his dreams and strange, partial memories.

Christopher stopped talking and Wallace said, "Listen Walter, you know how the Irish are. They're always making up stories that are better than the lives they lead. Their belief in fairies is far more serious than that of the Scottish peasants in Inverness. Most assuredly, your governess made up those stories to excite and entertain you."

Christopher thought Wallace sounded very adult, as he continued, "I'll wager your Mrs. O'Keefe won't respond to your questions because she cannot."

Christopher started to defend Mrs. O'Keefe, but thought better of it, and said only, "Perhaps you're right, Wallace."

The two walked in silence for a while and then headed toward their separate dormitories.

That night Christopher re-read Mrs. O'Keefe's last letter and puzzled over the riddle about twins and a butterfly. He could solve all sorts of math problems and riddles; but, he couldn't solve the one that was most important to him.

Spring ~ 1861

The Cavendish commencement occurred on a day considered balmy in the Scottish Highlands. The temperature was 67 degrees and a slight breeze blew from the northwest. Though Christopher was not graduating that year, his parents attended the ceremony because he had been chosen to represent the third level by giving the farewell speech to the fourth. Wallace's family was present because he was graduating. Having met the year before, the two sets of parents were looking forward to each other's company.

After the exercises, Christopher found Walter and Rose wandering outside the refectory where lunch was to be served.

Hugging her son, Rose breathed, "Ah, my boy!" His father shook his hand. "Good job, lad. Your speech was grand; and your delivery was eloquent."

A bit embarrassed, Christopher changed the subject. "Father, we should take our seats."

As soon as the Headmaster said grace after the meal, Christopher said, "Let's find Wallace and his parents."

Once outside the refectory Wallace suddenly appeared, greeted Walter and Rose, and said to Christopher, “I’ve been looking for you, Walter. Mum and Father are down front.”

Christopher stood on his tiptoes. “I see them. Say, Wallace, who’s that lass with them?”

"That would be my sister, Nessa.”

Remaining on his toes, Christopher said, “You told me Nessa was your ‘little’ sister!”

“She’s just shy of fifteen, I’m almost eighteen, she is my ‘little’ sister.”

Christopher said, “Aye, and what a bonny lass she is.”

As she walked closer Christopher noted the snow-white ruffles gracing the sleeves and hem of her purple dress. Tight dark brown curls, touching her shoulders, were revealed beneath her fashionable hat of purple, lavender and green hues. When Wallace introduced Nessa, Christopher stared into her eyes. They appeared to change from gray to steel blue as the scant breeze shifted clouds that shifted the sunlight on her face.

With Wallace’s help, Christopher and Nessa found themselves alone that afternoon. Though he had attended Cavendish social gatherings with young ladies, Christopher had never felt comfortable talking to them. But he had no trouble talking to Nessa.

The two families stayed at the College Inn that night. The next morning, Mr. Stevenson invited Christopher to come to Edinburgh for a month that summer to put his mathematics acumen to good work.

Christopher was elated with the thought that he would see Nessa again soon enough.

CHAPTER 26 ~ THE STORK'S KISS

Belfast ~ 1972

Tuck's eyes had almost had it, and he glanced through the next few pages. Seeing that Alice's account skipped through the years, he made a strong cup of tea and continued to read.

Edinburgh ~ 1861 to 1873

Throughout July 1861, Christopher and Nessa courted under her chaperone's watchful eye. They shared tea, attended Church together, and took boat rides on the Dùn Èideann. He wrote to his parents and Alice O'Keefe that he intended to marry Nessa Stevenson one day.

And he did.

In the fall of 1862, following his graduation from Cavendish, Christopher entered the University of Edinburgh, where, within one year, he was allowed to work toward a joint bachelor's and master's degree in mathematics. In his final year, Christopher and Nessa became engaged, and they married on Christmas Eve day 1865.

The following year their first child was born. They named her Sandra Rose in honor of both her grandmothers. On her second birthday, Christopher finished his first novel for children under his pen name, Alastair Ferguson, and dedicated it Sandra Rose. In 1869 he finished his second novel on the occasion of his son's birth. They named him Wallace after Nessa's brother.

Two years later, on a bright Sunday afternoon, Christopher was in his study when he heard Wallace suddenly start crying loudly. Miffed, Christopher wondered where his nanny could be. Suddenly, he heard an awful scream. He charged through the study door, almost tripping over his son.

Nessa was standing in the middle of the room, her face ashen. Unable to speak a full sentence, she sputtered, "Walter …Sandra is…"

"Nessa, what is it?"

"Our girl is …"

"For God's sake, woman! Where is she?"

Nessa got her wits about her, and ran up the staircase; Christopher followed. When he reached the top of the stairs, he was aghast to see Sandra Rose lying near the balustrade. Her neck was at a peculiar angle, her left leg impossibly hidden by her body. Pieces of Christopher's childhood rocking horse were strewn across the hallway. Instinctively, Christopher looked up to the third floor. Some banister rods were hanging as if by threads. The nanny was standing there, her face a mask of terror. Later she would explain that she brought the rocking horse into the hall in order to straighten the Nursery. She swore she was certain she sent 5-year old Sandra Rose down to the first floor.

For almost a year Nessa was unable to speak her daughter's name. She had become distant from Christopher and Wallace, an estrangement that would have a lasting effect upon the boy. Christopher eventually dealt with his wife's retreat by working at a feverish pace, often sleeping in his university office. And, when not working, he found solace in writing a book about a child's death with no intention of publishing it.

Late one night, Nessa knocked timidly on the study door. No answer, but she entered anyway. The candles were burning low. She stared for a moment at Christopher's back.

"Had he not heard me enter?" She asked herself. Softly, she said, "You will go blind in this light, Walter Macpherson."

He rubbed the grit from his eyes and turned toward her. He half stood; and when she reached out to him he did not rebuke her. They held onto to each other as if to save their lives. That night they made love with an intensity Christopher hadn't known since Sandra Rose's death.

Spent, Christopher snuggled into the warmth of Nessa's body. Her hands stroked the back of his neck. Then their bodies made some awkward twists and turns, and, as lovers often do, they made love again, and again. He landed on his stomach. She leaned over him, lacing her fingers through his hair. The candle light threw soft shadows onto Christopher's prone body. In the flickering light Nessa saw something on the nape of his neck. *Odd, she had never noticed it before.* She grasped a candle and held it close enough to see a light birthmark. She traced it with her finger.

"Darling Walter, did you know that you a have a stork's kiss on the nape of your neck?"

"What are you talking about?"

"We'll use mirrors in the daylight so you can see it."

She kissed the birthmark and soon they both fell asleep.

The next morning, true to her word, Nessa manipulated two mirrors so Christopher could see the birthmark. She said, "There! Can you see a wee butterfly with a bluish cast to it?"

Christopher saw it, but barely. He was intrigued, recalling Alice O'Keefe's riddle about twins and a butterfly. Alice had once told him that he had the stork's kiss; but, until that moment, that fact had been lost in the mists of memory. Even capturing that memory did not help him fathom the riddle's meaning.

Nine months after their reconciliation, Nessa gave birth to their second daughter. They named her Alice Rose, in honor of Alice O'Keefe and Christopher's adoptive mother, Rose Macpherson.

CHAPTER 27 ~ THE HIGHLANDER

Edinburgh ~1875

Christopher had been appointed full Professor of Mathematics at the University in 1874; and his novels had become a great success. In fact, a year later his stories were being compared to those of the English author and mathematician, Charles Lutwidge Dodgson, better known by his pseudonym, Lewis Carroll.

One dreary November afternoon in 1875, Christopher penned the last sentence of a novel he entitled *The Stork's Kiss,* dedicated to his two-year old daughter, Alice Rose. He stretched and smiled to himself. Then he went to the drawing room to tell Nessa and Rose, who was staying with them because her husband had planned to be away for quite a while. Walter senior had always liked the idea of adventure, and often threatened to accompany one of his liquor shipments to either Australia or America. Finally, having made good his threat, he was scheduled to sail with *The Highlander* bound for Australia.

Rose looked up from her knitting as Christopher walked into the room.

"Ladies!" He announced, "Alice Rose's book is finished!"

His mother fairly leaped from her seat. "Oh, Walter, read some to us."

"Later, mother. Right now, I'm in the mood for some sherry."

Nessa reached for the decanter, saying, "We've started without you."

Shortly, Rose grew pensive. "I'm worried about your father," she said.

"Your uncle and I both prevailed upon him not to go to off on such a long voyage in winter. He admitted that the weather is tricky; but, you know how stubborn he can be." She took a sip of sherry, and continued, "I can't help thinking about the ship that ran afoul on its way to Australia. What was its name?"

Nessa said, "*The Royal Adelaide* … and it sunk such a short distance from port."

Rose said, "And what a tragedy that was." She sighed. "Thank the Lord I've come for this visit, for I will be well occupied with you and the children. Otherwise, I dare say, I'd be doing nothing but worry."

She brightened and raised her glass, saying, "Here's to Alice Rose's book!"

Christopher and Nessa joined her toast, and said in unison, "Here! Here!"

Belfast ~ 1972

Tuck plopped the story sheets onto his lap, recalling the day his grandfather had given him his copy of *The Wreck of the Highlander*. He had read the book several times, and knew what Alice's story was about to relate. He swung his legs over the side of the bed, grabbed a Camel, lit it and dragged deeply. Then he snuffed it, and took the book from the bedside table and put it next to him on the bed. Caressing its cover, he picked up Alice's story.

University of Edinburgh ~ Two days later

"…therefore, one could say that Pythagoras was the…" The door of Christopher's lecture hall suddenly opened. Such interruptions were so unusual that the entire class turned as one toward the door. The students saw the headmaster give Christopher a high sign. The moment Christopher left the room they began to whisper among themselves. A few minutes later the headmaster came back into the room and dismissed them.

Christopher sat in the headmaster's office, holding a telegram in one hand and dangling a news sheet from the other. Its headline read:

Dorset, November 23, 1875

"Like the Royal Adelaide, The Highlander left London Port for the other side of the world; but got no further than the Dorset Coast."

The Headmaster said, "I am so sorry, Walter. The telegram naming your father among the missing arrived with the news sheet."

Christopher asked for a moment alone; and then he read the awful story.

After leaving London Port for Sydney, The Highlander ran into a fearsome storm, much like the one that capsized The Royal Adelaide *in 1866. The captain was unable to stay the course. Instead of heading for shelter, his ship was forced into Lyme Bay from which there is no exit. People on shore watched in horror as the ship struck the shoals. Men fashioned a line with a makeshift cradle and linked it from shore to ship. In this manner, many of the passengers and crew were rescued. But, we are told, the line broke and the last of the passengers fell into the sea and were swept away when the ship broke apart.*

The scene was illuminated by burning tar barrels. The rescue effort enthralled the growing crowd, which became even more excited when the ship's cargo was thrown upon the strand. The cargo, containing a grand array of goods, including casks of spirits, was soon strewn across the pebbled shore. Despite efforts of the local constabulary, many folks engaged in looting...

"Father..." Christopher whispered.

A few weeks after the disaster, Rose finally resigned herself to the fact that her husband's body had been taken by the sea, so she arranged for a memorial in his honor to be held at the family's church in Andover.

She was unable to bear the thought of remaining in their home, and eventually accepted Christopher's offer to come live with his family in Edinburgh. She sold the family home and asked her brother-in-law to manage Walter's Hampshire County's import/export business. He agreed, and placed his son in charge of the brewery located in London.

Edinburgh ~1876

"Wallace! Please, come down from there!" Nessa pleaded.

The boy was precariously balanced on the second floor banister. Nessa was paralyzed by the memory of her first daughter's fatal fall. Rose brushed by her daughter-in-law and marched up the stairs. She grabbed the 6-year old boy's arm, forcing him to the floor.

The crisis over, Rose said, "The child needs more fatherly discipline."

"Christopher has been busy at University," Nessa replied without conviction, for she knew that Christopher's absences had more to do with keeping the death of his father at bay.

Christopher's absences had had a deleterious effect on Wallace. By his fifth year, he had become difficult to handle; and by his sixth, his unruly behavior, particularly toward his little sister, seemed beyond control.

That night, as Nessa was preparing for bed, Christopher came up behind her. He placed his hands on her shoulders. "My dear," he began, "mother told me about Wallace's latest shenanigans. I know I've left too much of it for you. I cannot seem to get hold; even my teaching is affected."

He kissed the nape of her neck. "I've a sabbatical coming to me; I think a trip might do us all good."

She turned to face him. "Where are you thinking to go?"

"I've checked into our shipment headed for Australia...."

Nessa stared at him and he let his words fade. Then he sat on the edge of the bed, and said, "I know the idea might appear strange, Nessa. But, please, think about it for a moment. Father didn't make it to Australia; but we could go in his place … sort of a tribute, you know?"

As Nessa started to speak he put his finger to her lips. He said, “The trip might have a good effect on Wallace; and for mother as well. She may regain some of her natural good humor.”

He stopped talking for a moment. When she remained silent, he added, “We need to get away, Nessa.”

When she still didn’t respond, he said gently, “Well, I need to get away. I’ll go alone if you prefer.”

In the end, the whole family accompanied Christopher to Australia. Throughout the long voyage Christopher and Wallace took in every detail of the ship; and Wallace peppered the captain with questions about navigation. Once on land the family took side trips throughout Australia, marveling at the rugged terrain of the Australian outback; reveling in the excitement of Sydney and Brisbane. The entire trip proved to be the palliative Christopher sought. He soaked up the atmosphere; and on days too hot to move around, he worked on the outline of his new book, *The Wreck of the Highlander*.

He had decided the book would be a straightforward adventure tale for adults. It would not be a children’s book, sprinkled with symbolisms that only adults would understand that marked his earlier works.

The book was published by the Oxford Press in 1877, and in no time it was on thousands of bookshelves in the British Isles and on the Continent.

Belfast ~ 1972

“… and all the way from Alice O’Keefe to Will, to Seamus, to Granfar, and then to me,” Tuck mused. And then he read the final page of Alice’s story, which was in diary form.

December 1877, At last I have found dear Nelly’s son, William O’Connell. I will meet him on Friday after the New Year, 1878. And to him I will reveal the secret of the butterfly and the twins. Now, how I wish I had told dear Christopher. Was it an old woman’s folly? I don’t know. But, tis not too late to make it right. Alice O’Keefe

Tuck tapped the sheets of paper together and placed the sheaf into its plastic covering, turned off the light, and fell into a fitful sleep.

The next day he looked for, and found two of his Nationalist acquaintances in a downtown Belfast pub. He asked them to help him identify his family's murderer. They did not have time, they said, for they had bigger fish to fry. They were bent on achieving revenge for the massacre of unarmed Nationalist civil rights demonstrators by English soldiers in Derry on January 30, 1972, a day that had become known as "Bloody Sunday."

One of them said, "We can't help you, boyo. But, you should stop wasting your time. Why not join us? We know about your deeds in the States with the Neo2-Fenians. That's enough coinage for us, man."

Tuck considered the idea. Since his promise to Claire no longer held meaning, it didn't matter to him that these men belong to a radical splinter group that was not recognized by the Nationalists, and certainly not by the IRA. And so, he agreed to join them.

During the first raid in which Tuck participated, he killed an English soldier.

He felt nothing.

A couple years later, following a harrowing and unsuccessful raid, the gang dispersed. Tuck spent several weeks in Northern Ireland. Finally, he decided it was safe to return to Dublin under his own name. Within a few weeks he got his old job back working on the Dublin docks. And, for the next few years he led a quiet, if despondent existence.

CHAPTER 28 ~ HALF MOON COTTAGE

Dublin ~ 1978

"Say O'Connell, I've been holdin' a letter for ya." The Dockland's paymaster handed Tuck the letter along with his pay envelope.

Noting the return address, Tuck walked to the side and tore the envelope open, and read the short note:

"Where are you, lad? I got something to talk to you about. People at this phone number know where to find me. Your pal, Jack Coughlin."

A few days later Tuck walked into a pub north of Dublin and saw Jack toasting him from the back of the room. He walked over to him and regarded his old acquaintance. He noted that Jack had lost more than a few pounds, and lines of age – or was it decadence – dominated his once handsome face.

The man shifted his eyes and said, "Where the hell have you been, boyo? I've been tryin' to find you for years."

Tuck didn't answer; instead, he gave a high sign to the bartender.

Jack grasped the fresh Guinness. Tuck sipped his.

"Your note said you've got someting to tell me, Jack."

"I heard about your family and I know someting that might help get the bastard who killed them."

He grabbed one of Tuck's cigarettes, took his time lighting it and blew a few smoke rings.

Tuck peered at Jack through the smoke, and said, "What are you saying?"

"I'm saying I have a good idea who did it."

Tuck leaned forward, his arm brushing the Guinness bottle. He caught it before it tipped over. He said, "For Christ's sake, man, why didn't you say so?"

"Hey! I'm saying so now. If you'd hung around I would'a told you long ago." He paused and drank deeply.

Tuck spat, "Fuckin' get on with it Jack!"

Jack peered at him from the rim of his glass. "Hold your horses, man. I'm tellin' you." He took a quick sip, and said, "Back in '71 I shoveled horse shit at the estate of Lord someting' or other … related to the *grand* Lord Temple Palmerston, no less." He screwed his face at the mention of the hated name.

"One day I overheard my boss talking to his nephew, Jonathan someting. The guy said he had overheard you talking about … a captain I tink. And an Irish girl … don't remember her name."

Tuck, heart pounding, whispered, "Her name was Nelly."

"Yeah, Nelly, that's it. Anyway…"

Tuck interrupted him, "What was the guy's last name, Jack?"

Jack thought for a moment. "Cantwell, no, wait, t'was Caswell. That's it!"

"What did this Caswell look like?"

Jack's description fit to a "t" the man who had bumped into Tuck moments before the bomb blew his home and family to smithereens. Fighting to remain calm, he nodded to Jack to go on.

"Then this Lord tells Caswell to 'Take care of the matter.' I couldn't figure the guy's angle at the time; but after what…you know … after what happened to Claire and the lad, I put two and two together. I found out that Caswell was a … a, you know, like an embarrassment to the family. Tinking back on it, I figure he wanted to get in good with his uncle by shutting you up. Couldn't figure why to tell the truth."

"He wanted to shut me up because Nelly and the Captain are my ancestors, Jack."

Jack guffawed, dripping beer to his chin. He swiped his chin with the back of his hand, and said, "C'mon that's crap, son."

"No, tis not crap. Caswell knew about the relationship and that means he knew a Temple family secret. T'was a scandal that the blasted family tried to keep under wraps for more than a century." He paused, then, in measured tones, he said, "Jack, do you know where Caswell is?"

Jack took a deep swallow of Guinness, and then said, "What's this about a scandal?"

Tuck growled, "Forget about the scandal, Jack. Tell me you know where Caswell is!"

"I know he went off to America."

"Where in America?"

Holding his hand in mock surrender, Jack said, "Hey, c'mon, boyo, I'm helping here."

He took another cigarette, lit it and took a drag. Then, "Caswell's from an important family, right? To my way of tinking, his uncle probably got him a job at a British embassy in the States … or maybe not. I don't know."

"Which one?"

"Could 'a been New York. Hey, who the fuck knows where he ended up."

"Ah, Christ! Why the hell did it take you so long to tell me this?"

In a gruff, if petulant tone, Jack responded, "I couldn't tell ya 'cause you disappeared!"

It was an effort, but Tuck calmed himself, and said, "I'm sorry, Jack. It's just that my family's murder got me all tied up inside. To tink I might get the bastard is almost too much."

He motioned for the tab.

Jack said, "So that's it, is it?"

Tuck got up, pulled Jack from his seat and hugged him. "You have no idea how much this news means to me, but I gotta go."

He pushed money for the tab into Jack's hand; then held him at arm's length. "You need to take better care of yourself, Jack."

And then he left the man standing there, a look of complete confusion on his face.

As soon as he was able, Tuck went to the United States. He learned that Caswell had, in fact, been assigned to the New York British Embassy, but had been transferred to the Consulate in Boston. He went there and bunked with a friend of his late cousin, Paul Tibertus. For months he had stalked Caswell until he knew every move the man made. He knew the restaurants he favored; he knew his preferred drink; and, most importantly, he knew his schedule.

Tuck had begun to formulate a plan, which by November, 1978 was fully formed.

Haverhill, Massachusetts ~ Wednesday, November 10, 1978

Tuck swerved the rented motorcycle onto an exit and entered Haverhill, Massachusetts, the old shoe factory city his Uncle James drove through on the way to Country Pond. When Lake Kenoza came into view, he pulled over and stopped. He gazed through bare trees above the lake and spotted the turrets of Winnekenni Castle, and imagined its grounds, upon which he intended to complete his mission. His heart gave an odd tumble at the thought. Then he continued on his way to Country Pond, stopping to buy the supplies needed for his return on Friday.

Shortly, he took a left onto a narrow dirt road, indicated by a crude, arrow-shaped sign: "To Country Pond." He followed the road for less than a quarter mile and then killed the engine. He walked the cycle into a clearing and hid it in the bushes. He slung the saddlebag over his shoulder, tucked the grocery bags under his arm and carefully climbed down a steep trail to the beach. He stared for a moment at Half Moon Cottage. Built in the 1930's, the cottage had been deserted for a decade, except for his rare visits. Apparently, Aunt Agnes' family continued paying real estate taxes since the state had yet to seize the place.

As he walked up the three steps to the porch, he was relieved to see the ceramic half-moon still tacked over the door. He felt a familiar pleasant sensation at the center of his chest when he grasped the key nestled behind the half-moon. He opened the door, and watched the string he had secreted between the door and its jamb on his last visit, drop to the floor. He put the string in his pocket and stepped into the kitchen, which boasted a cast-iron stove and one large window over the sink. The rusted water pump on the edge of the sink once brought refreshing well water to the cottage.

He put the saddlebag on the table his uncle Jim had made from a large piece of butcher block and which occupied the wall opposite the sink. He opened the top door of the ice box, and filled the shelves with cheese, cereal, milk, fruit, two thermoses of water, and beer. He looked at the bottom door and realized he had forgotten to buy ice. Though chill permeated the cottage, he opened a bottle of Guinness, drank deeply, and walked into the living room, which contained a non-working stone fireplace, and a potbelly wood-burning stove. Two windows behind the well-worn sofa overlooked the woods on the side of the cottage.

He tossed some wood and papers into the stove, lit them, and soon felt the stove's warmth spread throughout the cottage. He sat down on the sofa, plopping his feet up on Uncle Jim's hand-made butcher block coffee table. He lit a Camel, and gazed at the dust motes dancing in muted sunlight streaming through two other windows facing the lake.

His gaze fell on the alcove where books and games once were stashed to be used on rainy summer days. The alcove was empty now, save for two fading pictures on the top shelf. One was of his Uncle Jim proudly holding a large pickerel; the other of Aunt Agnes surrounded by Tuck and his cousins horsing around.

He pictured the bedrooms up the narrow staircase, one for the grownups and the other for him and his cousins. With some distaste he pictured the commode that used to be under his bunk bed – to be used at night rather than the outhouse. Since he was the youngest, his job was to clean the awful place. He had perfected a method that consisted of three coffee cans filled with bleach that he would toss into the outhouse and then run like hell. He smiled at the thought.

Enough! Do what you need to do, man.

He strode to the kitchen and removed the wooden box and his copy of *The Wreck of the Highlander* from his saddlebag. He put the book aside and opened the box. He removed the sheaf of paper containing Alice O'Keefe's story and laid it aside. Then he picked up Aunt Stella's letter, picturing Claire's reaction when he told her about Stella's use of Christopher as a pawn. He felt a pang of regret that he hadn't had the chance to tell her the rest of Christopher's story.

He held Thomas' arrow head for a moment and then put it back. He put the captain's gold ring on his finger. Finally, holding Peg Mirran's note intended for Will O'Connell, he reflected upon the twists of fate that had determined his family's destiny.

Apparently, Peg had hid the letter, waiting for an opportune time to give it to Will – a time that never came. His grandfather had told him that Molly had decided that the West was too dangerous for the children after the death of Alice O'Keefe followed by Will's murder. So, he figured, Molly must have found Peg's letter while clearing out the cottage for the move south.

Now he read it through its protective plastic cover.

December, 1877- Dear Mr. O'Connell, t'was God's providence that you knew me as Miss Molly's attendant, and not as a neighbor of the Hughes family. T'was good too that your Uncle Thomas did not recognize me, for he was just a lad when I escaped the famine. I did not want you to know my history because it would have made it too difficult for me to keep a secret that I promised never to reveal. T'was told to me by my friend, Alice O'Keefe. But, now my days are short, and I need to tell you what you need to know.

Your twin, Christopher, did not die as told by Stella McBride. Alice's husband Terrance fetched Christopher from Galway and brought him home to Alice. Now, I was a midwife before the famine hit hard, so Alice sent for me that night to nurse Christopher, the poor little thing. Whilst doing so, I spied upon the nape of his tiny neck a strange, light blue mark left by the stork no doubt. It had a likeness to a butterfly, it did. I think you must have the same mark as your twin. Whenever your own nape was visible I would peer to see if it was there. But, t'was untoward of me to stare, so I don't know for certain. You should ask dear Molly to take a look. I think this sign will help in your search for Christopher.

I only know that Mrs. O'Keefe brought him to England to live in a place called Hampshire County. I am sorry I never told you before. But, only now it seems right to break a promise.

With blessings, Peg Mirran

Tuck recalled that when he was a boy his grandfather, Paul T. had read the letter to him. The birthmark intrigued him so he looked up the subject in the Encyclopedia. He learned that such birthmarks, sometimes inherited, were usually transient among Caucasian babies. The mark, deep pink or light blue in color, may appear on the eyelids, forehead, or the nape of the neck. They usually fade away within a few months, except on individuals with fair skin. Their mark can be faintly visible throughout adulthood. Whether the individual is fair skinned or not, if the mark appears on the nape of the neck above the hairline it tends to persist throughout adulthood.

During his second vacation at Half Moon Cottage, his Aunt Agnes had scolded him for not washing carefully enough. She had roughly rubbed his face with a wet cloth. When she began to rub the back of his neck, she paused, and said, "And what is this?" She told him that he had a stork's kiss in the shape of a tiny butterfly. "That means good luck, you know," she had said.

Then Tuck recalled the night he and Claire first made love in this very room, after which she squealed with delight: "Tuck, you have a wee butterfly stuck to the nape of your neck! Tis there plain as day, right above your hairline."

He smiled sadly at the memory, and put Peg's note in his jacket pocket. Then he left the cottage.

An hour later he returned, put a mimeographed copy of the note on the table, a block of ice into the icebox, and Peg's original note back into the wooden box. He stoked the fire and then sat at the kitchen table.

He drew a rough rendering of a butterfly on the mimeograph copy and scrawled one sentence: *"Get Boston's Detective Raleigh Buchanan, he'll understand."*

Though Peg's note was written in Gaelic, Tuck complicated things even more by tearing the copy in places, and pen-scratching through some words and sentences. Staring at his work he thought about the notes Raleigh and he had traded as boys. He recalled how ticked off he was when Raleigh hadn't left a response to his last note. Since he had mentioned a riddle in English, but wrote the riddle in Gaelic, he thought that Raleigh must've been pretty ticked off as well.

Smiling at the memory he put the copy of Peg's note in his jacket pocket and looked around. Satisfied that he hadn't forgotten anything, he put a new piece of string in between the jamb and the door, the key under the half-moon, and left Country Pond.

As he entered Haverhill, he knew he was pushing the cycle too fast. Suddenly a car turned onto Newton Road heading straight for him. He careened past the car, forcing it off the road. Adrenalin pumped through his body as he righted his cycle.

And he kept on going.

CHAPTER 29 ~ RALEIGH BUCHANAN

Boston - The Same day, Wednesday, November 10, 1978

Earlier that morning, Raleigh Buchanan had crammed suitcases into his red '72 BMW and, with great expectations, nestled skis into the roof rack. His town house in Boston's south end is a short walk to Copley Square where he and his wife Alana were having breakfast at Ken's Deli. The place was actually a restaurant with a 1920's feel to it – black and white tile on the floors, campy pictures, and famous for its incomparable blintzes.

Raleigh had started to take the first bite of his blueberry blintz when he stalled his fork in mid-air. He watched Alana attack her stack of pancakes. *A five-year old, holding the syrup bottle aloft, dripping circles into every tiny roadway made with her fork.*

That done, Raleigh knew she would slather butter all over the mess. This he couldn't watch. He closed his eyes and savored the first bite of his blintz – pristine save for a dollop of sour cream.

His blintz gone, he watched Alana finish off her pancake ritual, which is the only nod to excessive behavior she allowed. One more thing, he thought: *the woman is fierce in bed, though you wouldn't know it to look at her Grace Kelly countenance.*

Raleigh had cut his cop teeth with the New York City Police Department, but left for Boston when the BPD wooed him with an offer he couldn't refuse. Besides, Alana was from Cape Ann and missed the Boston area. In no time, Raleigh was promoted to Lieutenant Detective. He had "detected" for the better part of 20 years, and was pretty damned good at it. Apparently, though, he had been neglecting Alana. He figured that was why she insisted they get away to celebrate their 17th anniversary.

After breakfast, they left for North Conway, New Hampshire. They had driven about 30 miles from Boston when Raleigh asked Alana if she minded a little detour. She didn't. He took a quick right off an exit into Haverhill, whose northeastern border's elbow juts clear into New Hampshire. Raleigh knew the city fairly well, but hadn't been there in years. For several summers when he was a boy, he and his mother and sister would take a train from New York to Boston's South Station where they would meet his paternal Aunt Sandra who would drive them to Country Pond. As they drove through Haverhill, Aunt Sandra would entertain them with city's colorful history.

Raleigh said to Alana, "Granted, Haverhill's not as charming as Cape Ann's Magnolia; but it has a certain character and it has its characters. Aunt Sandra used to recite a litany of them when she drove us through the city on our way to Country Pond."

He then told her about Bob Montana's first cartoon drawing of the "Archie" comic book character on one of the high school's blackboards; the poet John Greenleaf Whittier; the master of the short story, Andre Dubus II; and Rowland Macy who, at his wife's urging opened his first store in Haverhill.

"He even held the first Macy's parade there, though Boston claims the honor," Raleigh explained. "And, Aunt Sandra loved telling us that Louis B. Mayer opened his first theatre in Haverhill's rundown burlesque house, which he had renovated. He named it the 'Orpheum,' and featured *From Manger to the Cross* to overcome the building's sleazy reputation."

Distracted by his story telling, Newton Road came up quicker than Raleigh remembered, so he had to turn the wheel quickly to the left. As he did so, a motorcycle was headed straight toward him. But the cyclist swerved past him such that Raleigh had to pull the car sharply into bushes lining the road.

He breathed an oath; Alana spat, "The jerk!"

She took the wheel while Raleigh pushed the car back onto the road. They continued north until they came to a side road Raleigh thought might take them to Country Pond. It didn't. After a while he confessed that he didn't remember the way.

"We'd better go back to the highway before I get us totally lost."

Alana put a cassette into the tape deck Raleigh had recently installed. He listened intently to the first movement of Verdi's *La Traviata*. The opera was special because, early in their relationship, he and Alana had taken turns reading aloud passages from Alexandre Dumas' *The Lady of Camellias*, on which the opera is based. Then Raleigh recalled the night he met Alana. It was July 1952 …

Raleigh and the kid from Ireland, who vacationed at a Country Pond cottage the previous two weeks, had been trading notes for two years. But at 15, Raleigh was pretty much over the thrill of finding notes behind the ceramic half-moon nailed over the cottage door. The last one was half written in Gaelic and had contained a riddle. The note had irritated him so he decided it was time to put childish things away. So, that night he went to the Country Pond dance.

The moment he walked through the Pavilion's swinging doors he saw Alana laying punch and cookies on a buffet table. She was the most beautiful girl he had ever seen. Her dress was soft blue, set off with a wide, black velvet belt. Her hair was drop-dead gorgeous: a darker blue ribbon held multi-shaded blond hair in place, stray ringlets escaping. He circled the dance floor, coming closer, feigning disinterest, but sneaking peeks. As he drew near, he saw that her dress's neckline was scooped, revealing translucent skin that he would've given his life to touch. She caught him staring, and smiled.

At that moment she turned to a boy calling her name. He led her to the dance floor and they danced to the Four Lad's, *Istanbul*, their first gold record. As she danced to the lively tune, Raleigh was transfixed by the sight of the hem of her dress whirling around her tanned legs. Then they danced to Patti Page's heartbreaking rendering of *I Went to Your Wedding*. Raleigh couldn't watch.

The disk jockey's voice boomed through the microphone, bringing the music to an abrupt end. "OK!" he yelled. "It's time for Country Pond's version of the Sadie Hawkins Dance! Gals get to ask guys to dance. Gals stand over here by me. Guys, you stand over by that wall."

Raleigh wanted to disappear; but, he stayed put for he was already where the guys were told to stand. After the dance floor emptied, the disc jockey said, "Ready. Get Set. Go!" and Jo Stafford's inimitable voice echoed *You Belong to Me* throughout the hall.

Alana headed straight toward Raleigh; and his heart dropped at least an inch. He couldn't believe she'd pick him. But, she did. She stood before him and simply stared for a moment. Her eyes were a shade of amber, almost copper. She took his hand and they began to dance. Though the song called for close dancing, Raleigh kept a respectable distance, lightly holding Alana's hand, barely touching her waist. They danced to the next two songs. Then the disk jockey played a fast tune. Raleigh held his hands up – no, he wasn't about to jitter bug. Swaying to the music, Alana asked him to join her outside for some fresh air.

It was a perfect summer evening, intermittent moonlight peeking through the pines. He couldn't believe how easy it was to talk to Alana. He was absolutely charmed by her accent, clipped in that New England way; and her voice deeper than he would've guessed. She told him that she lived in a town north of Boston. He would later learn that she lived on one of those horsey estates on Cape Ann. He would also learn that her father's family was "old Boston Irish," whose wealth was inherited money, earned by God knows what methods. She had clarified however that, by the time the money ended up in her dad's hands, it was as clean as a hound's tooth.

While they walked through the pines Alana told him that this was her second summer volunteering at a disabled children's camp across the lake. Raleigh was impressed. She looked at her watch and asked him to walk her to where the Camp's van driver was to pick her up. They walked in silence, enjoying the sweet summer night – until the van's headlights careened off the trees.

"The driver's a maniac," Alana said.

Then, without warning, she reached up and lightly kissed Raleigh's cheek, pressing a piece of paper into his hand. The van came to a stop in front of them, and she literally jumped into the front seat. She waved and he waved back. He held onto the paper and walked back to the cottage. Holding the paper up to the porch light, he traced his finger along the name and phone number she had written. He put the paper to his lips.

He knew he had just fallen in love.

Now, a blasting horn pulled Raleigh from his reverie. He had stopped at a red light, but hadn't noticed when it turned green. He wondered how the hell he'd driven safely into the center of North Conway. He looked in the back mirror just in time to see the guy give him the finger. Alana went into a thing about the dangers of daydreaming while driving. Ignoring her comment, Raleigh told her that he was remembering the night they had met, but, quickly changed the subject. "Well, will you look at that?"

Snow was coming down steadily in those face-stinging compact flakes, presaging one of those un-predicted New England blizzards. The storm was pummeling the White Mountains by the time they had settled into their room at the White Mountain Inn. Beautiful from the vantage point of the Inn's warmth and safety, they found being stranded in an early New England blizzard romantic even after 17 years of marriage.

Raleigh had splurged on their room. One large bedroom with a small sitting area near French doors that opened onto a balcony. A stone fireplace graced one wall, and on the other a huge picture window allowed a great view of the Presidential Range. The bathroom, which sported a Jacuzzi, was next to a walk-in closet. It was the same room they had had on their honeymoon, during which they might've gone skiing once. Now, given the intensity of the storm, he was sure they wouldn't be doing much skiing this time either.

After lunch he lit a fire; Alana poured two fingers of Hennessey for them. They sat cross-legged watching the fire, listening to its pop and sizzle; they sipped and talked for a while. She snuggled next to him, murmuring a satisfying "Mmm" sound. He maneuvered his left leg and shoulder to get more comfortable, she snuggled even closer. They both promptly fell asleep.

Raleigh awoke with a start; and adjusted his eyes to the muted light emanating from moonlit ice crystals sparkling on the windows. He shivered, untangled himself from Alana, jacked up the thermostat and put a log onto the dying embers. He sat cross-legged in front of the fireplace, and, rummaging through his knapsack, he removed a first-edition book, and then a journal filled with stories, which his father had read to him and Patricia. Laying them aside, he removed a photograph and held it the flickering fire light. Staring at the artist's rendering of his great-great grandfather, he whispered, "He was a handsome devil." The color of his eyes seemed Dresden blue, his dark blond hair curled a bit beneath his ears. His jaw was strong; a cleft chin added character. His full lips held the hint of a smile.

Other than the shadow of a cleft chin and blue eyes, Raleigh didn't think he looked much like him. *I'm more on the ordinary side.* Running his fingers through his hair, he thought, *Still thick and mostly dark brown, thanks God!*

Then Alana's voice broke into his thoughts, "Raleigh, what is all this?"

She lifted the book and caressed its cover. "I haven't seen this in a long time. It was displayed with other first editions in that darling alcove you made in our New York apartment."

She picked up the journal. Her look reminded Raleigh that she had never actually seen it, though he had once told her about the stories it contained. After a thoughtful pause she said, "Raleigh, except for your Aunt Sandra, you hardly ever speak of your father's family."

"Maybe it's time I did," he replied, much to her surprise.

She glanced at the clock on the mantel. "Sure, it's early enough ..." Looking out the window she added, "...and it looks like we're snowbound. Let's order room service first. I'm famished."

Raleigh regarded his wife. *My Alana, she can eat like a horse but never puts on a pound.*

He sucked in his stomach as he rose to call room service.

Early on, Raleigh had made a pact with himself that he wouldn't speak of his basic aches, which was why he spoke little about his father's family. Tonight, though, he was in the mood. Over dinner and dessert, over coffee and Hennessey he told Alana what he knew about his father's ancestors, some of which he guessed might be apocryphal, given his Aunt Sandra's penchant for exaggeration. He summarized the history that Alana already knew: His great-great grandfather had been a child prodigy in math and an accomplished author. By the time he died his wife, and then his son, Wallace, inherited quite an estate. According to Aunt Sandra, the son gave his sister, Alice Rose, their father's journal and his first-edition books, and little else. He did, however, offer a dowry upon her marriage to Ian McLaren, which McLaren urged her to reject.

Alice Rose and Ian had two children. The younger one was Raleigh's grandmother, Nessa, named after her grandmother. Aunt Sandra reported that Nessa had been a "feisty lass," whose penchant for being ahead of her time won her nothing but four years at an Anglican convent school in Scotland. When she was just shy of 17, she eloped with Duncan Buchanan.

Raleigh winked at Alana and said, "Not the usual nine months later, my father, Cameron Raleigh Buchanan was born."

He was silent for a moment. Then, "Actually, my father hardly spoke of Duncan. But, one day I heard Aunt Sandra tell my mother that the guy was a penniless fortune-seeking roué who married my grandmother for her money."

To this Alana raised an eyebrow and mocked, "Roué?"

He told her he'd always wanted to get that word into a sentence.

She told him to get on with the story.

"Shortly after my father was born, my grandmother became a shadow of her old self, so I've been told. After Nessa's father died, her mother prevailed upon her daughter and Duncan to come live with her on the family estate in Scotland. It turned out that she was a force with which Duncan had to contend. But, after she died, Nessa didn't have the strength or the heart to stand up to him … not even when he insisted they leave her ancestral home to emigrate from Scotland to New York City."

Then Raleigh stopped talking quite abruptly, and refreshed their drinks. He had come to the part Alana knew nothing about. He handed the glass of Hennessey to her, but said nothing.

After a moment Alana said, "Well?"

Raleigh said, "My grandparents hadn't been in New York long when Duncan used Nessa's inheritance to engage in the stock market boom following World War One. You know, Alana, the market was unregulated during that era, so Duncan's investments yielded enormous returns. He turned a relatively small family fortune into a fabulous one.

"I overheard Aunt Sandra tell my mother stories about Duncan. He wasn't interested in his children and had always been unfaithful to Nessa. By the late 1920's Duncan was rolling in cash, so he moved the family to an estate on Long Island and enrolled the children in a private school. He kept an apartment in Manhattan … for himself, his business partners, and his ladies. A year or so later he brought my father to live with him in Manhattan. Using his own money and a game he made up, he introduced him to the ebb and flow of the stock market."

Raleigh's voice dropped an octave.

"Though my father never experienced the thrill of real winning, he suffered the crushing results of losing. His father lost everything in the crash of '29 … including his life."

Then his voice cracked with emotion, he coughed went to the fireplace.

"One day my father came home and found his father hanging by his neck from the balcony inside his two-floor Manhattan apartment."

Alana's eyes grew wide. "Oh. My. God! Why have you never told me this before?"

He didn't respond; but, continued his story.

"The first thing my father did was remove Duncan's body, thinking he could hide the fact of suicide. Knowing Duncan had a habit of squirreling away cash, he rummaged through the apartment until he found as much money as he thought could be found. He stuffed it and some valuables into two suitcases and stashed them in the pantry. Only then did he call the police. After the police and the coroner left, he took the Long Island train home and broke the news to his mother, who told the other children.

"At the time Aunt Sandra was 13 and the twin boys were 10 – I never could get their names straight. To me, they were always known as 'the twins.' My father didn't reveal the facts surrounding Duncan's death. But, before my grandmother died, she told the family secret to my mother. She said she knew in her heart that Duncan had committed suicide, like so many during those dark days."

Raleigh paused. Alana waited. Then he said, "Before the auctioneer arrived at the estate, the family salvaged as many items of value that they could hope to carry, including my great-great grandfather's first edition books and his journal. There was very little money left after the auctioneer's commission; and hardly anything from the sale of Duncan's Manhattan apartment and the Long Island estate. So, the family moved to a small apartment in Manhattan's lower east side. My father became a bookseller sometime during the depression years. Aunt Sandra married James and the twins …"

Raleigh's pause was brief.

"Alana, you know about the five Sullivan brothers who were assigned to the same ship and were all killed when their ship was blown to smithereens." Alana nodded and he continued, "After that the Navy no longer allowed brothers to be on the same ship. But the twins enlisted in the Navy before that happened. They both were killed when their ship was sunk by a Kamikaze."

He noted dismay touching Alana's features. "You wanted me to tell you about my father's family, right?" He said in earnest.

"Yes. But, I can see why you don't talk much about them. Please don't stop now, Raleigh."

"When Patricia was born, my father needed more income than bookselling receipts, so he took and passed the Police Academy test, and joined the NYPD in 1936. The following year he moved the family to a small house in Brooklyn Heights. You know that's where I was born."

Alana nodded.

"Then one day Captain Murphy and our Presbyterian Pastor came to the house. Since it was my sixth birthday and all about me, I thought they had dropped by to wish me happy birthday."

Again Raleigh felt emotion rising.

Alana knew what was coming next, but whispered, "No."

"No, they didn't come to wish me happy birthday. My mother scooted me and Patricia into the kitchen and ushered the two men into the parlor. When the French doors shut, we immediately headed for them. Pressing my ear against the door, I heard the captain say, '… so you and the children will have his benefits; a small consolation, I know Mrs. Buchanan.'

"I wasn't sure what they were talking about, but Patricia started to cry."

Raleigh felt tears spring to his eyes. Alana got up and stood by him at the fireplace.

"When the men left the parlor, the minister touched our heads and gave us a sad smile. We peeked inside. My mother was sitting very still, holding a piece of paper up to her face, like a handkerchief. Patricia slowly walked toward her; but I hung back. But when my mother beckoned I went to her. She grabbed us and held us close. Though she did her best to hide her sorrow, I could tell she was crying. And so, I started to cry too."

Raleigh bent his head, lost in the memory of that day. When he looked back up, he saw tears in Alana's eyes. She wiped them with the back of her hand and with the other pulled him close. He thought he might actually cry. But he didn't.

He pulled back slightly and said, "Let's sit, Alana." He held onto her hand and continued, "My father's funeral was something. The ceremonial rifle shots echoed in my ears for a long time. Sorrowful bagpipe music still gives me pause. I think the majesty of it all motivated me to become a cop. I imagined that I would catch the man who murdered my father in a Brooklyn alleyway.

"Aunt Sandra came to New York to help us pack for our move from Brooklyn Heights to an apartment in Clinton Hill, a poorer section of Brooklyn. Patricia and I were assigned to pack stuff in the attic. My father's footlocker had always intrigued me. I could hardly wait to see what was in it. Nothing much was in there except the first edition books, my father's dress uniform and the journal.

"When I asked my mother about the stories in them she said, 'They're fairy tales, son, meant only to amuse children.' I believed her."

And with that Raleigh ended the story of his father's family. After a few moments Alana stood and took his hand. "Let's go to bed, darling."

That night in the White Mountain Inn Alana made love with an intensity she hadn't demonstrated before. Raleigh rolled over, caught his breath and said, "Maybe I should tell you sad tales more often." She gave his shoulder a playful punch.

They remained snowbound for another day; they skied the next day, and left the White Mountains on Saturday, November 13, the actual date of their anniversary. On the way home Alana replaced Verdi with Raleigh's personal favorite, Nikolai Rimsky-Korssakoff's *Scheherazade.*

Raleigh did not daydream on the way back to Boston.

CHAPTER 30 ~ REVENGE

Cambridge ~ Friday, November 12, 1978

The last day of his life dawned chilly and bleak. Jonathan Temple Caswell's radio alarm clicked on. He awakened to Rod Stewart's "Maggie May," remnants of his dream littered the floor of his mind. He shut the radio off, and plopped back onto the pillow, not used to rising at 5 o'clock in the morning. He thought about today's assignment. Though he was low man at the Consulate-General of the United Kingdom, by some snafu he was to represent his superior's superior at a meeting in Providence, Rhode Island. The Consulate covered the six New England States, and regular visits to them were required.

He stretched and swung his legs over the side of the bed. He went to the bathroom, dragging his bathrobe behind him. After a shower he decided to catch breakfast on the road and dressed quickly. He grabbed his overcoat, picked up his briefcase and went down the back stairway to his building's parking lot. As he walked to his black Mercedes a brisk wind whipped his briefcase painfully against his leg. "Shit," He murmured.

As he was about to unlock the car door an Irish-accented voice said to his back, "Nice car you have there, boyo."

Startled, Caswell turned to see a roughly handsome man needing a shave, wearing denim and tweed, and pointing a gun at his chest. In almost a single motion Caswell raised both arms, dropping his briefcase and keys to the ground. He opened his mouth to say something. Denim and Tweed held up a finger.

"Not a word, man. Do only what I tell you to do." Caswell nodded, as the man continued, "Quick! Open the trunk."

Caswell knew it was too early for his neighbors to see what was happening and he began to sweat despite the chill. He didn't move.

"Open the trunk!" The man demanded.

Caswell knew the ways of the Irish well enough not to argue, so he picked up his keys and opened the trunk. Then the man hit him on the head. Caswell blacked out, falling halfway into the trunk. The man lifted his captive's legs and toppled the rest of him into the trunk. He took several paces backward, picked up his saddle bag, grabbed Caswell's briefcase and placed both into the trunk. He looked around. Satisfied that no one had seen the assault, he took electrical tape from the saddle bag and quickly placed a strip across Caswell's mouth and bound his wrists and ankles.

Tuck O'Connell climbed into the car and started the engine. He drove onto Amherst Street, took a right onto Ames and a left onto Memorial Drive heading east toward the Tobin Bridge, which native Bostonians refer to as the Mystic River Bridge – just one of many ways that Boston confounds tourists. Crossing the bridge Tuck headed north liking the way the Mercedes handled. Forty minutes later he entered Haverhill. He kept to the speed limit as he drove up Main Street and onto Kenoza Avenue. Shortly, he turned the wheel hard to the right and entered a park to the right of Lake Kenoza. An Algonquin Indian name meaning "Pickerel Fish," the lake had been formed eons ago by glacier invasion. A 19th century physician had chosen a spot high above the lake for his summer home, which was built with stones in the style of an English castle. He christened the castle and its grounds Winnekenni, another Algonquin name meaning "very beautiful."

Winnekenni Park had suffered a terrible fire earlier that year, so Tuck was confident that the grounds would be deserted. He drove up a rutted road to the castle. Reaching the top he gunned the engine, causing the big car to skid over the crest where he expertly applied the brakes. He got out, opened the trunk, and looked down at Caswell's terrified eyes. He pulled him into a half sitting position.

"Swing those legs over, boyo, and be quick about it!"

He cut the tape binding Caswell's ankles and ordered him out of the trunk. Then he grabbed his saddlebag in one hand, and with the other shoved Caswell up an incline toward the Castle.

Tuck's re-creation of his great-great-grandfather's murder scene was proceeding nicely. He thought that Will O'Connell would approve, even thought Will O'Connell would approve, even though Haverhill is not Mullaghmore, and Winnekenni Castle is not Classiebawn. "Aye," he said aloud, "this'll do just fine."

When they reached the Castle's southwestern corner, Tuck slipped his gun from his waist band and with his other hand tore the tape off Caswell's mouth. Cutting the tape binding his wrists, he said, "Up with your hands, Mr. Jonathan Temple Caswell."

Caswell did so and only then did he recognize his assailant. He licked his lips and swallowed hard.

Tuck noted the look of recognition. "Ah, you know who I am. Tis about time we're face to face again, eh? Let's see … wasn't the last time back in '72? Aye, you almost bumped into me. Do you remember?"

Tuck's sarcasm controlled his impulse to hit Caswell. Spraying spittle from his lips, he continued, "Sure and t'was you that bumped into me; a coward running away from the scene of his crime."

Caswell murmured, "What do you want with me, man?"

"I want you to admit what you did to my family, you bastard."

At first Caswell denied knowing what Tuck was talking about; but he soon complied, hoping he'd have a better chance to survive.

"I … didn't mean the blast to cause such horror … meant only a small blast … I wanted to get you and the others out of the building."

"What foolishness is this?" Tuck spat.

"I left a note for you … in the cellar … door jamb … wanted you to meet me and if you didn't, something worse would happen." Then in a slightly stronger voice: "I misjudged the explosive. It's the truth, man, I swear."

Losing control, Tuck slapped Caswell hard across the face.

"You incompetent fuck! You couldn't get the job done right. Then your 'royal' family spirited you off to the States. Making sure you got a job you could actually perform. Ha! You're nothin' but a lackey to some English high mucky muck's lower mucky muck, eh?"

He dragged his hand across his mouth, and snarled, "Tell me why you killed my family!" Caswell said nothing.

"Cat got'cha tongue? Tell me you sonofabitch!"

Caswell looked as if he were about to cry.

Tuck laughed derisively. "No matter, I know why you did it." He did not check the anger rising in his chest, and snarled, "You were just another among your scum ancestors who murdered mine: Will O'Connell, Stella McBride, and Alice O'Keefe were murdered to keep them quiet just because they knew a secret about your family… and so do I. Tis why you meant to kill me. But you made a 'little mistake' didn't you, and killed my family instead. You're about to pay dearly for that."

Regaining his composure, he said in a milder tone, "Here we are a 100 years almost to the day and the hour that Will O'Connell was murdered – tis poetic justice, don'cha tink?"

He paused for effect.

"Take off the overcoat and shoes!"

Caswell hesitated; but, catching the look in Tuck's eyes, he did as he was told. Then Tuck motioned for him to remove his jacket. Caswell began to whimper as he removed his jacket.

"C'mon take off the rest, but leave your skivvies on."

Caswell removed his shirt and pants, shivering against the November morning chill. Tuck spat, "Shut your eyes." A beat, then: "Do it now, Caswell!"

Tuck stuck his gun in his waistband, and withdrew from his hip a long knife with a silver-filigreed handle. "Open your eyes, Caswell. Go on open them!"

When he opened his eyes Caswell was transfixed by the sight of the knife moving toward him.

A flock of Purple Finch, the state bird of New Hampshire, was perched on the limbs of a tree overlooking the ancient Lake Kenoza. A man's scream pierced the early morning quiet and the flock took flight over the southwestern tower of Winnekenni Castle. The murderer had driven a long, silver-handled knife into the man's chest, aiming for his heart. He placed the dead man's clothes in a neat pile, and tucked something into his jacket pocket. He removed a bag filled with dirt-like substance from his saddle bag and poured the stuff over the body. He got into his victim's car and gunned the engine, loving the way the big car handled the steep rock-strewn road. As he drove away, the November sun broke weakly through the cloud cover, sending its rays toward earth where they glinted off the ring on the dead man's finger.

Tuck exited Winnekenni Park in Caswell's Mercedes and glanced at Lake Kenoza, sparkling in the November sun that finally had emerged from cloud cover. Just as he made the left onto Newton Road, a sunbeam glinted off his gold ring, causing him to blink. He pictured the much newer version on the finger of the man he'd just murdered. Until that moment, Tuck hadn't thought of himself as a murderer. True, he was involved in the British Consulate attack back in '69, but casualties were unintended. Also true, he had killed an English soldier during that raid in Northern Ireland – but it was for a righteous cause. And so by his lights he had never committed murder. But, this time he knew that it was with malice aforethought that he had planned Caswell's murder; he knew he had just broken the Fifth Commandment.

"Ach, to hell with the guilt," he yelled, "vengeance is mine!"

Nevertheless his heart did an odd tumble, and his voice fell to a whisper, "But darlin' Claire, tis a bitter taste on my lips."

Soon he spied the wooden sign, but drove past it until he found the place he had selected on Wednesday to hide the big sedan. He got out of the car and opened the trunk, and removed a pair of gloves, electrical tape, and a rag. He began the task of ridding any trace of his presence. He kept track: wipe down the leather seats; run the rag along the steering wheel, gear shift, dashboard and door handles; drag the tape along the carpets and the interior roof to catch tiny bits of evidence that he had ever been in that car. Then he removed his saddlebag and Caswell's briefcase from the trunk. He dragged tape curled round his gloved hand across the trunk's floor and ceiling. He wiped the briefcase, only mildly interested in what it might contain.

Finally, he wiped the Mercedes keys, and tossed them and the briefcase into the trunk. He took a step back and mentally checked off his "to-do" list. Satisfied, he stuffed the gloves, rag and tape into his saddle bag and shut the trunk with his elbow.

Then he walked back to where he'd hidden the motorcycle thinking about the much longer walk he had taken on Wednesday to Haverhill's train station. *Amazing the difference a day or two can make in a man's life. Caswell's as well as my own.* He revved engine and headed for the cottage.

He put the saddlebag on the kitchen table and checked the ice, which had not melted in the unheated cottage. He ate a piece of cheese, a few grapes and took a long pull of water. Then he banked a fire in the stove. He stood there feeling at sixes and sevens, his mother's expression for "at odds with oneself." She had died in childbirth when he was 7 and it pained him to think of her, especially today.

He unhinged the alcove shelf, reached in and nicked his finger on something sharp. Withdrawing his hand he noted with some interest blood oozing from his finger. He sucked it for a moment. With his other hand he reached in and tugged loose the culprit – a metal frame holding a photo taken in the fall of 1968. He recalled that the kid, Frankie Gallagher, had taken the picture. Tuck gazed wistfully at Paul Tibertus hanging onto him in a playful choke hold; Kevin McAvoy standing with his arm around Alicia Burns, O'Shaughnessy standing behind. And there, Claire Sheain, kneeling in front, her lovely face in semi-profile. He noted the half- smile he would come to know so well. He tenderly traced her profile with his finger. A lump formed in his throat. He didn't want to think about Claire. He was bone tired and hungry, but knew he wouldn't be able to eat. He plopped onto the sofa.

As the sun dipped behind the clouds, Tuck fell into a deep sleep.

He awoke to the sound of shutters banging against the cottage. A cold wind was blowing sleet sideways through the window that he had opened to freshen the room. He jumped from the sofa, banging his knee painfully against the corner of the coffee table. *Fuck it!* He said as he limped to the window. He gazed for a moment at the white caps rolling across the lake. *Damned New England weather*. He shivered, shut the window and lit the mantel lantern. Holding his wristwatch to the light he realized that he had slept for hours. He tossed some kindling onto the dying embers, carried the lantern into the kitchen, made a sandwich and washed it down with water. He wondered if anything would ever taste good again; he wondered how long it would take before Caswell's body was discovered; and he wondered if Raleigh Buchanan would understand the meaning of the note he had left in Caswell's jacket pocket. He put fresh batteries into his flashlight and transistor radio, hoping to get reception so he could listen to the news.

Tuck dreaded the weekend ahead.

CHAPTER 31 ~ SCENE OF THE CRIME

Boston ~ Sunday, November 14, 1978

The ringing phone demolished Raleigh's dream. He grabbed it to his ear, and said, "What is it, Malcolm?"

"How'd you know it's me, Detective?"

Through a yawn Raleigh said, "I'm psychic."

"Well, sir, we caught ourselves a murder up in Haverhill."

"Haverhill! What's our interest in Haverhill?"

"It's a big one, sir, the victim lived in Cambridge, but the Cambridge PD handed it off to Boston because … um …"

Malcolm's pause was a beat too long for Raleigh. "Get on with it, Malcolm!"

The younger detective cleared his throat, and said, "The FBI's involved, too, and um … they found a note in the vic's pocket. It's written in Gaelic – or Irish, or whatever they call it. But one sentence is scrawled in English. It says, 'Get Boston's Detective Raleigh Buchanan. He'll understand'."

That woke Raleigh up. "Who's the victim?"

"The vic's English – ah, Jonathan Caswell's his name. He works, er, worked at the British Consulate at the Prudential. He's … let's see, I wrote it down… he's the Junior Assistant to the Assistant Deputy Consul-General of the United Kingdom Consulate General. Whadda handle!"

"Malcolm!" Raleigh barked.

"Yes sir, sorry sir. Caswell's body was found in a park near a – you won't believe it – near a *castle*."

"Winnekenni Castle. I know the place."

Alana rolled over. Raleigh turned toward her as she focused her beautiful amber eyes.

She said, “Winnekenni Castle! Years go by and now it’s Haverhill twice in one week?”

“Go back to sleep, Alana.”

“As if I could. You’ll need breakfast.” She leaned over and kissed his cheek, got out of bed, and went into the bathroom.

He said something to her back that she didn’t hear, but Malcolm did. “What’s that, sir?”

“Nothing, Malcolm. Get yourself over to Caswell’s apartment. I’ll go up to Haverhill.”

He dressed quickly and went into the kitchen where Alana was about ready to prepare breakfast. He kissed her forehead, and said, “I’ll grab something on the way.”

He nudged Walter, the cat, out of the way and left the brownstone.

Nick, the owner of the corner convenience store, was slitting the rope binding the Sunday newspapers. “Hey, detective,” he called, “here’s the paper. It’s on me.”

Raleigh took it, but put coins in Nick’s gloved hand. “Thanks Nick.”

Crossing Appleton Street he noted that his bright red BMW looked dreary to him on this bleak November morning. He drove quickly through the South End, entered Chinatown, and cut across to the Expressway north. He crossed the Tobin Bridge. Having come from New York, he never referred to it as the Mystic River Bridge.

As he drove into Haverhill he recalled Aunt Sandra’s stories about Winnekenni Castle, and thought, “An honest-to-God castle; an oddity in this old factory town.” He took the curves of Kenoza Avenue as only a BMW can, and then a hard right onto the road leading up to the castle. News vans and police vehicles blocked the way to the top so he parked off to the side and walked the rest of the way. To his left he could see Lake Kenoza peeking through the bare trees and in between the pines. Having seen it a few days before, and from his earlier experience, he knew that the lake is large and very beautiful, but flat and gray today, like an anvil.

On the hill to the right, he could see the granite antelope upon which, according to his Aunt Sandra, countless children had had their pictures taken. Then he saw several uniforms keeping reporters and squirrels at bay. He flashed his badge at an officer, who promptly lifted the yellow crime scene tape. He saw a woman dressed in a peacoat and jeans – without bellbottoms. *They're going out of style, thank you, God.* As he drew closer he could see that she wore no-nonsense hiking boots. The startling red scarf around her neck seemed out of place. He thought the woman might be the medical examiner, though a woman in that job would be unusual.

Extending his hand toward the woman, he said, "I'm Detective Buchanan, and you are the medical examiner, I presume."

"That's right," she said, taking Raleigh's hand. "I'm Doctor Connie Shaw, Assistant to the Medical Examiner." *Emphasis on the "to."* She pointed to a man who looked well over middle age, but might have been much younger. "That fellow's name is Albert Wysocki; he discovered Caswell's body."

Wysocki, who was seated on a park bench, wore a scruffy overcoat and rubber boots too large for his feet. His cap's muffs hung down the sides of his head. His dirty light brown hair, tangled with gray, beat the muffs to his shoulders by almost an inch. He sported a different color sock on each hand.

"Nice gloves," Raleigh observed.

Dr. Shaw gave him a look, and ignoring the comment, she said, "He's a local homeless guy, a Vietnam vet, actually."

Raleigh felt like a heel.

"Officer James Daniels spotted Wysocki walking along Kenoza Avenue at…" she paused, consulted her notebook, and said, "…at 4:16 this morning."

The woman's precise.

"Officer Daniels knows Wysocki." She waved her arm around, and added, "The poor guy thinks he's the caretaker of this place. Daniels didn't believe Wysocki when he said he had discovered a body, but checked to humor him. Good thing he did."

Then, looking over Raleigh's right shoulder, she said, "Here comes Haverhill's Police Chief. The fellow with him is FBI."

Raleigh extended his hand, "Hello, Agent Larrabee! Good to see you again."

"Hey, detective, haven't seen you in a bunch of new moons, eh. Not since …"

The chief cleared his throat. Dr. Shaw saved the moment, and introduced Raleigh to Chief Paul Madden. The man was tall and wide, and on the other side of 50. His bushy eyebrows matched the gray of his eyes.

He shook Raleigh's hand, saying, "Ah. So, you're the man of the hour, eh? I see you know Agent Larrabee."

"Yes, chief, he and I partnered on a terrorist task force back in the late '60's." He paused then added, "So, who's the lead on this one?"

Chief Madden held up his hand in a surrendering gesture, apparently having caught the note of consternation in Raleigh's voice.

"Hold your horses, man. You'll be the lead on this one."

He turned to Dr. Shaw, who nodded, and said, "Detective, the Northern Essex Lab will deal with the evidence and I'll do the post. Techs have already examined the note we found at the scene for fingerprints – and whatever else it can tell us. As we speak, a Bradford College linguist is working on it. He'll call in when he's finished."

To Raleigh's raised eyebrow, she said, "Not to worry, he'll use a copy to translate it. We've worked with Dr. McGrath before – I assure you, detective, he's very good at what he does."

She turned to Chief Madden, and said, "Wysocki's been up here a long time, and he's quite agitated. We have his statement, such as it is. We should get him back to town for some breakfast."

The chief agreed, but told her that Officer Daniels needed to stick around. He turned and said something to a young officer, whose cheeks, Raleigh noted, were the color of Dr. Shaw's scarf. He watched the officer walk over to Daniels and Wysocki. Wysocki suddenly stood, snapped his boot heels together and saluted. The guy didn't seem to notice that clicking rubber heels had no effect whatsoever.

Raleigh stifled a smile; Larrabee grinned.

The officer led Wysocki down the incline to one of the squad cars.

Then Chief Madden poked Larrabee's arm, saying, "C'mon, let's leave Dr. Shaw and the detective to their work." They walked toward the growing crowd of reporters, which now included Boston's WBZ-TV crew.

Raleigh turned to Dr. Shaw, saying, "I gather the techs preserved whatever tire tracks and shoe prints were here before the cavalry arrived."

"Officer Daniels took very good care of the scene," she responded.

"The weather's been typically New England. First a snow storm, then sleet, then bitter cold. But the techs were able make molds of a few good sets of tire tracks and shoe prints. The tracks are down there, above the crest of the hill. Come, I'll show you."

Raleigh had to jog a bit to catch up to her.

She turned and said over her shoulder, "From what we've gathered it appears that Caswell was abducted from his home and driven here most likely in his own car."

"How so?"

"Your Captain Furlong told Chief Madden that Caswell owned a Mercedes, which is nowhere to be found." She pointed to a set of tire tracks encircled with crime scene tape. "A tech identified these as German-made, most likely belonging to a Mercedes," and, she added thoughtfully, "Even so tires don't tell us anything about the car's model or year."

She started to walk up the hill toward the Castle; Raleigh had to jog again to catch up to her. Pointing to the ground, she said, "Those indentations might be shoe prints. But there are clearer sets nearer the castle."

A minute later she knelt, and said, "These prints were obviously made by Wysocki's boots; two fairly good sets are over there by the body. One set is a definite match to Caswell's shoes; the other most likely belongs to his assailant."

She stood, and glanced over at two morgue attendants leaning against their hearse. They were smoking and looking bored. She gave them a look, and began to walk. "Let's take a look so we can get poor

Caswell on his way. I've already examined the body, which I've left *in situ* for you detective."

She suddenly stopped walking, and Raleigh almost bumped into her. Un-phased she said, "We found tiny bits of stuff near the tire tracks that appears to be electrical tape. It's on Caswell's cheeks and wrists. Take a look."

She held back as Raleigh walked over to the body. He could see that Caswell had been a fit man in his early forties. His dark blonde hair was tangled with leaves and dirt. His eyes were open. Though opaque now, they may have been hazel or light brown.

Raleigh stared for a moment at the lifeless form. *His soul is gone.* Dirt covered part of his arms, legs and neck. This reminded Raleigh of something, but he couldn't say what. A silver knife had been thrust to its hilt into Caswell's chest. It wasn't hard for Raleigh to imagine the poor guy's death throes, including arterial splatter; then blood leaking from his body and pooling around his torso. He noted that, though dried, blood had drenched the winter grass, left-over patches of snow, and a portion of the uneven, brick pathway leading away from the body. Except for his boxer shorts, Caswell's clothes were lying on the pathway, held in place by a brick. Though the edges of the clothes had been tousled by the wind, Raleigh could tell they had been folded. That also felt oddly familiar to him.

Dr. Shaw knelt next to Raleigh. "See the pieces of tape on his cheeks and wrist. I sent the larger pieces to the lab – they might yield prints."

Raleigh stood and looked around. "What's that stuff on his body? I don't see anything like it near here."

"I have no idea. But, Caswell's body was almost completely covered with it. We had to remove most of it so I could examine the body. Once it's analyzed, we may even come up with a possible location of origin."

She paused and looked at Raleigh, clearly puzzled. "Detective, can you think of what the dirt 'shroud' might mean?"

"I don't have a clue; maybe some sort of ritual…" His words faded as he lifted Caswell's right hand. He craned his head toward Dr.

Shaw. She read his expression, and said, “I’ll remove the ring when I do the autopsy.”

Raleigh saw that the ring was engraved with a crest, and whispered an “Hmm” sound.

“Dr. Shaw, the ‘Temple’ on the crest – that’s Caswell’s middle name, right? The ring seems to be solid gold. Obviously, robbery wasn’t the motive.”

She said, “No, it wasn’t. His wallet wasn’t taken either.”

He gently placed Caswell’s hand back on the ground. “How long do you think he’s been up here?”

“I’d say maybe two days, maybe more. The weather was weird this weekend, so it will be difficult to determine the exact time of death.” Almost to herself she added, “A knife through the heart. Pretty damned cold.”

He asked her for a better look at the knife. Without hesitation the woman knelt, grasped the knife’s handle and pulled. The thing made an awful squishing sound as it left Caswell’s chest. She carefully placed it into an evidence bag and, with a black felt pen, wrote across the top: *Jonathan Temple Caswell, 11/14/78.* She initialed the bag and handed it to Raleigh.

He held the bag up and could see that the knife boasted a filigreed handle and at least six inches of bloody blade. He was almost certain that the knife was made of pure silver.

“Dr. Shaw, how old does this knife look to you?”

“Could be fifty or a hundred; or it could be a really good retro piece. Listen, I have to get this poor guy on his way.”

She gave a high sign to the morgue attendants. They shot her a look; but, she stared down their arrogance. Then in unison they dropped their cigarettes on the ground and crushed them beneath their boots.

She hollered, “Hey guys! Don’t mess up my crime scene!”

That look again; but, they bent and picked up the butts.

She watched as they lifted Caswell’s body onto a gurney. Then she said, “C’mon, Detective, let’s move this along.”

They approached Dr. Shaw’s green Cherokee. Raleigh said, “Nice wheels.”

She opened the tailgate, saying, “It does the job for me.” Then she placed the bag holding the knife into what looked like a hand-made footlocker lined with heavy plastic. *Here’s a woman whose job is an art form for her.* He liked Dr. Connie Shaw, and was trying to think of a polite way to ask the extent of her authority. She read his mind again.

“You’re probably wondering about my status on the case.”

“You could say that,” he said not unkindly.

“After Chief Madden contacted the FBI – because of Caswell’s affiliation, you understand – he contacted us at the Northern Essex Lab, and Captain Furlong. I arrived on the scene just before Agent Larrabee. But, to answer your question, I’m the assistant to the ME, Dr. Linnehan.”

There’s that emphasis on the “to” again.

“Dr. Linnehan is in New York at a conference and the assistant ME, Dr. Roland Metcalf, is otherwise tied up. So, you could say that I drew the short straw.”

Raleigh had lived with Alana too long for Dr. Shaw’s irony to be lost on him. Changing the subject, he said, “Boston’s British Consulate, the FBI, Cambridge, Haverhill, and the Boston Police department. What more do we need?”

“I got the impression that Chief Madden doesn’t want this in his backyard.” She looked over Raleigh’s shoulder. “Speaking of the devil …”

Raleigh turned and saw Chief Madden and who, he assumed, must be Haverhill’s mayor and his entourage headed toward the press. Agent Larrabee was standing discreetly away from the crowd.

Dr. Shaw placed a boot on the Cherokee’s bumper and began to tighten its lace. Raleigh said, “Dr. Shaw, we need to stay as close to the book as we can; but with a few exceptions.”

She raised her head, and an eyebrow. He said, “For now, can we keep the details describing the knife, the ring and the note under wraps?”

“I can do that, detective. Dr. Linnehan or Dr. Metcalf has to sign off everything I do. They’re not around. Ergo! No signed report for a while." She stood, saying, "I'll give you an unofficial report as soon as I complete the post."

As they exchanged business cards, Raleigh said, "Call me as soon as you have something."

She got into her Jeep, shot a glance in his direction and drove off.

"Not bad looking, hey, Raleigh?" said agent Larrabee, suddenly at Raleigh's side.

"Hey, Eric, glad to see we're back to first names. You feebies didn't waste much time getting involved."

"Well," he said dryly, "The victim did work at the English consulate, number one. And, number two, the perp did write a sentence on an old note written in Gaelic calling you to the scene." He paused. "So, I'm here; and my partner went directly to Caswell's apartment."

Catching Raleigh's look, he added, "Raleigh, Madden's already told the press that you're in charge. I'm in the back seat for now."

A young officer approached them. "Detective Buchanan, Dr. McGrath called in. He's got the note translated and wants to talk to someone about it. I got the feeling he's in a bit of a hurry. He said to meet him in front of Hazelton Hall. That's the main building, Detective."

"Call him back and tell him I'll be there in half hour."

Then Raleigh and Eric Larrabee joined the mayor, Chief Madden and the reporters. Following his introduction, Raleigh fielded a few questions; and then told them that a press conference would be held, and that they would be informed when and where once it was scheduled.

Raleigh whispered to Larrabee that he'd see him back in Boston. Then he took his leave. He walked down the incline and stopped. He looked back at the Castle and stood very still. *What does the Castle mean?* Caswell's English heritage, the ring, the dirt "shroud," the folded clothes, the knife, the note, and now the castle. Everything about this murder scene seemed familiar to him. But, he couldn't wrap his mind around the memory traces skirting the edges of his mind.

It was irritating.

He shook his head and sprinted down to the BMW, noting its red coat glinting in the sun. Finally, after a full week of gloom, except for a short while on Friday afternoon, the sun had broken through the clouds.

CHAPTER 32
"TIS A RIDDLE I GIVE YE" (Alice O'Keefe)

Dr. Gerard McGrath, a man on the sunny side of 70, was a study in rumple: Rumpled vintage London Fog; rumpled cheeks; long, rumpled ear lobes. He was holding an unlit pipe in his hand. Raleigh wondered if that was an affectation as he walked up the steps of Bradford College's Hazelton Hall. He introduced himself to the professor, and followed him into the building. They made small talk on the way to Dr. McGrath's office and Raleigh decided that the fellow was the genuine article.

The professor opened the door, and nodded for Raleigh to enter first. The first thing he saw was a small round table upon which lay a copy of the note found at the scene and its original.

Dr. McGrath picked up the copy, saying, "The technicians made a good copy for me to work on … see? They battered it up quite like the original, which itself could be a copy of a very old document. I warn you, detective, the note is not written in classical Gaelic, or even standard Irish. Slang here and there, words crossed out. Thus, my translation is not complete. But, I hope it will be helpful."

Raleigh said, "If there is an original document, we don't know if it is in the same shape or whether the perp is simply trying to confuse us."

"That could be, detective. Keep in mind as well that the note could be a complete fabrication. However, I must assume it is a copy of a real note written in real time, which, based on the choice of words and tone, I'd say mid-19th century Ireland, most likely the West Coast. Secondly, since the note is not written in classical Gaelic, I assume that the writer was not well-educated. He was probably a peasant who could write well enough to have been the village quill."

Raleigh stared at the version Dr. McGrath had translated into English. "This is so marked up and torn; it doesn't look any easier to understand than the original."

"Yes, I felt I should do it that way to keep faithful to the original. It appears that your bad guy scratched or tore anything we call 'identifiers.' You understand?"

"Names and places, and like that?"

"Right."

"I know you want to be on your way, Dr. McGrath, but would you stay a bit longer to help me complete some of these sentences?"

Twenty minutes later, Raleigh said, "I think we've done as much as we can. We've got a reasonable interpretation, but I can't figure out what it has to do with Caswell's murder."

Dr. McGrath sighed. "I regret I can't be more help to you, detective."

"No, no. You've been very helpful, Dr. McGrath."

After leaving the college Raleigh decided to take the relatively new route 495 that connected to Route 93 south to Boston. Bad decision, for he hadn't gone far when he saw nothing but red tail lights ahead. He thrust the mobile strobe light on the roof, and muscled his way through the traffic. He shot his badge out the window, and a police officer waved him on. He took a quick look through the rear view mirror at the mess of steel and chrome blocking Exit 31 in Medford.

Arriving in the vicinity of police headquarters, he saw Captain Furlong surrounded by the press. He made a sudden left and hustled around the block and parked by the lockup entrance. As he entered the detectives' squad room he bumped into Maggie, the squad's administrative assistant.

"Ha!" she said without a smile, "I saw that car of yours make a quick detour, lieutenant detective."

She liked using Raleigh's more formal title.

"Two very impatient British consulate fellows are waiting for you in the conference room. The captain's outside with the press." Raleigh interpreted that she meant he should get out there as well.

"Tell the consulate reps that I'll be with them shortly. Offer them tea."

The wink he gave her didn't soften her mood. She was not happy being called in on a Sunday.

When Raleigh stepped onto the front steps Captain Furlong said, "Here's Lieutenant Detective Buchanan now. Lieutenant, tell these fellas what's going on up there in Haverhill."

Raleigh was hit by a barrage of questions to which he held up his hand.

"Let me give you an overview and then I'll take your questions. As you know from early reports, a body of a Caucasian male, about 40 years old, was found early this morning in Haverhill. However, we have reason to believe he was abducted from his home in the Boston-Cambridge vicinity."

Not wanting to start a panic about random crime, he quickly added, "We also believe the victim knew his assailant."

A female reporter asked if the police had any suspects. Then Boston's popular TV personality, Jay Verrette, spoke up. "Lieutenant, the FBI is involved. What's that about?"

"I was getting to that, Jay. We're working the case with the FBI because the victim is an employee of a foreign embassy."

There was a low murmur from the crowd. Verrette raised his voice. "New York, Boston? What embassy, Lieutenant?"

"Jay, the victim's identity and his affiliation will be released after his family has been notified."

The reporter pressed, "When will that be?"

Raleigh glanced at Captain Furlong. His look said *I'll handle this*. The captain said, "We'll have an update at 5:15 p.m. tonight, right here."

"Less than three hours away," Raleigh thought. An amusing picture of Furlong's face with a muzzle crossed his mind.

Another reporter asked, "Chief, what about the Haverhill authorities?"

"Lieutenant Buchanan is working closely with Haverhill's Chief Madden and the Northern Essex ME's office."

Jay Verrette started to ask another question, but Furlong waved him off saying, "That's all we have for now, Jay. We'll see you tonight."

As Raleigh and the Captain walked into the building, Furlong said, "You're late, Lieutenant. Detective Schoenfeld came back from Caswell's apartment an hour ago; and those Brits have been waiting longer than that."

Raleigh picked up a paper clip up from the floor and began twisting it back and forth.

Furlong huffed, "We need to make progress sooner than later before those damned Feebies take over. Agent Larrabee beat you to the scene. His partner has already been to Caswell's place. I want this one, Lieutenant. And you should, too. You're the one the perp asked for."

He abruptly walked off. Raleigh stood there watching him walk down the hallway and up three shallow steps to his office. He waited until the office light tossed the Captain's shadow against the blinds. Though the man irritated him, Raleigh knew Furlong wouldn't last, and so he never let his irritation get out of hand. He put the paper clip in his pocket, and walked the opposite way.

After meeting briefly with the consulate reps, Raleigh went to his desk, at which Malcolm was sitting, sipping a cup of coffee. He gave Malcolm a nudge and peered into the cup. Maggie's special: awful stuff, hours old and looking like sludge.

Malcolm said, "I met Agent Michaels at Caswell's place." He took another sip, made a face, got off Raleigh's chair and tossed the stuff into the sink. "Michaels is pretty much on top of the case."

"Don't worry about it. We've got the lead on this, Malcolm. Agent Larrabee confirmed it."

Shifting gears Raleigh told the younger man that he met the agent in 1968, the year he was appointed the department's liaison to the FBI's Task Force on Terrorism.

"That was quite a time, Malcolm. I hope this case doesn't signal another mess."

Malcolm didn't press. Rather, he asked what the consulate reps had to say.

Raleigh responded, "The Consulate's publicist, Roger Langley, did all the talking. He said that Caswell always took the subway to work, arriving at 8:45 on the dot every single day for almost two years, except Friday. Caswell was supposed to be in Providence, but never made it. Apparently, his killer was waiting for him."

He paused thoughtfully.

"So, how did the perp know Caswell would be leaving early in his car? This was no random crime, Malcolm. No, no. It was carefully planned, right down to the dirt shroud."

"Shroud?"

"Dr. Shaw's expression for the dirt that covered the body. Apt, wouldn't you say?

"What did you find at Caswell's place?"

"When I got there Boston and Cambridge blues were all over the place. And a bunch of CSU techs were crawling around Caswell's apartment and in the parking lot. I talked with three neighbors who, of course, didn't see or hear anything on Friday morning. Though, one guy said he left earlier than usual ..."

He checked his notes.

"… the guy's name is Joel Aaron … he says Caswell's car was gone when he left for work around 6:30 Friday morning. The others, a BC grad student and a lawyer, didn't know much either, but said that Caswell kept to himself."

He stuck a piece of Juicy Fruit gum in his mouth and added, "Other than being a loner and the fact Caswell owns … er, owned a Mercedes, we got squat."

Just then Maggie strode over. Raleigh stifled a smile, thinking, "Maggie doesn't walk, she doesn't run. She really does stride."

"I've been looking for you, Lieutenant Detective Buchanan. That FBI man…"

"Agent Larrabee?"

"Yes. Well he's in the conference room. He walked right in and made himself at home." Clearly put out, she added, "He even had the gall to make coffee. And the Haverhill Police captain called in. They found Caswell's car. The Northern Essex people are checking it out."

"Thanks, Maggie."

"You're welcome." She turned and strode down the hallway.

Malcolm said, "That's good news, eh?"

"It's progress I suppose. But …"

The ringing phone interrupted him.

"Detective Buchanan here."

"That's excellent, Dr. Shaw." A pause, "Yes, we've got a pretty good translation. Don't know what it has to do with Caswell, though." He listened for a bit and then said "Thanks for your quick work."

Malcolm said, "Autopsy's done already?"

"Yes. The poor bastard died from a vicious knife wound to his heart's left ventricle. She said the stuff on Caswell's body appears to be some type of sod native to the British Isles. Also, print analysis indicates that both shoe prints were made by European shoes."

Raleigh paused, and added, "I have to call Alana."

He lifted the telephone receiver and dialed. "Hi Alana, it's …" He realized he was talking to the answering machine and started over. "Alana, it's me. How was the …" He stopped talking. Raleigh was still not used to home answering machines. Talking to them made him feel foolish.

He cleared his throat. "Alana, the case is complicated and I don't know how long I'll be. Don't wait up for me, darling."

As he placed the phone back in its cradle, he raised an eyebrow in response to Malcolm's smirk.

"What, you never heard a man call his wife 'darling' before?"

As they started to walk toward the conference room, Malcolm's phone rang. In a voice an octave lower than usual he said, "Detective Schoenfeld here."

Raleigh smiled. Malcolm had recently been promoted to rookie detective, and he really liked the sound of his title.

Malcolm put his hand over the receiver and pantomimed for Raleigh to go on ahead.

Later, when Malcolm walked into the conference room, Raleigh was saying, "… and that's it for the note, Eric. I don't think there's anything else we can do at the moment."

He looked at Malcolm, glanced at Larrabee and said, “I have to eat something. You fellas want to join me?”

Larrabee declined, but Malcolm agreed. They planned to meet at Raff’s following the press conference.

CHAPTER 33 ~ MEMORY TRACES

Raleigh gave enough fluff to give the talking heads plenty to report, and left the press conference, happy to leave the wrap-up and photo ops to Captain Furlong. The hint of snow was in the air as he crossed the street to Raff's. He had been on the case since 6:00 a.m., and was tired. And, he was irritated by the pesky memory traces playing havoc with him. Even more irritated now that the note's translation hadn't shed any light on the mystery of Caswell's murder.

Raff's was your regular cop hangout, owned and operated by a slip of a woman named Mary Rafferty Desimone. Malcolm was seated in a corner booth. As Raleigh entered, he gave Mary a high sign, which she passed along to her husband, Sally – short for Salvatore.

"Hey, detective, what'll it be?" Sally said.

Raleigh eyed Malcolm's chili. "Bring me some of that and a pilsner. Thanks Sally."

Sally plopped a bowl of chili and a pilsner in front of Raleigh, saying, "Seconds are on the house."

After a while Malcolm said, "You're pensive, sir."

"So much about this case seems familiar. The manner of the poor bastard's death, the notes; even the castle. But I can't wrap my mind around the thing."

"Maybe you saw a movie or something."

Raleigh gave him a look.

"Well, why not? That happens to me sometimes."

Raleigh smiled, thinking of his mother's saying: *A little simple, but he's a good egg.*

He said, "The note reminds me of summer vacations in New Hampshire. For two years I traded notes with a kid from Ireland who stayed in the cottage for two weeks before us."

He shoveled a spoonful of chili into his mouth.

"His last note was written partially in Gaelic and contained a puzzle or a riddle. I don't really remember. And I don't know why this case reminds me of that time. It happened long ago, Malcolm."

Malcolm's eyes remained focused on his food as he said, "That's a weird coincidence! Did you get the note translated?"

"I meant to, but never did. I met Alana that summer, and put away childish things, including the note. I have no idea what happened to it."

"Did you ever meet the kid?"

"Not exactly; but, I saw him twice. The year after I met Alana, she talked me into joining her as a counselor across the lake from the cottage. One night during a cookout for the kids, I overheard someone talking to a female counselor. He had an Irish accent, so I thought he might be the 'note kid.' But, as I started to walk toward him, someone called my name and I was distracted. By the time I turned around, he had disappeared.

"The second time occurred in 1968 when I worked with Larrabee on the task force. We were tracking a gang calling itself the Neo2-Fenians, which was a nod to the 19th-century Neo-Fenians, who were foolish enough to attempt an attack on Canada."

Malcolm choked on his beer. Wiping his chin, he said, "You're kidding, right?"

"Nope. The gang was disavowed by the 19th century Irish moderates, just as today's IRA disavowed the Neo2-Fenians. The Canadian Mounted Police and the FBI were waiting for them when they crossed the border. And that was that."

He took a long pull on his pilsner and signaled for another; but changed his mind, and ordered coffee instead.

Then he said, "Anyway, one night on a whim, I decided to drop into a pub where an Irish band was playing. They were good, but I couldn't hear the lyrics because a group of fellows was making a lot of noise. When I turned toward them, one of them looked familiar to me.

The music stopped and the band leader, Kirwan I think his name was, called out, 'Hey Chris McBride! This tune's for you, boyo.'

The guy stood up and toasted Kirwan, who motioned to his band. They broke into their version of 'Black '47,' a reference to the Irish famine.

"Anyway, the name 'Chris McBride' meant nothing to me, but his face was familiar. Though, it had been decades since I had seen the kid at the camp, I was almost certain he and the man named Chris McBride were one in the same. Just before he sat down, he glanced my way. I think he recognized me too."

Malcolm put down his fork and looked expectantly at Raleigh.

"In the middle of 'Black '47,' just as I had decided to go over to McBride's table two cops walked in the door. McBride took off in the direction of the bathroom. The policemen just stood by the doorway, looked around and then left. I was curious, so, I went to the bathroom. The window was broken and McBride was gone. I guessed he might be one of the Neo2-Fenians.

"I called Joe Pettingill, the task force Leader, and told him about the incident. But, we got nowhere. A few months later, though, we gathered Intel that a man named McBride had been associated with the Neo2-Fenians; but, he was now in the wind. We kept an eye on the gang, which was quiet until ..."

Raleigh nodded to himself. "... until they blew up Boston's British Consulate in '69. We ended up ..."

Then he abruptly stopped talking, finding it difficult to talk about that night. In fact, he'd never really gotten into it, even with Alana.

Then he said, "Listen, Malcolm, let's save it for some other time."

"OK, whatever you say, detective."

They finished their drinks and called for the tab.

As he turned the corner, Raleigh gave Malcolm a backhanded wave.

Malcolm called, "Yes sir. See you in the a.m."

CHAPTER 34 ~ MEMORY SPEAKS

Country Pond

The radio's consistent lack of reception was nerve wracking. Since Friday, when Tuck was able to get reception, he could hear only static from a Boston station, or country music from New Hampshire. After midnight, a Canadian news station came in loud and clear.

It was maddening.

Finally, at 8:15 on Sunday night he heard snippets of a re-broadcast from Boston. Through the static, he heard Raleigh's name mentioned. Pressing his ear close to the radio while fiddling with the antennae, he heard most of what Raleigh had to say, which wasn't much at all.

Tuck couldn't stand not knowing how much longer he'd have to wait before Raleigh figured things out – if he ever did.

Boston

Rounding the corner to the lock-up entrance where he parked the BMW, Raleigh suddenly stopped dead in his tracks. The note-trading story he had told Malcolm had shaken something loose in the recesses of his memory. He turned on his heel and ran back to the squad room.

He unlocked his desk drawer and grabbed the two versions of the note. He rushed to the projection room to see both versions of the note side by side. As he flipped the projector on, the sudden brightness stung his eyes, and his hands flew up to shade them.

He peeked through his fingers: English on the left, Gaelic on the right. His eyes adjusted, he scanned the English version, looking for a portion that he and Dr. McGrath couldn't figure out. And there it was:

Now I was a xxxxxfe before the famine hit hard, so Axxxe sent for me that night to xxrse Cxxxxxxxxx, the xxor xxxxxx thing. Whilst doing so, I spied upon xxx xxpe of xxx tiny nxxk a strange, xxxxx blue mark left by the xxxxx no doubt. It had a likeness to a bxxxxxxxy, it did.

Raleigh filled in the blanks: "A Butterfly!" He whispered. "A strange xxxxx blue mark left by the xxxxx ... It had a likeness to a butterfly ..."

He knew at once why the murder scene had seemed so familiar: This phrase had something to do with the kid's last note. He had to find that note.

He shut the projector off, grabbed the two notes, jogged back to his office and put them in his desk drawer. He raced back to the BMW. In no time at all he double-parked in front of his house, took the stairs two at a time, and dropped the house keys twice. Once inside, he ran upstairs to the attic, and, without hesitation, he unlocked his father's footlocker.

He carefully removed the dress uniform and his father's journal, and began to search through every folder and every box. With great anticipation, he picked up the old cigar box that held treasures he had collected as a boy. He paused before lifting its lid, hoping it contained the kid's note. A few baseball cards, old coins he'd found, including an early 20th Century silver dollar, and an arrow head he'd dug up in the back of his Brooklyn apartment house. Two notes lay at the bottom. He closed his eyes and whispered a quick prayer; but they were scribbled love letters never sent to a girl in his fifth grade.

He leaned back on his haunches, resigned. The only things left in the footlocker were his college text books. With mounting irritation, he assaulted the books. He flung his Logic textbook across the room, and as he did so, a piece of paper fluttered to the floor. He held his breath, scarcely believing it could be the note. Then, he picked it up and slowly exhaled: Gaelic written in a childish hand. The kid from Ireland, who he was certain was Chris McBride, had written "July 1952" on the top right edge. Like the day he first saw it, he was pissed that the first paragraph was written in Gaelic. He tried to decipher the first sentence. *"Má na póga Stork féileacán ar dhá bhuachaillí, cad iad na siad lena chéile?"*

No use.

He gazed for a moment at the crude rendering of the butterfly the boy had drawn. Then he skipped to the part where English began.

So, you see in a way, boyo, we could be related. Too bad about oul Will getting offed like that – they pinned it on the Fenians, those patriots I told you about last year. T'was the silver of the knife, the sod covering his body, and the clothes in a pile that tipped 'em. T'was the way the rebels would do it, ye see. But they didn't do it. My Granfar told me t'was the British rogue soldiers hired by the Captain's family that did the deed. Them were the bastards that killed ol' Will and left him near the Castle. And he never found his real Da (t'was the Captain you know); and he never found his twin. Sad, eh? You say that you want to be a detective, eh? I tink being what you called a rebel is much more exciting. But, when you become a detective, you might solve the riddle about twins and the butterfly. Maybe you and me will meet someday, eh? Maybe we won't. The kid from Ireland

.

Raleigh said aloud, "A silver knife; the victim's clothes piled neatly; his body covered with sod; a castle for Christ's sake." *Not to mention a riddle about twins and a butterfly! The woman in father's stories had told such a riddle.*

He became aware that he was rubbing the back of his neck. Then he made a sudden connection. Alana and he had been married a little over a year when their son was born on Christmas night, 1962. Alana was lying contentedly holding their newborn in her arms. She adjusted her hold and said, "Look, Raleigh! He has a birthmark on the nape of his neck. See? It's a tiny butterfly. That's good luck, you know."

Now he said aloud, "I don't have the mark, but my son did. So, kid from Ireland, am I making progress on your fucking riddle?"

He recalled how he had had visions that his son would grow up to be a famous mathematician or a writer, or both – like his ancestor.

But, the child died from some congenital disease they had never understood. The dates and the place of his birth and death were engraved upon Raleigh's heart: *Raleigh Cameron Buchanan II, b. December 25, 1962; d. 3:04 a.m., March 12, 1964, Saint Luke's Hospital in the City of New York.*

Alana had been completely undone for months. They never tried to get pregnant again.

He re-folded the note, taking care not to tear the creases. Then he placed it in his briefcase. He knew for sure that Chris McBride had murdered Caswell in the same manner that some ancestor of his was murdered. And, he knew where to find him. *I've got you now, McBride.*

He stumbled down the stairs calling Alana's name. By the time he was on the ground floor, he realized she wasn't home. *Of course not! A madman's tossing things around in her attic. Cops would be here by now.*

He grabbed *The Wreck of the Highlander* off the hall table; but stopped short, noticing the note Alana had left for him. He wrote on the back of the note, "Don't wait up. We've got a lead. R."

He knew that he should call for backup. But he didn't. In no time at all he had crossed the Tobin Bridge heading north. Memories of that night in '69 assailed him.

It was an absolute disaster from start to finish. The task force had obtained intelligence that the Neo2-Fenians planned an attack on the British Consulate located on the 47th floor of Boston's Prudential Center. They also learned that the gang had a safe house somewhere in southeastern New Hampshire. Though they had made painstaking preparations to be on the offensive, their time-frame information was off by less than half an hour. But, in that short time, a bomb had exploded on the Prudential Center's 47th floor, killing two cleaning crew members and a consulate guard.

Another consulate guard, who was assigned to the 46th floor by the exit leading up to the Consulate, was among the witnesses. The young man, whose name was Joseph Goudreault, told the task force leader, Agent Pettingill, that he had been struck from behind. He wasn't out cold long, and awoke just as the bomb detonated. He said, "I don't know how, but I had my wits about me and realized whoever hit me, had set the bomb. I wasted no time to pull the alarm. Then, I took the service elevator to the ground floor."

He went on to say that, when he ran onto the plaza, an hysterical woman holding onto her three crying children, grabbed his sleeve. In between sobs she managed to tell him her name, Monica Shellene, and that she had had seen four or five men, maybe one woman, on motorcycles heading north away from the Prudential.

After Pettingill interviewed the woman, he sent her and the children on their way. Knowing that the Neo2-Fenian terrorists had a safe house somewhere in southeastern New Hampshire, he alerted the Cambridge police and police departments in towns north of Boston. Then he and the other members of the task force took off in three separate cars.

They were joined by the Malden police and caught up to the motorcyclists in the town of Reading and joined the fracas already in progress. In the end, two agents and one Malden Police officer were wounded. One gang member was killed, and another one named Thomas Shaughnessy was captured. Raleigh found out later the name of the man who was killed – Paul Tibertus O'Connell. The others escaped, but they were pursued at break-neck speed.

Raleigh was in the back seat of the car Eric Larrabee was driving; Eric's partner was in the front seat. Eric drove like a maniac, and soon caught up to the terrorists. Without warning, Larrabee's partner leaned out the window and shot one of the men off his cycle. Eric swerved past the skidding cycle, never losing momentum. Raleigh didn't think the man even blinked.

A minute or two later, Raleigh saw the strobe-lights of a stationary police car and Eric swerved off the highway into the rest area. Three motor cycles, their engines still running, were on the ground; their owners were nowhere in sight. The police car belonged to the Reading police, and its occupants had already gone into the woods. Eric, the other agent, and Raleigh ran into the woods, taking off in different directions.

Raleigh had just entered a clearing when he heard yelling and gunfire. Turning toward the sound, a woman stumbled toward him, falling practically at his feet. He knelt to check her condition. She reached her arm up and tried to say something. The only sound Raleigh heard was blood gurgling from her mouth. Her arm slipped down, and she died in Raleigh's arms.

Hearing a noise he looked up. A man raced toward him, and tackled him. Raleigh's gun was no longer in his hand. They fought, pulling and punching and stumbling through the bushes. They toppled close to the edge of an embankment; and a second later down they tumbled. Raleigh landed hard on top of the man. Straddling him, he pulled his spare from his ankle holster and shoved it into the man's face, then pulled him to his feet. The man's arm hung limply at his side; blood dripped from a head wound. He smiled wryly, and said, "Did'ja ever figure out the riddle, detective?"

Now, speeding north, Raleigh recalled that he had had no idea what the guy was talking about. He was so amazed by the calm, personal way the man spoke to him that he let his guard down. The man twisted the gun from his hand, whacked him across the temple, and then ran into the woods – like a gazelle.

It was only later that Raleigh realized that he did recognized the man as the one he had seen in the pub the year before. But it was too late.

Raleigh had never been able to come to terms with what happened that night. He had never forgotten the face of that young woman dying in his arms; or the mangled body of that kid who was shot off his motorcycle. Most of all, he could not forget the one who got away – or, had he let Chris McBride get away that night?

For the second time in less than a week, memory had such a hold on Raleigh, he wasn't paying attention. He almost missed the Georgetown exit. He glanced in the rear view mirror and saw nothing, so he swerved the car into the exit. He put the mobile strobe light on the roof, not wanting the eager Georgetown police to stop him as he sped through their small town, slowing only at the one traffic light on the main street.

Shortly, he crossed the Groveland Bridge into Haverhill. It was after 9:00 p.m. and the city was shrouded in newly fallen snow. He thought back to when Alana and he had tried to find their way to Country Pond just a few days before. It had been 25 years since Raleigh had last seen the place. He wondered how the hell he'd find it in the dark.

But, he was on a quest; and memory served him well that night.

CHAPTER 35 ~THE BUTTERFLY LEGACY

Half Moon Cottage

After crossing into New Hampshire, by some atavistic instinct, Raleigh took turns that he had completely forgotten less than a week before. Soon his headlights beamed off a crude sign, he pulled over, got out, and read aloud, "This way to Country Pond." He peered down a half-hidden road. He remembered! He knew exactly how to find Half Moon Cottage.

The snow-covered road, lumpy with potholes, was no match for the BMW. Soon Raleigh was stumbling down a steep path, one hand hanging onto small trees, the other clutching his gun. The weather had cleared, and clouds raced across the moon, casting its intermittent reflection on the lake. He walked to the shoreline and looked over his shoulder, orienting himself. And then he saw the tip of a cigarette glowing in the night.

Tuck called out, "Hey there! I heard your car, Detective Buchanan."

Raleigh walked up the incline, holding his gun by his side. At the bottom of the porch steps he said, "So, who are you tonight, the kid from Ireland, or Chris McBride?"

Tuck didn't answer, instead he said, "Tis a bit nippy out here, detective, c'mon inside."

He flicked the end of his cigarette over the railing, and held the door open. But, Raleigh motioned for Tuck to go in first. Tuck nodded, saying, "No need for the firearm, detective."

Once inside, Raleigh could see Tuck's face in the warm glow of the kitchen lantern. He seemed much younger than Raleigh had imagined. A handsome man on the thin side, an angular face, a patrician nose – a profile that belonged on a coin. He noted the scar that ran from Tuck's eyebrow over to his temple. A couple days of beard growth barely hid full lips and the slight cleft to his chin. Dark hair curled beneath his ears. Though the soft light muted the color of his eyes, Raleigh could tell they were blue.

Shifting his gaze, Raleigh focused on the kitchen. Nothing seemed to have changed in 25 years.

Tuck pointed to the sink, and said apropos of nothing, "The pump doesn't work anymore." Then, "Take your coat?"

Raleigh didn't want to take off his coat, and suddenly he regretted his decision to come here. *I should've called for backup.* Nevertheless, he unbuttoned his coat, handed it to Tuck, and followed him into the living room. The room was exactly as he remembered it. Soft light from two lanterns flickering on the wall between two windows in back of the sofa. The pot-belly stove spread its warmth. The butcher-block coffee table, the alcove – sans books and games. It was surreal.

Shoving memories aside, Raleigh said, "Why did you kill Caswell?"

"Tis a long story, detective, take a seat. I'll get you a spot of – what is it you like? Ah, Hennessey! Tinking you might come, I have some for you."

That he knew his preferred drink rattled Raleigh. He noticed that Tuck's movements were quick, which added to his discomfort.

Tuck placed a glass and a bottle of Hennessey on a table beside an arm chair covered with loose damask ticking. Smiling, he said, "Here you go."

Raleigh remained standing, the gun hot in his hand. Tuck dragged another chair to the table. The light was better in the living room so Raleigh could see the tell-tale signs of sleep deprivation on Tuck's handsome face: smudges under eyes that were actually a brilliant blue; his hair, so black it too appeared blue, was tangled from lack of shampoo. He sat down. Raleigh remained standing, fighting with himself: Curiosity vs. his obligation to take the man in.

Curiosity won the night. Raleigh sat down, gun at the ready, ignoring the Hennessey.

Tuck took a long pull of Guinness, smiled wryly, and said, "My name is not Chris McBride, though the name has come in handy more than once. My name is William Tuckerton O'Connell. Friends call me Tuck."

Using his last name, Raleigh asked again why he murdered Caswell.

He didn't answer, and instead said, "I have a story for you, detective. I tink that's what you really came to hear."

When Raleigh said nothing, Tuck began to speak, and Raleigh listened.

Tuck told him about the murder of his wife and son. He said, "I almost bumped into the murdering bastard, detective. Our eyes met for a split second. His eyes were full of recognition; but he fled before I realized that I'd seen him before. Then that awful blast. When he killed my family, he killed someting inside me as well."

Tears welled in his eyes.

Despite himself, Raleigh was touched.

Tuck brushed the back of his hand across his eyes, and then lit a cigarette. He blew a few smoke rings, appearing to compose himself. Then he began to speak. He told Raleigh about his solo search for the murderer. He told him about Belfast without details; and, his meeting with Jack Coughlin.

"...Jack... no last names, eh? Jack told me all about Jonathan Temple Caswell. The family whisked him off to America so he could play in one of the Brit's embassies. I followed his trail to New York, and then to Boston. I bunked there with a friend of my cousin, the late Paul Tibertus O'Connell."

He peered at Raleigh through the wisps of smoke. Raleigh lowered his eyes, realizing that one of the people killed that night in 1969 was Tuck's cousin.

Tuck crushed his cigarette, and continued, "I had seen Caswell but 'course, I didn't know who he was then. I saw him on and off during the trip through Ireland that Claire and I took the summer of '72. Tis how the bastard heard me talking about Captain Tuckerton and Nelly!"

Raleigh felt his heart drop. *I know those names!* Involuntarily he sat up straighter, trying to remain expressionless.

"You see, detective, Caswell knew about their love affair and the birth of twins. Tis the secret the Temple family did everyting in its considerable power to keep under wraps … including murder. Tree of their victims were dear to me. Two of them were our ancestors."

Raleigh thought Tuck's use of the word "our" was a slip of the tongue.

"I was just another in a long line who threatened to reveal their secret," Tuck continued, "which is why Caswell's uncle told him to 'take care of the matter.' The matter being, get rid of me. But he fucked up, didn't he, and murdered my family instead."

He stopped talking and headed for the kitchen. Raleigh followed, hand by his side, holding onto the gun. Tuck glanced at it, and said, "I told you I have no firearms, detective. And there's not a piece of decent cutlery in the place."

He retrieved a fresh Guinness from the icebox. Back in the living room he said, "I stalked Caswell until the day before I took him off to Haverhill."

He moved the Guinness bottle to the side of his face, saying, "I don't mind tellin' you that I took great pleasure in the stalking alone. I knew every move the weasel made, including his assignment in Providence on Friday."

He was silent for a moment, and then: "That's why I killed Caswell, detective. Do you want to know the how of it?"

He didn't wait for an answer, saying, "Caswell's ancestors hired rogue soldiers to kill my great-great grandfather, Will O'Connell. They did so in the rebel manner. I killed Caswell in the same way … sod and all. Poetic justice, wouldn't you agree?"

Raleigh simply stared at him.

Then Tuck said, "So, Detective Buchanan, that's it. Tis why Jonathan Temple Caswell is no more." He raised his arms, and said, "Now you can turn me in."

And Raleigh knew he should; but he didn't. Instead, he said, "Why me? How did you know I'd come here?"

Tuck dropped his hands to his side, and calmly said, "I've known who you really are since 1952, detective. I vowed that I would meet you one day. And I did, twice. But you know that, don't you."

"Memories of the pub in '68, and the woods in '69 had assailed me all day," Raleigh thought.

"I'm good at stalking. I looked you up every time I came to the States. As a boy, as a man, as a … what did you call it in your last note? …was it rebel? Well, terrorist will do. I knew when you married Alana; I knew when you'd made a name for yourself; and I knew when you left New York for Boston. When I planned Caswell's departure from this world, I planned to get my favorite detective to the scene."

Raleigh was about to ask why; but Tuck read his mind, it seemed. "I wanted you to find me so I could tell you what you've always needed to know."

Impatient, Raleigh said, "I want you to explain that fucking note. Who is P.M., the person who signed the note you left?"

"I'll tell you who she is." He walked to the mantel, looking so haggard that Raleigh almost felt sorry for him. He picked up the wooden box. No longer feeling a threat, Raleigh stuffed his gun into the folds of the chair's damask covering, and took a sip of Hennessey. As the silky warmth slid down his throat, he blessed the man who cured it.

Tuck opened the box and retrieved an old piece of paper. Waving it slightly he said, "This is the original of the note I left for you to find."

As he leaned toward Raleigh's chair, Raleigh thrust his hand into the damask and grasped the butt of his gun. But Tuck merely handed him the note, and said, "I mean you no harm, detective."

Raleigh took the note with his other hand, holding it delicately. Tuck pointed to "P.M."

"See there? Tis Peg Mirran. She wrote this note to Will O'Connell. But he never got it. He got murdered instead, you see. The note was passed down from his wife Molly to their son Seamus, and so on down to me."

Then he pointed at another name that Raleigh knew as "O'K." "There!" He exclaimed, "Tis Alice O'Keefe."

Alice O'Keefe! A woman in Raleigh's father's stories had that name. Tuck caught the look of recognition in Raleigh's eyes. In a voice Raleigh hardly recognized, he managed to say, "O'Keefe's a common name."

Tuck stood close, and Raleigh tightened his grip on the gun.

Tuck said, "Tis true, O'Keefe's a common name. But how about this one?" He pointed at the "C" that Raleigh and Dr. McGrath had puzzled over. "Tis Christopher, Will O'Connell's twin."

Twins! Raleigh raised his hand to his brow. Tuck straightened, and lit another cigarette. Raleigh had lost count.

Peering at Raleigh through the swirl of blue smoke, Tuck said "Tell me, detective, why do you tink all this is familiar to you?"

He didn't wait for an answer. "Look here!" With his finger he traced words Raleigh had partially deciphered, and translated Peg Mirran's words.

Now, I was a midwife before the famine hit hard, so Alice sent for me that night to nurse Christopher, the poor little thing. Whilst doing so, I spied upon the nape of his tiny neck a strange, light blue mark left by the stork no doubt. It had a likeness to a butterfly, it did. I think you must have the same mark as your twin.

Tuck raised his voice, and said, "You would not have come here if you didn't know what this all means."

And then, before Raleigh could react, Tuck was behind him. Raleigh pulled the gun from the damask. Tuck wrapped his hand around Raleigh's. "I say again, no need for the firearm."

Raleigh felt Tuck's other hand on the nape of his neck. He said, "You don't have it. But I do. Aye, I have the stork's kiss"

Raleigh thought of the birthmark on the nape of his newborn son's neck. Rattled, he twisted his head. Tuck's hand dropped to his side. Raleigh felt the man's other hand lessen its hold on his.

He held onto his gun.

"I'm going to explain everyting to you, detective. But eat someting because it will be a long night."

Raleigh followed him to the kitchen, and watched him make two sandwiches, and garnish the plates with grapes and orange slices. Standing there Tuck ate his sandwich. Raleigh left his untouched. Tuck's calmness infuriated him. Then he followed him back into the living room, telling himself he'd take him in any moment, knowing it was a lie.

They sat, Tuck with grapes, orange slices and Guinness; Raleigh with the gun in his hand, feeling foolish.

"Alice O'Keefe had told Peg Mirran about our story, detective. Tis no coincidence that Alice was governess to Christopher, your great-great grandfather."

"My grandfather's name was Walter," Raleigh retorted.

"Tis only what you were told. No, no. Alice O'Keefe preserved our true history through the tales she whispered to Christopher. Years later she told the same to Christopher's twin, Will O'Connell, who told his son, Seamus, who told his son, my Granfar, Paul T. O'Connell, who told it to me. I bet Alice's stories came down through your family as well."

Raleigh's thoughts swirled with remnants of his father's stories, as Tuck continued talking.

"You and I have the same blood, man."

Then he put Peg Mirran's note back in the box and took off his ring. "Here hold onto it."

Raleigh took the ring, which looked exactly like Caswell's, except much older.

"Our story begins with this ring, detective."

He peered into Raleigh's eyes, apparently to see whether he was getting the drift. Raleigh had begun to believe his story. Tuck knew he had his attention.

"This ring is the original the Captain gave to Nelly," Tuck explained. He then went on to tell Raleigh about the Hughes family; their endurance through Ireland's Great Hunger; the love affair between the Captain and Nelly; and the birth of twins in a Galway convent. Raleigh could almost hear the blood pulsing through his veins, as his father's stories came alive.

Tuck spoke of things not in the stories: the description of Nelly's horrific journey in the hold of a coffin ship; her life with Seamus on Prince Edward Island. Tuck concluded with Nelly's death, which brought tears to his eyes. Raleigh held back a few of his own.

Then Tuck took the ring from Raleigh and put it back on his finger. He handed Raleigh Thomas' arrowhead, and told him Will O'Connell's story.

Tuck O'Connell was a very good story teller: Will's exploits; his marriage to Molly O'Casey; the awful betrayal and suicide of her father; and Thomas' appearance, and ultimate death.

Raleigh became aware that the arrow head was digging into his hand. He loosened his grip.

Then Tuck motioned for the arrow head, Raleigh gave it to him and watched as he put it back into the box. He stood by the mantel for a while. Raleigh poured himself an inch or two of Hennessey, but changed his mind. He pulled the gun from the damask and shoved it into his shoulder holster, stood and went into the kitchen. He ate the sandwich, now stale. He leaned his head against the ice box, emotionally drained and exhausted. But, he needed to hear more. He poured himself a glass of water from the thermos and went back into the living room.

Tuck was holding an old piece of paper, wrapped in plastic. He said, "Years after Will settled in County Sligo, Alice O'Keefe caught up to him. She told him about Nelly's Aunt Stella and her treachery."

Handing Raleigh the paper, he said, "Stella lied about the captain, and she lied about Christopher; but that was not the worst of what that woman did."

Raleigh gazed at the paper, not comprehending a word of the Gaelic script.

Tuck said, "Tis the letter Alice O'Keefe kept, not knowing that one day she would give it to Will. She could not have known it would be preserved for us."

Then he said, "A few days before she was murdered …" His words hung in the air. Tossing the end of his cigarette into the stove, he muttered, "…and just a month before Will himself was murdered, she gave him that letter."

He took the letter back, telling Raleigh that it was addressed to Lord Palmerston. Raleigh knew the name – a famous man, revered as a war hero.

After Tuck translated the letter, Raleigh felt shocked to the root of his soul. He could hardly breathe, appalled as he was by Stella's colossal blackmail attempt against Lord Palmerston. He felt anger rise in his chest as he absorbed the full meaning of her treachery: Her son's freedom in exchange for Christopher and her silence. This was the cause of the travesty brought down on the descendants of Nelly Hughes and Captain Tuckerton. He began to understand what Tuck was really telling him.

What a legacy, he thought, but did not say. Instead, in a voice weaker than he thought possible, he said, "What happened to Christopher?"

"My Claire asked the same ting, but she didn't live to hear it." Tuck said, as he placed the letter and the wooden box into his saddle-bag, which he put on the kitchen floor. Then he walked back to the mantel and picked up a very old looking sheaf of paper an inch thick. He said, "Tis all here, detective. Alice O'Keefe wrote down everyting she knew about Christopher, and gave this to Will O'Connell."

Then, exaggerating his Irish accent, he said, "I tink me tongue is tied as well. So, I'll just tell ye a wee bit more of the story, and ye can read the rest for yourself."

He lit another cigarette. Raleigh had stopped smoking seven years before; but tonight he was tempted.

Tuck blew smoke in the air, and began to speak, his voice cracking with emotion and fatigue. He talked of things Raleigh knew about his great-great grandfather, who Tuck referred to as Christopher. And he talked about things Raleigh only knew from his father's stories, which his mother had told him were mere fairy tales. He finally understood the riddle of the twins and the butterfly. It was the story of the kid from Ireland and the boy from Brooklyn, descendants of identical twins separated at birth. He wanted to hear more, but Tuck simply stopped talking.

Raleigh thought he was finished; but, he wasn't.

Tuck said, "Granfar told me that Will gave the story sheets to his son, Seamus. When he grew up, Seamus tried to find his Uncle Christopher. And he almost did, detective. Because of Will's murder, Molly and the children moved away from County Sligo. That's when she found Peg Mirran's note, which she apparently hid, waiting for the proper time … a time that never came.

"Anyway, when Seamus was 16 or so, he got a job on a ship headed for England. T'was against Molly's wishes, of course. But, he was determined to find Christopher. One of the first buildings he saw when he arrived was the Macpherson Brewery. Within days he was working there as a stock boy. A month later, Christopher's son, Wallace …" He paused and said, "Name sound familiar, detective?"

Raleigh said nothing.

"Christopher's son, Wallace came to the brewery to work for the summer. Seamus' fellow workers had developed affection for the Irish lad, which did not sit well with Wallace."

He went on to say that Wallace took an immediate dislike for Seamus and often tried, unsuccessfully, to get him in trouble. Seamus, on the other hand, knowing Wallace was his cousin, longed to talk to him about their relationship and, especially about Christopher. But, by August their relationship had become hopelessly strained.

"Aye, detective, t'was a bad fellow that Wallace. The rascal stole some money. And sure didn't he blame it on Seamus. The constable was summoned and he hustled the lad into his wagon. And wouldn't you know Christopher had arrived a day earlier than expected to bring Wallace back to Scotland. Now, as Granfar's story goes, the wagon's back window was open and Seamus heard a voice, much like his father's. Listen …"

"Say! Wallace, what's the constable doing here?"

Aghast, Wallace came quickly to his father's side. He glanced at the carriage as it started to move and said, "Father you're a day early!"

At that moment, Seamus leaned out the window and, seeing a man that looked exactly like his father, he cried, "Uncle! Uncle Christopher."

The constable turned around. "Shut up, boy. Mind yourself or things will go badly for you."

Seamus pleaded with the constable, "He's my father's brother, I swear."

The constable shrugged, urged his horse forward, saying, "Go on with your nonsense, that's Mr. Walter Macpherson himself."

As the wagon drove pass Christopher, his eyes briefly met Seamus' eyes.

And then the carriage was gone.

Christopher had heard the lad yelling, and watched the wagon until it turned the corner. Wallace said, "It's just in Irish stock boy who stole some money, father."

Christopher wasn't listening. His mind was on the boy in the carriage.

The following morning as Christopher was helping Wallace pack, a bundle of money fell to the floor. "Wallace! What is this?" Wallace started to reply, but Christopher interrupted, "Do not lie to me. I won't have it."

He took hold of Wallace's arm and dragged him from the room. "We're going to see the constable and you will tell the truth."

Seamus was seated near the chief constable's office. When his guard went to the necessary room, the boy saw his chance and took it. Within minutes he was outside the jail, fleeing in an easterly direction. He ducked into an alleyway, and didn't see the carriage carrying Christopher and Wallace turn into the street.

The boy hid for the rest of the day and slept in the loft of the blacksmith's barn. The next morning he headed for the brewery. When he arrived one of the men who had befriended him from the first day told him that Christopher and his son had already left for the ship. Seamus ran to the docks in time to see the ship heading out to sea.

Now, Tuck abruptly stopped talking.

Raleigh said, “Twists of fate seem to mark your family.”

“A twist or two of it binds you and me, detective. For tis your family as well.”

Raleigh stared at him for a few seconds; and then he made up his mind about something and motioned toward the Hennessy. Tuck nodded and Raleigh poured an inch or two for both of them. Tuck took a sip; and then told Raleigh that Seamus went back to Ireland. After Molly died, he went to Dublin where he worked in the shipping industry, and eventually married.

“Seamus told his son, my Granfar Paul Tibertus, the family story and gave him the wooden box. It was Paul T.’s turn to search for Christopher … this time for his descendants. But Granfar never found Christopher’s family. But, he did find out that Christopher’s daughter, Alice Rose and Ian Maclaren had a daughter named Nessa. But, you know that. Ting of it is I know that as well. I know that Nessa married Duncan Buchanan, your grandfather, cousin.”

Using Tuck’s first name for the first time during that long night, Raleigh said, “So then, Tuck, that means we’re cousins to, what, the 5th power?”

“Close.” Tuck said. And then, from memory, he recited an Encyclopedia entry: “If your great-great-great grandparent (great + great + great + grand = 4) is another person's great-great-great grandparent (great + great + great + grand = 4), then you are 4th cousins. There is no ‘removed,’ because you are on the same generational level, that is, 4 - 4 = 0. So, Raleigh, what do you tink?”

Raleigh had to smile at Tuck’s use of his first name.

“Granfar Paul T. found out that Buchanan had taken his family to the States. And that’s where the trail ended until …” He waved his arms around. “… until you and I traded notes from this very cottage. That summer in 1952 I heard Aunt Agnes speaking to a neighbor. She mentioned the name ‘Buchanan.’ I had seen that name in the story sheets Granfar had given me. Tis how I guessed that you and I might be related; tis why I added the riddle in the note I left behind the half-moon. Sorry about the Gaelic part.”

Then he lit a cigarette. Raleigh didn’t weaken.

Tuck blew several smoke rings. Through the wisps of smoke, Raleigh could see Tuck's eyes move with memory.

"Paul T. never told my Da anyting about the family history. Cornelius was a difficult lad; I don't tink Paul T. even liked him. When Cornelius was just 15 he had taken to the drink; and soon the drink took him."

He coughed. Raleigh thought it might be the cigarettes, or Tuck's attempt to shed the memory of his father.

In a voice touched with sadness and fatigue, Tuck continued, "Anyway, tis why Granfar gave me Will's wooden box, and why he told me, not my father, the story about our true heritage."

Tears glistened in his eyes.

Composing himself, he said, "People were murdered because of what they knew about the love of two young people, and the twins born of their union." Then he recited a litany: "Alice O'Keefe, whose death was suspicious; Will O'Connell, whose body was found on the grounds of Classiebawn Castle; sure and they murdered Aunt Stella, whose mangled body was found at the base of Maeve's Knockneara; and my Claire and son killed by a blast meant for me."

Neither said anything for a long moment.

Then Tuck broke the silence, "So, that's the story, detective."

Raleigh was overwhelmed with exhaustion. He became aware of a chill settling deep in his bones. Nevertheless he said, "But you haven't told me everything about Christopher."

"Tis true enough," he said, and gave Raleigh Alice O'Keefe's story sheets. Raleigh felt the weight of them, and handed them back. Tuck slipped them into his saddle bag, and said, "Tis a bit nippy in here for story tellin' I tink. Time for more firewood."

He put on his jacket and left the cottage.

Raleigh went into the kitchen and, with the ice box open, ate a few grapes. Suddenly he stopped chewing. He'd noticed a thick, legal-sized envelope on top of the ice box. He turned quickly and saw that Tuck's saddlebag was gone. Then he grasped the envelope. "For Detective Buchanan" was written in a bold hand across the front of it.

He knew Tuck was not coming back.

He slammed the ice box shut and ran out of the cottage, almost tripping over the firewood Tuck had placed on the porch. Then he heard a motorcycle revving in the distance.

Tuck O'Connell had escaped once again. *No, I let him go... again.*

Raleigh knew he should go after him. Instead, he picked up the fire wood and went back into the cottage. He stoked the fire and removed a sheaf of paper from the envelope. On the first page Tuck had written, "Tis Alice's story, Raleigh Buchanan. I translated it for you. Maybe someday we'll meet again, maybe not. Never can tell."

Raleigh sat heavily on the sofa, and began to read Alice's story about Christopher, who he'd always known as Walter. But, he felt a thrill when he noted that, throughout the pages, Alice O'Keefe referred to his great-great grandfather as "Christopher."

As dawn peeked through the window, Raleigh finished reading the last sentence of Alice's account of Christopher's life. He put the sheaf of paper back into the envelope, and put that into his briefcase. He made sure the embers were extinguished and turned off a lantern, the other having died over an hour ago. He looked around the cottage, picked up his briefcase and walked out the door.

The eastern sky was beginning to glow pink and red as he climbed the hill to his car.

EPILOGUE

"The human voice can never reach the distance covered by the still, small voice of conscience."

~M. Gandhi

Raleigh found a phone booth at a gas station in Kingston and called Malcolm. "I've got a lead on Caswell's murderer. Don't look for me until late this afternoon." He hung up the phone.

Then he went home and told Alana most of what had happened that night. Later, at the station, he told Malcolm and Captain Furlong that he had lost the bead on the guy.

To the captain's query as to why he hadn't called for backup, Raleigh merely replied, "It was a hunch, captain, just a hunch. A lead, I thought, but one that led nowhere – zilch, zero, nada."

For the next few months he worked the case in a desultory manner, allowing his colleagues to believe whatever they wanted to believe: domestic trouble; an illness; depression caused by their lack of progress on the British Consulate case. And when he took a leave of absence, no one was surprised.

That act of letting Tuck go was eating him up inside. So, he decided to take a journey hoping it would assuage his guilt. Alana was none too happy about it; but, she understood.

He visited some O'Connell relatives in Prince Edward Island; then off to Ireland. He took a tour through Dublin. Donavan O'Casey's house was actually on the tour. With relish, the guide revealed that O'Casey had been a notorious traitor to both the English and Irish causes.

On his own he went to Stable Lane looking for Will's rooming house. But the whole block had been destroyed by fire in 1907. Then he followed Will's journey from Dublin to Wicklow; and from there west to the River Shannon.

He took a ferry boat across to *Ros Comain* where he spent the night. The following morning he looked for the spot where Thomas breathed his last. Not a sign Thomas or the others had ever been there. Not a sign of the place where Thomas was buried. No wooden cross, no nothing.

Then he rented a car, and drove to Galway City. He went straight to the park across from Nun's Island. As he watched the ducks, he thought of Tuck's son, Will, chasing a duck on this very spot, while Tuck told his story to Claire. Gazing at the ancient convent across the narrow waterway, he thought of Nelly seeing it for the first time. He thought of the birth of her twins, and of her sorrow when she had to leave one behind. He whispered a prayer for – or maybe to – his great-great grandfather.

Then he drove north through the magnificent Connemara mountains. With some trouble, he found the Inn that Tuck said was the one where Stella McBride had crafted her blackmail letter. *I wonder where ol' Stella's soul ended up after losing her life at the base of Maeve's Knockneara.* The next day he bought a Connemara marble ring with matching earrings for Alana. Then he took off north to Mullaghmore, County Sligo.

For two weeks he toured the area, visiting the memorials to those who lost their lives in coffin ships; and the mounds of stone, under which lay the bones of famine victims. He wondered which one of them covered the bones of Michael Hughes, Mr. Ryan, Kathleen, and Maeve. Tuck had told him that Aunt Stella and Fiona Hughes were buried in proper graves. He did not find Fiona's grave; but he did find Stella's. Despite himself, he whispered a prayer that the woman had finally found peace.

His hotel room in Mullaghmore had a magnificent view of Donegal Bay. From the veranda he could see Maeve's Knockneara; and a side window allowed a glimpse of Classiebawn Castle. For years, the Castle had been owned by Lord Louis Mountbatten, who happened to be present in the village that week. Raleigh gazed at the bit of the Castle he could see from his room. He pictured Will O'Connell's body on its grounds. And he felt sad. The Castle brought to mind Jonathan Caswell's body on the grounds of a different castle in a different land.

He did not feel the least regret for him.

The day before he was to leave, August 28, the weather was simply magical. Brilliant sunshine washed across the bay. A perfect day for a late breakfast on the hotel's veranda. As the waiter placed coffee on his table, Raleigh heard a commotion. He got up and leaned over the railing. He saw a man walking among the citizens and tourists.

The waiter joined him at the railing and said, "And there goes a good man. Tis none other than Lord Mountbatten himself. He was a war hero, you know. During World War II he was the admiral of the fleet in Southeast Asia. And didn't he take Burma back from Japan!"

Lord Mountbatten was dressed simply in faded corduroys and a cable-knit sweater. The people seemed to love this man who, the waiter told Raleigh, had vacationed at his Castle for over 30 years.

"See there," the waiter said, pointing at the docks, "that's his yacht. The Lord is on his way to check on his lobster pots."

Less than half-hour later Raleigh could see the *Shadow V* as it slowly passed beyond the harbor's protecting walls. The waiter joined him to watch the yacht proceed along the coast, still only a few hundred yards from shore. Then it stopped, apparently to check the lobster pots.

Suddenly a terrible explosion shattered the peaceful afternoon. The waiter's surprise knocked him off balance and he tripped over Raleigh's chair. And Raleigh fell to his knees. After the initial shock they realized they had just seen the *Shadow V* blown to smithereens.

They watched as a fisherman rushed to the site where the yacht had so recently been. Later they were told that the fisherman pulled Lord Mountbatten into the boat; but the man had died almost immediately. Both his legs had been nearly blown off.

Then they heard two men shouting orders to other men who had gathered to help. They carried doors to be used as stretchers, tree limbs and broken broomsticks for splints, and ripped-up sheets to bind wounds. Raleigh and the waiter went down to help the effort. Soon ambulances began arriving to take the victims, alive and dead, to County Sligo's General Hospital.

In the end, only Lord Mountbatten's daughter, Lady Patricia Brabourne, her husband and their fourteen-year old son Timothy survived the vicious attack. Timothy's twin, Nicholas, and the Irish boat boy, 15-year-old Paul Maxwell, had been killed in the blast. Doctors worked tirelessly to save the life of Lady Patricia's mother-in-law, Lady Brabourne. She died the next morning.

The Provisional wing of the Irish Republican Army claimed responsibility for the "execution" of Lord Louis Mountbatten. Their news release, which referred to "Bloody Sunday," stated that their intention was to bring their cause to free Ireland to the attention of the English people and to the world.

Pandemonium reigned for several days, so Raleigh was unable to leave as planned. Sickened by the senseless assassination of Lord Mountbatten, and the murder of the others, like Tuck's Claire, Raleigh often wondered aloud, "When will this madness end?"

Finally he was able to leave for Boston from Shannon Airport. Melancholy had replaced the ounce of solace he had achieved through taking his journey. Upon his arrival at Logan Airport, he called Alana to tell her that he had landed safely, but that he needed to do one more thing before coming home. She was not happy.

He rented a car and headed north.

After he parked the car on the road above Country Pond, he followed the steps he had taken the previous November. Holding onto small trees, he half-skidded down the steep trail. This time without his gun. He reached the shoreline just as the sun dipped behind threatening clouds. It was barely dawn when he left the cottage the last time he had been there, so he was not prepared to see the great change that had taken place since he had vacationed on Country Pond as a boy.

He turned from the shore and was brought up short: he saw only piles of rubble where the cottage should have been. He guessed immediately that Tuck must have burned down the place as if to burn everything else from his memory.

He circled the crumbling fireplace chimney that once was the center of Half Moon Cottage. The sun peeked through the cloud cover casting a sunbeam or two off an object near the chimney. He bent and picked it up. Aside from the edge the sunbeams had caught, the object was filthy. He wiped it as clean as he could. A sigh escaped from his lips – the kind of bitter-sweet sigh that sometimes accompanies memory. He gently folded his palm around the charred remains of the ceramic half-moon.

He walked toward the neatly manicured pine grove, which was what had become of the wilderness he remembered from his youth. A deep sadness washed over him. Then he walked to the water's edge. Sail boats were tacking back and forth, heading toward shore ahead of the rain.

Not a rowboat or a raccoon in sight.

Then he felt a few sprinkles of rain so he headed for the trail leading up to where he left the rental. He turned back for one last look and saw one fat rain drop splatter a miniature crater into the charred hearth of the chimney.

It was all that was left of Half Moon Cottage.

THE END

TUCK O'CONNELL'S ANCESTORS

County Sligo, Ireland: Tenant farmers, **Michael and Fiona Hughes** had five children, one of whom was **Nelly** who had a brief affair with an English Captain, **William Temple Tuckerton.** The affair resulted in the birth of twins, Will and Christopher, who were separated shortly after their birth in 1846.

Prince Edward Island, Canada: Nelly and the stronger twin, Will, survived crossing the Atlantic in a "coffin ship" where she entered into an arranged marriage with her distant cousin, Seamus O'Connell. He adopted Will and gave him his last name, **Will O'Connell**.

Ireland: Following Nelly's death, Will went to Dublin, became a printer and married **Molly O'Casey**. Their son, **Seamus O'Connell,** was born in 1867.

Ireland: Seamus married **Mary Maxwell.** Their first son, **Paul Tibertus O'Connell,** was born in 1886.

Ireland: Paul Tibertus (Paul T.) married **Sinead Rea.** Their third child, **Cornelius O'Connell**, was born in 1910.

Ireland: Cornelius married **Monica O'Brien.** Their only child, William Tuckerton O'Connell **(Tuck)**, was born in 1942.

RALEIGH BUCHANAN'S ANCESTORS

County Sligo, Ireland: Tenant farmers, **Michael and Fiona Hughes** had four children, one of whom was **Nelly** who had a brief affair with an English Captain, **William Temple Tuckerton.** The affair resulted in the birth of twins, Will and Christopher, who were separated shortly after their birth in 1846.

England: Christopher was adopted by a Scottish couple, and re-named after his adoptive father, **Walter MacPherson II.**

Edinburgh, Scotland: Christopher/Walter married **Nessa Stevenson**. They had several children, one of whom, **Alice Rose MacPherson**, was born in 1873.

Edinburgh, Scotland: Alice Rose married **Ian Maclaren**. Their daughter, **Nessa Maclaren**, was born in 1895.

Edinburgh, Scotland: Nessa married Duncan Buchanan and had four children. Their second son, **Cameron Raleigh Buchanan,** was born in 1915. Duncan moved the family to New York City.

New York City: Cameron Raleigh Buchanan married Regina Gabrielle Legare. They had a daughter, Patricia, and a son, Cameron Raleigh Buchanan II (**Raleigh**), born in 1937.

10563986R10175

Made in the USA
Charleston, SC
14 December 2011